PRAISE FOR ERIC BROWN

"*Necropath* was a real success for me:
the depth of the characterisation; a very alien,
yet deeply sympathetic life-form; the authenticity
which Brown gives to the society on Bengal Station.
This is a place that you can see, hear and virtually smell."
SF Crow's Nest

"The writing is studded with phrases I had to
stop and reread because I liked them so much."
Fantasy

"Eric Brown's *Helix* is a classic concept – a built world to
dwarf Rama and Ringworld – a setting for a hugely imaginative
adventure. *Helix* is the very DNA of true SF. This is the
rediscovery of wonder."
Stephen Baxter

"*Helix* is essentially a romp – a gloriously old-fashioned
slice of science fiction... What gives the novel a unique spin
is its intertwining parallel plots. It's smart, fun, page-turning
stuff, with an engaging cast and plenty of twists...
A hugely entertaining read."
SFX

"He is a masterful storyteller. Eric Brown is often lauded as the
next big thing in science fiction and you can see why..."
Strange Horizons

"SF infused with a cosmopolitan and literary sensibility...
accomplished and affecting."
Paul J. McAuley

E.M. BROWN
BUYING TIME

First published 2018 by Solaris
an imprint of Rebellion Publishing Ltd,
Riverside House, Osney Mead,
Oxford, OX2 0ES, UK

www.solarisbooks.com

ISBN: 978 1 78108 508 0

10 9 8 7 6 5 4 3 2 1

A CIP catalogue record for this book is available from the
British Library.

Designed & typeset by Rebellion Publishing

Printed in Denmark

E.M. BROWN
BUYING
TIME

SOLARIS

PROLOGUE

HE WAS DAZZLED by a white light and felt a sudden heat in his head. He reached out for the wall to steady himself as he crumpled to the floor, his consciousness dwindling. He was aware of nothing else until he awoke in a hospital bed, hooked up to various bleeping machines.

Anna sat beside the bed, leafing through a fashion magazine and looking supremely unconcerned at his fate.

He wondered if he'd suffered a heart attack.

CHAPTER ONE

January, 2017

RICHIE PREPARED THE evening meal, then poured himself a glass of Burgundy and waited for Anna to arrive home from work. He moved into the lounge and crossed to the picture window.

It was a week since his hospitalisation. He recalled the white light, the sudden heat in his head: he'd passed out and awoken a day later in hospital. A neurosurgeon told him they'd run every test and scan imaginable, but had found nothing physiologically amiss. An idiopathic cerebral episode, he'd said, which Richie had interpreted as meaning that the specialists didn't have a bloody clue what had happened to him.

He'd taken it easy since getting home, easing himself back into work over the past couple of days. Anna had told him that it had been a sign, that at his age he should be drinking less and watching his diet. Richie had put it down to overwork, and told himself that he was as fit now as he had been ten years ago.

Still, it had been a sobering experience. His father had died of a massive cardiac arrest just months before his sixtieth birthday. Maybe he should heed Anna's words.

He dismissed the thought.

Dusk was falling and a full moon was rising over the copse on the horizon. The first snow of the year had fallen unexpectedly that afternoon, and he'd stopped writing at three and watched it through the study window. The grey sky and gently sifting snow had suited his mood, that indefinable melancholy which always afflicted him in the yawning hiatus between the travesty of Christmas and the perpetually belated coming of spring. It did not help that the script he'd just finished rewriting had changed from something he would have been proud to see under the by-line of Ed Richie to a piece of utter hackwork, thanks to the input of an inept director and an actress with a hypertrophied ego.

Now he stared out at the transformed countryside. A landscape blanketed with snow usually engendered in him a certain optimism. What was familiar, predictable, was metamorphosed into something other. A perfect record of passage covered the land, pristine and unblemished, and in the past it had spoken to him of fresh starts, new opportunities. He wondered whether that had been a carry-over from childhood, when snow betokened the wonder of Christmas and the joy of the new.

Now he could only see the slush that the snow would soon become.

A gritter had trundled up the lane an hour earlier, broadcasting salt, so the road from the station would probably be passable. He wondered if Anna would call from Leeds and use the snow as an excuse to stay the night at a hotel; he hoped so. He would enjoy a meal alone, then his usual Friday night pint with Digby at the Black Bull.

He drained his wine, poured himself a second glass, and returned to his station before the window. The snow was still falling – bigger, puffier flakes now – and the fields across the lane were covered, silvered in the moonlight. From far off he heard the high insistent barking of a fox.

The telephone rang in the hall. He hoped it was Anna, ringing from Leeds to say she wouldn't be back. As he picked up the receiver he felt a niggling guilt.

"Ed, I haven't dragged you away from anything?" Digby Lincoln's baritone resounded down the line.

"Only the contemplation of my mortality on this witheringly bleak January evening."

"Ah. How are you feeling, after…?"

"Surprisingly well, as a matter of fact. I'm on some pills to lower my blood pressure, which was rather high. Otherwise… fit as a fiddle."

"That's good to hear. You gave us a hell of a fright."

"Gave myself a bit of a fright, too. But I'm fine now." He changed the subject. "How's Caroline?"

"Caroline's Caroline, Ed. Never happier than when complaining about the vicar or the harridans at the local WI. Anyway, that's why I'm ringing. She just phoned to say she'll be late back from some meeting or other, so I won't be at the Bull until around nine-thirty."

"I'll have them in."

"Good man," Digby said. "Let's have a bit of a late one and make the most of Bob's disregard of the licensing laws, hmm? I'm celebrating."

"Celebrating?" Richie echoed. Then, "Oh, you got it?"

"Just back from a meeting in London with that fuckwit Traverson. Well, that's how I always thought of him. Strange how one's opinion can change, isn't it? No, on reflection, Ed, he still is a fuckwit – irredeemably old school. I'm sure the BBC wheel him out and dust him off to put the kibosh on any project that whiffs of radicalism."

"I feel a 'but' coming…"

"But for some strange reason he likes my outline and has commissioned six scripts."

Richie was genuinely pleased. "Great stuff. The beer's on me."

"Hell of a surprise," Digby said. "You know how much I've invested in this project. This means a hell of a lot to me, and with Traverson's backing I can scale back work on the execrable *Henderson's Farm*."

Richie smiled to himself. For the past five years Digby had made a very good living from knocking out thirty-minute scripts, at fifteen grand a time, for ITV; provincial hackwork, he'd said, that not only prostituted his talent but made London producers reluctant to commission more serious work from him. What he failed to mention was that the dozen episodes a year kept him and Caroline in luxury and earned him more than the Prime Minister's annual salary.

Richie, scrabbling around the studios for crumbs – writing three episodes a season of the godawful *Morgan's Café,* and a few radio plays for the BBC – was envious. And now Digby had his own hard-hitting prime-time drama to look forward to.

Perhaps, he thought, the Theakstons should be on Diggers tonight.

He heard the grumble of Anna's Range Rover as it crawled up the drive. "That's Anna. See you tonight, Digby, and congratulations."

He was replacing the receiver when the front door opened and Anna stamped into the hall.

He leaned against the wall and watched her struggle from her raincoat. "And how was your day?" he asked.

"Shit, if you must know."

He winced. He would be walking on eggshells tonight. "Care to elucidate?"

She stopped in the process of unwinding her scarf. "As if you're really bothered." She looked at the phone. "And who was that?"

"Digby. He got the commission he's been working on."

"Great," she grunted. "How is it that the talentless slob is rolling in it while you can hardly make ends meet?"

"Digby isn't talentless," he said. "For your information, he's a damned fine writer. It just happens that he's been working on a crap show. Also, he works hard at getting scenarios out there."

She hung up her dripping coat. "Well," she said pointedly, staring at him, "why can't you do the same? We could do with a few extra thousand. Then you might be able to afford that Caribbean holiday you promised me six months ago."

Six months... Was it really that long since Anna had moved in with him?

She saw the glass in his hand. "And I hope you've poured me one of those?"

"Right away," he said, moving to the kitchen and adding *sotto voce*, "my little Gauleiter."

He poured Anna the last couple of inches of some cheap Bulgarian plonk he'd opened yesterday, then filled his glass from the Burgundy. He took four huge mouthfuls and doled out the dinner: chicken chow mein with egg fried rice.

They ate in the oak-beamed dining room, warmed by the wood-burner which Richie had had the foresight to light just after the snowfall began.

Anna's ill-temper communicated itself through lack of eye contact and her silence; then later, through comments. She started with: "Jesus, this is like vinegar," hoisting her glass. "What is it?"

Richie lifted the bottle of Burgundy and showed her the label.

"Well, I don't like it. How's yours?"

"I must admit, it is rather on the tart side."

"I don't want any more. You can finish the rest of it. Get me a glass of water, would you? I'll have a gin after the meal."

He dutifully fetched a bottle of Perrier from the refrigerator and resumed his meal.

"So, why was work so bad?"

"You don't want to know."

"No, go on."

"No, I said you don't want to know." She looked at him over a forkful of noodles. "I know you couldn't give a damn about what I do."

He shrugged, let it go. The meal continued in silence.

Anna was tall, blonde, forty-two, and attractive. She wore expensive clothes very well and had a certain elegant hauteur, which was what had attracted him a little over six months ago. They'd met at a party arranged by the production company of *Morgan's Café*. Anna was the accountant hired by the company, and the party, with copious champagne, was one of the many corporate freebies Coromandel Cable had written off as a tax expense. Ed and Anna had hit it off immediately; he liked her wry sense of humour and her intelligence – although she worked in a dry-as-dust profession, she had artistic sensibilities and left-of-centre political leanings. He'd asked her out for a meal the following day, ringing her at work, and had suggested a weekend in the Lakes a few days later. The sex, he recalled now with chagrin, had been amazing.

A month after first meeting her, he'd suggested she move into his moor-side barn conversion twenty miles north of Leeds, and for the first three months everything had gone to script.

Then Anna had started griping about his apathy.

Now she hung her fork over her meal, stared at him and said, "Jesus Christ."

Shocked out of his reverie, he looked up at her. "What?"

Surprising him, she said, "Sultanas."

He smiled, genuinely nonplussed. "What?"

"You've put sultanas in the chow mein." She said *sultanas* the way you'd say *arsenic*.

He kept his calm. "I always put sultanas in chow mein."

"You know I hate sultanas."

"I..." Did he? He shrugged. "Sorry... Look, just leave them to one side."

"You did it deliberately, didn't you?"

Her stare was glacial and she had her mobile jaw clicked to one side in an expression that almost frightened him. "You put the bloody sultanas in the chow mein to provoke an argument."

"Anna, for chrissake... What's to argue about? If you don't like them, leave the damned things."

"You did it deliberately."

"Look, I forgot you didn't like them. I cooked this on auto, hardly thinking."

"I don't believe you. You used them deliberately to provoke me, to push things."

He sighed and took a huge gulp of wine, trying to calm himself. "I don't want to argue," he said, ashamed that he hadn't spoken more forcefully. The words had come out in barely a whisper.

She pushed the plate away. "You don't want to argue. Why am I not surprised? That's you all over, Ed. You just don't want to communicate, end of."

"No, Anna, I just don't want to argue."

"That's the contradiction. For a so-called writer, you're signally inept in the communication department. I've never met a more emotionally inarticulate man in all my life."

He stared at her, feeling himself starting to shake. "What do you want me to talk about?"

"You. Your emotions. Us. What you feel about me."

"You know what I feel about talking about emotions. It's a trite concept –"

"Christ, just listen to yourself." She paused, marshalling her words. "Do you know what I wondered, not long after we met?"

He centred his wine glass on its coaster. "No, what did you wonder?"

"I wondered if the only thing you wanted from me was the sex. I told myself I was being ridiculous. Now I think I was right."

"Anna…"

"And now that our sex life is dead," she cut in, "you're about as communicative as a corpse."

"And whose fault is that?" he snapped.

"What?"

"I said –"

She interrupted, "You think it's my fault? My fault we don't make love like we used to? Have you ever considered, you conceited bastard, have you ever considered for *one fleeting second* that I feel nothing for you because you're not only apathetic but emotionally constipated? How can I bring myself to feel anything for someone who sits in silence most of the time, never tells me how he's feeling, and never – not once – tells me what he feels for me?"

He was on the verge of saying, "I'm sorry," but that would have been an admission of guilt.

She pushed her chair back and hurried from the room, a hand to her mouth.

He sat in the sudden, resounding silence. The tick of the grandfather clock in the hall was very loud. He heard her moving about upstairs. He raised the wine to his lips and drank, drained the glass and poured himself another. The Burgundy was fine, rich and velvety. He felt only slightly guilty at his deception, then told himself, no, that was a lie. He didn't feel in the slightest bit guilty about giving her the dregs of the Bulgarian.

At moments like these, he was very aware of himself sitting on the cusp between one moment and the next. It was as if time were slowed down, as if he had an age in which to access and take stock of his emotions. Anna might accuse him of never communicating those emotions, but the truth was that his emotions, his feelings, were incommunicable, known only to himself, and then only nebulously, and reduced to cliché if he tried to make them understood to a third party.

He heard Anna come down the stairs and enter the kitchen, heard the fridge door rattle open and the gasp of tonic water being opened. She pulled at the cupboard door where the gin was kept, swore when it stuck, then poured herself a good measure. The following silence told him that she'd carried her drink through to the lounge, where she'd be curled on the sofa, feet drawn up, the bottle lodged between cushions.

"Well," she called from the next room, "aren't you going to say anything?"

He rose from the table and carried his glass and the bottle through to the lounge.

With the pretence of normality, he said, "Lawley rang this morning, wanting more changes." He stood by the window, staring out at the snow-covered countryside, his back to Anna.

"And are you going to make them?" Her question was brittle.

"Of course. I have to."

Before Anna, he'd lived with a woman called Sam Charlesworth, a well-known actress he'd met on the set of *Morgan's Café*, in which she'd guest-starred. Sam had been wanton, and demanded he make love to her before the picture window, the curtains open, every night for months – as if the room were a stage and their love-making was watched by an audience of thousands: her risqué exhibitionism was only slightly undermined by the fact that the sweep of terrain was totally uninhabited and the window not visible from the lane below.

The memory of her body, and the lust they'd shared, almost brought tears to his eyes.

"*Why* do you have to? Why can't you stand up for yourself?"

"Because it doesn't work like that. You make the changes or you're out. You'd be the one complaining, then."

"So you bend over and take it?" she said. Didn't she listen to a word he said? "I can't see your chum Digby taking any of that bullshit."

"Digby is a bigger name than me," he explained patiently. "And anyway, it isn't the director's changes I object to. Apparently he's screwing the actress, who wants a bigger part. That's the galling thing."

He closed his eyes, cursing himself, knowing that he'd provided her with further ammunition.

She used it. "Oh, so that's your gripe? It comes down to male ego. You can take being buggered by this Lawley chap, but coming from a mere woman…"

"It's not like that at all."

"Like hell it isn't. You're fragile, Ed. That's what I've noticed about you. Behind that big man-of-the-world front, you're about as confident as a teenager –"

He turned to face her. "You certainly have had a shit day at work, haven't you? And does that justify coming home and taking it out on me, with your illogical arguments? Or are you approaching that time of life?" He stopped.

She was staring at him, her mouth open as if in shock. He'd pushed her too far, this time.

"You shit!" In one fluid movement she was on her feet and throwing something. He only realised that it was the half-full gin bottle when he ducked and the chunky, ice blue missile hit the table and slid onto the floor, miraculously unbroken.

"What a thing to say! You fucking shit!" The glass followed. This time her aim was more accurate, and the glass glanced off his forehead, hit the wall and shattered.

He stared at the shards on the carpet, then turned in surprise as she came at him. Her first blow hammered off the side of his head, her second caught him across the jaw.

In the bubble of slowed time he seemed to inhabit, a part of him wanted to pull back his fist and show her how it should be done. She stared at him, tears blurring her make-up, her lips re-arranged, skewed in rage, waiting for him to react. She came at him again, raining blows on his chest with small, ineffectual fists. It would be laughable if it weren't so pathetic. He caught her wrists, less to stop her hurting him than to prevent her from hurting herself. She made inarticulate straining noises as she tried to escape his grip. Aware he was hurting her, he manoeuvred her across the room and pushed her into the sofa. She hit the padded backrest and used the momentum to launch herself at him again, screaming.

He caught her by the shoulders and held her at arm's length, counselling himself not to lose his temper. She wept, clawing at his arms, and he shut his ears to her railing and again pushed her into the sofa. She hit, struggled, and came back at him. He gripped her upper arms and said, "This is getting stupid. Calm down, for chrissake!"

He pushed her once more and this time, fuelled by vindictive indignation, made sure that the small of her back connected with the arm of the sofa. She screamed at the impact, fell to the floor and, sobbing, picked herself up and hurried from the room.

He stood for a time, breathing hard, then pushed stray hair from his brow, realising that he was sweating inordinately. He drew a few deep breaths, working to calm himself, while all the while his heartbeat matched the mantra going through his head, *The bitch, the bitch, the bitch...*

He picked the shards of glass from the carpet by the wall, ensuring that he had every last sliver, and deposited them in the kitchen bin, then returned to the lounge. Not wanting to be seated when she returned to instigate the next round, he moved to the window and stared into the darkness.

The moon was up and brighter now, laying its platinum light over the spinney on the hillside so that every gnarled branch and arthritic bough was etched individually. The snow had ceased, and the upholstered land rose and fell in great gentle swathes. Sounds came muffled through the cold air; a distant car moving up the lane, the barking of a farm dog.

He heard Anna moving about upstairs, banging doors as she went from room to room. What the hell was she doing? In her rage, was she looking for the airgun he'd for some reason kept from his youth – did she know about that, or was it Sam, or Gemma, he'd told about the weapon?

He wondered how she'd escalate the conflict. Their arguments had never reached this level before; had always ceased at imprecations. Her physical attack was unprecedented: he half expected her to come storming down, take a carving knife from the kitchen and launch herself at him.

He found himself thinking about Sam, and saw her undressing, smiling, seductive, in the arch of the floor-to-ceiling window; she had been tall, willowy, long-limbed, a blonde Scandinavian ice-maiden... except there had been no ice in her passion, but a hot, raging inferno of lust that had sometimes frightened him with its animal violence.

As a contrast to that passion, he recalled how their affair had ended. Three years after moving in with him she'd come back from a shoot in London and told him, dispassionately and without the slightest show of emotion, that she'd met 'someone,' and before he could gather his stupefied wits and demand an explanation, she left in the same taxi she'd arrived in. He'd heard nothing more from her since, not a word, not a letter or an email. She had excised herself from his life as if she'd never existed, leaving only a few perfumes and toiletries, and a freight of painful memories.

From time to time he caught glimpses of her on TV, before hurriedly switching channels, and once he'd inadvertently read a headline about her torrid affair with an American movie star.

He heard Anna descend and bang through the kitchen. Something dropped to the floor behind him and he turned to see her framed in the archway, two cases on the floor at her feet.

"You can push me just so far, Ed, but no bloody further. I'm going."

He stared at her. He knew, as the silence stretched, that he had it in his power to prevent her departure. All he had to do was to climb down, say sorry, tell her that he was thoughtless and unfeeling, and did she want another gin?

They had been here before, twice, and he'd relented, and things had been fine for a while – almost back to the rosy days at the start of their affair – until the next altercation.

Her face was blotched, made ugly with tears. She'd applied make-up hurriedly, and her face's lack of perfection was an accusation.

She said, "Well?"

He felt empowered, and without a word turned his back on her and stared through the window.

He heard a sound, an almost inaudible gasp, and the scrape of cases on the stone-flagged floor. He heard her footsteps pass down the hall, the front door open and slam, then saw her tramp through the snow, burdened, and throw the cases in the back of her Range Rover. She reversed at speed down the gravelled drive and into the lane, almost hitting the gatepost on the way, slewed round to face down the hill and raced off.

He raised the glass to his lips and took a long drink of wine.

Always, at times of heightened emotional tension, Richie felt as if he were an actor on a stage: there was something abstracted and artificial about his inhabiting this rarefied reality, as if an audience were watching him and judging his performance.

He picked up his mobile from the coffee table, found Anna's name, and deleted it. He moved to the dining room and stood before the painting hanging above the hearth. It showed a country scene of wild North Yorkshire. Early in their affair last summer, at a gallery in York, he'd vaguely admired the painting at Anna's prompting. A week later she'd presented it to him for his fifty-sixth birthday, and he'd made the required noises of appreciation.

He unhooked the painting from the wall and stuffed it behind a stack of cardboard boxes in the cupboard under the stairs, then saw the bubble-wrapped canvas that had hung on the chimney-breast before the Yorkshire landscape: an oil depicting the Cretan coastline, which he loved. He pulled it out and leaned it against the wall, intending to hang it later.

He made his way through the house, looking for signs of Anna's erstwhile presence. He was gratified to find that she had been thorough in removing all evidence of herself: she had even gone so far as to sort through the linen basket in the upstairs bathroom and take her dirty clothing. The only trace of her that remained was the faint ghost of her perfume.

He returned to the lounge and finished his drink.

He knew from experience that, over the course of the next few days – maybe even weeks – he would be afflicted by unpredictable mood swings. For no apparent reason he'd feel, as he felt now, the heady euphoria of liberation, of being freed from a relationship in which he'd felt bound, imprisoned: then, again without any obvious cause, he'd be overcome by an oppressive sense of melancholy, loneliness, and self-pity. In the past he'd self-medicated a course through the emotional roller-coaster with the soothing balm of alcohol, and it had always worked. He'd come through the other side, telling himself that he was better off alone... And then he'd make the same mistake again; lust and loneliness would overcome reason and he'd inveigle another fair, beautiful woman into the wreck of his life.

He considered opening a second bottle of Burgundy, then looked at his watch. It was just after nine, time he was pushing off to the

Black Bull. The thought of spending a few hours with his best friend propelled him into the hallway. He pulled on his thick winter coat, then saw that Anna had even left her copy of the key in the door. She'd thought of everything with that calculating, analytical accountant's brain of hers.

He left the hall light on, to guide his drunken return in the early hours, locked the door and tramped down the snow-covered drive.

He turned his collar up against the sharp wind. The stars were out in profusion, their incandescence undimmed by city lights. He'd moved to Yorkshire fifteen years before, after living in London for twenty years, and it had been one of the best moves of his life. The thought of the city now, with its incessant noise and bustle, filled him with horror. Where else but in the country could he retire to a good pub that wasn't overcrowded and which served fine ale till the early hours?

The Black Bull was a cheerily lighted old building in the main street of the village, its ill-painted sign showing a cross-eyed bull above the proclamation: *Free House*. That had been another boon, he'd discovered on moving to Harrowby Bridge: the pub served regular Theakstons, along with three guest ales every week.

He pushed into the snug and was enveloped in the heat belted out by the open log fire. Half a dozen regulars, all men and all knocking on – local farmers and a few in-comers like himself – occupied their regular seats around the oak-beamed room.

Richie buttressed the bar, nodded to a taciturn farmer whose response was a cryptic, "Hey-up."

"Service here!" Richie called out.

Cindy popped her head around the door of the store cupboard. "Oh, it's you. Well, you can wait your turn. I'm trying to find the bloody pickled eggs for Alf." Her tone was harsh with the granite-sharp local dialect, at odds with the lovely smile she bestowed, like a blessing, on all her regulars.

He saw that one of the guest ales was Taylor's Ram Tam. "A pint of the Taylor's when you've done with Alf, Cindy."

She emerged from the cupboard with a huge glass jar of pearlescent pickled eggs, spooned one into a bun case and slid it across the bar to the farmer, who asked her how she was enjoying university.

"I'm loving it." Cindy was a third year English student at Durham, back in the village for the Christmas break. Richie watched her pull him a pint of Ram Tam.

"Working hard, I hope?" Richie said.

"I never stop."

"I remember my far off student days. Would you believe I graduated thirty-five years ago?"

"You've told me at least ten times before. What do you want me to say, that I'm gob-smacked you're really fifty-six?" Her lovely smile tempered her words.

He laughed. "No, Cindy. I look in the mirror every morning and I'm reminded of the ravages of time."

"Well, you're the cheery one tonight," she said, placing the settling pint on the beer towel before him.

He relished the prospect of the first mouthful. "And I've every reason to be cheery, my sweetness. Anna has left me."

She cocked an eyebrow at him. "You're kidding me, right?"

"I jest not," he said. "She saw the light, saw what a mirthless, apathetic, self-centred bastard I really was, and packed her bags. Cheers!" He lifted the beer to his lips, took a long draw, and sighed. "By Christ, that's nectar."

She was watching him, her head on one side. "Straight up, Ed? Anna's walked out?"

"No word of a lie, child."

"So... how do you feel?"

He took a second mouthful. "Never better." He closed his eyes as the Ram Tam slid down.

Cindy said, "I remember you coming in with what's her name – not Sam, the one before her...? What was her name?"

He thought back. "Hell... what *was* her name? I can see her clearly enough."

Cindy laughed. "'See her'? They're all the same, Ed. You only go for one type: slim, blonde... Me dad says you order them from a catalogue. Hilary! That's her."

"Of course, Hilary. How could I forget Hilary?"

"Anyway," Cindy went on, "you came in and announced that you'd been released from Purgatory – or was it Hell? Hilary had left you. You're odd, you know that, Ed?"

"I know it better than you."

She said reflectively, "But I liked Sam. She was lovely."

"I liked her too. I loved her. Still, these things happen, water under the proverbial."

She stopped mopping the bar and looked at him, then shook her head in mock despair.

He stared at her. "What?"

"I've known you for about five years, Ed. And in that time you've lived with a dozen women."

"You exaggerate."

"Not much, I don't. When do you intend to settle down?"

He gestured to her with his half-empty pint. "Ah. Intend? I intend to settle down with every fair maiden I lose my heart to. I fully *intended* to spend the rest of my life with Samantha."

"Likely story!" Cindy snorted. "Anyway, where's Shakespeare tonight?"

Richie glanced at the back-to-front clock behind the bar and worked out that it was a minute off nine-thirty. "Diggers will barrel through the door the very second you place a pint of Old Peculier on the bar, if you start pulling now. Nothing if not punctual, old Diggers."

She took a pint glass from the shelf above the bar and drew a pint of Old Peculier. She let it settle, topped it up, and lifted it onto the towel just as the door opened to admit a huge, rubicund figure, along with a flurry of snow.

"There," Richie said. "What did I tell you?"

Cindy poked her tongue out at him and moved off to serve another regular.

Digby Lincoln stamped up to the bar, brrr'd his lips, and clapped Richie on the shoulder. "Cheers, my man. You're a life saver."

He necked half the pint, smacked his lips, and gestured across the room to a table beside the fire.

"Great news about the commission," Ed said as they sat down.

Digby laughed. "God, I'm one lucky old bugger. Didn't expect to get it, you know that?"

"Even when they hauled you down to London for the meeting?"

"I assumed Traverson wanted me to do something else, one of his bloody pet projects. Or get me to pitch him another bloody idea for a drama set in a restaurant."

"So when he said he liked your synopsis...?"

"I had to lift my triple chins off the floor."

Richie smiled. He'd met Digby Lincoln at Cambridge way back in '78. Richie had been a fresh-faced, naive lower-middle class lad from Nottingham – Digby the privileged scion of minor aristocrats from rural Shropshire. With nothing at all in common apart from the desire to write great novels and plays, they'd surprisingly formed a deep and abiding friendship that had not only survived the torrents of student life – including the obligatory fallings-out over girlfriends – but also the dangerous rapids of working in the same business for thirty years... with one exception which Richie tried not to think about.

Digby had been a tall, big-boned, good-looking youth at university, with debonair pretensions and an appalling taste in cravats. In recent years he'd grown bigger, rounder, and his consumption of alcohol had, improbably, increased even from the mammoth feats of inebriation of his student days. And he still sported garishly loud silk cravats.

He was borderline alcoholic now, and somehow managed to keep his sanity together despite hacking out sub-standard soaps for an opiated TV audience. Richie hoped the new series would give him a well-needed dose of self-respect.

"Anyway," Digby said, "how're you and Anna?"

"I'm fine. Anna's buggered off."

Digby halted his drink halfway to his mouth. "Come again?"

"We had a showdown an hour ago. She threw a few things at me and walked out."

"You're joking."

"I jest not." He pointed to Digby's almost empty glass. "Drink up."

He took their empties to the bar, dragged Cindy's attention away from a craggy young farmer, and ordered two more pints and some dry roasted peanuts.

"So," Digby said when he returned, "how are you feeling? Want to talk about it?"

"Cheers." Richie wiped foam from his top lip. "I'm fine. Not much to talk about. It's been going downhill for ages. We're best shot of each other."

"What happened? Excuse my prurience. Research for the next series. One of the characters is a serial philanderer."

Richie lowered his pint. "You don't have me down as a – ?"

"I was joking, Ed. Anyway, what happened? I know things between you two'd been a bit rocky of late."

"Rocky is an interesting euphemism, Digby. You know how it is: the glow wears off, the sex becomes routine, then non-existent... and you wonder what you first saw in the woman."

"I don't know how it is, though you've told me often enough." Digby regarded his pint. "You know, there have been times when I look at you, contrast my life with what you have... and I wonder if I'm missing something. I've been with Caroline for twenty-five years, now. Twenty-five bloody years, and I've never so much as bloody looked at another woman."

Richie smiled. "And I sometimes look at you and Caroline and wonder what *I'm* missing. Of course, you always covet what you don't have."

They sat in companionable silence for a time, warmed by the flames of the fire, tossing peanuts into their mouths and washing them down with beer. Did life, Richie wondered at one point, get any better, with good company and alcohol to take the sharp edge off reality?

Digby said, "Sometimes you amaze me, Ed."

"How's that?"

"All those women. The emotional freight… And yet it doesn't seem to upset you. I mean, Anna walking out. Okay, okay… I know you two had issues in the" – he hiccupped – "in the bedroom, but then there was Sam, and Hilary, and Pamela, and before her… what's her name?"

"What was her name? I've no idea." He could see the woman, small, pixie-like… an American solicitor at a big firm in Leeds.

"Susan," Digby said. "And before her…" He waved. "God knows. Dozens of them, ever since…"

"What's your point?"

"My point is… when they walk out, you affect this nonchalance, water off a duck's back. Even with Sam. Okay… a few tears in your beer for a day or so, and then what did you say, 'Good bloody riddance'? The thing is, Ed, are you kidding yourself? Are you kidding the world? Brave front, kind of thing? Macho defence mechanism? Is that what you're hiding behind, or are you really an unfeeling bloody bastard?"

Richie laughed, when he would rather have winced. "My round. Whisky chaser?"

"Why the hell not?"

At the bar he ordered two pints and a couple of whiskies, downed his Glenfiddich straight off, and signalled for another. He returned to the table and hoped that Digby had lost the thread of his argument.

But he should have known better. Old Diggers was like a terrier worrying a bone when in pursuit of a notion.

"Well?" Digby said, consigning the scotch to oblivion. "Which one is it?"

"Neither," Richie said. "Or both." He downed his whisky. "You want the honest truth?"

"Please."

"Then I'll tell it. It's both. I alternate. I swing between regret and euphoria, melancholy and joy." He took a long swallow of Ram Tam. "And the bloody stupid thing is, I don't know which feeling is the... the genuine one. So maybe I am an unfeeling bloody bastard. Am I making sense?"

Digby blinked. "I think so."

"Tonight... tonight I'm on a high. Anna walked out on me and I feel liberated. Tomorrow... tomorrow there'll be moments when I'll miss the bloody woman, followed by the realisation that I'm better off without her. And it was the shame... the *same* with all the others."

"Even Sam?"

He ignored that. "So who knows what I *really* feel, Digby? I swing between poles. Maybe I don't cope as well as I seem to. Maybe I'm schizoid." He laughed without humour at the idea. "So maybe sometimes I feel the pain but I'm too weak to show it, and at other times I'm a bloody unfeeling bastard."

Digby raised his glass. "That'll do me, Ed."

For the next hour or so they wandered back and forth over the agreeable no-man's-land of business gossip, punctuating character assassination with further rounds, plus chasers, then wending their way back to the topic of the little shits in charge of the production companies that ran things these days. Richie became steadily and remorselessly more inebriated. The pub filled up with familiar faces. The publican, Cindy's portly father Bob, threw a couple of logs on the fire and stopped to chat with Richie and Digby. Someone put The Cure on the jukebox... except they weren't called jukeboxes any more... and the 'eighties tune, *Boys Don't Cry*, reminded Richie of a girl he knew in '88, and a woman standing across the room put him in mind of someone else, a woman he'd worked with in a bookshop in London.

Digby was saying, "Christ, you know what'll happen to the next project?"

Richie sighed. "Don't be so pessimistic."

"Down the fucking toilet like all the others."

"Oh... I don't know. If... if you stick to your guns."

"Down the fucking toilet!"

"... stick to your guns."

They stared into the flames and downed their pints, and then Digby was back from the bar with another two pints and chasers.

Richie tried to focus on his friend. He had three or four chins, which Richie only really saw when he was drunk. The rest of the time he didn't notice how absurd those chins were. They were just Digby Lincoln, part of the great, dishevelled man that Diggers had become. But he noticed the wobbling soufflés of flesh now, and the greying straggle of his moustache, and Digby's bulbous red nose, his poor dental work...

"How the hell did it all end up like this, Ed?"

Richie blinked. "Like what?"

"Like us two, writing complete and utter shite for the god in the corner?"

"But the new commission...?" Richie began.

Digby swept on, "Prostituting what little talent we possess for oodles of cash. Ed, tell me truthfully. How many TV pieces can you tell me, hand on heart... hand on heart, man... how many pieces are you *proud* of? How many?"

Richie thought about it, cast his mind back over the years, over the dozens of TV credits to his name – though of course he recalled nothing like that number, just the crap. He tried to think of one series, one episode even, he could claim was excellent, a finished product that lived up to his original conception.

"Well... there were a few radio plays."

"No! No, TV... I'm talking about TV, Ed."

"Very well. You win. Nothing. Not a thing."

"Touché."

"But... but I never heard you or Caroline complain about the money, Diggers."

Digby stared into the flames. "I'm complaining about it now, Ed. You know what I wish?"

"I know... I know. You've told me before. You wish you'd kept at writing novels."

"Too bloody right. I had talent, you know? Okay, so I wasn't getting anywhere, but I should have stuck at it. Written for radio and TV alongside the novels."

Richie looked away. "Never too late..." he began, lamely.

"Of course it is! I'm old, over the hill. Worn out. Jaded. Fucking cynical. And..."

To Richie's amazement, then, Digby began weeping.

He stared at Diggers, quite at a loss to know how to respond. He half reached out, meaning to tap his friend's meaty, corduroy-clad thigh in a consolation – but the gesture died, half-completed, inappropriate.

His friend hung his head, his shoulders shaking, and tears fell onto the rumpled shirt that swelled over his belly.

"Digby, what the – ?"

Digby said, "Caroline's having an affair." It came out in a rush, and Digby looked up and smiled at Richie through his tears.

The pronouncement came as a profound shock to Richie, almost sobering him. Digby and Caroline were fixtures in his life, inseparable; they carped and complained about each other from time to time, but behind the words abided a deep affection. Richie knew that Diggers had found, in the solid, dependable, homely Caroline, something that he, Richie, had never managed to find in anyone.

He found himself wishing that Digby had never mentioned Caroline's unfaithfulness, for it upset him, set his world off-kilter. Then he realised how selfish the thought was, and said inadequately, "An affair?"

"Thought there was something wrong. Or rather I suspected. But I told myself I was being paranoid."

"How do you know?"

"Found a letter. A note in her handbag when I was looking for change. You know she takes pottery courses in Gargrave? Well, she met someone there. Arty type. Bohemian. And he's younger than her. Thirty-sodding-five."

"She told you this, admitted…?"

"I confronted her. She admitted it."

"So… what'll happen?"

His friend took a long, juddering breath. "I asked her… asked her if she was leaving me. She said…" He stopped suddenly, shook his head and murmured, "She said she didn't know. She said she loved him, this Jonathan character. I never did like the fucking name… Said she loved him but that she still felt something for me." Digby looked up at Richie and tried to smile. "The hell of it is, Ed, the terrible thing is: not knowing, the uncertainty. Not knowing what the bloody hell she'll do. And the fact that I still love her, and yet hate her for what she's done."

Now Richie did reach out and pat Digby's ham-like thigh. "The thing not to do, Digby, is… is act rashly. Take it easy. Don't push her. My guess is it's just a fling, an infatuation. It'll blow over."

Digby gave a gusty laugh. "That's what I keep telling myself. It's a fling. She's become jaded with me, the routine. Christ, I admit it, Ed, I'm no Adonis. I mean, look at me, just *look* for fuck's sake. A fat, fucking alcoholic wreck…" He sighed. "Another round?"

"I don't see why not, Diggers."

Later, still reeling from Digby's bombshell, Richie recalled looking at the clock behind the bar and working out that it was not eleven o'clock, but after one… And he was blasted, shit-faced, and he'd have one hell of a sore head in the morning.

The next thing he recalled, Digby was on his mobile phone, calling for a taxi, and then Richie lurched to his feet. He staggered, felt himself falling, reached out and knocked something from a shelf to uproarious comment from a knot of regulars… and he saw a globe hit the floor and shatter. He stood swaying over the broken world, apologising to Bob who was picking up the pieces and telling him not to worry…

Then he felt Digby's hand on his arm and they stumbled from the pub, and the cold wind hit him in an icy, sobering blast.

They stood swaying in the street, beneath the packed stars, waiting for the taxi.

Diggers was saying, "But you, Ed... about Anna. I'm sorry."

"'Sokay. Don't worry. I'm fine."

"Fine?" Diggers stood before him, rocking back and forth. "You're just saying that, Ed. You're not fine. Not really... How can anyone be fine when... when their woman's just walked out?"

Snow began to fall again, spangling his friend's long hair and balding pate.

"You know what it's all about, Ed? Your women...? Why you move from one to the next, all the same..." He reached out, gripped Richie's shoulders. "It's... it's because of... of what's her name, back then. It's all about what happened back then."

"No."

"It is, Ed. You can't deny it."

A car swept around the corner, bathing them in the glare of its headlights, and braked beside the pavement.

Digby said, "Come back to my place. A nightcap."

"I... I've really had enough... Going home."

"C'mon. A little nightcap. I have a bottle of... of something."

"No, really, Diggers."

Richie eased his friend into the taxi. "I'll see you later... give you a call."

And then the taxi was driving away through the falling snow, and Richie was left with his friend's words ringing in his ears.

It's all about what happened back then...

He turned up his collar, out of habit, against a cold wind he no longer felt, and turned this way and that to orient himself.

He trudged home, along the main street and then left, up the steep lane towards the moors – stopping once to relieve himself in the ditch – then onward through the packed, squeaking snow. Ahead, on the crest of the hill, he saw the apex of his barn conversion, like the prow of a ship against the stars, and then the hall light came into view, guiding him. He made his way up the sloping drive and saw that the tyre tracks from Anna's Range Rover had been filled in by the evening's fresh snow, obliterating her retreat.

At the door he turned and stared down the valley to the glinting lights of the village, crudely mirroring the constellations overhead. *It's all about what happened back then.*

Annabelle.

No...

He found his key, managed to unlock the door, and pushed his way inside.

He stopped dead, staring. He tried to cry out, but the sound died in his throat. At the far end of the hall, standing at the foot of the stairs, was a slim, fair woman smiling sadly at him.

Richie pitched forward, engulfed in a sudden white light, and fell to the floor unconscious.

From Ed Richie's journal, 9th January, 2017

THIS IS A verbatim account of the dialogue I had with Anna when she came to visit me in hospital a few days ago.

Anna: How are you feeling?

Me: I'm fine

Anna: You don't look fine. What did the doctor say?

Me: That I suffered an idiopathic cerebral episode...

Anna: And what does that mean?

Me: It's medicspeak for 'they don't have a bloody clue.'

Anna: You need to cut down on the booze, Ed. You're not the man I met...

Me: I'm certainly not the man you met. I'm older, wiser, and more jaded.

Anna: And what's that supposed to mean?

Me: It means, my sweet, that I'm older, wiser, and more jaded.

Anna: And apathetic.

Me: I've always been apathetic, but I didn't let you see that when we first met.

Anna: You admit as much?

Me: I admit everything. I'm an imposter.

She just stared at me, hatred in her eyes.

Anna: Fuck you, Ed!

And she stormed out.

Is it any wonder that our relationship is on the rocks?

CHAPTER TWO

January, 2030

ELLA SHAW STOOD in the observation lounge of Edinburgh International Airport with a dozen other reporters and three TV crews and watched the first plane of Operation Rainbow Airlift touch down. As the Scottish Airway's strato-liner, its fuselage emblazoned with rainbow insignia especially for this flight, taxied along the runway and approached the terminal building, Ella hurried from the lounge and took the lift to the arrivals area, seriously conflicted. It was a tragedy that the airlift was necessary at all, yet gratifying that the Scottish government had offered a safe haven for the refugees. Even on a personal level, Ella didn't know quite how she felt about being reunited with an old lover who, seven years ago, she had walked out on.

She moved to a window overlooking the freezing tarmac. She'd already written a preliminary story and squirted it to her editor at ScotFreeMedia, backgrounding the airlift and describing the landing and the emotions it aroused. Later, after interviewing Kit, she'd write a piece for release first thing in the morning. It would be something of a scoop for her newsfeed; she hoped Douglas would be suitably impressed.

She watched as ground staff drove the step-vehicles to the front and rear of the plane. It was freezing out there – her wrist-com reported temperatures in the capital of minus five – and the workers' breaths billowed in the air. Frost scintillated on the tarmac like pulverised diamond. The sickly pale sky over the Forth promised the first snowfall of the year. What a welcome for the refugees, Ella thought, many of whom had made the long trek across the US from California to JFK.

To her right, a young woman with a Glasgow accent talked to camera; other reporters murmured into microphones or wrist-coms. Ella was glad she'd got all that out of the way and had to do neither; she was too nervous about the imminent meeting to compose an objective report.

The door in the aircraft's bulbous nose cracked open and pivoted back, and the first of the refugees appeared at the top of the steps. Ella watched them file down the staircase and hurry across the glittering apron towards the terminal building, choking up at the thought that it had come to this. In stark contrast to the last time she'd seen a number of her LGBTQ brothers and sisters *en masse* – last summer at the Gay Pride festival in Stirling – there was nothing joyous or celebratory about the sorry gaggle of men, women and children filing from the plane. Some of them were draped in rainbow flags, but they resembled the bedraggled plumage of storm-battered birds, once gaudy, now defeated. A few of the refugees smiled and waved, but for the most part the atmosphere was sombre.

Ella spoke into her wrist-com, making a few *ad hoc* observations, descriptive details she'd splice into her report this evening.

The last of the refugees left the plane and trooped into the terminal building. Ella moved from the window and positioned herself behind the barrier in sight of the exit. She hadn't seen an image of Kit for almost five years; she wondered if she'd recognise her old lover. *Old*, she thought; hell, she and Kit were the same damned age: both sixty now, though Ella tried to tell herself that she looked ten years younger.

Her wrist-com chimed and Douglas's big face filled the small screen.

"Ella, we've secured an exclusive with the PM about the airlift and its consequences. We're leading with that at nine. Will you have something to follow that, by midnight?"

"You said a long piece by the morning..." she began.

"That was an hour ago, Ella. You think you can get an exclusive with Kit Marquez?"

"I'll do my best, but I can't promise anything."

She'd worked it to her advantage, not telling her editor that Kit was an ex when she mooted the outside chance of getting an exclusive with the one-time Director of the now-defunct Civil Liberties Organisation. It'd be kudos for her when she presented the package; she just hoped she had time to compose something hard-hitting by midnight.

"And have you seen the latest from the States?" Douglas asked.

"Go on." She'd killed her wrist-com's news update while waiting for the landing, the better to concentrate her thoughts and compose herself.

"An off-air comment by the President of the good ole US of A. Caught by a by-stander and squirted two minutes ago. I'll patch it through."

Ella heard a squall of static followed by President O'Ryan's lazy Texan drawl: "*We're best rid of the queers, bud. Pity the plane didn't ditch in the Atlantic.*"

Douglas looked up at her. "What do you think?"

"Deliberate," Ella said. "O'Ryan might be a bastard, but he's smart. It'll go down well with cretins in Fucksville, Idaho. The midterm elections are later this year, remember?"

"We're getting together a montage of his inflammatory statements over the past year, then doing a contrast piece with the PM's latest statements."

"Hey," Ella said, "the first of the refugees are coming out. Catch you later."

She cut the connection and scanned the drawn faces of the men and women emerging to a scatter of cheers and ragged applause.

Representatives of various aid organisations and charities were on hand to meet the refugees; those without friends or family in Scotland were to be housed in temporary refugee centres outside Edinburgh and Glasgow. Over the course of the next week, a further six planes were scheduled to leave the US, and civil liberties groups were chartering more flights next month. Many people had left the US of their own accord over the past couple of years, but after the bombings of gay nightclubs in New York, San Francisco and Phoenix, and the murder of over a hundred LGBTQ people across the States last month alone, the mass exodus had begun.

Ella felt a rush of blood to her face as she caught sight of Kit Marquez. But Jesus, she looked old... Ten years ago, Kit had been tall, broad, and straight-backed, an athlete and an intellectual. She'd worked as a lecturer at UCL in London, and then in Edinburgh, a towering figure, both physically and intellectually. Now she appeared shrunken, bent over, her hair iron-grey and her face lined.

The press-pack tagged her and swooped, cramming mics in her face and jabbering for sound-bites. At that second, Kit looked up through the melee, caught Ella's eye, and smiled – and the years rolled away.

She barged her way through the press with her old determination, dropped her bag and stood facing Ella. They embraced.

Ella found herself unable to speak.

"I never thought," Kit whispered fiercely into her ear, "that our reunion would be like this, in such dreadful circumstances. But we make the best, girl, we make the best."

Ella pulled away and brushed tears from her cheeks. She shook her head, words still beyond her.

Kit said, "You look good, El."

How could she return the sentiment, utter a flagrant lie? She smiled through tears and then, annoyed by the buffeting, said, "Let's get out of here. I have a taxi booked. As I said in the last email, you're staying at my place for as long as you like."

"El... One thing. There's someone... I hope you don't mind?" Kit turned and indicated a tiny young woman with a shaved scalp and a thin, scowling face, hanging back. She looked no older than twenty-five.

Ella felt relieved and smiled at the young woman. "You should see the size of my place, Kit. I have an upper villa in Morningside. Plenty of room."

"This is Aimee," Kit said. "Aimee, Ella."

Aimee gave a guarded smile and a thin, cold hand. "Kit's told me a lot about you, Ella," Aimee murmured.

"It's good to meet you. Come on, let's get out of here. I did some cooking this afternoon. You must be famished."

They squeezed through the crowd and took the elevator down to the car park.

"Not one of your famous curries?" Kit said.

"How did you guess? It's the only thing I cook with anything like competence."

As the taxi carried them through the rapidly descending twilight, from a still frost-white countryside around the airport to the brightly illuminated city, Aimee said, "You have a strange accent, but not Scottish?"

Ella laughed. "I'm from London, Aimee. Peckham. I came up here when things started getting bad down south."

"From what I read," Kit said, "things are almost as bad down there as they are in the States."

"You know what they used to say," Ella said. "When America sneezes, England catches a cold."

Aimee looked shocked. "But we'll be okay up here?" She glanced from Kit to Ella, a frightened rabbit.

Kit squeezed her hand with maternal affection. "We'll be fine, Aimee. Trust me."

They arrived in Morningside and Ella showed them around her spacious villa with pride; from Ella's top-floor lounge they looked across the lighted spread of the capital.

After the meal, which Aimee picked at but Kit devoured, they sat in the lounge before the multi-fuel stove as, through the picture window, the first fat snowflakes began to fall. Ella told them about her life in Scotland, her friends in the capital, and her job for ScotFreeMedia.

Kit said at one point, "You have a rich life, El."

She nodded. "I'm reasonably happy."

Kit looked around the room. "You're here alone?"

"That's right."

Ella changed the subject.

They talked politics, with Kit dissecting the situation in the US and giving a bleak forecast of what was to come, contrasted with the fortunes of Europe. Aimee, Ella noticed, fell silent and stared into her wine; she wondered if the girl found the talk boring, or couldn't keep up.

Then Aimee yawned and said she'd turn in. Ella gave her the choice of bedrooms, a single or the double she'd set aside for Kit. "Are you two...?"

Kit said, "We'll take the double, if that's okay?"

"That's fine." She indicated the room. "En suite. I think you'll have everything you need. Just shout if not."

Kit kissed Aimee. "I'll stay up, okay?"

When they were alone, Kit sat cross-legged on the sofa, her relaxed posture bringing back memories.

Ella said, "I feel I need to apologise... walking out the way I did."

Kit shook her head, smiling. "Don't apologise. I understand."

Ella stared, surprised. "You do?" How could Kit understand what had motivated her back then, when Ella herself could hardly make sense of why she had ended their relationship?

Kit smiled and gestured with her glass towards the bedroom. "Hey, I must apologise for landing Aimee on you like that."

"Really, there's no need."

"She's a great kid, but she's... I met her last year. She's from a Mormon family in Utah, and you can imagine their reaction when she came back from university one vacation and announced she was seeing someone, and a woman at that. They disowned her." Kit shrugged. "I think I'm a surrogate mother figure."

"You'll be good for her."

"She's... she has problems, El. She's traumatised. Her lover at uni... this was eighteen months back... Her lover was out late one night, on the way back from a party... Just her luck to run into a vigilante gang of AWs."

Ella repeated the acronym. "Meaning?"

"Aryan Wolves, they call themselves. White supremacists."

"And this girl... she was black?"

Kit nodded. "And the little fool had a rainbow badge. So when the pricks saw it... El, she didn't stand a chance."

El swallowed and stared at her wine.

"They killed her, but not before..." Kit paused, then went on, "Aimee fled to New York, then tried to take her own life. A cry for help. I helped." She took a long drink of wine. "You know something, El? I thought long and hard about leaving the States. In the early days, I was determined to stay. I looked down on the people who'd had enough and decided to get out. I said it was best to stay, to fight the hatred and prejudice. I really thought I could do something, I thought that, together, the voice of reason could change things." She stared into the flames of the stove. "How fucking wrong was I there, El?"

She fell silent for a while, then went on, "So, I'm sorry about hauling Aimee along, but I hope you understand."

Ella smiled. "Of course I do."

In fact, it made things easier for her.

When Kit had contacted her a couple of months ago, out of the blue, and told her she was leaving the States and seeking asylum in Scotland, Ella had offered her a place with her, and sponsorship, without really thinking through the emotional consequences of her altruism. It had been the right thing to do for an old lover in trouble.

Only later, when the reality of Kit's return kicked in, had she feared that her old lover might want to resume their relationship on more than just a friendly footing.

Ella turned the talk back to her work, and then asked, "Have you thought of what you might do here?"

Kit shrugged. "Write. Try to pick up a bit of lecturing…"

"As I said in my last email, I think I can help there. With the writing, anyway."

"That'd be great."

"My editor at the newsfeed wants me to do a piece on the airlift, and you, for midnight. I'll knock out something about what you told us over dinner, your take on the situation over there and where it's heading. And I'll include a suitably altered version of what you said about the murder of Aimee's lover, if that's okay, as an emotional hook."

"That should be fine, but let me check with Aimee. No names."

"Of course not. Trust me," Ella said. "The thing is, my editor doesn't know about you and me, so when he asked me to try to get an exclusive, I said I'd try. He'll be ecstatic."

Kit smiled over her wine glass. "Just where is this leading, El?"

"He'll be even more knocked out if I say I might be able to get you to write for him."

Kit looked dubious. "For a *newsfeed*?"

"Don't pooh-pooh it, Kit. Do you know how much they pay?"

"Go on."

"Two pounds a word," Ella said. "And you could wrangle more from them if you sign an exclusivity deal. They run everything from a few hundred-word opinion pieces, to full articles of two thousand or so. It'd give you a voice, a platform, and a foot in the door. If you sign for a year, at the end of it you could look around for other things."

"But a *newsfeed*, El?"

"It's a prestigious outlet. Obama and Monbiot do pieces for them; it's the future."

Kit regarded her wine. "It's tempting, The money is good."

"If you like, I'll arrange a meeting with my editor, Douglas Munroe. I'm seeing him in the morning. I'll mention your name.

He'll snap my hand off, of course, and you'll have all the bargaining chips on your side. What do you say?"

"Very well," Kit nodded. "As you say, it's a platform, and I have a *lot* to get off my chest."

Talk, inevitably, drifted back to the political situation in the States, and Kit's feelings about leaving the place of her birth, for good. She rounded off her peroration with a line that Ella knew she would use in her article: "You know, El, some people think that America in the twentieth century was a social experiment: a nation founded on liberty, equality, and freedom of speech; a nation whose motto was the American Dream, where anyone, no matter what their social status, origin, race or gender, might enjoy an equal status and equal opportunities... And that experiment has ended in failure."

Later, Kit drained her wine, said she was dog-tired, and paused on the way to the bedroom. "El, you still planning on writing your book on that writer guy?"

"Still planning, Kit. In fact, I hope to get down to it pretty soon now. Pity I have to go to England to do the interviews."

"Into the lion's den, El. Good night."

"Sleep well."

Ella sat for a while when Kit had retired, thinking about the book and her meeting with Douglas Munroe tomorrow. She had a proposal to put to her editor, and she was not at all sure how Douglas might take it.

She considered another glass of wine, but abstained: she still had the fifteen hundred words to write on Kit Marquez and the airlift.

For the next hour she curled in her armchair and tapped away at her laptop. She read the article through, toned down a few of the purple patches, then squirted it off to ScotFreeMedia minutes before the midnight deadline.

Then she did have another glass of wine and sat thinking about Kit.

*   *   *

IN THE MORNING, after a leisurely breakfast, she left Kit and Aimee to explore the city and took a taxi into the centre of town.

The head office of ScotFreeMedia was on the third floor of the old Royal Over-Seas building on Princes Street, overlooking Princes Street Gardens and facing the imposing monolith of Edinburgh Castle.

Ella's wrist-com told her it was seven below zero, and as she stepped from the cab into the keening wind she marvelled that it was as much as that. She crunched across the gritted pavement, hurried into the warmth of the Over-Seas building, and took the lift to the third floor.

Douglas Munroe was seated in an old armchair with his feet lodged on a coffee table. Like Douglas himself, the building was old and decrepit, the oak panelling and plaster cornices pitted and crumbling. Douglas was vastly overweight, his face empurpled, and his long hair grey and unkempt. In contrast to the old room, a dozen state-of-the-art smartscreens hung at every height, relaying images from around the world. The editor worked at a laptop, wobbling on his meaty thighs, a mic and earpiece emerging from the tangle of his hair.

When Ella entered the room, he looked up briefly and grunted, "What the hell are you doing here?"

Ella pulled up a dining chair and sat before him. "I made an appointment, remember? Yesterday morning, for eleven today?"

Douglas grunted again, his eyes flickering across the screen. Without looking up, he said, "Fine piece you filed last night." He dispensed praise with bad grace, like a miser parting with pennies. "But how the buggery, I asked myself, did you do it?"

He slipped the laptop onto the worn carpet and tugged the mic and earpiece free, giving her his full attention. "You didn't pay the woman?" he asked, almost wincing in anticipation of her reply.

"Called in an old favour."

"That's what I like to hear, Ella. Now, why the hell are you wasting my time? If you've come for a pay rise, no way. If you want a transfer to sunny Australia, on your bike."

"I don't know why I put up with you, Doug, you old curmudgeon."

"You love it. You know where you stand with old Dougy. Say it as it is. Now, out with it."

"I think I can do you a big favour."

He narrowed his eyes. "This sounds ominous. I don't like favours. In this business, favours are a debt. Go on, girl."

"What would you say to having Kit Marquez writing for ScotFreeMedia?"

"Couldn't afford her," he grunted.

"I think you could."

"She wouldn't work for us."

"But she would, if you gave her free rein to express herself. I even think she'd sign an exclusivity clause. For a year."

"You sure?"

"I think I can swing it."

"I'd need to meet her, sound her out."

"I can arrange that."

Douglas raked a hand through his thatch and bared nicotine-stained teeth at her. "So, Ella... What's in it for you?"

"I want a month off."

"I can't pay you."

"That's fine."

"What?" He feigned shock. "Let me repeat: I can't pay you."

"And I said: fine. I don't need paying."

"Well... that puts a different complexion on the matter. I'll miss you, but I suppose I can give Bob and Letty more hours. Okey-dokey, you've got it."

"You're a star, Douglas."

"Don't tell me, you're going to sunny Thailand or some such tropical clime?"

"I'm going to England."

"That cess-pit? You must be bloody mad." He stopped and pointed at her. "I get it. That damned book of yours? You're finally going to write the bloody thing."

"Well, start the research, interview a few people."

"As I keep telling you, there's no market for biographies of English writers – or writers of any nationality, for that matter. I don't know what you see in him."

"A lot, Douglas. Not least that for thirty years he wrote middling TV dramas and radio plays, and then chucked all that in and wrote eight novels that dissected the modern Western world and foretold, with utter prescience, the rise of fascism."

"And then he vanished."

Ella nodded. "Then, five years ago, he disappeared without trace. That's part of the allure, Douglas – what the hell happened to Ed Richie?"

Douglas sighed. "Right, you've got what you want. A month off. Arrange Kit Marquez to come and see me and we'll be quits. Now bugger off!"

"I'm on my way, Douglas," she said. She felt like kissing the foul-mouthed, miserable old xenophobe, but restrained herself.

She left the headquarters of ScotFreeMedia and rewarded herself with a coffee at her favourite café on Charlotte Square. She sat at a high stool in the window, looking out at the muffled, hurrying crowd outside, and contemplated the trip south. She hadn't ventured over the border to the country of her birth for five years, and a part of her dreaded the prospect.

But Ed Richie's story fascinated her – and she had a personal connection to the author that she hadn't bothered mentioning to Douglas.

Her wrist-com chimed, and Kit smiled out at her. "Meeting over, El?"

"All sorted."

"Great. Listen, we've just found a wonderful café on Nicholson Street, The Sorority, and it's full of sisters. Get yourself over here, girl."

Ella smiled. "I thought it wouldn't take you long to find it, Kit. I'm on my way."

From Ed Richie's journal, 2nd August, 2005

FALLING... AGAIN. DEBS stars in *CrazyMadLoopy*. She's thirty, small, crew-cut, feisty, tattooed, studs all over the bloody place. Not my type at all, but shorn of ironmongery and tribal markings, just the ticket. I know what Diggers will say: he'll call me a bloody fool and tell me to grow up. Anyway, Debs lives over in Manchester, and she's meeting me in Leeds for dinner next week. We'll see what happens. It's three months since Ophelia walked out and I noticed the other week that I've started talking to myself again.

From a review of recent children's programmes in Whazzup Kids? *25th November, 2005*

AND BBC'S *CRAZYMADLOOPY* goes from strength to strength. The set up is bats-in-the-belfry: brother and sister Ben and Liz are packed off to their uncle's rambling country pile by squabbling parents, only to find that mad uncle Montague is dead and his ghost is haunting Montague Hall. Rather than tell the authorities and have their holiday come to an end, Ben and Liz conspire with their uncle's ghost to keep the hall running as a stately home open to paying guests. Madcap shenanigans follow. Super fun! We'll have an interview with the show's creator and chief writer Ed Richie in the next issue.

CHAPTER THREE

April, 2016

RICHIE WOKE IN the morning to find himself in his bedroom.

He must have somehow staggered up the stairs, undressed, and put himself to bed. That in itself was something of a minor miracle, and another was that he wasn't suffering from a raging hangover. The last thing he recalled was stumbling into the house... After that, nothing.

He wondered how Digby was feeling, if he'd gone home and made inroads into the bottle of 'something.' He remembered what Diggers had told him about Caroline – and only then did he recall Anna leaving him.

He stared at the ceiling and tried to work out how he felt about her departure. If he was perfectly honest with himself, he was fine. He still felt the sense of liberation he had experienced last night, and none of the incipient loneliness. The last couple of months with Anna had been hell, so perhaps he would be spared the melancholy and regret, this time.

He glanced at the clock on the bedside table and was surprised to find that it was after eleven. Well, he deserved a lie in; he'd finished the damned script yesterday, and promised himself some time off. He'd mosey on down to the Black Bull, have a pint and a ploughman's to celebrate regaining his freedom.

He looked back at the bedside table and wondered what was wrong. Then he had it: the novel he was currently reading was not in its usual place beside the alarm clock. He wondered if in staggering to bed last night he'd knocked it on to the floor.

He sat up and swung out of bed, expecting his head to start throbbing. To his relief he felt nothing – well, nothing aside from the twinge of arthritis in his ankles and right knee.

He stared at the dining chair next to the bed. His chinos, shirt and jumper were folded neatly along with his underwear on the chair. He had expected to find them strewn across the carpet. He reached out, picking up his shirt, and stared at it, and then at the trousers and jumper.

But he'd been wearing black jeans last night, a rugby shirt and a thicker jumper than this one. He must have ditched what he'd been wearing in the laundry and set out these clothes for the morning...

He dressed and made his way downstairs. He'd have a quick coffee to kick start his metabolism, then wander down to the Bull.

It was strange, after living with Anna for months, to have the kitchen and the morning to himself. She'd been an early riser, showering and dressing before Richie stumbled out of bed much later, and she'd always insisted on making breakfast and brewing the coffee.

He made coffee, marvelling at the well-stocked fridge; Anna must have been to the supermarket during the last few days, as he found his favourite cheeses and a fresh jar of piccalilli.

He poured himself a black coffee and drank it standing up, staring through the kitchen window at the farmer's field rising towards the spinney.

The snow was gone and the sun was shining. That was unremarkable in itself – he'd become accustomed to rapid variations in the weather away from the city – but it was obviously warm out: old Alf was in his shirt-sleeves, mending a drystone wall next to the lane.

He finished his coffee and considered the weekend that lay ahead. When he got back from the pub he'd call Digby to see how he was after last night, maybe even suggest he drive over. Leeds United were playing and the game was live on TV. He'd pop down to the Bull at four and watch it with a pint or two, then stay on for an evening meal.

Anna had detested football, and in the early days of their relationship, with the hypocritical diplomacy of the freshly infatuated, he'd foregone the pleasures of the beautiful game; only later, over the past couple of months, had his abstinence begun to rankle, and he'd drifted back to watching the odd game and staying up on Saturday nights for *Match of the Day*.

He found his winter coat hanging in the hall – not decorating the floor, where he'd expected to find it – and picked up the *Guardian* from the doormat. He set it on the table beside the door, deciding to read it later rather than take it with him to the pub. He liked to absorb himself in the paper, not have his reading interrupted by conversation with regulars.

He locked the door behind him and set off down the drive, then stopped in his tracks. Hell, it *was* warm, and he was wearing his thick winter coat. He returned to the house, flung the coat on the table by the door, and set off again.

Maybe he'd call Diggers from the pub and see how he was, he thought as he strolled down the lane, marvelling at the unseasonable warmth in the air. It was more like spring than the bitter January of last night.

He still found it hard to credit what Digby had told him. Caroline, having an affair with a bohemian potter? That the homely Caroline would be unfaithful to Digby with *anyone* was amazing enough, but with a young, arty potter...? He recalled trying to reassure Diggers last night with platitudes like, "It's just a fling..." and "It'll blow over..." and while he'd fully believed his words, he knew they'd done nothing to reassure his friend. He really should drive over that afternoon.

Old Alf was fastening the gate at the bottom of the field as Richie passed.

"Beautiful morning," Richie said.

"Aye, 'tis that."

"The snow didn't last long."

Alf gave him an odd look, said something in his broad accent that Richie didn't catch, and climbed up into the cab of his tractor.

He expected the village to be busier than it was; there was usually a market in the square on Saturday morning, and people drove in from miles around to stock up on fresh provisions. This morning, however, there was no sign of the market, and only a few cars were parked in the street around the square.

The Bull was also quiet, with just a handful of regulars occupying their usual places.

"Place is like a ghost town," he said to Cindy as she waited while he scanned the guest ales.

"Is it?"

"Usually bustling, and what's happened to the market? Serve Nigel while I make up my mind."

Nigel, a prosperous solicitor in a Burberry overcoat, asked for a half of Tetley and said, "You're a gent, Ed. Spoilt for choice?"

Richie indicated the ranked beer pumps. "I can't decide between the Landlord and the Goose Eye."

"The Landlord's good today, Ed," Cindy said.

"In that case make it a pint. I was going to limit myself to a half," he said to Nigel, "but what the hell?"

"That's the spirit, Ed. Whenever have you stinted yourself in the ale department?"

"Had a bit of a bender last night with old Diggers. Thought I'd better take it easy today. But the head's feeling fine, none the worse. Oh, and I'll have a ploughman's too when you're ready, Cindy."

He looked around the snug and saw the globe intact on the shelf beside the empty hearth.

"I see your father's mended the globe," he said to Cindy as she placed his pint before him.

She looked confused.

"The globe," he said. "I had an altercation with it last night, knocked it for a Burton. Bob's obviously fixed it – or do you have a stock of the things?"

"Last night? But you weren't in here last night."

He stared at her, pint poised before his lips. "Are you kidding? You served me and Diggers all night."

Cindy looked at Nigel and raised her eyebrows. "Ed," she said as if talking to a child, "you weren't in here last night. And neither was Shakespeare."

"You're joking, right? Taking the proverbial? I was blathered. Old Diggers insisted on whisky chasers. We left around one, but not before I shattered the world."

Cindy braced her arms on the bar and leaned forward. "Ed, I don't know what you're talking about. You weren't here last night, but I was. It was dead – the usual Sunday night –"

He interrupted. "Sunday? Did you say Sunday night?"

"Of course I did."

He shook his head as if to clear it. "Sunday…? So what day is it today?"

She made her eyes massive. "Duh. Monday?" She moved off to serve another customer.

"Sweet Jesus…" Richie breathed.

Beside him, Nigel chortled. "You ought to write a film about it, Ed. Call it *The Lost Weekend* – or has it been done?"

"Monday," Richie said in wonder. "Bloody hell. Well, that'd account for how quiet it is."

So he'd got home pissed to the gills on Friday night – or rather in the early hours of Saturday morning – stumbled his way to bed and miraculously slept all Saturday *and* Sunday, waking up this morning, *Monday*… No wonder he didn't have a hangover – but surely he would have woken up at some point to go to the loo, or had he been so paralytic that he'd relieved himself on amnesiacal autopilot?

"My God," Nigel said, "that session must've been a corker. I knew you liked the sauce, old boy, but you really ought to go easy. Losing complete days like that? Not healthy, not healthy at all, Ed."

Richie said, "You know who you remind me of when you sneer like that? Your namesake, Nigel Farage."

Nigel hoisted his half. "I'll take that as a compliment, sir."

Richie took a delayed sip of his Landlord, sighing. "Bloody hell, that's good."

"Now not too many of those, Edward. Don't want you losing the rest of the week."

"Ha-bloody-ha."

"So how's the delectable Sam, these days?" Nigel asked.

Richie sighed. Surely he'd seen Nigel since Sam walked out. He lodged a shoe on the foot-rail and stared at upside-down bottles of spirits behind the bar. "Sam? I wouldn't have a clue."

"What do you mean?" Nigel said, then, "My God, don't tell me you two have...?"

"She walked out on me many moons ago, Nigel."

He saw the solicitor exchange a worried look with Cindy, who was pulling a pint further along the bar.

Nigel stared at him. "But... but, bloody hell, Edward. She was in here just the other day. Both of you –"

"You must have mistaken her for Anna," Richie said.

Nigel looked mystified. "Anna? Who on earth is Anna?"

"Are you taking the piss?" Richie said, becoming annoyed. "Anna, the blonde whose cleavage you're always drooling over."

"Sorry, old boy, you've lost me. You were in here last Wednesday with Sam, celebrating the part she'd landed in a police drama. That's where she is now, Edward – or have you forgotten? Filming in London? Ring any bells?"

His pulse hammering, Richie stared at the solicitor, then turned his back on the bar and gazed across the room without seeing a thing.

Last year Sam had been cast in a prestigious crime serial for the BBC. They had indeed spent a drunken Wednesday evening in the

Bull, celebrating; then Sam had left for a month in London, filming the first couple of episodes.

And, when she returned, she'd dropped the bombshell that she was leaving him...

Cindy said, "Your ploughman's ready, Ed. Where you sitting?"

Richie indicated a table on the other side of the room, well away from the bar and Nigel. He carried his pint to the table and sat down, and Cindy slid his plate onto the mat.

She paused, hovering. "Ed, are you okay? I mean..."

He looked back at the bar, where Nigel was sharing a joke with a farmer. "He was taking the piss, wasn't he, Cindy?"

She bit her lip.

He went on, "I mean, about Sam. Me and Sam being in here...?"

"No... Look, Ed, you were in here with Sam last Wednesday. Don't you remember? You ordered a bottle of champers."

He nodded absently. "Oh, I remember. It's just... Look, that was last year. Sam went to London, did the shoot... When she came back... she told me she was leaving... You must remember that, Cindy? I was in here, crying into my beer."

Cindy gnawed at her lip, shaking her head.

"Then I met Anna, about six months ago. We were in here a lot, to begin with. You must remember her?"

"Anna?"

"Your height, blonde," he said, almost desperately. "An accountant."

"I'm sorry, Ed. Look, you've had so many women, I lose track."

"But you must remember Anna? I recall you saying that you had a sister in Wales, not far from where Anna's brother lived."

Wide-eyed, Cindy shook her head.

Christ, he thought, *what's happening to me?*

Cindy pointed vaguely over her shoulder. "I'd better get back..."

Alone with his ploughman's, he found he'd lost his appetite. He bit into the pork pie and chewed without tasting a thing. Even the beer tasted flat.

At the bar, Nigel drained his half, said toodle-oo to Cindy, then gave an unsure wave to Richie as he departed.

They think I'm losing it.

He finished his pint and left the pub.

Head down, he hurried through the village. Without really knowing why, he didn't want to bump into anyone he knew. The encounter with Cindy and Nigel had been enough to destabilise him. He recalled his exchange with old Alf in the lane earlier, the farmer's odd reaction when Richie had mentioned the snow...

He arrived home and let himself in. He saw his bundled winter coat on the small table, and knew the *Guardian* would be beneath it. Taking a breath, he pulled the paper from under the coat. Why hadn't he noticed it before? The paper was not the Saturday edition, fat with supplements, but the thinner, Monday issue. He stared at the dateline beneath the masthead.

18th April, 2016.

His vision blurred. He dropped the paper on the floor and leaned against the wall, dizzy.

"Okay," he said, "if this is really happening..."

He moved to the stairs and climbed, then stopped on the second step and backed down until he was staring through the door into the dining room. Last night, when Anna had walked out, he'd removed the landscape she'd bought him, leaving a yawning expanse of magnolia in its place. Now the space above the hearth was occupied by the Cretan coastal scene by Emmi Takala. He stared at the painting, suddenly sweating.

Slowly he climbed the stairs. He paused outside the bedroom, frightened at what he would find, now that he was really looking – or perhaps, he thought, afraid of what he might *not* find.

He pushed open the door and stepped into the room.

A superficial inspection suggested there was nothing amiss, that the room was as it had been when Anna had been in residence. He moved to the wardrobe and reached out, his hand shaking.

He opened the door and reeled.

He took a handful of dress and pulled it to his face, inhaling Sam's scent. He unhooked the hanger from the rail, staring at the dress in disbelief: Sam's yellow summer frock, with the shoulder straps and low hemline, which he always thought made her look like a Swedish schoolgirl, especially when she wore her hair in pigtails. He replaced the dress and pulled out another, and gave an involuntary gasp: the dress she'd been wearing on the first night they'd made love. He recalled turning her around, very gently, and pulling down the zip, easing the padded velvet epaulettes from her pale shoulders and kissing the nape of her neck. She had moaned, turning to him...

He pushed the dress back into the wardrobe and slammed the door shut.

He backed towards the bed until his legs collided with the mattress and he sat down heavily, holding his head in his hands.

Then he looked up and stared at his reflection in the wardrobe mirror.

"No..."

He stood up and approached the mirror like a sleepwalker.

He touched his top lip. His moustache was gone. He'd only started growing the thing when Anna had said she thought men with moustaches were sexy, six months ago... He examined his hair; was there a touch less grey in his sideburns?

He backed away from his reflection and turned, taking in the room as if for the first time.

Now that he looked, really *looked*, he noticed other tell-tale signs of Sam's presence. Her old hairbrush on the mantel-shelf above the empty hearth; a pile of her scripts on the bookshelf under the window; the toes of her slippers peeping out from under the bed.

"Oh, sweet Jesus Christ..."

He sat down on the bed again, gripped his head in his hands and tried to make sense of what was happening.

The only explanation he could think of, the only possible rational answer to the situation he'd found himself in, was that he was going mad. This was a psychological reaction, perhaps engendered by Anna leaving him, and everything he'd experienced today since waking was taking place inside his head. He was living through a very convincing hallucination. Perhaps he was still unconscious from all the drink on Friday night; perhaps this was his subconscious, punishing him, and soon he would wake up to blessed normality.

He felt the sunlight that slanted through the window and warmed his hands; he felt his trousers beneath his fingertips. He heard the ticking of the alarm clock and inhaled: he detected, faint in the warm air, the subtle musk of Sam's perfume.

If it were an hallucination, it possessed a fidelity beyond anything he'd ever experienced...

It was no hallucination.

But what else *could* it be?

He'd heard about people being hypnotised, reliving what they thought were past lives. They reported the absolute reality of their experiences, the thoughts and feelings of the person they had been, the scents and sounds and sights of that earlier reality... So if the brain could convince itself while under hypnosis, then perhaps he *was* imagining all this?

It was a frightening thought – but more worrying was the alternative, that this experience was real.

He needed a drink. He recalled the 'idiopathic episode' he'd suffered a week ago... Perhaps that was responsible?

He hurried downstairs to the kitchen. The wine rack was full of the chianti and prosecco that Sam favoured. He opened the fridge and reached for a beer, then stopped himself. What he needed now was coffee.

He filled the kettle and sluiced the dregs from the cafetière, rinsed the mug he'd used that morning and made himself a black coffee.

He sat at the table, mug in hand, and tried to think through what was happening to him.

He pulled his mobile phone from his pocket and stared at it. Should he find Sam's number and call her?

He activated the phone, scrolled down to her name.

He pressed the call button and held the phone to his ear.

"Just to hear her voice again," he promised himself, "then I'll hang up. I won't even speak to her... What would I say, anyway? What *could* I say?"

The dial tone sounded.

His heart thudded.

There was a click, then a voice, *"I'm sorry, the person you called is unavailable. If you would like to..."*

Relieved, he cut the call and dropped the phone on the table.

Had Sam picked up her phone and spoken, he would have been unable to maintain his silence. Would he have told her that he loved her, knowing what would happen when she returned home?

The phone rang – the theme tune of Sam's last TV show – startling him.

His hand shaking, he reached for the device and said, "Hello?"

"Eddy, did you just ring?" A pit opened in his gut at the sound of her voice, her light, modulated Home Counties accent.

"Sam," he heard himself saying. "Just wanted to see how it was going."

"Just finished for the day. It's great. The director's a pussy cat. Did I tell you I'm working with Sally? You know, the lead in the Ayckbourn we saw in Leeds in November?"

"Great."

"We've got the afternoon off. I'm going into the West End with Sally, doing a little shopping. How're you? Getting along without me?"

He could have wept. "Just about."

"Don't drink too much, Eddy. Only kidding. Eeek! That's Sally. Must dash. Loves. Bye-eee!"

She rang off and he sat staring at the phone in stunned silence.

There was so much he had forgotten about her. The softness of her voice, her pet phrases. *Loves. Bye-eee...*

Three weeks, he thought, standing up suddenly and striding to the window. He stared out at the fields in anger. Must he endure three weeks of soul-destroying purgatory, isolated here in the house, knowing exactly what would happen when she returned?

She had sounded so normal just now, so natural... *Loves. Bye-eee...* Had she met her lover yet, the detested anonymous 'someone,' or was that to come? Did she still love Richie?

He sipped his coffee, pulled a face on finding it too bitter, and decided that he needed a beer after all.

He took an Italian lager from the fridge and sat at the table, drinking from the bottle.

He pulled the phone towards him, scrolled down to Digby's number, and called his friend.

For the second time a pre-recorded voice told him that the person he'd called was unavailable.

He cut the call and tried Digby's home number.

"Hello?"

"Caroline. It's Ed."

"Edward! Lovely to hear from you. When are you coming over? I haven't seen you for weeks."

"As soon as possible. You okay?"

"I'm well, Edward. Are you wanting Digby?"

"If he's there?"

"He's just popped over to Manchester, delivering that script for Rogers. You know what he's like – he doesn't trust emailing things. But he set off early, and said he'd be back mid-afternoon. Look, why don't you come over and we can have a drink? Digby shouldn't be long."

"Would that be okay?"

"Of course. I'm kicking my heels here all alone. And why not stay for dinner, Edward? Steak and kidney pie, your favourite."

"I'd love to. See you in half an hour."

He rang off and smiled at the phone, at the blessed, mundane normality of the exchange with the woman he'd known for almost twenty-five years; Digby's staunchly loyal wife and companion who...

Who in nearly a year from now would have an affair with a bohemian potter.

He still found it almost impossible to believe.

Almost as impossible as what was happening to him.

This is insanity, he thought as he found his car keys and left the house.

DIGBY AND CAROLINE lived thirty minutes away over the moors on the border of Yorkshire and Lancashire, one of the most beautiful areas in all England. Fifteen years ago they'd moved from London, bought a tumbledown farmhouse on the edge of a small town, and lived in a caravan while the house was being renovated. After enduring a smallish study in their Islington town house, Digby wanted a huge room in which to work and house his extensive library. Caroline, a legal secretary in London, had worked for a few years in Manchester after the move, before giving it up and devoting herself to, in her own self-deprecating phrase, 'good causes.'

They had a son who'd long flown the nest and worked as a graphic artist in London. Now they lived with a pair of hyperactive red setters which Digby claimed kept him fit, though judging by his friend's waistline and omnipresent wheeze, Richie doubted that.

He pulled his battered Rover into the drive and braked next to Caroline's Mazda run-about. The dogs galloped from the house, a deranged welcoming committee, flopping and bounding around him as he climbed from the car. He endured their slobbering attention until Caroline appeared at the door and called them off.

She beamed and held out her arms, a tall, matronly woman, handsome and greying; she reminded him of a character actress from the 'fifties – no-nonsense, kindly, and very English.

"Come here, you," she laughed. "What have you been doing with yourself? It must be a month or more. What are you working on at the moment?"

They hugged. Richie ransacked his memory for what he'd been

writing this time last year. "The same damned script as the last time I saw you," he temporised.

"I thought that was almost finished?" she said, leading him through the stone-flagged hall to the sitting room, a vast, low-beamed room overlooking the rolling green countryside.

"Rewrites," he said.

"I hope you don't mind my saying, Edward, but you don't look well. Are you okay?"

He smiled. "Fine. Just burning the candle at both ends."

"Can I get you something? Digby bought a crate of Theakstons the other day."

"If you don't mind, I'll just have coffee."

"You must be under the weather. Black, isn't it?" She pointed to a small table near the hearth. "I'm on my first sherry already."

She moved to the kitchen to fix his coffee, and Richie strolled around the room and examined the bookshelves where Digby kept his travel books. Too lazy to travel himself, he told friends, he loved reading about the exploits of intrepid travellers to exotic, far-flung climes. It was his comfort reading, he claimed.

Caroline returned with the coffee and they sat on an old sofa redolent of dog. "And how's Sam?" she asked. "Enjoying the shoot?"

Richie sipped his coffee. Odd how the mere mention of Sam's name was like the twisting of a blade. "She's fine. I spoke to her an hour ago. The filming is going well and she was just about to indulge in some retail therapy in the West End."

He wanted the conversation to move on from Sam, but Caroline had other ideas. "I like Samantha, Edward. I really like her. She's a good woman."

Richie smiled and sipped his coffee.

"You know, when you first met her, and you introduced us... I wasn't sure."

"In what way?"

"Well, she was so much like all your other women – your harem,

I often say to Digby. That is, physically. And she was an actress...
I've met enough of them to know what they're like."

He smiled. "Surely you can't lump them all –" he began.

"Most actresses I've met are all of a certain type, Edward. For the
most part egotistical and vain, and not a little neurotic."

"Not Sam."

"No. No, I realise that now. She's... this might sound trite,
Edward, but she's truly devoted to her craft, and she's a generous,
warm-hearted person."

Richie maintained a lockjaw smile, wondering where this might
be leading.

Caroline went on, "And I think she loves you."

He felt himself give vent to a mental wail of despair. "You do?"

"Believe me, I know about these things. I've watched her when
you're together. The way she looks at you... it's love."

He shrugged, uncomfortable. "I don't know."

"The thing is," Caroline said, "how do you feel about Samantha?"

He stared down at his coffee, thinking that coming here today had
been a big mistake. "Well, naturally, I feel a lot for her."

"How old is she, Edward?"

He thought about it, wondering where this might be leading.
"Forty."

Caroline smiled, looking more than a little self-satisfied. "The
sort of age when she might be thinking of settling down. I was
talking to Digby the other day... I said that you really ought to pop
the question."

He laughed. "Pop the question? That sounds so..."

"Ask her to marry you, Edward."

Oh, Christ... He floundered. "I'm... I'm way too old for her. The
age difference, sixteen years."

She corrected him, catching him out. "Fifteen, Edward. Don't
make yourself out to be older than you actually are."

Fifty-five, he thought. *I'm fifty-five now...*

"You do love her, don't you?"

He hesitated. "I don't know. I thought I did, and then..." And then Sam left me.

"And then?"

He shrugged. "I don't know. You know me. I'm not the marrying type. The idea of settling down with one woman..." He let the sentence trail off.

"You're a strange man, Edward Richie. I've known you for so long, and yet there are times when I wonder if I really know you at all."

"I'll take that as a compliment." He smiled. "Clearly I'm deep and mysterious."

She held his gaze. "Or insecure." She stopped and looked away. "I'm sorry, I shouldn't have said that."

"If you can't be honest with friends..." he said. "Actually, I think I will have that beer now."

"Good."

While she fetched it from the kitchen, Richie glanced at a newspaper on the sofa. It was open at the sports pages, and he scanned a preview of tomorrow's Premiership match between Newcastle and Manchester City: it came to him that he knew the score.

He stood and moved to the picture window. The sun beat down on farmland dotted with sheep and grazing cows. A tractor patrolled a distant field, so far away it resembled a child's toy. A vortex of crows, like vultures, trailed in its wake. For some unholy reason – if he were *not* going mad – he had been pitched back in time to inhabit the body of his younger self, supplanting his younger self's memories with his current, fraught neuroses. He tried to think back to this time last year, as it were, and work out what he had done on this day. A Monday, so he would have been at work on a script... He certainly hadn't driven over to Digby's and had this conversation with Caroline.

She returned with a bottle of Theakstons best and a glass.

She started a new topic, probably thinking it politic. As he poured himself the beer, she sat down on the sofa and said, "I've been trying to persuade Digby to take up novel writing again."

He joined her. "I think that'd be a good idea."

"You do?" She sounded surprised. "The last time I mooted that idea, you said you thought he was happy enough knocking out TV scripts."

He shrugged, caught out again. He'd said he thought it might be a good idea because of what Digby had told him on Friday night… or *would* tell him… about being so pissed off pounding out hackwork.

"When I first met Digby," Caroline said, "he had dreams of becoming a novelist. Science fiction."

He smiled. 'Speculative fiction' was the term Digby had preferred, while Richie had dismissed the genre as sci-fi. "You're going to blame me, now, for putting him off that idea."

"Certainly not. You helped him out no end in the early days. He was getting nowhere writing novels, and you opened up new avenues."

In London, in their late twenties, he'd criticised one of Digby's early novels so caustically that it had caused a rift in their friendship that had lasted for years. Later, in their thirties, he'd introduced Digby to a few BBC bods he'd written radio scripts for, and gradually, over the years, his friend's career had taken off, moving from radio scripts to TV work.

"So what makes you think – ?" he began.

Caroline interrupted. "That he needs to write novels now?" she asked. "He was complaining the other day about how demeaning he found it, working on the current series. So I suggested he write a novel. He's had more experience; he's lived, and he has contacts."

"What did he say?"

"Well, he didn't dismiss the idea out of hand. He said he'd think about it."

Richie drank his beer, then said, "Caroline, do you think Digby's happy?"

She opened her eyes wide, as if she found the question strange.

"Why... I must admit I haven't really thought about it. Or if I have, then..." She shrugged. "Then I assumed he's happy enough. We're comfortable. We have a nice place here, and we get along..." She looked away and sipped her sherry.

"And you? Are you happy?"

She smiled, and to Richie she looked like someone putting a brave face on a situation that could be far, far better. "Let's say that I'm accepting, Edward. I often think that that is far more important than being 'happy,' whatever that might mean."

He nodded. She was 'accepting'... for the time being.

A car engine sounded outside, and Caroline jumped to her feet as if with relief. "Digby's back," she said, moving to the window and waving.

The front door slammed and Digby's booming baritone sounded. "Is that Ed's jalopy I espied in the drive?"

He appeared in the doorway of the lounge, filling the frame with his girth. Dressed in a navy blue business suit, he looked constrained and sweaty.

"Come here, you old reprobate. I see Caroline's been trying to get you pissed."

Richie hugged his friend and hoisted the glass. "My first," he said.

"Uncharacteristically, he started with coffee."

"The man's ill," Digby opined. "Myself, I could kill a beer. Another, Ed?"

"I'd love one. I'll take a taxi home."

He fetched two bottles from the kitchen. "And to what do we owe the honour, Ed?"

Richie temporised. "I have... an idea I'd like to try out on you."

"Ideas? Meat and drink," Digby proclaimed, taking a long swallow straight from the bottle. "Christ, that's better. I had a long meeting about the storyline on *Henderson's*. Pure bollocks. But I'll tell you all about it later."

"Edward's staying for dinner," Caroline said. "Steak and kidney pie."

"Wonderful. And why don't we crack that bottle of Beaujolais we've been saving?"

"I'll get the dinner on and let you two talk shop," Caroline said. "Oh, there's just one thing before you go."

She crossed the room and sorted through a few pamphlets on an occasional table. She came back with a leaflet and sat on the arm of the sofa where Digby had slumped. "You know how I've been toying with the idea of doing an evening class?"

Richie stood before the empty hearth, watching the couple.

"Well," Caroline went on, "I can't decide between these two. They're on different evenings, Mondays and Wednesdays. Mondays it's pottery, and Wednesdays a watercolour class for beginners."

Digby gave the leaflet a cursory glance. "Well, which do you prefer?"

Caroline pulled a face. "I'm torn."

Richie found himself saying, "Oddly enough, I was talking to a friend of Cindy's in the Bull the other day. She did the pottery course, and regretted it. Apparently the bloke who runs it is a bit of a seedy character, with roving hands."

"Is that so?" Caroline said. "Well, I was veering towards the watercolour course anyway. I did a little painting many moons ago, before Digby came along. That settles it. I'll ring and book the course first thing in the morning."

Caroline moved to the kitchen and Digby said, "I'll grab another couple of beers and we'll go through to the study."

Richie followed him from the sitting room, along the hall to a spacious room overlooking a rising pasture at the back of the house. Digby's study was stocked with books on three walls, the one facing the door displaying what he proudly claimed was the county's finest collection of SF paperbacks from the 'fifties through to the 'nineties, when he'd taken against the genre – disgruntled, Richie suspected, at having his masterpiece rejected so often.

Digby removed his suit jacket, hauled off his tie like a man ridding himself of a noose, and opened a few buttons of his shirt, revealing a mat of grey chest hair. He flung himself onto a battered sofa and Richie sat on a comparably careworn armchair. Across the study, Digby's Apple Mac sat incongruously on a mahogany Queen Anne desk.

"Ed, are you okay?"

Richie looked up from his beer and stared at his friend. "No. No, I'm not."

Digby swallowed. "Oh, Christ... The test results?"

Richie was momentarily flummoxed. The test results? Then he remembered. "Oh, that... No, no. Everything's fine on that score." Last year he'd seen his doctor, complaining of chest pains, and the medic had packed him off to Harrogate General for further examinations. "No, that turned out to be referred pain from a suspected irritable bowel. I'm on peppermint pills."

"Christ, that's a relief. So... what's wrong?"

"You're not going to believe this."

"Try me," Digby said. "Hold on – the thing about story ideas was just what you told Caroline, right? Only, I like to know when to take my writing hat off."

Richie smiled. "No, I'm not here to bore you with my half-baked ideas."

"Out with it, then. If you don't mind my saying, by the way, you look bloody dreadful." He stopped. "Hell, it's Sam, isn't it? You've given her the old heave-ho?"

Richie grunted a humourless laugh. "No. *I* haven't... but *she* will."

Digby frowned. "Sorry, Ed, you've lost me."

How the hell to explain what was happening to him? "You won't believe a word of this, Digby."

"So you've said. I'm intrigued. Fire away."

Richie took a mouthful of beer, considered his words, and then said, "I'll tell you this as it happened to me, Digby. I'll tell you what happened and see if you can make sense of it."

"Very well."

"It was last Friday night... Subjectively, for me, the 13th of January, 2017. I'd just had a god-almighty spat with Anna."

Digby held up a hand like a bemused traffic policeman. "Whoa! 2017? *Anna?*"

"I know, it sounds crazy. I'm with you there; it *is* crazy. I hardly believe it's happening. But later this year, in July, I meet a woman called Anna Greaves, and in January 2017, we have a row and she walks out, and the same night I see you for our usual Friday night session."

"Later this year you meet...?" Digby echoed.

"That's right."

His friend nodded, playing along. "Okay... but what's happened to Sam in the interim?"

"Sam will get back from London and tell me, as calm as you like, that it's all over between us. She's met someone in London and she's leaving me."

Digby was sitting very still, the beer forgotten in his huge right hand, watching him. "Right," he said at last. "Go on."

"So Sam walks out, and in the summer I meet Anna Greaves."

"Let me guess, Ed," Digby said with an attempt at levity. "She's blonde, slim, smart, and very pretty?"

"Right on every count. Anyway, we get on fine at first, and then things go belly up."

"Par for the course."

"And on this particular night, last Friday – my last Friday, not yours – we row and she packs her things and walks out, and I meet you in the Bull, and..."

"And you proceed to get shit-faced?"

"We both get hammered," he said. "And I wend my way home and collapse in the hall... And when I wake up I'm in bed, and it's not Saturday morning in January 2017, but a Monday morning in April, 2016. Now. Today."

Digby nodded. He took a long drink, then lowered the glass and stared at Richie. "Do you know something, if I didn't know you better I'd say that this is your way of dramatising an idea for Perkins over at Open Box Productions. Weren't they casting about for a science fiction series recently?"

"But you *do* know better?"

"I know you're not pitching me an idea, certainly," Digby said. "You really believe what you're telling me."

"That," said Richie very deliberately, "is because I'm telling you exactly what happened to me."

"And you expect me to take it as gospel? You somehow... time-travelled back from January 2017?"

"I know, it's impossible. I'm somehow inhabiting the body of my younger self, but all my thoughts and memories are those of my 2017 self."

They sat in silence for a while. Richie stared at his half-empty glass.

At last he looked up and said, "Digby, what the fuck's happening to me?"

His friend pursed his thick lips and settled his three chins on his chest in contemplation. "It's psychological, Ed," he said quietly. "You've suffered some... I don't know what the term would be... mental aberration."

Richie nodded. "Last week – in my time, that is – I collapsed and was hospitalised for a few days. The medics said it was a 'cerebral episode,' and packed me off home." He paused. "So maybe all this isn't really happening?" he said. "You, me, this conversation? Or rather, it's happening in my head."

Digby smiled. "Well... I know what *I'm* experiencing, as far as I can be certain of anything. But what didn't happen, what hasn't happened yet, is what you said occurs from now until January next year. Sam leaving you, you meeting this Anna, her walking out and you getting arseholed with me on that January Friday night." Digby tapped his head. "*That's* happening up here. False memories, as it were. They seem convincing to you, subjectively. You have these memories, yes, but they have absolutely no basis in fact."

"So I'm going mad?"

"I wouldn't put it quite like that," Digby said, uncertainly.

Richie finished his beer. He sat clutching the empty glass, staring down at the carpet.

"Another?" Digby asked, pointing at the glass.

Richie held it out without meeting Digby's eyes.

While his friend was fetching the beers, Richie reviewed his memories of the intervening nine months. He recalled Sam's announcement that she was leaving him, the row with Anna... Hell, they were real, branded into his consciousness with real pain and trauma. They were not some make-believe recollections fabricated by his failing sanity.

He recalled what Digby had told him last Friday night, nine months in the future, about Caroline's affair.

Digby returned and handed him a beer. Richie tipped it into his glass, waited until his friend had seated himself, then said, "At the moment you're working, on and off, on the synopsis of that 'sixties counterculture series, right?"

"What about it?"

"You pitch it to the Beeb later this year, in August as far as I recall, and next January Jeremy Traverson summons you to London and commissions the series."

Digby stared at him. He tried not to smile. "Traverson? That –"

"Fuckwit," Richie got there before him. "That's what you called him last Friday, when we met to celebrate Traverson commissioning the series. You were as surprised as I was, called him a fuckwit who the BBC rolled out to put the kibosh on anything radical, as I recall."

"With all due respect, Ed, this doesn't really prove –"

"When did you intend to send the Beeb your outline, Digby?"

"Sometime this summer, maybe later."

"August?"

"Maybe."

"So how did I know that?"

Digby smiled. "An educated guess? Or maybe I mentioned it over a pint?"

Richie shook his head. "No, it's because that's when you submitted it."

"It's a far from convincing argument, Ed," Digby said, gently.

"Christ!" Richie said.

"I'm sorry."

The silence stretched, both men looking anywhere but at each other.

"Okay. Okay..." Richie said, leaning forward. "I'll tell you something else. Why do you think I told Caroline about the pottery class being run by a seedy type?"

Digby looked nonplussed. "I've really no idea, Ed."

Richie stared at his friend. "It's because if I hadn't, then a few months from now Caroline would start the pottery course on Monday nights and she'd meet someone there, and they'd have an affair."

"Caroline?" Digby almost laughed.

"You recall I said that we both got hammered? Well, you told me that you'd found out about the affair, and you were devastated."

Digby was shaking his head. "But Caroline wouldn't..."

"That's what I thought, but she did." He pointed at Digby. "Except that now, as she'll not be attending the pottery class, she won't meet the arty potter. Why the hell did you think I said what I did about the instructor?"

Digby sighed. "Because," he said with infinite patience, tapping his head, "because of what's going on up here, in that crazy, mixed up cranium of yours."

Richie screwed his eyes shut and swore to himself.

"Perhaps you're right," he said, near to tears. "Perhaps I'm losing it." He stopped, staring at his friend, and smiled suddenly.

"What?" Digby said.

"Christ, why didn't I think of it before? It's obvious!"

"What is?"

"How to prove that I'm right – that what's happening isn't just going on up here."

"Go on."

"It's Monday the 18th of April, right? Tomorrow, Tuesday, Newcastle play Manchester City in the league."

"Live on Sky," Digby said.

"And I know the score. I remember the game because we watched it at the Bull."

Digby narrowed his eyes. "Okay, right…"

"It's a 1-1 draw," Richie said. "Unfortunately I can't recall who scores. But I know the result."

"You *think* you know, Ed."

"Tomorrow, Digby, we'll watch the match, okay, and if it's a one-all draw, you'll believe me?"

"O…kay, if it's one-all." He nodded. "Then I'll have to rethink the 'Ed Richie is a madman' scenario."

Richie smiled. "Thank you. That's all I wanted to hear."

"I'll see you at the Bull tomorrow," Digby said. "But not a word of this to Caroline, hmm? She sometimes worries about you, you know?"

Richie grunted a laugh. "She told me earlier that I should pop the question to Sam."

"We discussed it the other night. You could do worse, you know, far worse. But of course you'll do no such thing. That wouldn't fit into your subconscious, self-destructive impulse."

Richie recalled, dimly, that years ago Digby had broached this topic when very drunk. Now he said, "You think I'm self-destructive?"

Digby shrugged, uncomfortable. "It's something Caroline once said to me. And I must admit, going on the evidence…"

"The evidence?"

"How long have we known each other, Ed?"

"Over thirty-eight years. At least, I've known you that long. You've known me nine months less."

Digby smiled. "At any rate, a hell of a long time."

"So?"

"So you know I wouldn't say anything to hurt you. But I must say..." He paused, licked his lips, and went on, "Ed, you have this self-destructive impulse when it comes to women. You drive them away."

"*I* drive *them* away?"

"I know you're going to deny it. But I've watched you. Every time – every time, without fail – you undermine your relationships so that, eventually, your partner can't take it any longer and they walk out. But it's your fault, Ed, and I'm sorry to have to tell you this."

Richie shrugged. "Okay, a couple of times... I admit it."

"Every time, Ed. How many woman have you lived with over the years? I lost count after a dozen. And they all end up leaving because of how you destabilise the relationship."

"'Destabilise'? You sound like a marriage guidance counsellor, Diggers."

"I've had to be, on occasion. Except that you're never there."

Richie cocked his head and stared at his friend. "Meaning?"

Digby said, "Sam, Hilary, Marsha, Pam, Emma... they all spoke to me, at the time, told me how you treated them."

Richie swallowed. "You should have tried living with them," he quipped. He shook his head. "But what about Sam?"

"You're still with Sam," Digby said. "But even she's mentioned things... to Caroline, not to me."

Richie felt sick. "Things... about me?"

"About how you treat her. It's small things, not so much cruelties as an inability to open up, to show your emotions. She thinks you're apathetic, about her, about your relationship."

"I had no idea."

"Of course not... consciously."

He stared at his friend. "But subconsciously?"

"Subconsciously," Digby said, "you're punishing yourself for what happened all those years ago. And that might even be the reason for what you *think* is happening to you now."

Punishing myself, Richie thought, staring down at his half-empty glass.

He was saved further soul-searching by Caroline, calling them to dinner.

FOR THE REST of the evening they kept off the subjects of the missing nine months, and Richie's self-destructive impulses, but he ate without really tasting a thing. Conversation revolved around work, mutual acquaintances, and politics – but Richie's attention wandered, and a dozen times he found himself trying to work out what might be happening to him.

By midnight he was more than a little inebriated, and he was willing to consign the events of the day, and his conviction that he'd somehow slipped back in time, to some unaccountable mental aberration. Even this acceptance, thanks to the alcohol, was painless.

Only later, after taking a taxi home, did he consider what Digby had said about his punishing himself.

He sat in his study in the early hours, staring out at the moon-silvered countryside, and thought about Anna and their final altercation. Had he manufactured her discontent, by adding sultanas to the meal, by giving her the Bulgarian wine – and then goading her, and saying nothing to make her stay?

And Sam, Hilary, Marsha, Pam, Emma and all the others?

He was too drunk to recall the details of their departures, but perhaps he had been responsible.

But Sam?

He thought he'd loved Sam.

But if he were *subconsciously* undermining his own peace of mind...

No!

He made his way to bed.

He would wake up in the morning, he told himself, and everything would be back to normal. It would be January 2017, and Anna would have walked out on him, the latest in a long line of unsuccessful lovers. And it would be the first day of the rest of his life.

He slept the sleep of the hopelessly inebriated and woke with only a slight hangover at nine in the morning.

He rolled over and kept his eyes shut tight. When he opened them, he told himself, he would look out and see a snow-coated land, and it would be January again, in the year 2017.

He sat up, opened his eyes, and swore to himself.

The sun was shining across rolling farmland shy of snow, and lambs gambolled in the meadows. Sam's play-scripts still sat on the bookshelf.

Richie found his mobile and got through to Digby.

"Diggers?"

"Ed, how are you?"

"What's the date?"

Digby sighed. "Tuesday, April the 19th, Ed. 2016. See you tonight for the match?"

"I'll be there."

"Ed, are you okay?"

"I'm fine," Richie said, and cut the connection.

He sat on the side of the bed and stared down at his hands.

He had another three weeks to endure before Sam returned, and left him, and then he would be alone again. Three weeks of knowing what she would say, of anticipating that sick-to-the-stomach sense of rejection.

He stood up and moved towards the bathroom, then staggered as a sudden, searing heat passed through his head.

Blinded by a flash of bright white light, he fell forward, unconscious.

From the *Guardian*, 20th June, 2015

Q&A
Edward Richie, script-writer

Born in Nottingham, Richie is an award-winning TV and radio scriptwriter. Over the past twenty-five years he has written more than a hundred scripts for shows such as the children's comedy *CrazyMadLoopy*, the crime drama *Beat Up*, and the BAFTA nominated series set in a psychiatric institute, *All In A Day*. His one-off radio play *The Ten Sleepers* won the Radio Critics' award in 2005. He currently writes the BBC hit soap opera, *Morgan's Café*. He lives in North Yorkshire.

When were you happiest?
Crete, June 2008.

What is your greatest fear?
Terminal illness.

What is the trait you most deplore in yourself?
Apathy.

What is the trait you most deplore in others?
Greed.

Which living person do you most admire, and why?
My friend the scriptwriter Digby Lincoln: he doesn't let the bastards grind him down.

What was your most embarrassing moment?
Stumbling over my acceptance speech for the 2005 Radio Critics' award.

Property and cars aside, what's the most expensive thing you've bought?
A computer.

What is your most treasured possession?
A photograph.

What makes you unhappy?
The greed and short-termism of politicians.

What would your superpower be?
The ability to heal and cure.

What is your most unappealing habit?
Talking with my mouth full.

What do you most dislike about your appearance?
My constant five o'clock shadow.

What is your favourite word?
Replenish.

What did you want to be when you were growing up?
A footballer, then a writer.

Which book changed your life?

I never read a novel until I was fifteen, when my father gave me Orwell's *Nineteen Eighty-Four*, and instantly I understood the power of fiction.

What or who is the greatest love of your life?
Annabelle.

What is the worst thing anyone's said to you?
An old girl-friend, who was also my editor at the time, told me that my work lacked psychological insight.

What is your favourite smell?
Curry.

What does love feel like?
A kind of pain.

Who would you invite to your dream dinner party?
Digby Lincoln, Germaine Greer, Noam Chomsky, Doris Lessing, and Jonathan Miller.

What is the worst job you've done?
Working as a kitchen porter while I was a student.

If you could edit your past, what would you change?
Pass.

When did you last cry, and why?
A month or so ago, thinking about Annabelle.

To whom would you most like to say sorry?
To Annabelle.

How do you relax?

Watching football.

How would you like to be remembered?
As an honest writer and loyal friend.

What do you consider your greatest achievement?
Two or three of my best plays.

What is the most important lesson life has taught you?
To keep on.

Where would you most like to be right now?
I'm fine here, sitting in the Black Bull with a pint, completing this questionnaire.

CHAPTER FOUR

January, 2030

ELLA STARED DOWN at the Northumberland countryside far below. The land was covered with snow, the black lines of dry-stone walls dividing fields into separate squares on a vast, undulating grid. It looked as if the countryside was being prepared for a great game of noughts and crosses. She smiled at the notion, and wondered if she could use it in her book about Ed Richie: the country as a board-game, divided by competing national interests over the last decade into autonomous states, with Scotland and Wales seceding, and Northern Ireland yet again torn apart by sectarian imbecility.

The sun was high, and the plane's dark shadow rippled over the snow, arrowing south.

She had taken the eleven-thirty flight from Edinburgh to Leeds-Bradford airport, where she would pick up a hire car and drive towards the border with Lancashire. On the way to Digby Lincoln's place she would stop off at Harrowby Bridge, where Ed Richie had lived for twenty-three years until his disappearance in 2025.

She returned to her book, *Interesting Times*, Richie's first novel, published when he was fifty-eight. It was a semi-autobiographical account of the life of a screenwriter, his increasing dissatisfaction with the trade, and his midlife-crisis as he searched for a fulfilling means of artistic expression. It was also an astute analysis of the prevailing political climate in the mid-teens of the century, and a bleak forecast of what was to come. It had sold reasonably well, but it was his second novel, *Statecraft,* a near-future dystopia about a world-wide fascist state controlled by multinational companies, which had become an international hit, selling twenty million copies in English alone and being translated into more than thirty languages. Richie had written a further six novels combining penetrating psychological insight with astute political foreboding. And then, one morning in July 2025, he'd left his house and never been seen since.

She turned to his photograph on the inside flap. It showed a long-faced, dark-haired man in his mid-fifties, with a drooping moustache, five o'clock shadow, and dark, intense eyes. She could have characterised the face as being haunted, but wondered if she were reading too much into subsequent events. She recalled meeting Richie once or twice when she was twelve: a darkly handsome, driven young man in his early twenties, forever either ranting about the political situation or tapping away at a play on his portable typewriter. He had lived with Ella's sister, Annabelle, in a poky Hackney flat, which Ella dimly recalled from family visits.

She shut out those memories and lost herself in the novel, smiling at a scene in a pub and the banter that passed between the brilliantly drawn characters.

The plane landed just after twelve; she passed through passport control, ignored the touts hawking cheap rooms and hire cars, and picked up a battered Nissan from the Hertz office.

The bored girl behind the counter, whose name badge identified her as Rizwana, her face heavily made-up with purple eye-shadow, passed Ella the keys and said, "Where you going, luv? Only the York road's closed and so's the M62."

"I'm heading west, but not by the M62."

"Be careful on the smaller roads, then. The councils don't do owt these days to clear the roads."

"Thank you, I'll take care."

Her wrist-com told her that it was two below zero and the Nissan, standing out in the open, started on the fifth attempt. Ella inched her way out of the airport precincts and headed west on winding country roads, passing through pretty stone-built villages and out into beautiful countryside. There was no satnav in the car, and the program on her wrist-com was experiencing limited connectivity. Fortunately she'd memorised the route to Harrowby Bridge.

Compared with the well-maintained roads north of the border, even the main roads of West Yorkshire were pot-holed and crumbling. The towns she passed through were silent and depressed, with rows of shop-fronts boarded up and covered with posters advertising Romanian circuses and UK Front rallies.

England had suffered a gradual economic melt-down, starting with the lean years of the '20s, with the ever-increasingly draconian austerity measures of the Conservative-UK Front alliance. Ella had watched with mounting incredulity as the ultra-right-wing UK Front came to prominence on a wave of popular support. With the rise of the right had come the invidious influence of Christian fundamentalist churches from the US, the ban on abortion in '22 and the repeal of same-sex marriage. Ella wondered how long it would be before England followed the lead of the US government and declared homosexuality illegal.

Her wrist-com pinged and she pulled into the side of the lane and took the call. Kit waved from the tiny screen. "How's England, El?"

"A delight. And cold and bleak. How did it go with Douglas?"

"Very well, but he's a miserable prick, isn't he?"

"It's a front," Ella said. "He's really a pussycat."

"I'll believe you. Anyway, I signed up for a year and I'm due to deliver a daily diary, five hundred words a slot, from tomorrow. He also wants longer, in-depth political pieces every week. It'll keep the wolf from the door. Thank you, El."

"I'm glad I could help."

"Oh, and Aimee's found a job. Short-order cook in a Cantonese place on the Royal Mile. It'll do till she finds something better."

"Great."

"I'm amazed at all the tourists in the city, El. The place is packed. And most of them seem to be Chinese."

"That's where the money is these days. They've opened a chain of authentic restaurants in Edinburgh and Glasgow, not happy with the standard of Chinese food the locals were doling out. And they've just moved their car manufacturing plant from Middlesbrough to Aberdeen. That did nothing for Anglo-Scottish relations."

"But everything for Scottish-Chinese accord." That was the direction Europe was looking, these days, as it turned its back on the US.

"I'd better be going," Kit said. "I'm treating Aimee to a steak, in celebration."

"Catch you in a couple of days."

She cut the connection, restarted the car and pulled out onto the icy lane. Rizwana of Hertz was right: the councils had done nothing to make any of the roads less of a death-trap, and in many places Ella was forced to inch along at ten miles an hour.

She tuned her wrist-com into the ScotFreeMedia newsfeed for the next hour and listened to the news pinging in from around the world. The civil war in Nigeria was entering its fifth year with no end in sight, and each side accusing the other of atrocities. The Australian government was brokering an aid deal with India to supply Malaysia with food and agricultural infrastructure following the ceasefire between government troops and Islamic rebels. In the US, President O'Ryan, as the third Operation Rainbow Airlift plane touched down in Edinburgh, announced a state visit to England to discuss trade deals between 'our great countries.'

Swearing to herself, Ella killed her 'com and concentrated on the road.

One hour later she edged the Nissan over the brow of the hill and braked.

Down below, nestled in a snow-clad valley, was the village of Harrowby Bridge, a cluster of honey-coloured stone houses with grey slate roofs, smoke drifting vertically into the windless winter sky. Nothing moved, not even traffic, and the river threading its way through the village was frozen, the ice shattered and whitened along fracture lines.

Ella scanned the hillside to the west of the valley, looking for the converted barn that had belonged to Ed Richie. There were perhaps half a dozen likely candidates; she'd ask directions at Richie's local, as the satnav on her wrist-com was still down. She wanted a photograph of the house, and to get a feel for the place where he'd lived for twenty-three years.

She eased the car down the lane that descended steeply into the village, located the Black Bull, and parked behind the pub.

A blazing coal fire warmed a traditional bar-room decorated with horse brasses, paintings of the area, and a couple of mock-antique globes. Three or four locals sat at tables, drinking by themselves, and an old man in a Burberry jacket and flat cap stood at the bar. Ella noticed that he was reading the Breitbart daily bulletin on a softscreen rolled out before him.

A smiling, auburn-haired barmaid in her late thirties, welcomed Ella with, "Freezing out there, luv. What can I get you?"

"A coffee, and do you do food?"

The woman pointed to a specials board. It was mainly meat, with a lone vegetarian option. Ella ordered the cheese and onion pie with veg.

"That'll be fifteen minutes. And here's your coffee."

Ella remained at the bar, warming her hands on the cup. When the woman returned from the kitchen, she asked Ella, "Come far?"

She refrained from saying she was down from Scotland, for fear of arousing hostility. "From Leeds."

Along the bar, the old man looked up. "Staying in the area?"

"Just passing through," Ella said. "I'm trying to locate where the writer Ed Richie lived."

The barmaid stopped polishing a glass. "Are you a detective?"

"A writer. I'm planning a book about Richie."

"Who'd've thought it!" the old man laughed. "Fame at last, if belatedly."

The barmaid bridled at this. "Ed was famous in his lifetime, Nigel. You should have read his novels."

"Novels?" Nigel snorted. "Don't read claptrap, Cindy. 'Specially not the tripe Ed trotted out. Stick to the truth." He tapped the screen before him.

Ella had wondered why the old man seemed familiar, then smiled to herself. He resembled the long-forgotten Nigel Farage, President Trump's gurning gimp.

"Ed lived in the converted barn on Old Smithy Lane," Nigel said. "Head west out of the village and it's the first turning on the left. Ed's old house is the second you come to, on the crest of the hill."

Ella looked from Nigel to the barmaid. "Did you know him personally?"

Cindy said, "Ed was a regular here for years, when my mum and dad ran the place. Came in with Shakespeare – well, that's what I called him because he looked like Shakespeare, only fatter. He was called Digby. Ed called him Diggers."

"Digby Lincoln," Nigel said, not looking up from his softscreen. "Another bloody champagne socialist, just like Ed."

"You didn't see eye to eye with Ed Richie?" Ella asked.

"Oh, we rubbed along well enough. He always bought his round. But he was like all the rest of his kind, artists and writers. Heads up their bloody arses when it came to politics. I put him right a few times. Christ, he'd be spinning in his grave if he could see what's become of his beloved Labour party, eh? Not that old Ed's in his grave... But Cindy knows what I think on that score."

The barmaid rolled her eyes. "Nigel has a pet theory. Thinks Ed did a runner."

"A runner?"

"Saw the writing on the wall, the fall of the left, so he got out," Nigel said. "Probably sunning himself in Bali as we speak."

"I think we'd have heard about it, if that were so," Ella said.

Cindy nodded. "That's just what I said."

Nigel drained his lager, rolled his softscreen, and saluted with it to Cindy and Ella. "See you around. Good luck with the book. And remember, try Bali."

"Don't take any notice of that old fascist," Cindy said when Nigel had departed.

"You must have known Ed Richie quite well," Ella said.

"I'd never met a writer before I started working here," Cindy said. "And Ed wrote some of my favourite TV shows. He came in here three or four times a week, and always on Tuesday and Friday nights for the lock-ins. Ed and Shakespeare liked their ale. There was quite a crowd of them at one point, a few local artists and potters, and Nigel hanging around on the fringes ready to stir things."

"What did you make of Ed?"

"I liked him. He was a real gentleman, and very quiet. I mean, sort of quiet in a sad way. Melancholy, that's the word. I often wondered if he suffered from depression, not that he ever let it show in how he treated people, though he did get a bit irate with Nigel once or twice."

"I suppose the political situation would have depressed anyone of the left," Ella said. "You must have known him a long time."

"Years, apart from when I was away at uni. I came back and ran this place when my dad retired. Ed came in every week, without fail, him and his many women."

Ella smiled. "I hope to interview some of them, if I can trace them after so long."

"Strange thing is," Cindy said reflectively, "they were all very much the same. Blonde, pretty, slim as you like. I never had a chance, did I?"

"Were you attracted to…?"

"Ed was one of those men who made you want to take care of him. I suppose that's what all his women thought, to begin with."

"And then? Why do you think all his relationships came to nothing?"

"I don't know. Maybe Ed only loved one thing – his writing. I mean, he worked long hours up there on the hill. I'd see him at his study window, tapping away, when I was out walking the dogs. And he'd often come in here with his laptop. Maybe that didn't leave him enough time for his relationships?"

"Maybe," Ella said. Her food arrived and she ate at the bar, chatting with Cindy in between customers.

In a lull, she said, "Were you around when Ed disappeared?"

Cindy had been wiping the bar, and she slowed down, her eyes taking on a faraway look. "Do you know something? I served Ed the day before he vanished. That's why I know he didn't do a runner, despite what Nigel says. He was just the same old Ed as always. I remember we chatted about my dog. He'd just had an operation on his spine, and Ed was asking after him." She shrugged. "Ed was the same as usual, in for his lunchtime pint. Just one, and then home to rewrite what he'd written that morning. Same old routine. You'd have thought, if he was thinking of doing a runner, that he'd say something to me: not exactly goodbye, but..." She shrugged again.

"What do you think happened?"

She thought about it, then shook her head. "I honestly don't know. I don't think he was... Well, I don't think anyone *did* anything to him."

"You mean murdered?"

"Mmm. You see, there was no evidence of a struggle at the house, nothing missing." She shrugged. "It's a mystery. His car was still in the drive, and the front door was unlocked. He just... vanished."

Ella nodded. She'd read all the news reports; the coverage had been extensive in the first week or so, and then had died to nothing as the months elapsed with no trace of the missing writer.

Cindy began wiping the bar again, then stopped and looked up at Ella. "I just hope..."

"Yes?"

She shrugged. "Well, I just hope he didn't do anything silly. He hadn't lived with anyone for a few months, and he'd just finished a book, and he once told me that he always felt a bit down after working for so long on a novel, and the UK Front were doing well in the polls... I just hope it didn't all get too much for him and he walked into one of the tarns. But surely they'd have found his body, wouldn't they?"

"I'm sure they would have," Ella said.

"In the weeks after Ed vanished, Shakespeare came in and he'd question me about that day." Cindy smiled sadly. "Digby was so upset. They were great friends. They'd known each other since uni. He was desperate to find out what'd happened. He stopped coming in here after a month or so. I suppose it held too many memories."

"I intend to drive over to see him this afternoon."

"Say hi from Cindy at the Bull, and tell him to pop in for a pint on the house."

"I'll do that."

"It's strange," Cindy said, "but Ed disappeared five years ago, and yet I still expect him to come striding in through the door and order his pint. The place isn't the same without him, you know?"

Ella finished her coffee and made to leave.

"I'll look out for your book," Cindy said. "Good luck, and I hope you find out what happened to Ed."

Ella thanked her for sharing her memories of Richie and left the pub. The air was still and freezing, and a milky grey sky was releasing its load of fat snowflakes. She hurried to her car and drove from the village.

She found the first turning on the left and accelerated up the steep lane, then came to the crest of the hill and braked. To her left, a low, double-winged barn conversion bulked against the louring sky. A light burned orange and welcoming in a front window, and Ella imagined Ed Richie sitting in his study, working on the novels that made him famous. She climbed from the car, waited for a pause in the snowfall, and then took a few snaps of the house and its surroundings on her wrist-com.

She drove west, overcome by a strange melancholy. She'd read a lot about Ed Richie the novelist over the years, but that had been mainly about his work and his politics; those commentators who had ventured to say anything about the man himself had quoted people calling him an introverted, rather dour character. It was gratifying to have spoken to someone who had known and liked the writer. She trawled her memories of the times she'd met Ed Richie, but she'd been very young, and not much interested in the dark, withdrawn young man with whom her sister had been in love.

A mile outside Gargrave, Ella was halted by a police road-block. She feared for a minute that the snow-swept road was impassable further on, and that she might have to turn back and find an alternative route. A body-armoured officer toting a black machine gun strode towards the car, making a negligent winding motion with his gloved right hand. Ella obediently wound down the window.

The cop met her smile with a blank look. "Identity."

She reminded herself that she was in England now, where the police were armed and malefactors were as likely to be shot in the back as arrested.

She dug out her ID card from inside her parka and passed it through the window.

The cop slipped the card into a reader belted to his waist and examined the tiny screen.

"A Scottish national. What're you doing down here?"

Ella shivered in the icy wind. "Visiting friends."

"Who are?"

Her first impulse was to tell the prick to go take a flying fuck, but she restrained herself. She gave Digby Lincoln's name and address, and then the details of an editor friend in London.

A second cop, she noticed, was moving around the car, holding a device that looked like a mine detector and sweeping it under the chassis. The cops conferred over the car roof, their words whipped away in the wind.

"What seems to be the problem, officer?" she asked.

The cop returned her card. "No problem at all," he said. "On you go."

The barrier was lifted and Ella drove through, telling herself that security would have been ramped up after the terrorist bombing of Manchester airport six months earlier. Still, the sight of the machine gun had spooked her.

She drove on into Gargrave, then followed her satnav back onto the B-road that wound its way through the windswept hills towards Digby Lincoln's converted farmhouse.

Ten minutes later she drove up a gravelled driveway and parked in front of the house. What had been the barn door was now a huge, arched plate-glass window, and beyond it an open fire burned, reminding Ella of the pub she'd just left. A hyperactive red setter pup bounced up and down at the window, barking to announce her arrival.

Ella saw a big, balding, pear-shaped man struggle out of an armchair before the fire. He peered through the window at her, then limped from the room. She approached the front door and waited.

Digby Lincoln would be seventy now, with a chequered career as a scriptwriter stretching back to the mid-'nineties. His satirical sitcom, *The State We're In*, had been a huge hit and had run for five years. Following the attack on Heathrow Airport in August '22, the UK Front government had imposed 'temporary' military rule and brought in draconian legislation that included press and media censorship. The independent production company that had made *State* was forced into liquidation, and Lincoln had found himself blacklisted. With the election of the Tories last year, Lincoln was working again, co-writing a bland sitcom set in a retirement home for vicars in the Channel Islands.

She heard a succession of bolts being drawn and chains slid back, and the door opened a grudging six inches. Lincoln's beefy face peered out, his small mouth parenthesised by a drooping grey moustache. What few strands of hair remained on his bald pate were grey and hung to his collar.

"Can I help you?"

"I'm sorry to bother you, and I know I should have called beforehand to ensure you were available for interview..."

His eyes narrowed. "Interview?"

"I'm Ella Shaw, and I'm writing a biography of your friend, Edward Richie."

The suspicious eyes widened a fraction at her name. "Shaw? Ella Shaw?"

"That's right. I –"

"You wrote Corbyn's biography?"

She smiled. "I did."

"And you do pieces for ScotFreeMedia."

"You're well informed."

"I read your column all the time," Lincoln said, opening the door fully. "Hell, you can't trust the BBC these days." He hesitated. "Look, I can give you an hour. I have to set off at three for a meeting."

"That would be lovely, Mr Lincoln."

He stood back. "Digby," he said. "Come in, you must be perishing."

He led her into the lounge where she suffered the attention of the bouncing pup until Lincoln called it off. "Tea or coffee? Or would you prefer something stronger?"

"Black tea would be fine."

He came back bearing a tray and poured two cups. She sat on the sofa while he resumed his place in an armchair before the fire, the dog curled at his feet. She glanced at the photographs of a smiling grey-haired woman lining the mantelpiece.

Lincoln said, "My wife, Caroline. Passed away last summer. She was sixty-eight. No age at all. Brain haemorrhage. Just like that." He snapped his fingers. "We were in the garden, pruning roses. Died in my arms."

Ella made futile noises of commiseration. "I'm sorry."

"Nearly thirty-eight years, we were together. She made me a very happy man." He smiled. "Still, we soldier on. I didn't mope, threw myself into my work."

"I see your latest is doing well."

He laughed and shook his head. "Thanks, but it's not up to much, between you and me. Typical of the stuff the Beeb's putting out these days. Still, I was surprised the BBC would sully their hands with me, after what happened... Anyway, it keeps the old mind occupied. Also, I'm writing my autobiography for Canongate in your neck of the woods." He sipped his tea and gave her a penetrating look. "I'm glad someone's doing a book about Ed, and I'm glad it's you. He deserves it."

"How long did you know Ed?"

He pointed at her wrist-com, and said, "Are you recording this?"

"I'm not, but if I have your permission...?"

"Go ahead."

She gave a voice instruction to her wrist-com to record their conversation.

"How long did I know Ed?" Digby went on. "Just under forty-seven years. Met at Cambridge back in '78. We got along like a house on fire. We both wanted to write, change the world."

He stared at the flames, then looked up at her. "Ed was a good man, Ella. The best friend a man could have. He had a great brain, wasted on TV: he didn't have enough creative freedom. TV's okay for third rate hacks like me, but it was too limiting for the likes of Ed." He smiled. "But he proved that to the world when he wrote his novels."

Ella was tempted to ask about the early days, but decided there would be plenty of time for that in subsequent interviews, if he agreed to them. "What prompted him to make the transition, so late in life?"

Lincoln smiled. "What else? The bloody awful political situation. This was in '17. What with Brexit and the election of Trump the year before... He just couldn't go on turning out soaps for the Beeb. He talked it over with me in the Bull one night. He wanted to take a year out to write a novel about a television scriptwriter set in the near future, charting the worsening political situation. The damned thing was, Ella, I tried to talk him out of it. I said no one reads serious novels these days. I tried to persuade him to do it as a TV script, try it with a few independents. But, bless him, he wouldn't listen to me, took a year off and wrote the book… and look what happened. The first novel did okay, and his second sold a million copies in the first year."

"I've read somewhere that you wanted to write novels when you were younger." Ella hesitated. "How did you feel at Ed's success?"

"I was honestly the happiest man alive when his novels became best-sellers. I was old enough, and wise enough, to rejoice in his success. The dedication in the first book… It still brings tears to my eyes."

"I'm quoting from memory, but wasn't it something like, 'To Digby, the best friend a man could wish for: thanks for all those bull sessions in the Bull'?"

"That's it, almost to the word. Ed ran the plots and ideas by me before he began writing – not that I'm taking any credit. It just quickened the process of gestation, that's all." He shook his head. "The exquisite irony of it was that, back in our twenties, I wrote a big, fat – and very bad – science fiction novel, showed it to Ed, and he pulled it to pieces – rightly so, I admit now. Not that I saw it like that at the time. I was livid, it almost ended our friendship. I was immature and egotistical back then…

"I can't recall how we patched it up – I think Ed tracked me down and told me to grow up. Anyway, we sorted it out and later Ed introduced me to a producer at the BBC, who took some of my early plays. And the rest, as they say, is history."

"And then when you moved up north, you returned the favour by getting him work with Yorkshire TV?"

"He moved up here soon after Caroline and I left London, and we had twenty-odd years as near neighbours, and enjoyed thousands of pints at the Bull."

Ella noticed Lincoln glancing at his old-fashioned wristwatch; she had about twenty minutes before he was due to set off.

"If you're agreeable, Digby, I wonder if I could meet you again over the next few months? I have someone interested in the book, and there's a chance that I could pay you for the interviews."

"I don't want paying, for God's sake. I'll do it for Ed. He deserves someone to write a good book about him, before... I was about to say before he's forgotten. I know, I know... his novels are still in print, but for how much longer – and how much longer will it be before they're banned? We're living in a post-literate world, Ella, a post-intellectual, post-scientific world. The truth no longer matters. Or rather it's swamped by lies promulgated by vast industries and governments with vested interests. There's so much misinformation that people don't know what to believe nowadays. Is it any wonder that the electorate votes for fascist celebrities?" He stopped. "I'm sorry. I'm ranting."

"No, I quite understand. And I agree."

The silence stretched, filled only by the crackle of the fire. At his feet, the puppy whimpered in its sleep.

After a while, Ella said, "I hope you don't mind my asking, but do you think Ed killed himself?"

Lincoln stared into the flames for a long time, then looked across at her and said, "Do you know, Ella, I've asked myself that question on and off for the past five years. Ed's books sold well, and were very well reviewed... But did they change anything; did they influence anyone? Ed wanted the books to change the world. To make people wake up and see what they were sleepwalking into. In those eight novels he outlined an affectless society more bothered about celebrity, possessions, and personal wealth than about culture, art, literature... or about a pluralistic, inclusive, caring society." He lifted a hand and gestured through the window. "And look what we've got."

"So... do you think this was what drove him to – ?"

"No," Lincoln said. "No, on reflection I don't think Ed took his own life. He... he wasn't that kind of man. He was stronger than that. And anyway, he had an idea to turn his first three novels into TV dramas, and he wanted me to co-write them. Okay, the climate was against the project, what with the Beeb under the thumb of the UK Front, but we had plans to tout the synopsis around the few remaining independent production companies."

"So... what do you think happened to him?"

Lincoln bit his bottom lip, regarding the fire. He was silent for a time. Somewhere a clock ticked. At last he said, "I don't know, Ella. I honestly don't know. But..." He hesitated, then went on, "In the last few months, before he vanished, he was in touch with someone we both knew at Cambridge. We were close, the three of us, which was a bit odd considering that Ralph Dennison was a scientist with not the slightest interest in literature or the arts. Anyway, we lost contact with Ralph after we graduated, went our separate ways... Only in the last few months, before Ed vanished, Ralph contacted him and they met up."

"And?"

"They met three times, as far as I recall, and after every meeting Ed got back and was... He wasn't himself, Ella. He was lost in thought, miles away. I'd ask how it went, how Ralph was, and he'd fob me off with some story about how they had a few drinks and nattered about their student days."

"And you think... what?"

He shook his head. "That's just it. I don't know what to think. I do know that Ed seemed incredibly preoccupied after meeting Ralph, but he wouldn't open up and tell me what was wrong, and I suppose I resented it. But whether it could have had anything to do with what happened to Ed, I honestly don't know."

He glanced at his watch again.

Ella said, "I mustn't keep you. It's been fascinating... I'll be in contact, if that's okay, to arrange further meetings – entirely at your convenience, of course."

Lincoln seemed not to have heard her. He was staring at the dog at his feet as if lost in thought. Surprising her, he struggled from his armchair and said, suddenly, "Come with me."

He wheezed from the room, the puppy in hot pursuit. Ella followed them through the house, along a corridor to a book-lined room looking out over the snow-clad moorland.

Lincoln crossed the room and removed a landscape from the only patch of wall not covered by books, revealing a small safe. He turned the combination lock, swung the door open, and pulled out what looked like a fat, battered ledger.

He stood with it clutched to his chest, staring at her.

"A few days after Ed vanished," he said, "I was getting worried. We were in contact almost daily, and met at the Bull two or three times a week... Then – nothing. He didn't answer my calls, either to his mobile or his home number. So three days later I drove over to his place. The front door was unlocked and I went in, expecting to find him... Well, you can imagine what I expected. But there was no body, no indication of anything amiss, and no clues as to where Ed might have gone. I searched the garden but found nothing. The fact that the front door was unlocked worried me. I found the spare front door key where he kept it in the kitchen, made sure the place was secure, then contacted the police. A few days turned into a week, then two. I went over again, with Caroline this time, to really search the place, and go over the garden again. But no, nothing. I did come across this, however, on his desk in his study. A hand-written journal going back years, full of day-to-day jottings, names and addresses, story ideas... I began reading it, thinking it might shed light on..." He shook his head. "I found it too painful. It was Ed, speaking to me, his voice in my head, while the real Ed was... *gone*. I couldn't take it, and had to stop reading. Anyway," he went on, "I think you might find it invaluable if you're going to write a book about Ed's life. Please, take it." He passed her the journal.

"Why, that's... thank you. I'll take great care of it and get it back to you when I've read it."

He nodded. "There's no hurry. Take your time. I don't think I could..." He gestured. "But I'd love to read the biography when you've completed a draft you're happy with."

"You'll be my first reader," she promised.

He escorted her back through the house and along the hallway. "Now, I really must get ready for that blessed meeting. Script conference over dinner in Leeds," he explained. "Last minute changes to the opener in season seven of the appropriately named *Oh, My God!*" He laughed. "But what next for you?" he asked as she pulled on her parka.

"I'm booked into a hotel in Manchester," Ella said, "then I'm taking a train down to London tomorrow. I've arranged to interview the actress, Samantha Charlesworth. One of Ed's old flames."

"Ah, the delectable Sam." Lincoln smiled, as if in reminiscence. "Remember me to her, will you? And next time we meet, Ella, I must tell you all about Ed's women, and a little theory I have about them."

Ella thanked him once again and hurried out to her car.

She laid Ed Richie's journal on the passenger seat and started the engine, wondering what Lincoln's 'little theory' might be.

As she drove from the house, she turned to wave at him. He was a portly figure filling the doorway, the puppy seated obediently at his feet.

He lifted a hand in farewell, then retreated inside and closed the door.

From Ed Richie's journal, 20th May, 2020

So THE PEOPLE of Scotland have voted for independence. I'm not sure how I feel about this. One part of me is against the breaking up of functioning political units (no matter how dysfunctional those units might be!) for fear of fomenting unrest and even warfare fifty, a hundred years or whatever down the line... Then there's the other part of me that rejoices in the referendum result. I think the socialists up there will make a decent fist of it and rejoin Europe. Compared with what we have down here, with the rise of the UK Front and the encroaching totalitarianism... Scotland's prospects seem rosy.

Reading *Enemies and Lovers*, the second volume of Olivia Manning's *London Trilogy*. Wonderful stuff.

From Ed Richie's journal, 17th November, 2023

LAST WEEK I received a letter – a real, snail-mail letter, and hand-written – from the daughter of an old lover. She wrote that her mother and I had had an affair in the late nineties, lasting some three months. The woman, Sherri Morton, told her daughter that she cherished her memories of our time together, and still felt a great fondness towards me. The reason the daughter was writing was that Sherri had recently passed away, aged 60, after battling with cancer for three years, and she thought I'd like to know.

I wrote to the daughter expressing my commiserations, and telling her that I, too, harboured wonderful memories of our affair...

The terrible thing is that it was a lie. Worse: I have no memories whatsoever of anyone called Sherri Morton, still less of our affair.

It's sobering to think that twenty-five years ago I had an intimate relationship with someone who left no impression on me. I can't have lived with Sherri Morton – surely I would have recalled that? But apparently I had an affair lasting three months. I made love to Sherri, perhaps even said that I loved her – and perhaps at the time I truly did! – and yet *nothing* of our time together, now that Sherri is gone, remains.

CHAPTER FIVE

September, 2013

WHEN HE CAME to his senses, Richie was sitting at his desk in his study, staring at the computer screen. He looked up, through the window, at the fields across the lane; bright sunlight glinted off rain-wet trees and sheep munched contentedly. The last thing he recalled, he'd been in his bedroom, a little hungover, having just spoken to Diggers on his mobile. Now he had a clear head, and it appeared to be the middle of the day. He looked down: he was wearing the brown cords he'd long ago thrown away, and a faded blue rugby shirt – his casual writing gear.

He reached for the mouse and dragged the cursor to the clock – 12.35 – and clicked. A calendar appeared.

It was Tuesday the 10th of September, and the year was 2013.

So he'd jumped again, over two and a half years this time.

His heartbeat seemed to slow in his chest, as if it were pumping treacle instead of blood. He felt light-headed, a little hysterical. His first urge was to laugh out loud at the absurdity of the situation; his second to rage tearfully. He did neither, just sat very still and stared at the screen.

He clicked the calendar away and read the words on the screen. The outline of a one-off radio play about an illegal immigrant he was working up for the BBC. They commissioned the play later that year, and he'd spent the following November and December writing the first, second and third drafts. Work that he recalled doing, sweating over... The play was produced and broadcast the following year, to universal indifference.

September 2013...

He'd met Samantha Charlesworth in April 2013, and about now would still be in the honeymoon period of total infatuation. He recalled those first few months as joyous, carefree – he thought he'd met the woman with whom he'd spend the rest of his life, and Sam had given him all the signs of reciprocating these feelings. Even later, three years into their affair, he'd worked to convince himself that theirs was a long-term relationship... despite what old Diggers might have thought.

He left his study and moved through the house.

The 10th of September... He had a bad memory at the best of times, and had no hope of recollecting what he might have done on this particular day. As an actress, Sam's working routine was arbitrary at best: she might be away for a few days, back for one or two, then off again... Or she might be away for weeks at a time, or at home for just as long. He had no idea where she might be today.

He entered the bedroom and found her cases on top of the wardrobe. So she was at home, or rather not at work. He moved from room to room, anticipating coming upon the woman he thought he'd loved, and wondering at his reaction if he were to find her. But Sam was nowhere in the house, thankfully, and he experienced a sudden release of tension.

In the kitchen he poured himself a bottle of Landlord, then saw that the answerphone was flashing.

Her high, bright voice filled the room. *"Eddy, darling. Don't cook. I'll pick up a Thai take-away on my way back, and a bottle of white. Should be in around four. Loves. Bye-ee."*

He played the message again, her words conjuring an image of the woman; slim and slight, in her late thirties now but looking ten years younger. She often wore her hair in plaits wound around her head. She sported navy blue velvet waist-coats, faded blue jeans, and Converse trainers. He recalled the heft of her in his arms, her perfumed slightness, her insatiable sex drive.

He found himself fearing her return. He was totally unprepared, psychologically, for the encounter: she had walked out on him around nine months ago, subjectively, and to the best of his ability he had dealt with the rejection, and moved on. Now, to be shunted back to near the start of the relationship, when Sam had been at her most passionate, and he had mirrored that passion with an almost incredulous sense of gratitude, he was like an actor pitched into an unfamiliar role, in a play he barely remembered.

He took a long drink to steady his nerves, then swore out loud as if to do so might provide some form of catharsis.

He carried the beer back through to the study and sat down at his desk, staring through the window without seeing a thing.

There was a lot more to think about, he realised, than the mere fact that in a few hours he would be reunited with Sam.

That was a massive enough consideration – how he might conduct himself, without letting slip to her that all was not as it should be – but the more weighty concern was what might be happening to him.

It had been difficult enough to accept when he had assumed the first jump had been a one-off. He might, had he continued to live in 2016, have come to some acceptance of what had happened, maybe even shrugging it off as a mental aberration, and got on with his life.

Now that was not an option.

He had jumped back twice, once to a point nine months before what he still thought of as the 'present,' and the second time to now, to September 2013, three years and four months before January 2017.

His first thought was, where might this end? A one-off he might have been able to live with, but the second jump made the phenomenon random, unpredictable, and therefore terrifying.

He would be able to take nothing for granted, from now on. His day to day reality was fundamentally destabilised; how could he plan ahead, look forward to tomorrow, when faced with the uncertainty of there ever *being* a normal 'tomorrow'? Potentially, from now on, his tomorrows would be always in his past.

Was he doomed to relive snatches of his earlier life, as if to atone...?

He recalled what Digby had said, yesterday... or would say, two and a half years from now.

No... No, he could not accept that he was being punished, or was punishing himself.

But he was faced with the very real fact that in three subjective days he had been pitched back in time more than three years ...

His hand shaking, he snatched up his beer and moved outside. His study was claustrophobic, limiting: he needed to be outside, in the open.

He carried his beer into the back garden and walked up the sloping lawn to the picnic table, from which he had a bird's-eye view over the slate roof of the house to Harrowby Bridge and the widening valley beyond.

The village had been here for centuries, essentially unchanged, and the valley dated from the last ice age, gouged out by the relentless forces of glaciation. An eye-blink in the entire span of geological history, perhaps, but a long time in human terms. The view provided Richie with a sense of solidity, a familiar, reassuring landmark against which to assess his own small, egocentric problem.

Where might it end, he asked himself?

Did his time-shifts to date indicate a set rate of progression? Nine months, then thirty months... and then what...? Or were they purely random, so that all he could be sure of was that he would, again and again, find himself inhabiting the body of ever younger versions of himself, in past times he had already lived through?

Until?

In their student days, when Digby Lincoln had harboured dreams of writing groundbreaking science fiction novels, he and Richie had exchanged drink-fuelled speculations long into the early hours. Digby had possessed a thorough working knowledge of the sciences, an active imagination, and an envious ability to extrapolate current trends. He had spun fantastic futures, creating post-human scenarios long before that sub-genre became popular, and stunning Richie with his bizarre storylines.

He wondered what Digby would make of what was happening to him; if he could accept the phenomenon as fact, and not some psychological defect, as he had yesterday, or rather more than two years in the future?

So he was travelling, little by little, back in time. He would move gradually through his forties, thirties, twenties, into his teens and earlier... Would he eventually come to his senses in the incontinent body of his new-born self, with fifty-six years of memories intact, but with no way of communicating with the outside world?

And then? What then?

Richie marvelled, drinking his beer and staring out across the sun-dappled landscape.

Digby might push the speculation further, envisage his temporal regression to... where? ...into a past life? What if reincarnation were a fact, he could hear Digby saying – you'd inhabit past lives, but backwards, spinning back through history, surfing down the centuries, the millennia, until... until you ran out of humans to inhabit and you found yourself in the consciousnesses of animals, apes, and then lemurs, then shrews... right back to the time some form of legged-fish crawled from the primeval ocean...?

He stopped himself, his head spinning.

He had never believed in an afterlife, and he had no reason to believe that there had been a life before this one. He thought all religions ludicrous, wish-fulfilling fantasies. As far as he was concerned, this life was all there ever would be. You lived, then died, and then your consciousness expired. It was a harsh thought, especially when it hit you in the cold, empty early hours, but he'd come across no evidence to suggest any other, happier resolution.

So when, at last, he inhabited his new-born self, he envisaged no existence beyond that. He would expire, his consciousness extinguished, forever.

It was a sobering thought because it meant that if his previous two jumps were any indication, he had a very limited time left on planet Earth.

If he lived through a day or two at every jump and there were, say, another twenty jumps remaining... then he could measure his life-expectancy in weeks, not decades.

A *very* sobering thought.

On reflection, he preferred the mental breakdown theory. Perhaps he was in a coma in hospital, and this was a very realistic dream?

His mobile went off, startling him with its long forgotten ringtone. He quelled the *Thunderbirds* theme tune and said, "Hello?"

"Ed," Digby said. "Still on for tomorrow night?"

"Tomorrow?"

"Don't tell me you've forgotten, Ed? Dinner at ours, followed by the match? I know you hate Man U., but even you appreciate good football, or should..."

He smiled. Now he remembered: he'd gone over to Digby's and watched United play in the European Cup – a game Manchester won, he recalled dimly. Sam was seeing a friend in Leeds, granting him furlough.

"I'll be there. What time again?"

"Six. Caroline's cooking an Indian," Digby said. "And how's the delectable Sam?"

"She's well. Gone shopping."

Digby hesitated. "I thought you told me she was reading for a part in a play?"

Jesus! "Ah... No. That was called off. Re-scheduled. She decided to go shopping instead."

"Attagirl! Got to keep herself looking beautiful. See you tomorrow, Ed."

Tomorrow evening, at Digby's, he'd tell his friend for the second time what was happening to him – and this time he would have proof: United would beat Bayern one-nil, scoring in the second half. He'd tell his friend the score and perhaps Diggers might believe his bizarre story.

If, of course, he didn't time-jump again before tomorrow evening...

He drank his beer and reflected that there would be time for a couple more before Sam arrived home. He decided that the best way to prepare himself for the potentially traumatic encounter would be to be well-oiled. If he played the part of his old self, in love and in lust, Sam would suspect nothing.

As he sat and drank and stared down the valley, thoughts of his 'old' self made him wonder about his future self: that is, the Ed Richie who had woken up two-years-plus down the line, the day after he, the Ed Richie of now, had jumped back in time. Like a mental usurper, he had briefly inhabited the body and mind of that future Ed, supplanting his thoughts for the duration of his brief tenancy – but the day after? Did Ed wake up with a blank in his memory of that day?

He considered the events of this day, more than three years in his past. He would have written all morning and into the afternoon – but he was sure he'd not had a beer or three on that occasion. He tried to think back that far, but had only the faintest recollection of Sam's returning with a Thai take-away, insisting they make love before dinner, and again afterwards.

His own consciousness was overwriting the old Ed's, he thought. He could alter what he did on this day if he chose to: place a hefty bet on Manchester winning tomorrow night. bequeathing himself a few extra thousand pounds. Then when next he jumped, leaving this iteration of himself, his future self would be a little richer, but with, presumably, no knowledge or memory of how it had happened.

He could alter history – or rather alter his future – by creating events in the here and now that never occurred originally... But what, then, of the 'past' events that he, the Ed Richie of the future, recalled as established fact? What happened to *that* reality?

His head was spinning again. He'd put it to Digby tomorrow and see what his friend came up with.

He went back to the kitchen and returned to the garden with another beer, and only when he sat down and opened the bottle did it hit him. Normally he took the stone steps from the patio to the rear lawn, but this time he'd jumped up onto the low retaining wall without the slightest spasm of pain from his usually arthritic knees. He held out a hand and examined it closely. The crepe paper texture of his metacarpus was not as pronounced as it would be three-plus years down the line; in general his body didn't ache as much, and he felt no twinges from his knees and ankles. He'd begun a course of methotrexate for his arthritis this coming December, and though it had slowed the progress of the disease, he'd still been plagued, over the following two years, by periodic bouts of pain.

It was little compensation for the malaise now afflicting him, but at least he wasn't in pain.

He polished off the beer and the world began to take on a rosy glow.

He wondered when he'd time-jump again, away from the here and now, wondered how long he might have in this present. The coming encounter with Sam would be a bitter-sweet experience, on one level a recapitulation of the love and desire he had felt for her, maybe, combined with a sense of betrayal at her ultimate rejection. He told himself to treat it as a short fling that would soon be over, to enjoy the moment, and not to invest emotionally in the *affair*... but he knew that that would be impossible.

He heard the grumble of an engine and looked up to see Sam's sky-blue E-type Jaguar race up the valley road and turn into the drive. She gunned the engine and accelerated the last ten metres, coming to a sudden halt in a spurt of gravel. That was something he'd forgotten about her, how her driving had mirrored her recklessness, her impulsiveness.

He felt his throat tighten as she climbed from the low car, her long fair hair flowing and her short skirt dancing around her legs. She saw him and waved, clutching a carrier bag to her chest.

"My God, she's beautiful."

She disappeared as she entered the house, then emerged through the back door carrying a bottle of Chardonnay and a glass.

She climbed the sloping lawn, and he watched her as if seeing the woman for the first time. It was little wonder that she was a sought-after actress with dozens of TV credits to her name; her fresh, Nordic beauty turned heads, and yet she was more than just a pretty face: fifteen years on the London stage had taught her how to act.

She deposited the wine and her glass on the table, dropped into his lap, and kissed him; and not just some pleased-to-meet-you peck. She straddled him, held his face in her hands and pressed her chest to his. "Missed you," she breathed between kisses. "Been thinking about this all the way home. Christ, Ed, you make Woman so damned hot..."

He laughed, not in pleasure at her attention – though it *was* pleasing – but in recollection of another thing that had slipped his memory: how she sometimes dropped the personal pronoun and called herself Woman. It was one of the many idiosyncrasies that he told himself he'd loved about her.

She pulled away, breathing hard, and looked around, a mischievous glint in her eyes.

"No," he said, pre-empting her suggestion.

"Why not, Ed? You prudish? Woman not."

"But people will..."

"What people? There's no one for miles around. And if someone turns up..." She shrugged. "So what? Let 'em watch."

She began unbuttoning her waist-coat, and then her shirt. She reached up behind her and unclipped her bra. She pressed her breasts to him and they kissed, Richie groaning with the pain of lust as he slipped his hands up her ribcage, gripped the back of her neck and pressed her lips to his.

She jumped up and danced away and, with one quick twist, divested herself of her skirt. She curtsied, a demure movement belying wanton intent as she pulled down her panties, then kicked off her trainers and rose up before him, gloriously, uninhibitedly naked.

They made love on the lawn for an hour until, exhausted and spent, he rolled off her and sprawled on the grass; she came to him on all fours and flopped on top of him, breathing hard and laughing.

"Sleepy now. Bed. Then dinner, mmm?"

"Mmm."

"Carry Woman to bed, my man."

"Don't know if I have the strength."

She poked his ribs with a pointed nail. "Carry!"

Another recollection: her demands, often backed up with minor violence. He'd found them perversely fetching at first, the slaps and blows, digs and nips, surprising himself with his masochistic acceptance of her low-key sadism.

He knelt and scooped her into his arms, surprised anew at how light she was, child-slight, as he carried her from the lawn and through the house to bed.

They made love again, and then she fell asleep against his chest, and Richie held her, stroked her long hair and wept.

IT WAS EIGHT o'clock before they descended to the kitchen and ate.

Richie watched her, this woman who had walked back into his life, and his love-cum-lust was tempered by something else. He was surprised that he could feel so dispassionately about her; he could see what had attracted him to her, what had made him love her, but at the same time could detect, now, the small things that would in time become annoyances.

She played on her beauty, her sensuality, to manipulate; she was egotistical and demanding, and ultimately selfish. Perhaps with hindsight he should blame himself for it, blame himself for being the passive audience to her act, of lapping up her performances and proffering no criticism.

"Finished the outline?" she asked at one point, licking a stray noodle from her lip.

He recalled the outline he'd seen on the PC earlier. "I think so."

"Great, want to read it."

"I'll give it a final polish tomorrow and you can give it the once-over before I send it to Carter."

"Big part for me, I hope?"

"The biggest. Anyway, how did it go...?" He was purposefully vague, as he only had Diggers' word for it that she had auditioned today.

She shrugged. "Who knows? Casting directors are a law unto themselves. But I met Shelly afterwards and we went shopping. Bought that little watch I've been promising myself ever since that notice in *Stage and Screen*."

He remembered that; the magazine had singled out her performance in a TV play, calling her portrayal a grieving mother moving and profound, *a performance that elevates Ms Charlesworth to the first rank of British actresses.*

He recalled her being hyper for days afterwards, recalled how she'd carried the clipping with her wherever she went, forever pulling it out and reading it to herself, her lips silently moving. He'd been touched by it back then, only later wondering at her need for such approbation.

His own reaction to reviews was severely pragmatic; he'd had enough of them over the years, good and bad, to know that neither really mattered, and ignored them.

She finished her pad thai, drained her Chardonnay, and said, "Know what I want?"

He almost winced at the thought of going back to bed: she'd wrung him dry.

She went on, "Let's have a session at the Bull, okay? See who's down there? A couple of pints and a bottle of pinot blanc, and a long lie in tomorrow, hm?"

He nodded, relieved. "Let's do that."

With the ill-deserved wisdom of retrospect, he understood now that it was more than just pride he felt when showing Samantha off to the regulars at the Black Bull: it was egomania. He was an overweight hack on the wrong side of fifty and he'd managed to pull a well-known actress who looked twenty years his junior.

This realisation hit him in a flash as he hauled open the door to the public lounge of the Bull and ushered Sam in before him. Heads turned; Nigel, propping up the bar, declared, "What an entrance! The Beauty *and* the Beast. We're honoured... What'll you have?"

Sam kissed him, standing on tip-toe to do so – she liked making a show of kissing acquaintances; it was part of being an actress.

"A bottle of Prosecco, Cindy," Sam said, "and the Beast will have a pint of Theakstons."

Paul and Debbie, artists recently moved to the village, arrived soon after, followed by Charles and Greg, an older couple who'd become part of the Tuesday night group; they repaired to a table beside the empty hearth and a long night of boozing and banter began.

At one point Nigel wandered over, raised his pint and beamed. "I was out on the moors earlier, with my old binocs."

"Bird-watching?" Sam asked, with a grin at Richie; she knew where this was heading.

"You could say that," Nigel went on, "and guess what I was lucky enough to spot?"

"That pair of buzzards?" Charles said.

"A pair of mating... I don't know quite *what* they were," Nigel said, "but they were going at it hammer and tongs. Happened to be in your back garden, Edward."

Richie found himself colouring, while Sam was lapping it up. He stood abruptly, gesturing to the empties. "My round."

As he moved off, he saw Sam leaning into Nigel as she said, "Tell me more? Did you get a close up?"

He heard no more as he sought refuge at the bar. He caught Cindy's attention and ordered, then watched as she pulled the pints. She was still adolescent with puppy-fat, yet to become the pretty twenty-one year old he recalled.

When he returned with the drinks, Debbie said, "We've heard all about it, Ed. Sam's making a dishonest man of you."

"He loves it!" Nigel chortled.

"Slowly bringing Ed out of his middle-aged shell," Sam said, squeezing his knee, "though it takes some doing."

Please don't mention the picture window, he thought...

To his relief, Paul asked Sam about getting tickets to a play she was starring in at Manchester, and the conversation turned to other matters.

The evening wore on. Richie downed five pints of Theakston bitter and felt pleasantly abstracted from proceedings. He was happy to sit back and watch as Sam held the floor, downing the Prosecco all by herself but not letting it show.

He remembered something Digby had said at their last meeting, that Sam had been to see him and Caroline and had complained of Richie's apathy, his lack of emotional openness, or some such. He had been offended at the time, and surprised.

But perhaps he'd been rightly accused.

When he'd first met Sam Charlesworth, he'd been beguiled by her ego, her ebullience, seeing it then as an attribute, not a defect. Now, having known her for three years, he could see through her act after just a few hours.

So perhaps old Diggers was right, and he had worked subconsciously to undermine his relationship with his lover.

Midnight came and went; the night fragmented into drunken recollections, stray images: Sam insisted on showing Charles how a real woman kissed, sitting on his knee and planting a smacker on the old gay's shocked face. Nigel called out, "My turn next!" and received a rather too forceful smack across the cheek for his trouble. Sam called for another bottle at one o'clock, and Richie recalled gripping her arm and saying, "I think you've had quite enough, my girl."

"No! Woman wants wine!"

And then they were outside, in the late autumn warmth, and saying their drunken goodbyes as if they might never meet again, and Sam was pulling him back and insisting, with blows about his head, that he give her a piggy-back all the way home.

He recalled panting up the drive, almost slipping once or twice, and her riding him like a jockey into the house and urging him up the stairs with prods of her heels. He dropped her on the bed where she struggled from her clothes, and he undressed. In bed she tried to raise his passion, with little luck, then gave up and turned her back on him.

And Richie passed out.

In the morning he woke to an empty bed, reached out and encountered a tundra of cool sheets.

He wondered, for a second, if he'd jumped again, then heard noises from downstairs: music on the radio, and Sam singing along.

He looked at the bedside clock. It was after eleven. He sat up, surprised that he only had a medium-bad hangover. After all the beer last night, he'd expected a real beauty; he was relieved he'd stuck to the Theakstons, and not mixed his drinks.

Sam joined him a while later, carrying a plate of toast and a mug of coffee. She looked fresh-faced and bright-eyed, as if the wine had affected her not at all.

She sat cross-legged beside him, munching her toast.

"And where's mine?"

"You don't deserve breakfast in bed," she said.

He was genuinely surprised. "And why not?"

"After last night's performance?"

"Last night's...?" he began, nonplussed.

"You were awful, Ed. You hardly said a word, just sat there in gloomy silence with a face like thunder, watching."

"Well, you did act up a bit."

She stopped eating and stared at him. "'Act up'? What the hell is that supposed to mean?"

"Come on, I know you like to be the centre of attention, but there's a limit."

She shook her head. "I don't know what you're talking about."

"Egging Nigel on about seeing us making love... snogging Charles... insisting that Paul paint your portrait... naked. And did you really need to drag out that damned review and read it aloud? And another thing, I don't like being assaulted in public."

She widened her eyes. "Assaulted?"

"All those slaps and pinches and digs in the ribs. What the hell got into you?"

With downcast eyes she said, "I was just trying to get your attention, Ed."

"Well, there are better ways of going about it."

She leapt off the bed and ran from the room, still gripping her mug and spilling coffee.

He lay back and stared at the ceiling.

He thought back to their time together, wondering why they had never argued then. Perhaps the fact that he knew it was going to end was making him boorish now.

She returned bearing a fresh plate of toast and coffee in his Leeds United mug.

She knelt on the bed beside him and murmured, "Woman sorry. Peace offering. Your favourite: Marmite. Forgive me."

He took the mug and the plate and placed them on the bedside table. He kissed her small hands. "Sam..."

"I'm sorry. It's... I know it's wrong, Ed. I..." She shook her head. "I think there's something wrong with me, you know? You're right – I like to be the centre of attention. It's as if... the more attention I get, the more I need. I'm insatiable. I can never get enough. I crave more and more attention and will do anything to get it. Why the hell do you think I act?"

He squeezed her hand. "But why the craving?"

"Because..." She stared down at his hands. "I've never told anyone this," she said in a small voice. "My father... He and my mother separated when I was six. He visited every month. When you're a kid, a month's a year. It was as if he never came, and then only for a few hours, which were always over too soon. I lived for his visits, Ed. And when he did come, I had to make the most of it."

"You acted?"

"I suppose I did, but I didn't realise I was doing it. I was hyper, craving his attention, his... what's the word? You've used it... Approbation, that's it. I craved his approbation. I really wanted his reassurance that I was the centre of his world, just as he was mine."

"And... did you get it?"

She shook her head minimally. "I found out that he was living with another woman. She had twin girls, a little older than me. He didn't tell me, but I saw them together in town one day. He was holding their hands, laughing. They were having a great time." She was weeping, now. "How do you think that made me feel?"

"I'm sorry."

"So the next time I saw him, I acted all the more, put on a show, tried to make him love me, want me. I didn't understand his... his reluctance at the time, of course. Only now..." She smiled through her tears. "Now I can see that he was protecting himself. I lived with my mother, and he could never get her back, or me, so he was distancing himself, protecting himself. I wish he'd lived long enough for me to tell him that I understood. But he died when I was ten." She blotted her eyes on the cuff of her pyjamas.

He pulled her to him and kissed her forehead. "I'm sorry. I understand."

"Do you?"

"I think so."

"I don't think you do, Ed. You see, all this craving attention, needing to be the centre of things... Why do you think I love you so much?"

"I..." He swallowed. He knew what was coming.

"You remind me so much of my father," she said in a small voice. "I'm not wrong, am I? I'm not sick for... for searching for what he couldn't give me?"

He smiled. "I don't think so, Sam."

She leaned forward and kissed his lips, then moved down his body, kissing his chest, his belly, then taking him in her mouth.

"Oh..." he said.

She looked up at him. "What's wrong?" she said.

"Strange. Sticky with jam and scratchy with toast crumbs."

They made love with a passion he recalled from the early days of their relationship, then dozed in each other's arms.

He woke before her and held her head to his chest, stroking her hair and staring through the window at the sun on the distant spinney, thinking over what she'd told him.

They'd never had this conversation during the time they'd been together; he had never understood her. Sam's craving for attention, for *his* attention, had slowly begun to annoy him, and he realised in retrospect that he had withdrawn, become apathetic. No wonder Sam had gone to Digby and Caroline with her worries; no wonder she had left him for someone else.

And now?

Would he soon jump from this time, shunted into a younger version of himself? Or might he never jump again, might he live on with Sam Charlesworth, understanding her now, so that she never had reason to leave him? And, if so, how did he feel about it?

A painful thought occurred to him. He considered what Digby would tell him, two and a half years down the line. If he did remain on this time-line, then would something deep and buried within him seek a way to undermine his relationship with Sam, despite his new understanding of her? Would he drive her from him?

Or perhaps, he thought bitterly, perhaps I was right when I wondered if I was in a coma, and all this is my traumatised brain's way of coping...

But Sam felt so real in his arms, and he knew he was not hallucinating.

He slipped into a troubled sleep, and was jerked awake later by Sam's startled exclamation. "Look at the time!"

It was one o'clock.

She danced from the bed, a naked sprite, and ran into the en suite bathroom. "I said I'd meet Kath in Leeds at two," she called. "Retail therapy, and then a meal at Angelo's."

She returned ten minutes later, dressed and applied a little make-up. All set, she knelt on the bed and said, "You're going over to see Diggers?"

"Caroline's cooking an Indian, then we're watching the match. Well, me and Diggers will."

"Staying the night?"

"No, I'll be back."

They kissed, staring into each other's eyes for seconds. "Loves," she murmured.

"Loves," he said.

She hurried from the house and he heard her E-type reverse down the drive and roar off along the lane.

HE DOZED AGAIN, then at four forced himself to get out of bed and shower. At five-thirty he drove over the moors to Digby's farmhouse, pulling in along the way to admire the armada of bruise-blue cumulus piled over a valley; it was raining in the distance, and with the late afternoon sunlight a startlingly vivid rainbow had appeared, arching from one side of the valley to the other.

He decided that he should tell Digby all about the time-jumps, and risk his ridicule – no, not ridicule, Digby was more sensitive than that, but his incredulity, his concern. Or maybe he should spare his friend the worry that he might be losing his marbles. After all, there was nothing Digby could do to stop what was happening, only come up with a theory that might account for the phenomenon.

No, he had to unburden himself, he decided, to take the weight from his mind. A problem shared...

The dogs bounded out when he pulled into the drive, the setters two years younger and bouncier. He kneaded their ears, waved to

Caroline on the doorstep. She was younger, too, and the difference was appreciable.

They embraced, kissed cheeks. "Dinner's almost ready. Dall paneer, Edward. Isn't that your favourite?"

"Love it."

"And chicken saag, Digby's favourite. Did I tell you I was putting him on a white meat only diet? He's getting a bit paunchy in his middle age. Wish I could do something about his boozing, though."

Was that said with real concern, he wondered, or with mock despair? "You're looking well, Caroline."

"I started a keep fit class a month ago," she said, leading him into the house. "I'm feeling great."

He calculated that she was forty-eight, and the lines around her eyes had not yet appeared; she seemed slimmer, her hair not as grey.

"Digby!" she called. "Edward's here!"

Digby emerged from his study. His beard and hair were trimmed, shorter and much neater than the last time Richie had seen him. He looked well, despite the paunch that preceded him into the lounge.

He opened a couple of bottles of Black Sheep and they drank while Caroline put the finishing touches to the curries.

"How's the outline coming along?" Digby asked.

Richie said he'd almost finished it, and was happy with how the synopsis had worked out.

He thought back to this evening, recalled enjoying a superb Indian meal and talking shop, then watching the match. Although he knew the score, the other details of his visit were lost. He had no idea what they chatted about, though he guessed that it was business, as now: Digby regaled him with an account of his script-conference with the other writers on *Henderson's Farm*. Richie had an odd sense of deja vu: he recalled, dimly, Digby telling him about a couple of new writers on the team.

Caroline called them in and for the next hour they ate, Richie falling quiet as he savoured the meal. The dall was cooked to perfection, the chicken tender and suffused with spice without being overwhelmingly hot. Caroline made her own chappatis, which melted in the mouth.

"This," he declared at one point, "is sublime." He lifted his glass. "If you weren't already shackled to this old reprobate, Caroline, I'd ask you to marry me."

"I don't think I could compete with your harem, Edward," Caroline laughed.

"Speaking of which, how's the latest?" Digby said. "The wondrous Samantha?"

Richie smiled. "She's a delight," he temporised.

"So this is serious?" Caroline asked.

Digby laughed. "As serious as Ed will ever be, I'll wager," and Richie joined in with the laughter and spared himself from replying.

After the meal, he helped clear the table and then Caroline excused herself. Digby replenished their beers and led the way to his study. He switched on a flatscreen television, muted the sound on the pre-match build-up, then settled himself in his armchair and turned to Richie.

"So... what's wrong, Ed?"

Richie lowered his beer, surprised. He wasn't aware that he'd let anything show. "Wrong?"

"Last Friday at the Bull you were full of beans about the synopsis. Best thing you'd ever done... Now you seem lukewarm. Carter hasn't pulled the plug on the project, has he?"

Richie sighed. Part of him wanted to say nothing about the time-jumps, despite his earlier decision; another part wanted to get it off his chest, although he feared Digby's reaction.

Then he said what he'd say three years in the future. "You're not going to believe this, Digby."

And his friend replied as he would do then. "Try me."

He took a deep breath. "Okay... Three days ago it was 2017," he said, "and I woke up one morning to find myself in 2016."

He detailed what had happened to him over the course of the past few days. He described his first jump, from January 2017 to April 2016, and then his second, from 2016 to the 'present,' September

2013. He told Digby all about Sam leaving him, and then about Anna... He said that he'd already told the Digby of the future, in 2016, about his first jump.

At this, Digby interrupted, "And what was my reaction?"

"What else? You thought I'd gone mad. I sometimes wonder myself. That'd be the easy explanation. Or maybe I've had an accident and I'm lying in hospital, and all this is a hallucination. Though a bloody real hallucination, I must say."

Digby was wearing his non-judgemental expression, the straight face he assumed when listening to Richie outline a story idea: he would reserve judgement, let Richie get to the end of his tale, and only then pronounce on the feasibility, or otherwise, of the outline.

Richie went on, "But I *know* it's happening to me, Digby. Listen... In almost three years from now, Sam walks out on me. She goes to London, shooting some crime drama, and when she gets back she tells me she's met someone, and off she goes. Yesterday afternoon I came to my senses in my study and found that I'd jumped back two and a half years, and I'm a few months into the relationship with Sam. And..." He shook his head. "And it's cracking me up, knowing how it'll end, and knowing that soon, in all likelihood, I'll find myself shunted back to God knows when."

Digby said, quietly, "How long did you remain in the 'present' the first time, in 2016?"

Richie thought about it. "Around a day, just over."

"And now you've been in this time for...?"

"Just over a day. I 'woke up' yesterday afternoon, around twelve-thirty. Of course, it might not follow the same pattern."

"You might," Digby said, "remain here for good."

Richie shrugged. "Christ knows. I might. But... the jump to 2016, and then to now... Why? Why the hell did it happen, just to stop *now*? Logically it should go on forever, shouldn't it, or at least until... until I run out of life to relive."

"When you told me last time, and I thought you'd gone mad... did I try to offer some kind of... rationale, other than insanity?"

Richie shook his head. "No, and I don't blame you. It's a hell of a thing to land on a friend. I don't know... perhaps I was hoping..." He made a sweeping gesture at the ranked science fiction paperbacks on the shelves. "Perhaps I was hoping you might be able to come up with an explanation, however outrageous."

Digby stroked his chin, for all the world like a TV psychoanalyst. "And you say you have all your memories of the intervening years, of all the events you experienced?"

"Well, those that I recall," Richie said. "I can't remember everything, the minutiae of day to day life. And that's another thing... There are things I do recall, but which don't happen this time around. Like yesterday. I remember Sam coming back with a take-away. After the meal, last time, we went to bed after watching a film. This time, Sam wanted to go to the pub, and we did. So... so what happened to the night we spent at home? Has that ceased to exist? Did it ever exist, despite my remembering it?"

Digby took a long drink of beer, as if buying himself time. "Other than the two explanations you've suggested, insanity or a hallucination, I can't offer an explanation, no matter how far-fetched, to explain what's happening to you."

"So you think I'm crazy?"

"I didn't say that. I said that I can't offer an explanation."

"Should that make me feel better?"

Digby smiled. "I'm glad you've still got your sense of humour."

"Despite losing my marbles."

He saw the television, flickering away silently. He stared at the emerald green pitch and smiled to himself. "Before I was whisked away from 2016," he said, "I'd arranged to meet you at the Bull the following day and watch the Newcastle v Man City match. I could prove what was happening to me, you see, because I knew the result, a one-all draw."

Digby nodded towards the screen. "Don't tell me. You can remember tonight's result, right?"

Richie smiled, pleased that his friend was going along with what must sound, to him, like the rant of a psychotic. "I think so. Your beloved Man U beat Munich 1-0. Rooney scores late in the second half."

Digby laughed. "One-nil? I'll take that," he said. "And if you're right, and if Rooney does score, late on..."

"Yes?"

Digby shook his head. "Then I might have to rethink what little I know about the workings of the space-time continuum... Another beer?"

While Digby was fetching the beer, the match kicked off. Richie found the controls and increased the volume, but kept it low. Digby returned and passed him a bottle, and they settled down to watch the match.

"If it is one-nil, and Rooney scores," Richie said, "then I'll know for certain that I'm not going loopy. And to be honest, I don't know what I'd prefer. If I *am* being shunted back in time, then..."

Digby looked across at him. "Then where might it end?"

"I'd rather not think about it."

Digby was silent for a while, absorbed in the to-and-fro of the match. United were doing all the pressing, but Munich absorbed the pressure and looked dangerous on the counter-attack.

One eye still on the game, Digby said, "And another thing, what happens to the 'you' of now while you're in possession of his mind? I mean, if you do jump again tomorrow or whenever..."

"Then what will he recall of today and yesterday from twelve-thirty?"

"Exactly."

Richie shook his head. "I don't know. Will he have a blank in his memory, or will he recall..." – he paused, following a new line of thought – "or will he recall the events that *would have* happened, had I not shunted back to occupy his mind?"

"Intriguing."

"Because I did come here in 2013," Richie said, "and sat watching the game after having a fine Indian with you and Caroline. But of course we didn't discuss anything about the time-jump business, because it hadn't happened then."

"So the you of tomorrow might recall the original version of the visit?"

"Maybe."

"It's mind-boggling," Digby laughed.

"How do you think I've felt for the past few days, trying to make sense of it all?"

They watched the match. It was one of the very few occasions, he reflected wryly, when he wanted Manchester United to win.

At one point Digby asked, "Have you mentioned this to Sam?"

"What? And have her think I'm a nutcase? No way."

"Wise man. You do realise, of course, that if you're right and we do win the game one-nil, then I'll have you racking your brain for every result you can remember for the next two years. Pity you aren't a racing man."

Richie chugged on his beer. "I can tell you that in 2016, David Cameron will call a referendum on whether or not Britain should stay in Europe – and by a narrow majority the good citizens of the country, in their wisdom, elect to get out."

Digby squinted at him. "You're joking?"

"I jest not," Richie said. "Oh – and you might not believe it, but in November 2016 Donald Trump is elected President of the USA."

Digby stared at him. "What? The multiple-bankrupt, TV celebrity shyster? Come on, even the Americans can't be that stupid!"

Richie smiled to himself. "And Leicester will win the league in the 2015-16 season."

"You're talking rugby union, I take it?"

"No, football. Leicester win the Premier League in 2016."

Digby laughed. "And now I *know* you're crazy."

Richie smiled, shaking his head. "Whatever happens to me, Diggers. Remember my prediction and put a hundred on Leicester. They were five thousand to one against at the start of the season."

They returned their attention to the match.

Half-time arrived with the score still nil-nil. Digby muted the sound and told Richie about an idea he'd had for a police drama series set in a northern town.

"Have you done anything with your 'sixties counter-culture idea, set in London?" Richie asked.

Digby stared at him. "I can't recall telling you about that." He tapped his head. "It's still in here, gestating. I must have let it slip when we were pissed."

Richie smiled. "No, you'll tell me, in great detail, over a few beers in a month or so... as far as I recall. But three years down the line, the BBC like the idea and commission six episodes. Please believe me, Diggers."

His friend grunted. "Like I should believe you about Trump becoming President and Leicester winning the league?"

The second half kicked off. They downed more beer and concentrated on the game. United pressed, and ten minutes from time Rooney headed them into the lead from a corner.

Digby punched the air.

"There," Richie said. "What did I tell you?"

His friend peered at the time in the top left corner of the screen. "Still ten minutes to go."

But despite German pressure, Manchester held out and won the game 1-0.

Digby killed the screen.

"So?" Richie said.

Digby looked uncomfortable. "A lucky guess?"

Richie sighed. What else had he expected? "I know, I know... I must sound crazy." He stared at his friend. "Bloody hell, Diggers, what's happening to me?"

Digby shrugged, uneasy. "Perhaps... perhaps it's down to stress, the series you're working on? The workload is pretty constant, isn't it? And the relationship with Sam...?"

The door opened and Caroline poked her head in. "Match finished? How did it go?"

"One-nil to the Reds," Digby said.

"And that's good?"

Digby smiled. "I'm happy enough."

Caroline nodded. "How nice," she said, with the blithe condescension of those blessed with the knowledge that football was, after all, only a game. "I'm turning in. Lovely to see you again, Edward. And next time bring Sam, hm?"

"I'll do that, and thanks for a great meal." He climbed to his feet and hugged her goodnight.

He and Digby sat drinking for another hour, Digby assassinating the character of a director they both knew, and around midnight Richie called a taxi to take him home.

"You're welcome to stay here tonight," Digby offered.

All Richie wanted was to get home and hold Sam to him, a locus of reassurance in an uncertain world. "Thanks, but Sam's expecting me."

"You lucky man."

The taxi arrived fifteen minutes later, and in the hallway Richie turned to Digby and said, "Maybe this is all my own doing, Diggers? Me, punishing myself?"

"Come again?"

"You once told me... in the future... you told me I have a self-destructive streak."

Digby winced.

"Said I drive all the women away, because... because of what happened to Annabelle."

"Ed," Digby said, gripping his arm.

"So perhaps you're right, and I am punishing myself," Richie finished. He opened the door and hurried out to the taxi.

THE CAB DROVE through Harrowby Bridge, climbed the hill and turned into the driveway. He paid the driver and made his way into the house with the exaggerated care of the hopelessly inebriated.

He undressed as quietly as possible, slipped into bed and pulled a naked Sam to him. She was as warm, and as reassuring, as he'd hoped. She murmured something, which Richie told himself was, "Loves…" before he fell asleep.

He awoke with a start in the morning, to bright sunlight streaming in through drawn curtains. He sat up, relieved when he saw Sam emerge from the bathroom. She dressed quickly, applied lipstick, and explained, "Must dash. Read-through of the play in Manchester. Be back around six."

He pulled her to him and kissed her. "I'll cook something."

"Okay, bye-ee."

That morning, feeling more than a little cut adrift from reality, wondering if he were insane and whether it would be for the best if he were, he took the *Guardian* down to the pub for a pint or two before lunch. He wanted to do nothing but get drunk, anaesthetise his senses with the balm of alcohol, and forget everything…

He carried the beer across the snug to his favourite table beside the hearth.

He was assailed by a sudden premonition, a forewarning that reminded him of the time, years ago, when he could tell that he was about to suffer a migraine.

A sudden pain shot through his head, followed by a blinding white light.

From Ed Richie's journal, 9th June, 2015

I SOMETIMES WONDER about Sam's state of mind. I don't mind her exhibitionism – and I like making love to her in the picture window – but when she started slapping me as she climaxed the other night... I really got the impression that she was enjoying hurting me more than she was enjoying what I was doing to her. And another thing... a few nights ago, after making love, she told me that her friend Kath fancied me, and Sam looked at me and said, "Have you ever wanted to make love to two women at the same time, Ed?"

Call me a traditional old fart, but I said that it was all I could do these days to make love to one woman.

I think she was disappointed in me.

Extract from the review, by T. J. Laisterdyke in The Times, *of* Towards Oblivion *by Edward Richie, March, 2022*

RICHIE TAKES ONE of the well-worn tropes of sci-fi, nuclear armageddon, and tries to construct a fable for our time. One of the main problems with this approach, quite apart from the fact that it's been done a thousand times before, is that Richie's cast of characters is thoroughly objectionable and runs the risk of alienating the reader. Richie has been praised for writing strong female characters, but this is a superficial analysis. His women lack in-depth psychological portraits, and a case in point is the female lead in *Towards Oblivion*, Kate Lerner, a domineering neurotic without a single redeeming feature...

CHAPTER SIX

January, 2030

Ella looked up from Ed Richie's hand-written journal as the train slowed and came to a halt. They were somewhere in the Midlands, three hours into a journey that should have taken two and a half hours. This was the fourth unscheduled stop due to, respectively, snow on the rails, signals failure, track maintenance work and whatever excuse would soon be announced over the public address system. It was a white-out beyond the window, with snow drifts obscuring the walls and hedges between the fields, and only electricity pylons visible as they marched across the undulating landscape. The mood in the packed carriage was almost mutinous, the occasional comment giving rise to a general babble of discontent. At one point the door at the far end of the carriage slid open, and heads turned in expectation of an official; the passengers fell silent as a brutish police officer strode down the aisle, clutching a machine gun to his chest.

He was followed by an announcement. "Due to an unforeseen bomb threat at Peterborough Station, this train will be delayed by approximately twenty minutes. The revised time of arrival at King's

Cross is now five forty-five." Wondering if there might be such a thing as a *foreseen* bomb threat, Ella was grateful that she wasn't due to meet Sam Charlesworth until seven that evening.

The armed officer passed through the carriage, and it was as if his proximity stifled protest. People communed with their wrist-coms, mobiles, and softscreens, and a silence settled over the becalmed carriage.

Across the aisle from Ella was a family of three seated around a table: the little girl, perhaps twelve years old, was slight and blonde and the sight of her – so similar to Annabelle at that age – produced a hard fist of pain in Ella's chest. She shut all thought of her sister from her mind and resumed reading Ed Richie's journal.

It was a fat ledger, made even fatter with loose pages. The combination of Richie's small handwriting, and the fact that he rarely wrote more than a dozen or so lines per entry, and then only two or three times a week, meant that the journal covered a period of almost thirty years before his disappearance in 2025.

She had begun reading near the end, covering the period from 2020 to 2024, when Richie's greatest success as a novelist corresponded with the most draconian period of English politics under the UK Front. Under their inept stewardship, the United Kingdom became disunited, losing Scotland and Wales in close succession, followed by a period of military rule when the troops were called in to quell civil unrest in major cities from Newcastle to London, Bristol to Norwich.

Richie spent little time detailing his political discontent – saving that for his novels – but instead wrote about his day-to-day life.

15th June, 2022: *Saw Diggers for a lunchtime pint in Leeds. One turned to five. Glad I went by train. Word is that the bastards at the Beeb are caving in under pressure from the Cabinet to axe* The State We're In... *I tried to reassure D that it wouldn't happen, but he wasn't sanguine. He has it on good authority, from his contact at the BBC, that this series*

*will be the last. D in a hell of a state… pun unintentional.
He doesn't need the money, but that's hardly the point. It's
far bigger than personal careers. This is state interference in
culture. Where will it end? Christ, had anyone told me ten
years ago that we'd be under military rule…*

2nd July, 2022: *Sue is becoming irritating. Two months is
all it took – is that a record? She was going on the other day
about my slovenly habits. I told her that when I'm writing,
everything goes out of the window – I really don't give a damn
that I've been wearing the same fucking shirt for days… Sue
was out with friends last night so Diggers invited me over.
I got pissed as per usual and displeased Caroline. I'd been
moaning about Sue, and then talk turned to Diggers' old dog,
Archie. I have a dim recollection of saying something along
the lines that no matter how badly you treat a dog, they never
hold it against you. Caroline gave me a frosty glare and said,
"No, they don't, do they?" I was too blathered to twig, but
it came back to me this morning. A bottle of gin as a peace
offering, methinks.*

15th September, 2022: *Sue left me last night. Said she couldn't
stand living with a fat drunken slob any longer. We didn't
row. I'm past arguing. I won't miss her. After a period of
melancholy reflection – lasting all of an hour – I looked on
the bright side: I was free again. I went to the Bull for lunch
today, in celebration. The Old Peculier was like nectar. And
more good news: Cindy's secured the leasehold of the Bull
after her father retired. That's what I want in this uncertain
world: continuity.*

11th October, 2022: *Diggers was gloomier than usual last
night at the Bull. The pusillanimous bastards at the Beeb have
caved in and axed State… Diggers and his co-writer are out*

on their ears. And to add insult to injury, some jumped up little ponce at Broadcasting House suggested they apply for a couple of vacancies that've just come up on the team writing the fucking Archers. Diggers, in his own inimitable fashion, told the young man to introduce his smug face to his lower intestinal tract. This was at a packed meeting. Didn't go down well. Talk about burning one's bridges. Good old Diggers!

Ella smiled and continued reading.

21st December, 2022: We're here again. My favourite time of the year, that appalling reminder of humanity's susceptibility to greed and gullibility. Diggers and Caroline are buggering off to the soon-to-be Republic of Wales to share the festivities with their son. I'll hole up here with plenty of frozen curry and a drop of the cup that cheers. And the Bull will be open every bloody day, thank Christ. Note for a one-off radio or TV play, not that anyone would commission it: Miserable sixty-something curmudgeon, sick to the gills of the farce of Xmas, pisses off to Malaysia or some other country where they don't celebrate the bloody thing. Only… the proprietor of the guest-house where he's staying takes pity and arranges Yuletide festivities to cheer our hero… I like it, but there's a big BUT: where on Earth doesn't do Xmas these days? Of course there's all those blighted Islamic holes, but there the drink doesn't flow… And with the fall of communism in Cuba and the uptake of Mammon… North Korea? Bloody hell, has it come to that? Our hero flees the totalitarian regime of ye jolly olde England for another even worse. Must rethink.

Ella laughed to herself and turned the page.

5th January, 2023: Deep in our cups at the Bull last night, Diggers suggested we emigrate to Scotland. Pros: it's liberal, democratic; its publishing industry, though small, is free, and

TV and radio likewise – and its links to Europe are a bonus. Cons: we'd be running away, and I don't like that. Diggers, well blathered by this time, says that it's all very well for me: my publisher hasn't been got at by the Cabinet, yet. But the fact is that old D is on a blacklist, not that anyone would admit as much. He's applied for work on a couple of shows in the past month or so, to no avail, and his last three outlines have been quietly shelved. I suggested he write a novel, but he just shook his head and stared into his beer like a dyspeptic bulldog.

Ella looked up from the page and stared through the window.

Ten years ago, she had met Kit Marquez and fallen hopelessly in love; Kit had just landed a lectureship at Edinburgh University after three years languishing at UCL, and had wanted Ella to move in with her. *Fait accompli.*

Only later had she worried that she was guilty of what Richie had suggested, running away. Wouldn't it have been more honourable to stay in England and fight the erosion of civil liberties, however ineffective her opposition might be? But she'd rationalised her decision by telling herself that she could just as effectively oppose England's regime from a base north of the border – in fact, given the free rein offered her by ScotFreeMedia, her opposition would be far more effective.

The train started up and trundled south. Sheep stood stoically in undefined fields, grey-white against the backdrop of driven snow.

Ella flipped through the journal, dipping into Ed Richie's thoughts. She counted references to a further three live-in lovers, and three break-ups. She came to the entry mentioning Ralph Dennison, and recalled what Digby Lincoln had said about Richie meeting with an old university friend.

4th December 2024: Bolt from the blue. Ralph Dennison emailed this morning. It's been over forty years since we last

met. Hard to believe that we three, Ralph, Ed and Digby –
Diggers had made much of the acronym at the time – had been
inseparable at uni, and then lost contact. I followed R's career
for a few years, and then he seemed to fall off the radar. It's
odd, but last year I was wondering what had become of him.
Not that he gave much away in the email, the same old Ralph.
Simply said he'd enjoyed my books and would like to meet up.
He'll be in Leeds next week, so we've arranged lunch.

Ella scanned the following entries, looking for mention of Richie's
old university friend.

12th December, 2024: *Lunch with Ralph at Venner's on the*
Headrow, then a pint around the corner. He looks well, and
he's taken care of himself. Could pass for fifty, not nearly
sixty-five. He told me a little about his research.

She jumped to the next entry, but it was a brief description of
a woman he'd met at the Bull. She turned the pages, looking for
reference to Dennison.

25th April, 2025: *Met Ralph for lunch.*

She turned the page, looking for more.
A month before Richie's disappearance, she came across one of
the last entries.

21st June, 2025. *Lunch with R. He wants to know what I*
think. I told him I need time.
Time? Time for what?
The last entry concerning Ralph Dennison was dated the 26th
June, 2025: *Ralph came to see me. Lunch at the Bull.*
And no more, no detail, no description of what transpired at that
lunch.

There were three more brief entries in the journal, all dated July 2025, the month he vanished: a note for a story idea, a description of dinner with the woman – Francesca – he'd met at the Bull, and the last entry of all, on the 7th of July: *Hell of a session last night with Diggers. Can't recall a bloody thing.*

And then nothing, just a wad of blank pages denoting the future into which Ed Richie had vanished.

She accessed her wrist-com and Googled Ralph Dennison, only to receive the message that connectivity was poor. That was another thing about England; cyber-infrastructure had suffered during the economic recession of the late 'twenties, and word on the street was that the government, eager to crack down on the dissemination of information over the net, had done nothing to improve the service in the years following.

She scrolled down a list of names and got through to Kit.

Thanks to the poor reception, it was a voice-only connection. "El, how's it going? Where are you?"

"On a cold train north of Coventry. I'm not interrupting anything?"

"Just finished a piece for old misery-boots. I'm about to pop out for lunch with Aimee at the Chinese place where she's working."

"Look... I wonder if you could do me a favour? There's no hurry at all, but the net's crap down here. I'm trying to trace an old friend of Ed Richie's. They were at Cambridge back in the late 'seventies. He's called Ralph Dennison, and he's a scientist of some kind. Any info at all would be welcome."

"Of course. As soon as I come back after lunch, I'll work on it."

"You're a star, Kit. Enjoy your lunch, and say hi to Aimee." She cut the connection.

The train snailed through the grey suburbs of Coventry, a succession of dour, Victorian estates, red-brick factories and pre-fab warehouses – and a cowed and shuffling populace that put her in mind of Lowry's dark, malnourished wraiths.

Colour was provided a little later as the train pulled out of the station. The door at the end of the carriage slid open to reveal a tall young man dressed as a nun, with a blue-painted face, ethereal, otherworldly, and quite beautiful. He glided along the aisle, handing out leaflets, arousing muttered comments and cat-calls to which he responded with blown kisses and batted eyelids. Ella smiled at the foolhardy soul and took a leaflet, printed with a rainbow arching over the legend: *Queers Against the Front.*

The nun passed a leaflet to the family seated around a table across the aisle from Ella; the little blonde girl took it. Ella was gratified that her parents did nothing to prevent the exchange. In fact, the mother gave the nun a covert smile. As the nun passed on down the aisle, a middle-aged woman seated behind Ella stood up and approached the family.

She hissed something to the mother, who replied, "I don't see what business..."

"It's disgusting," the woman said. "Perverts like that should be..." And unable to finish the sentence for sheer rage, she snatched the leaflet from the bemused child and returned to her seat.

Ella made a show of leaning over to the family and saying, "If it's okay with you, she can read mine."

The mother smiled. "Say thank you to the nice lady, Kathryn."

The child thanked her and took the leaflet, and Ella was gratified to hear an outraged muttering from the woman seated behind her.

She glanced across the aisle, to the person occupying the fourth seat around the table; a man in his mid-forties whose cold expression told Ella exactly what he thought of her.

She heard a commotion at the far end of the carriage, and turned in time to see two armed guards dragging the nun through the sliding door. He was waving and blowing kisses, defiant to the last. Ragged cheering greeted the arrest. Ella couldn't work out if it was in derision of the police or the nun.

She returned Richie's journal to her bag, then sat back and closed her eyes as the train gained speed towards London.

*   *   *

THE MATINEE PERFORMANCE of *Puss in Boots* had just finished and the well-muffled audience was filing from the Old Vic when Ella alighted from the taxi and hurried down the side-street to the theatre. London depressed her, and she would be glad to be away from the place as soon as possible. She didn't particularly like the atmosphere in the city – with its xenophobic graffiti, openly racist Mayor, and sense of superiority and privilege – but much of her dislike was a result of her memories of the place: being kettled by the police at protest rallies and Gay Pride marches; being knocked over by a police horse and spat on by passersby; being evicted from a squat in Streatham by bailiffs.

She approached the stage-door, told the doorman she had an appointment with Samantha Charlesworth, and was admitted into a dark, narrow corridor smelling of sweat and greasepaint. She asked a cloakroom attendant where she might find the actress, and the woman said, "Third door along the corridor. Can't miss it. Look for the big silver star."

She found the star on the third door and knocked.

A contralto, loud with post-show adrenalin-rush, called out, "Come in!"

Ella opened the door a crack and peered inside. A young man in doublet and hose was seated before a dressing-table.

"Sorry!" Ella pulled the door shut and retreated.

The door opened instantly and the youth laughed. "Ella Shaw?"

Ella peered. "Good God – Sam Charlesworth?"

"Underneath all the face-paint and this bloody ridiculous costume, yes. Come in."

Ella followed the actress into the dressing-room, marvelling not only at what a transformation make-up and costume could achieve, but that the woman standing before her was in her mid-fifties.

"Would you be an absolute darling and help me out of this damned thing?" She indicated the criss-cross laces across the back of the bodice.

As Ella pulled at the laces, loosening the bodice, she glanced over the actress's shoulder at her face in the mirror. Samantha was applying cleansing cream, stripping away the make-up to reveal a face that seemed innocent of the ravages of time. Her skin was translucent, without a single wrinkle, and the flesh of her neck was taut and firm. It had been a long time since Ella had undressed a beautiful woman, and she found herself flushing.

"When I'm human again, we'll scoot off to a cosy little bistro around the corner. There's no evening show tonight, thank God, so I'm all yours."

"That sounds great."

The laces undone, Samantha pulled off the bodice. She turned and said, "Would you look at that..." revealing small, high breasts imprinted with red weals from the bodice. "The things one does for one's art." She touched her pixie-cut hair and went on, "And would you believe I had to have my tresses shorn for the part?"

She ducked, easing down her pantaloons and knickers and kicking off a pair of pointed shoes. Entirely naked, she leaned against the dresser, lit up a joint, and inhaled gratefully. "Hell, I needed that. I've been gasping. Do you know, this is one of the few places in London I feel free to indulge. You know what the pigs are like these days. No one dares enter here, you see."

On cue, the door opened and a slim young man walked in.

"Well," Samantha said, "almost no one. But Timmy is a darling."

"Hark at Lady Godiva," Timmy said, scooping the Dick Whittington costume from the floor, and in an aside to Ella, "She keeps a picture in her attic, she does." Then he was gone.

"Hold this while I have a quick shower," Samantha said, passing the joint. "And help yourself."

Ella watched the lithe woman step into a shower cubicle. She took a hit, felt dizzy and sat down on a chair, staring at the actress's blurred outline through the glass.

"You're probably wondering," Samantha called out above the noise of the water, "what Sam Charlesworth, star of many a West End hit way back when, is doing slumming it in an extended run of *Puss in bloody Boots*?"

Ella's head whirled. It was a while since she'd last indulged. "Not at all."

"Since you asked for a candid interview, warts and all, I'll tell you. There's precious little else being performed, these days; I love acting, and I need the money."

"It must be galling – that there's so few serious plays being performed, I mean?"

"Galling isn't the half of it, darling. It's a crime. The public don't know what a serious play is. Pinter? Churchill? Poliakoff? Who're they? And Shakespeare? Do you know when the Bard was last performed at London?"

"Go on?"

"Three years ago, darling. What do you think of that?"

"What do you expect, with Westminster full of career criminals?"

Samantha poked her head from the shower. "I'm so glad we're on the same wavelength, Ella. But then I knew we would be. I Googled you before I consented to be grilled. Pass me the towel."

The actress stepped from the shower and dried herself; Ella had to look away.

"What I don't understand, though," Samantha went on, "is why someone who usually writes polemic and political articles for ScotFreeMedia wants to interview a washed-up has-been 'starring' – I laugh! – in a third-rate panto? Then I had it: you want to know what a jobbing actor really feels about the political situation south of the border." She peered out of the towel as she dried her hair. "Look, I'll tell you on one condition: anonymity. I don't like myself for the stipulation, but I want to work in this town, and there are people out there who'd make damned sure I never trod the boards again if I started bad-mouthing certain ministers-of-the-arts-who-should-remain-nameless... *Comprenez-vous?*"

She pulled on a pair of tight-fitting faded jeans, buttoned a white blouse, and looked at Ella enquiringly.

"I'll be honest with you," Ella said, taking a long pull at the spliff and passing it to the actress. "I'm going to do a fluffy celeb-piece for SFM's entertainment strand, and if you want I'd be more than happy to do a more serious article about being an actress in today's political climate – source anonymous, of course."

Samantha quirked her lovely lips and peered at her. "I sense a 'but' coming. But... you want something else, hm?"

Ella nodded. "I'm writing the biography of Ed Richie, and I'm interviewing everyone I can who had anything to do with him."

Samantha closed one eye theatrically and drawled, "You're interviewing *all* his women? How long have you got, darling?"

Ella smiled. "As long as it takes," she said. "And I quite understand if you don't want to rake over the past. I'll still do the other pieces, but I'd be grateful..."

"No." Samantha leaned against the dresser and folded her arms, peering through the smoke rising from the joint. "No, I'm quite happy to talk about Ed. On that score, I have quite a lot to get off my chest."

"I'm very grateful, Samantha."

"Please, it's Sam," the actress said. "Hokay. I'm famished, and I could kill for a drink. Let's go." She pulled on a fake sheepskin jacket, wound a long knitted scarf around her neck, and led the way from the theatre.

Le Moulin Bleu was a steamy, atmospheric cafe-bistro tucked down a nearby sidestreet, the haunt of students and the odd nostalgic French diplomat and business-person.

"Would you believe," Sam said as they seated themselves at a tiny, marble-topped table, "that this place was trashed when England lost to France in the quarter-final of the last World Cup?"

"Why doesn't that surprise me?" Ella said.

Sam recommended the French onion soup followed by ratatouille, accompanied by sparkling white wine.

"So... Ed," Sam said.

For the next hour, as they ate, Sam told Ella all about her first meeting with Ed Richie, and their subsequent affair. "It came at the right time," she said. "I'd been single for a year, and I think I was looking for someone. And then this handsome, intelligent man walks into my life."

"Love at first sight?"

"Certainly wild attraction. And it was mutual. The love came later, but not much later, say a couple of months after I moved in. It was pretty wild. We seemed made for each other. He was a bright cookie, and I was no slouch. Our politics meshed. We both loved theatre and books... And the sex. Jeez."

She went on, explaining how she felt about the man and describing their time together. Ella smiled as she listened, and it was as if Sam were describing her own feelings, in the early days, for Kit Marquez.

"It was a very equal relationship, Ella. He really loved me. I hope that doesn't sound corny."

Ella shook her head. "In his novels, his portrayal of women is exceptional. But..."

"Go on." Sam lodged her chin on her hand, watching Ella.

"I can't claim to have known Ed Richie at all well, but I sense a contradiction. For all his ability to write about strong women, why was it that he couldn't find someone who would remain with him? I've read his journal, and read the pieces about him in magazines and the better papers... and it seems that his life was just one long series of affairs."

"One thing" – Sam reached out and touched Ella's hand – "he might have had lots of affairs, but he never cheated on any of his women."

"As far as you know, surely?"

"No, I knew Ed. He was an honest man."

Ella tried not to smile. "Sam, he was a *man* –"

"Don't give me any of that sisterhood bullshit, Ella. Credit me with a little insight into someone I lived with for three years. Ed didn't cheat. That's not to say he was perfect, far from it. He could be surly and uncommunicative at times, and damned sarcastic, and he flew into rages... But he didn't look at another woman while he was with me."

Ella nodded slowly. "Okay. So... why didn't it last? And why were there so many other women down the years? At a conservative estimate, going from what people have told me... I'd say that he lived with at least twenty lovers in around thirty years."

Sam was silent for a time, staring at her beer. At last she said, "Ed wasn't easy to live with. He was... uncompromising. He had his routines, his writing routines, and woe betide anyone who tried to change things. He didn't suffer fools gladly, and he had no time for anyone not of his political persuasion. Also... Look, the fact that he had so many lovers, one after the other, suggests to me he was searching for something, and never finding it. I once asked him about this, towards the end. I... I kind of sensed his dissatisfaction in our relationship. You know how it is, that terrible, nebulous sense that's almost impossible to define, when you know that something isn't right but you have absolutely no idea what to say in order to fix it?"

"You felt that?"

"It was just before I landed a part in *Dark Heart*, the crime drama that was big back then. So I got the part and went away to shoot it for a month, thinking that that was all it would take – a few weeks away to allow me to think, to look back and assess our relationship."

"And did you come to any conclusions?"

Sam frowned. "Well, I did wonder if Eddy was happy with me. He seemed to be pushing me, goading me." She shrugged. "But I was confused... I realise that this might be no more than self-justification on my part. You see, I met someone on the set, someone I'd known for a couple of years as a friend. And..." She shrugged. "There was no going back to Eddy, after that. I... I'm not proud of how I ended it, Ella. I should have... We should have sat down and talked honestly, but... I wanted out. And at the back of my mind I was telling myself that Eddy would be okay, he'd find someone else pretty damned quick, as per usual. But, no, it wasn't honourable. I... I came back that day, told him I was leaving, and off I went."

She shook her head. "No, I'm not proud of myself, Ella. I'd do it differently, now."

"You never saw him again?"

"Never. I saw him being interviewed on TV – this was after his novels became best-sellers, and do you know, I was pleased for him. Really pleased. And of course I read the books." She smiled. "I even thought I recognised myself in one of them. Jessica, the posh sculptress in *Endeavour's Harbour*."

"And five years ago...?"

"I read the newspaper reports, saw the TV coverage." She shrugged. "I don't know. I was shocked, but not as shocked as I thought I might have been. It was years since we'd been together..." She fell silent, then asked, "Do you have any idea what might have happened to him?"

Ella sighed. "No. No, I haven't. None at all. But I hope to find out, in time."

"If you do, I'd like to know, okay? Before it becomes public knowledge."

They ordered coffee, as the snow came down in incessant flurries beyond the plate-glass window, and Ella asked the actress about Ed Richie's reaction when Sam had told him she was leaving.

"What I'd like to know, Sam, is whether he was jealous?"

"Any man who tells you they aren't jealous, Ella, is a liar. Of course he was, but whether he would have been any more jealous had he known who it was I was leaving him for..."

Ella looked at the actress. "You mean, it was someone he knew?"

Sam smiled; she shook her head. "No, it was a woman."

Ella opened her mouth, but no words came out.

"You're shocked. Disappointed in me."

"Disappointed?"

"That the well-known Sam Charlesworth, actress, is bisexual but never had the guts to come out and admit it? Well, guilty as charged. But you see, my mother was still alive at the time, and she was a strict northern Methodist. It would have killed her. And later..."

She shrugged. "I was briefly married to a man ten years ago, and he didn't know about my past. I suppose I could have come out after the divorce, but then Front came to power and repealed same-sex marriage, and things began to get nasty... So," she said, staring Ella in the eye, perhaps challenging her, "so no, I wasn't as strong as I liked to think, and I wanted to work. I'm sorry if I've disappointed you."

Ella shook her head. "Jesus, Sam... I know how hard it is. And I don't blame you for a thing, okay? Now let's have another drink."

She was more than a little drunk, an hour later, when they left the bistro and stood facing each other. Snowflakes settled on Sam's face, melted and turned to diamonds, glittering in the street lights. She was beautiful, and Ella felt a sudden clutch in her heart.

"I was wondering..." Sam began, touching Ella's hand. "My flat's just around the corner. Maybe you'd like to...?"

Something caught in Ella's throat. "Thank you, but –"

Sam waved. "But you have someone? That's okay."

Ella squeezed the actress's hand, relieved at being let off so easily. "I'm sorry. I hope you don't mind? If we could meet again, to talk...?"

Sam smiled. "Of course."

"I'll be in touch."

They parted with a brief kiss and Ella watched the actress walk away through the quickening snowfall, her heart still thumping. She took a taxi to her cheap hotel in Earl's Court, but walked the last half mile when the driver lost his way: she needed to clear her head, anyway.

She hurried through the snow, thinking over her interview; she relived the sensation of drawing the laces from the woman's bodice, and wondered what it would have been like to make love again, after so long.

As she turned into the street where her hotel was located, she looked behind her, moved by some intuition – and she was right. A dark figure slipped into a doorway thirty yards back.

Ella made it to her hotel, took the lift to her room, and locked herself in.

She made a strong coffee, opened her laptop and began the first of two short articles about Sam Charlesworth.

She was interrupted by the chime of her wrist-com.

"Hope it isn't too late?" Kit said, smiling out at her. "But I have something on that scientist you mentioned, Ralph Dennison."

"Go on."

"He graduated from Cambridge in '81, then did a doctorate there. In '87, he was snapped up by an independent research company in Oxford. He worked for them for twelve years or so, then left around the turn of the century."

"And then?"

"Well, he fell off the radar for a while, then disappeared completely in 2010."

Ella blinked. "Disappeared?"

"Vanished into thin air. Reading between the lines, it's possible that he was snatched by the Chinese – or went of his own accord. He was always a bit of a Red, apparently."

"Christ, okay... What exactly did he work on?"

"He studied natural sciences at Cambridge, and did his PhD in quantum physics at Oxford. The research team he worked with in Oxford was all very hush-hush – and oddly he published no papers during his time there. And according to a couple of people I've spoken to, he was a brilliant physicist who should have published reams of research work. Anyway, that's it for now. I'll keep digging."

Ella thanked her and cut the connection.

So Dennison disappeared in 2010... but had met up with Ed Richie in Leeds in 2025, according to Richie's journal.

She wondered if it were merely a coincidence that Richie and Dennison, two university friends, had both vanished.

She made herself another coffee and tried to concentrate on the article about Sam Charlesworth.

From Ed Richie's journal, 9th September, 2007

TALK ABOUT KICKING a man when he's down... Traverson axed *Beat Up* a month ago, citing falling viewing figures – even though it was nominated for a TV Guild award last Spring – and now Coromandel Cable has pulled the plug on *CrazyMadLoopy*... which was fun to work on. I've gone from having three shows running or in production, to one – the sequel to *Catweazle*, due to start filming next spring. I'm not getting desperate, just yet... The odd radio commission brings in a couple of thousand a year, but the big money is in TV. And it's drying up. And my bloody agent is worse than useless. I need a serious talk to her about what she's doing for me.

From Ed Richie's journal, 14th September, 2007

IN A BID to try to earn a crust and pay the sodding mortgage, I approached Dave at the *FT* last week to see if they had any openings for reviewers. As luck would have it, they did. As bad luck would have it, the first bloody book they sent me was a reprint of Ballard's *Crash*. My initial instinct was to contact Dave and say that I didn't do automobile porn... But I decided to bite the bullet and read fifty pages before I had to put it down. So I Googled Crash + Ballard + reviews, and proceeded to cobble together four hundred words cribbed from online reviews. Ker-ching, three hundred quid better off.

CHAPTER SEVEN

June, 2008

RICHIE CAME TO his senses and wondered where the hell he was. Something was covering his eyes, rendering him blind. He reached up and touched a pad of soft material. He was surrounded by a constant droning, a vibration that conducted itself through his body, at once familiar and yet disconcerting. He felt a little woozy, as if with alcohol, but somehow knew he hadn't been drinking. It was a different kind of wooziness, and he tasted no trace of alcohol in his mouth. He felt as if he'd been drugged.

His first shocked thought was that he was being held captive somewhere, quickly followed by a more rational explanation. He pulled off the blindfold and saw that he was right: he was aboard a plane, the small window to his left showing an expanse of glittering ocean far below.

Richie feared flying and avoided doing so whenever possible. When there was no other option, he dosed himself up on sleeping tablets and wore a blindfold for the duration of the journey.

He tried to recall when had been the last time he'd flown anywhere, then remembered and looked around in panic. Sure enough, Marsha was sitting next to him, fast asleep. Digby and Caroline sat across the aisle, reading the Saturday supplements of the *Guardian*.

So it was June 2008 and he was flying to the Greek island of Crete with his friends, and lover, for a two-week break. He felt no fear of being aboard the plane, this time – after all, he had survived the flight, hadn't he?

He'd jumped back five years. He was forty-eight, and felt better than he had for a long, long time. His body was not beset by the nagging pain of arthritis, and he'd lost a little weight since 2013, or rather had yet to gain it.

He tried to work out how many relationships he'd gone through between 2008 and 2013. After Marsha was Liz, which had lasted for a year, followed by Hellena, which had been a brief, tempestuous affair of a few months; after that… the American, Susan, then Pam, and finally Hilary, before he'd met Sam in 2013. These women had lived with him at the barn for varying periods, but there had been other affairs in between which had never graduated to live-in status.

Now he found himself re-living the very last days of his disastrous liaison with Marsha Mallory.

The start of 2008 had been a bad time for Richie. Last year, two of his shows had been axed, and half a dozen proposals for one-off dramas, and the synopses for a couple of films, had all come to nothing. Digby had come to his rescue like the true friend he was, loaning him five thousand pounds and in June taking him, and Marsha, on holiday to Crete. Richie, overcome by Digby's generosity, felt it would be churlish of him to refuse the break on the grounds of his fear of flying – he wished he could have gone without Marsha, though.

They'd met just after Christmas at a party thrown by the director of the kids' show – a bash at his Manchester loft-conversation just a week before the show was axed. Richie had been immediately attracted to the short, vivacious fair-haired woman in her early thirties who introduced herself and said that she loved his work. He suspected at the time, and found out for certain later, that it was not his scripts she admired so much as his position on the writing team: Marsha was an aspiring screenwriter, with a degree in film studies, and assumed mistakenly that he might be a way into the profession. He should have realised this and advised her to bed the director – for all the good it would have done her, given what happened to the show.

Something else he should have realised, early on, was that the mutual attraction was purely physical and destined to end in tears. They had little in common, and Marsha liked nothing more than ridiculing what she called his wishy-washy liberal leftism.

He recalled that they'd spoken hardly a word to each other on the first day of the holiday, and the following day Marsha had told him that their relationship was over and had moved to an apartment along the coast in Rethymnon. As soon as they'd returned to Yorkshire, she'd packed her possessions and left.

Two days after arriving in Crete, he'd met Emmi Takala; she'd seduced him – there was no other way to describe it – and he'd enjoyed a blissful holiday romance. It had been the start, he told himself, of the improvement in his fortunes that year: he'd landed a job writing *Morgan's Café* and sold a string of radio plays to the Beeb, allowing him to pay Digby back the five thousand by Christmas.

He wondered how long he might have here, this time, before he was shunted off again?

The period between jumps had increased. One year, then three, and this one, the third, five... If they continued at that rate, how long before he came to his senses as a new-born?

Of course, there was always the explanation that this wasn't really happening to him, and he was going mad.

He glanced through the window. The wing, stretching out for thirty feet, seemed to be vibrating dangerously. He heard a clunk as the landing gear unfolded: it all seemed very industrial to him. Far below he caught a glimpse of a green coastline, shimmering in the afternoon sun. Their destination was in sight.

Marsha woke up and made a show of casually flipping through the in-flight magazine while he gripped the arms of his seat, sweated, and endured the bumpy landing.

She maintained an icy silence throughout disembarkation and the passport check, and Richie tried to recall the reason. They'd had so many set-tos over the past week, over no doubt trivial things, that he had no hope of remembering what had set her off this time. No doubt Digby would have said it was all his fault.

A six-seater taxi carried them from Iraklion Airport to a village nestling in the hills. Their sprawling stone-built villa, over a hundred years old, stood on a rise just above the village which boasted, according to Digby, three good tavernas and several bars. The villa was owned by a writer friend of Digby's, who rented it out at a peppercorn fee to friends and acquaintances. He'd even left the keys of an old Volkswagen Beetle for their use.

"This is idyllic!" Caroline declared, dropping her case on the patio and admiring the view down to the coast.

Richie stared at her. She was, he realised, now in her early forties and very attractive. She had yet to put on the weight that would later make her matronly, and there was not a grey hair on her head.

"How about we freshen ourselves up," Digby said as they entered the villa, "relax a while, then mosey on down into the village for a drink before dinner? Apparently, there's a taverna called Spiro's that does excellent food."

Digby was a svelte, slimmed-down version of the man he'd last seen in 2013. His stomach was flat and the bald patch at the front of his head was not as established; he wore his dark hair long and sported a Zapata moustache which rather suited him.

They entered the villa.

"And then," Digby said, "we must find somewhere with a TV."

Caroline made a show of raising her eyes to the heavens.

"What?" Digby said, mock-surprised. "Cut the boys a little slack. Holland play Russia in the quarter-finals tonight. We have the rest of the holiday to do the cultural things."

"Sounds like an idea to me," Richie said. He glanced at Marsha. Under her breath she hissed, "Typical!"

"I'm sure we'll find a nice bar to enjoy ourselves in, won't we, Marsha?" Caroline said.

Richie watched Marsha pick up her case and move off through the villa, selecting a bedroom and closing the door behind her. Digby made a face in her direction, questioning Richie; Richie just smiled and shrugged.

He recalled that he'd shared a bedroom with Marsha on that first night. Well, he would spare himself the pain, this time. He carried his case across the open-plan ground floor, up a short flight of stairs, and found a room overlooking the village.

He was unpacking when the door burst open.

"What the hell are you doing?"

Marsha stood on the threshold, staring at him with murder in her eyes.

"If you're going to shout," he said patiently, "then please come in and close the door behind you."

He found that the best way to counter Marsha's intemperance was to assume an air of unruffled calm: it also had the pleasing effect of infuriating her.

She slammed the door. "Well?"

"Well?" He continued transferring his clothes from the case to the chest of drawers.

"I've found us a lovely double room with a view over the mountains, and what do you do?"

This conversation, of course, had never happened the first time; back then he had followed her to the bedroom and unpacked in uneasy silence.

"After today's behaviour, alternating between silence and blazing invective, what did you expect me to do?"

She looked incredulous. She really was at her most striking when angry; she was slim, with bountiful ragged-cut hair, fierce green eyes and an expressive mouth.

"*My* behaviour? It's *you* who've been ignoring me for the past week. Ever since the party…"

"The party?" He must have looked stupidly vague.

"Christ, don't be so dense! The do at Nigel's last Saturday. Is this all about Jonathan?"

He cast his mind back over the years and tried to recall the party that, for Marsha, had occurred just last week. Jonathan was a chunky, good-looking farm-hand popular with certain married women in the village. He recalled that he'd seen Marsha flirting with him; she'd flattered herself, at the time, that Richie had cared a damn.

"Jonathan? Oh, the Young Tory farmer you find so fascinating? Marsha, let's be grown up about this… If you want to rediscover your long-lost youth chasing farm labourers, I have no desire to stop you." That wasn't in the script, either. "I chose this bedroom for the simple reason that I'd rather sleep alone, if you don't mind."

"You bastard!" she said.

She stormed from the room and slammed the door behind her.

He was unpacking, a little later, when he heard a tap at the door, then Digby enquiring, "You okay, Ed?"

"Come in."

Digby slipped into the room and leaned against the door. "Are you two – ?"

Richie interrupted. "It's over between Marsha and me."

"Oh, I'm sorry."

"I'm not. I'm fine. I should never have…" He shook his head. "Anyway, I intend to enjoy the holiday."

"That's the spirit."

"I'm sure I'll meet someone."

Digby laughed. "You're incorrigible! Come on, I need a drink. Did I tell you that Caroline's had me on a diet – not a drop of alcohol for the past week, in preparation for the next two."

"Well, you look good on it, Diggers. Maybe you should abstain a little more."

"You're beginning to sound like Caroline," Digby said, and led the way from the room.

They wandered down to the village, Marsha lagging behind with Caroline. They dined at Spiro's, sitting around a table in a raised courtyard overlooking the hillside that tumbled down towards the coast. The sun was slipping into the sea, turning the horizon molten, and the thrum of cicadas was a constant accompaniment. They ate grilled swordfish caught that morning, with fava beans and Greek salad, washed down with bitter retsina. Marsha maintained an obdurate silence during the meal, making a point of finding the view more interesting than the conversation. Richie tried to draw her out a couple of times, asking her about a screenplay she was writing, but she replied in monosyllables and, when she did deign to speak, addressed herself exclusively to Digby and Caroline. His friends affected not to be fazed by the icy atmosphere at the table.

Towards the end of the meal, Richie sat back and looked along the hillside. Beyond their own villa was the tumbledown farmhouse where Emmi Takala lived and worked, a rough outline of grey bricks in the moonlight. He recalled that he'd met Emmi one morning when he'd taken himself off for a long walk. A slight blonde woman in a brilliant white cheesecloth dress had been painting at the side of the road. He'd stopped to admire the view, told her that her painting was wonderful, and their conversation had flowed as naturally as if he'd known the woman for years. He'd suggested they meet for a drink, and for the rest of the holiday they'd been inseparable.

Now Richie sat up. A slim figure had appeared on the cart-track below the level of the patio. He watched Emmi Takala stroll, with casual elegance, past the taverna and towards the village. She was wearing the cheesecloth dress, which set off her slightness and emphasized the golden tan of her arms and legs. He looked away, aware that he had broken out in a sweat.

Digby glanced at his watch. "The match starts in ten minutes. According to a brochure back at the villa, there's a TV in a bar just down the road. Do you girls want to come along?"

Caroline said, "I think we're fine here for a while. We'll have another drink or two and then come to find you. Is that okay, Marsha?"

"I could stay here all night," she said, directing an acid smile at Richie.

They escaped.

Richie thought back to the first night of the holiday. They had dined at Spiro's as they had tonight, though Marsha had been a little more amenable. He was sure he'd not seen Emmi – he would have remembered doing so. He tried to recall if Caroline and Marsha had joined them at the bar later that evening, and thought that perhaps they had. He hoped they didn't bother, this time.

He recalled the match because it had been an excellent end-to-end affair, and because Digby, who'd been following Holland throughout the tournament – as England had failed to qualify – had bet Richie a fiver that his team would beat Russia. Richie, who had enjoyed Russia's open, attacking football in the tournament so far, had taken him up on the bet, and won.

As they approached the bar Richie said, "Still fancy Holland to go all the way?"

"Why not? They're one of the best teams in the tournament."

"A tenner says Russia beat them tonight."

"You're on."

They shook on it and entered the bar.

A gallery of gnarled Greeks, clutching walking sticks planted between their boots, lined the walls and stared at the television, tiny glasses of raki on the tables before them. Richie ordered two Amstel lagers and carried them back to the table by the door. Greek bars reminded him of open garages, with wide doors to admit the breeze on hot summer evenings; he was rather pleased with this arrangement, as it allowed him to scan whoever should pass by outside. He hoped to see Emmi again before the night was over.

The game kicked off and Richie took a long drink of ice cold beer. "Another tenner on whoever guesses the correct score, or gets closest to it?" he said.

"You're on. Holland'll hammer the Ruskies three-nil."

"And I say it'll be three-one to Russia," he said. "After extra time."

"In your dreams."

For the next hour, Richie forgot the strange phenomenon that gave him foreknowledge of the match's result and enjoyed a succession of beers with his best friend. The bar filled up with a mixture of local Greeks and mainly German tourists.

It was nil-nil at half time, with all to play for. There was no sign yet of Caroline and Marsha.

"I'm sorry you and Marsha haven't hit it off," Digby said. "I sometimes wonder if you'll ever settle down."

"As I said earlier, I'm not in the least bit sorry. I should have known better. What could I have been thinking about, chasing a Tory?"

"The tyranny of biology over common-sense."

Richie raised his glass. "You said it."

"You've had a tough year, Ed."

"The tide is turning. There's that possible opening on the soap, and I have a few ideas with the Beeb's drama department. I'm sure something will turn up. But I couldn't have gone on without the loan."

"What the hell are friends for?"

"I'll be able to pay you back by the end of the year."

"Don't worry about it. There's no hurry."

"Five grand, plus interest, before Christmas, okay?"

"Forget the interest, Ed, for pity's sake."

Richie smiled across at Digby. "Thanks."

"Get another round in," Digby said. "They're about to kick off."

The second half panned out as he knew it would. Russia scored ten minutes after the break and he nudged Digby. "That's the first, Diggers."

"And the last," Digby said.

"We'll see about that," Richie scoffed. "Holland will equalise with just minutes to go, and Russia will score two in extra time. Arshavin will get the last one."

On cue, with four minutes to go until full time, Holland equalised and the game went to extra time.

Fifteen minutes later, Caroline and Marsha turned up. Richie, more than a little drunk by now, offered his seat to Marsha with what she took to be sarcastic gallantry. "I'll stand at the bar," she snapped.

Caroline joined her and ordered beer.

Digby whispered, "You're in for an earful in the morning, old boy."

"I'm past caring." He nudged his friend and said, "Here it comes."

He recognised the Russian build up down the right wing. The cross came in and the forward prodded it home. Two-one.

Digby held his head in his hands.

Richie patted his back. "Just one more to go, then your agony will be over."

"Holland will get back into it. Still ten minutes to go."

"Just time for Arshavin to make it three, mark my word."

Right on cue, with just four minutes to go before the whistle, the forward slotted the ball home from a tight angle and Richie punched the air.

The final whistle went and Digby, muttering, made a show of reluctantly pulling a handful of euros from his pocket and throwing it across the table.

"Take the filthy lucre. Any other predictions?"

"Yes, how about Spain to beat Germany one-nil in the final? Oh, and I'll have a fling with a Finnish artist called Emmi Takala before a few days are out."

Digby squinted at him. "That... that's rather definite," he hiccuped.

"I'm feeling lucky."

Digby shook his head. "I don't know how you do it."

"A lucky guess."

"No, you bloody fool. All those women falling at your feet, one after the other. It'd tire me out. Give me one dependable, loving woman, any day." He gazed across the bar to where Caroline was laughing with Marsha and a group of German tourists. "She's bloody wonderful, isn't she?"

Richie nodded. "She's a fine woman, Digby," he said. "Don't you take her for granted, okay?"

Digby smiled. "As if I'd ever do that."

"No..."

Richie looked up, through the wide door of the bar, and was amazed to see a vision in a white cheesecloth dress stroll past the bar and up the hill.

"Jesus..." he said. "Diggers, be a pal and cover for me, okay? Keep the girls talking while I sneak out."

"What the – ?"

Richie pointed. "Emmi, the Finnish angel."

Digby muttered, "You'll get me hung, drawn, and..." but he moved to the bar and asked the women what they were drinking as Richie slipped out and hurried up the hill after Emmi.

She was ten yards ahead of him, a distinctive figure amidst the gaggle of promenading tourists and locals. She wore delicate sandals bound with leather thongs in helices around her slim golden calves, and Richie recalled the first time he'd made love to her, almost nine subjective years ago.

He wondered what compulsion was drawing him to her; their affair had been nothing more than a holiday fling, sensual and fulfilling though it was; so why did he feel the overwhelming urge to reacquaint himself with her now? Was it solely because he knew that their affair was predestined, or was he simply driven by the need to prove something to himself?

Am I really that shallow, he wondered?

She turned into a bar at the top of the hill and, taking a breath, Richie followed her.

The room was long and low, and opened at the far end onto a

patio overlooking the hillside and the distant sea. Emmi leaned against the bar and ordered a drink. Richie stood a little way from her and ordered an ouzo with ice; he caught her eye and smiled.

He feigned surprise. "Emmi Takala, isn't it?"

He recalled her smile from all those years ago, cool yet amused. "It might be. And you are?"

"I'm sorry. I'm Edward Richie. I was admiring your work in the gallery down the hill earlier today, and this evening my friend pointed you out. I hope you don't mind my saying that I love your paintings."

"That's kind of you, Edward."

"You capture the essence of the landscape," he went on. "I don't know how you do it, but you manage to convey the heat of the place."

"Ah, that would be the colours I use. And also I blur my paintings by tempering the paint with chalk, to achieve a heat-haze effect."

"Well, it certainly works. But should you be divulging the tricks of your trade?"

She laughed prettily. "You don't look like an artist who would steal my secrets."

"I don't know whether to be flattered that you don't think me a thief, or hurt that you think I'm not an artist." He tried to recall what they talked about at their first meeting all those years ago; he was sure he was extemporising now.

She was perhaps five feet tall, and impossibly slim and elfin. Her skin glowed, as if she were beaming back the Greek sun absorbed during the day in some uncanny kind of photosynthesis. She pressed her glass to her bottom lip, watching him closely.

"What do you do, Edward?" Her English was precise and unaccented, but occasionally she framed her words in a way that was odd and becoming.

He told her he was a writer, and recalled how easy it had been, talking to her, eight years ago. Now it was just the same, and he wondered why had he not sought her out again, the first time round, returned to Crete and continued their affair?

He finished his drink, saw that her glass was almost empty, and asked if she would like another drink.

"Thank you, yes. Perhaps ouzo like you, this time."

When they had their drinks, she said, "And now shall I tell you a little about myself?"

"No, let me guess."

She smiled. "Very well."

"You're thirty-three and from a small town in the far north of Finland. Impressed?"

"No," she laughed. "You've read the pamphlet in my gallery!" Her victorious smile was wicked.

"Very well, then; I see I'm going to have to employ my telepathic powers." He took a long drink, watching her as she smiled at him with amusement, and said, "Okay... you paint in oils, but you're considering moving into acrylic; in fact you've been experimenting."

She opened her mouth, appearing shocked; then playfully slapped his arm. "Oh, you! You have been talking to people in the village – no, in the gallery?"

"And also," he went on, "you've recently signed a deal to supply a gallery in Marseilles with a dozen paintings."

"But no one but me and the dealer knows anything about that!" she said, wide-eyed. "Perhaps you *are* telepathic, Edward."

"Ed," he said. "And I *am* telepathic, and I know you want another drink and would like to sit outside, on the patio, under the stars."

They carried their replenished glasses outside and found a seat near the rail. The Mediterranean glimmered in the distance. A full moon was out, its silver light etching the olive trees which stippled the hillside.

"How long will you be here on Crete?" she asked.

"Another thirteen days," he said. He fell silent, sat back and stared up at the pulsing canopy of stars. If only it were thirteen days, he thought; he would be lucky if he had two days with Emmi Takala.

"Then we must meet again and I will show you the island, and my studio, and my paintings." She stopped. "You seem sad."

He laughed. He had the ridiculous urge to tell Emmi what was happening to him, to pour his heart out as if appealing to her for help. But he knew better than to scare her.

"I'm not sad at all," he said, "just bewildered." He surprised himself with this admission. "Life is so damned short, and you make so many mistakes. It'd be bad enough, wouldn't it, if you didn't make mistakes – if you knew the right decisions to make, all the time. You'd still grow old and ill and die, with nothing accomplished that you really wanted to do." Where was all this coming from, he wondered; and what was it about this woman which made him open up like this?

"But we have to make mistakes, Ed, and learn from them."

He stared at her. "Perhaps that's it," he said, trying to keep the bitterness from his voice. "Perhaps it's because I've made so many mistakes and never learned from them."

She said gently, "What kind of mistakes?"

He thought about that. "To begin with, abandoning serious plays when I should have persevered, instead of giving in and writing rubbish for TV. And..."

"Go on."

He regarded the distant sea. "And I've allowed myself to fall in love – or what I think is love – with too many women... hurting them, and myself. You think I would have learned from my mistakes by now, wouldn't you?"

She was silent for a time, twirling her glass.

"It's never too late to learn," she said. "Perhaps you should write your plays, and find a suitable woman."

He gave a hollow laugh and shook his head. "It is too late, for... for various reasons. There isn't enough time, Emmi."

"You're wrong, Ed. There is always enough time."

He felt the sudden urge to weep, but stood quickly and pointed to their glasses. "I'll get them in."

He returned with the drinks, and Emmi smiled up at him. "Thank you. This is nice."

He smiled at her. She sat back in her chair with her legs crossed, the hem of her dress riding up over her unblemished knees. She wore a fine gold necklace around her neck. He wanted simply to reach out and stroke her cheek, nothing else; to simply show her his affection.

She went on, "It is so easy being with you, Ed. It is as if we've met before."

"Perhaps we have."

She told him about her childhood, growing up in a tiny snowbound village beyond the Arctic Circle; told him about her father, who was a woodsman, and her mother who hunted for food, shooting elk deep in the forests, and who told her Finnish folk tales by the fire at night. It was another life entirely from anything he could have imagined. He wondered if she'd told him this, eight years ago, but thought not. For some strange reason, even though he had made love to Emmi Takala every night for ten days back then, he felt closer to her, more intimate, now.

It was midnight when she finished her drink and said, "I really must be going."

"Can I walk you home? I'm staying in the villa just below your farmhouse."

They left the bar and strolled up the hill and out of the village. There was no street-lighting along the rough track that straggled up the hillside, but the uneven surface was illuminated by the moon.

"I'm working on a series of paintings depicting the landscape at dawn," she said. "I would like you to see them tomorrow."

"I'd love to."

They stopped by the turning to the track that led to her farmhouse. The silence was absolute here, and a warm breeze lapped in from the sea.

"Come for lunch at noon. I will show you my studio, and then we'll go swimming. A little way up the hillside there is a gully with a stream, and a natural lagoon. It is beautiful, and no one but me and the local shepherds know about it."

She stood on her tiptoes, quickly, and brushed his lips with her own, the merest touch, then hurried off into the night.

He watched her go, the pain in his chest intense.

He turned and made his way towards the villa.

He wondered if the reason he hadn't followed her was that he did not want to torture himself; what they might have, briefly, was doomed. He should really not see her tomorrow; he should remain in the villa, get drunk, and await the time when fate would whisk him off to another time, another life. But he knew, of course, that he would do no such thing; he would meet Emmi at noon, and swim in the lagoon, and would that be another mistake?

A light was illuminating the patio when he returned. Digby was sitting outside with a bottle of beer clutched in his hand. "Nightcap?" he asked.

Richie fetched a beer from the fridge and joined his friend.

"And how was she?" Digby asked. "Is she Finnish, and called... what did you say she was called?"

Richie smiled. Digby was a little drunk. "Emmi Takala," he said, "and she is Finnish, yes."

Digby shook his head. "But... how the hell did you know?"

Richie thumbed over his shoulder in the direction of the lounge. "I read about her in a pamphlet. She's an artist."

"Ah..." Digby said. He fell silent for ten seconds, then recalled something. "But... the match? Three-one, extra time... How the hell...? How the hell did you get *that* right, Ed?"

He considered telling his friend, yet again, about the time-jump phenomenon, but knew he'd be wasting his time. Digby would only think him mad, again.

"A bloody lucky guess, Diggers." He took a long drink of beer, then said, "I'm seeing Emmi tomorrow, for lunch."

"That's fine. Marsha said she'd like to take the car, drive into Iraklion to see friends."

Richie fetched two more beers from the kitchen and they sat and talked.

At one point Digby said, "You know something, Ed? I've never been happier in all my life."

Richie felt a strange pressure in his chest. "I'm glad to hear that."

"I have everything, you know? A decent, well-paid job I enjoy – well, most of the time."

"What about that great sci-fi novel you always wanted to write?"

"Science fiction," Digby corrected. He shook his head. "I know my limitations, Ed. That's beyond me, now. I'm happy writing for TV. And..." He pointed at Richie. "And more importantly than anything else, I'm married to the most wonderful woman in the world."

Richie lifted his glass. "Let's drink to that," he said.

They sat in companionable silence and drank beneath the pulsing stars.

SHE WAS PAINTING in the field beside the farmhouse when he arrived the following day. He paused before the gate, watching her. She was sitting on a folding seat with her back to him, leaning forward and applying very delicate strokes to the canvas. He pictured her tongue, trapped in concentration between her small white teeth.

She sat back, pressed a hand to the small of her back, and stretched. Then she packed up her canvas and brushes and turned towards the house. She saw him, smiled radiantly and called out, "Ed! How long have you been standing there?"

They kissed briefly, cheek to cheek. "I just got here. I didn't want to interrupt."

She led the way to the house. "Shall we have lunch?"

After the glare and the heat of the sun, the interior was darkened and cool. She led him through to an old dining-kitchen with French windows at one end looking out towards the sea.

"Tiropita, Greek salad, and home-made humous," she said. "And beer to drink."

"You think of everything."

"I hope you're hungry."

"Famished. I didn't have breakfast."

He'd awoken early with a pounding head, having sat drinking with Digby until two in the morning. He had little recollection of what they discussed, other than how happy Digby was now, and something about his latest project. This morning, the last thing he'd felt like eating was the fried eggs and bacon Caroline had prepared.

As they ate, Emmi said, "I came to Greece with friends when I was twenty, to the island of Zakinthos. After northern Finland, can you imagine what I thought of Greece, the sun and the stark landscape and the warm, warm sea? I knew I would come back one day, and paint it. I have been here for five years now, and I have no plans to go back."

"What about your family?"

"My parents are both dead."

His throat caught. "And lovers?"

She looked at him through long lashes. "No one who is important," she said. "And you? Your family?"

"My mother and father died when I was in my twenties, within a few months of each other."

She smiled at him, then jumped up, grabbed his hand, and dragged him from the kitchen and through the house. She led him into her studio and watched his reaction. He stared around him in wonder. "So many canvasses..."

A hundred or more, some completed and stacked against the walls, others in various stages of completion, on easels or leaning against tables and chairs. The smell of oil paint and turpentine mingled with the lavender hanging in swatches from low, oaken beams.

She had never showed him her studio, eight years ago. He had made love to her night after night in the cool, ground-floor bedroom. He had been more intent on her body than her art, and had not asked to see her work in progress.

He watched her move around the room, showing him piece after piece, explaining why she had come to paint this canvas and that...

"And these are my dawn paintings, Ed."

"They're very beautiful."

"I'm proud of them."

They showed the rocky coastline bathed in the incendiary pinks and crimsons of sunrise, highlighted with dashes of silver; he knew that from now on he would see the familiar seascape with new eyes.

Just as he was seeing Emmi, again, but as if for the very first time.

"I will just get a bottle of wine from the refrigerator, and then we will go swimming. The lagoon is shaded by trees, so we will not burn."

They walked through the searing afternoon heat, up the hillside and over an outcropping of rock towards groves of olive and carob trees. They passed through the vegetation and there, before them, a green lagoon shimmered.

Emmi set the wine on a flat stone in the water, shaded by ferns, and turned to him. "Shall we swim?"

Without waiting for his reply, she turned away, unbuttoned the front of her cheesecloth dress, and let it fall to the floor. He watched, his pulse loud in his ears, as she walked naked into the water, then eased herself forward and swam the length of the lagoon.

She turned, treading water and laughing. "Come in," she called. "It's wonderful!"

He undressed, stepped into the water, and swam towards her. He reached where she had been, but she had darted off, a mischievous naiad, laughing at him. He swam towards her again and she approached a large flat rock and levered herself from the water. She turned, crouching, and smiled at him, shaking water from her hair.

He came to the rock and settled his forearms on the warm, striated sandstone, staring at her.

She stared back, a half smile playing on her lips.

He felt his throat constrict. He knew that soon they would make love, and it would be bliss, and he knew with the same terrible certainty that at some point he would be taken from her.

She sprang to her feet, dived over him and entered the water like an arrow. She swam the length of the lagoon, emerged from the water and walked into the shade of the trees, turning to face him.

He swam towards her and strode from the pull of the water.

They stood facing each other for long minutes, Richie staring into her blue eyes. She came towards him, reached up, and they kissed. He embraced her, pulled her body towards him, and lifted her onto him.

They made love, and swam, and drank wine all afternoon, and Richie was sure that for the entirety of their time at the lagoon they hardly spoke a word.

The sun went down and the breeze cooled, and they dressed and made their way back to the farmhouse.

At one point Emmi stumbled, cried out, and lifted a hand to her temple. Richie reached out to steady her. "Are you all right?"

She shook her head, as if to clear it. "A little dizzy." She looked at him, as if seeing him for the first time, and smiled. "The effect of the heat, I think."

They entered the farmhouse and ate the leftovers from lunch, supplemented by slabs of moussaka and glasses of cold retsina. Then Emmi took his hand and led him to her bedroom and they made love again by the light of an old bedside lamp.

He lay beneath her, and she traced patterns on his chest.

She looked at him and said, "Why are you crying, Ed?"

She wiped tears from his cheeks with her thumb, licked them and smiled. She kissed him, and whispered, "I can help you."

He stroked her cheek with the back of his hand. "I doubt it, my darling."

"I can. I know what you're going through."

He tried to laugh. "You have no idea..."

She straddled him in silence, staring down, her lips curved into a gentle smile.

And then she said something which sent his pulse racing.

Very quietly, in almost a whisper: "We have done this before..."

He felt dizzy; had he not been lying flat on his back, he might have collapsed. He shook his head, unable to find the right words.

"I know what's happening to you," Emmi said, "because the same thing is happening to me."

How could she know, how could she *possibly* know, unless she were telling the truth?

"Ed, I was sent here, to you," she said.

He stared at her. "Sent?" He shook his head, dizzy again.

"I was sent here, to you, to explain."

He felt some strange unnameable emotion swelling in his chest, part joy, part apprehension. "Sent to explain?"

"Sent by the scientists, Ed."

He repeated the word. "Who the hell," he asked, "are the scientists?"

"They are the people responsible for what is happening to you."

She placed a finger on his lips. "But we need a drink." She jumped from the bed.

He watched her dance through the door, then lay back and stared at the ceiling.

Emmi was undergoing what he was experiencing; she had been sent to explain the experiment being carried out by the scientists...

He sat up suddenly, alerted by a familiar pain in his head.

He called out her name, fear clutching at his chest, and tried to climb from the bed.

"No!" he cried. "Emmi!"

He reached out, staggering towards the door.

The heat in his head increased, followed by a blinding white light, and Richie passed out.

From the Daily Mail, *20th March, 2014*

MEANWHILE, MORGAN'S CAFÉ limps from one lame cliché to the next with a cast of dull characters matched only by the banal ineptitude of the script. So far this season we've had our lead characters surviving a gas explosion, a train crash, attempted murder and life-threatening illness. If that were not enough, the café itself was threatened with closure in episode seventeen – and I for one was praying for the bailiffs to move in! Veteran lead writer Ed Richie needs to look long and hard at where *Café* is heading, before the Beeb do the honourable thing and scupper their flagship soap.

From the Guardian, *July 18th, 2025*

Best-selling Author Missing

ED RICHIE, THE author of eight best-selling and critically acclaimed novels, was reported missing from his North Yorkshire home yesterday. TV scriptwriter and friend Digby Lincoln contacted police yesterday, concerned as to the writer's whereabouts. "It's quite unlike Ed to go away without telling me," said Lincoln.

Richie, 65, sprang to fame in 2019 with the publication of his second novel, *Statecraft*. It became an instant best-seller, was translated into thirty languages, and short-listed for the Booker

Prize. He went on to write six more novels, lauded for their realistic portrayal of the political situation in Britain and the West. Mr Richie was also a TV scriptwriter...

CHAPTER EIGHT

January, 2030

ONE OF THE most forbidding sights in nature, Ella told herself, was an expanse of cold grey sea without any sign of reassuring, encompassing land. From the comfort of the old Airbus rattling high above the Baltic, she stared down on a cold, grey sea. It was so still and barren, with not even a fishing boat to give a sense of scale to the vastness, and she half expected to see ice floes down there. Was it any wonder that the artist Emmi Takala had forsaken her northern homeland for more than twenty years and set up a studio on the island of Crete?

Takala, both the woman and her work, had obviously held a deep fascination for Ed Richie. According to his journal, he'd met her in the summer of 2008 when he'd accompanied Digby and Caroline Lincoln to Crete. He'd gone with his then lover Marsha Mallory, their relationship already on the rocks, the holiday paid for by Lincoln as Richie went through something of a lean time: commissions had dried up and he was finding it hard to make the mortgage repayments on his barn conversion.

One particular entry caught her attention.

3rd July, 2008: *Our last full day on Crete. My last day with Emmi. We made love all afternoon, dined at her farmhouse, and then went back to bed. She has said nothing about our affair, about the possibility of my coming out here to live with her, and I know I'll do nothing of the kind. The simple fact is that Emmi Takala is too good for me, and I don't want to hurt her – and if I were to pursue the relationship, that is what would happen: I would hurt her, as I have all the others.*

Ella read the entry again, then stared down at the grey sea.

The passage was remarkable for being the only place in the journal when Ed Richie admitted to himself that the fault in his many failed relationships might be his own.

The simple fact is that Emmi Takala is too good for me, and I don't want to hurt her.

He had returned home and hung her painting in his house and often sat before it, reminded of his time with Emmi on the sun-soaked Greek island.

1st December, 2010: *Greta walked out this afternoon, and I helped myself to a few large measures of Glenfiddich and stared for an hour at Emmi's* Plakias at Sunset, *dreaming of what might have been but knowing that, had I returned to Crete, what was beautiful would, in time, have spoiled.*

25th February, 2012: *Emmi's painting sings to me. It springs to life at my every glance. It's infused with her personality. Today I remembered an afternoon towards the end, when I outlined to her the plot of a radio play I'd been thinking about for a year or more. And Emmi, with devastating insight, told me where I was going wrong. Physically, and intellectually, she reminds me so much of A...*

10th October, 2017: *I wonder if Emmi Takala is still living on Crete? She will be forty now, and no doubt still beautiful. Should I fly out there, on the off chance... or am I thinking this because Jessica has just left me and I'm very, very drunk at the moment?*

It was obvious to Ella that though he'd been with Takala for just ten days, her influence on him had been profound – perhaps all the more so because he had followed his intuition and not pursued the affair.

The simple fact is that Emmi Takala is too good for me, and I don't want to hurt her.

Back in London, Ella had decided that she must meet the woman, the only woman, to her knowledge, who'd provoked such self-critical insight from Ed Richie. She was intrigued by her, and wanted to view her paintings at first hand. There were examples of her work online, but precious little about the artist herself. All she knew of her recent whereabouts was that she had left Crete in 2026 and returned to Finland. When Ella tried to contact Takala for an interview, via a gallery in Helsinki that stocked her paintings, she was informed that the artist valued her privacy and did not encourage contact with the press.

All the more intrigued, Ella had made arrangements to fly to Helsinki in an attempt to track down the artist.

She took a taxi from the airport to the old centre of the city, passing through seemingly endless suburbs of squat grey residential blocks that brought to mind the brutalist architecture of Soviet Russia. This impression was not helped by the weather: the sky was a monotone grey, a shade darker than the buildings, and snow came down in wind-whipped vortices. Old snow formed levees in the gutters of wide, tree-lined boulevards. In the back of the taxi, Ella shivered and wondered why Takala had come back to *this*.

All the more odd because in 2025, the year before Takala returned home, the People's Party had swept to power in Finland, promising an end to immigration and a ban on all asylum seekers. They had made good on the promise, and instituted harsh austerity measures besides, to no beneficial effect.

Ella was booked into a small hotel in the old Kruununhaka district of the city, and after a coffee and sandwich in the snack bar on the first floor, she took another taxi to the harbour.

The car, an unheated, clapped-out Skoda driven by a gnome lagged in a bulky overcoat and a balaclava, pulled into a cobbled quayside. She paid the fare, braved the keening wind that blew off the icy sea, and ran across a gritted pavement and into the rosily illuminated refuge of the gallery.

A well-dressed elderly couple stood before a huge abstract, speaking in low tones to a young woman assistant. On the far wall, bringing Ella to a sudden halt, were half a dozen large oils, unmistakably the work of Emmi Takala.

She could see why the paintings had struck such a chord with Ed Richie, and the effect could only have been enhanced by knowing the artist. All but one were scenes of a sun-soaked landscape, rocky coasts with olive trees, shimmering sea, and setting suns; the colours were extraordinary.

The only painting not of Crete showed a bleak winter landscape and a distant, setting sun. Ella wondered if it were the artist's comment on the state of her nation.

She heard a soft voice at her side, speaking Finnish.

She smiled at the young woman. "I'm sorry..."

"The work of Emmi Takala," the woman murmured in perfect English, "one of Finland's finest, if most overlooked, artists."

Ella nodded. "They're... beautiful, striking," she said. "I wish I could be a little more original, and articulate, in my appreciation. The colours are remarkable. I feel as if I'm there, under the sun in Crete."

The woman moved to a counter and returned with a brochure. "Takala's full catalogue. These hanging here are only a small sample of her work we are selling."

Ella took the catalogue. She stood back and examined the paintings on the wall, then looked for the price tags. Anticipating her question, the woman said, "They are colour coded." With her little finger she pointed to tiny coloured dots beside each canvas. "You will find the prices in the catalogue."

She retreated tactfully to the counter as Ella leafed through the catalogue, finding the page where half a dozen multi-coloured dots indicated the various prices in Euros. She stared, wondering if there had been a misprint. She had expected the paintings to cost thousands: the largest, she saw – a sunrise over a tiny harbour – was priced at just over three hundred Euros.

She moved to the counter. "I'd be very interested in purchasing one," she said. She pointed to the paintings reproduced in the catalogue. "Is there any chance I could see these in the flesh, as it were?"

"I could arrange for you to visit Emmi Takala's studio. It is only ten kilometres out of town, along the coast. A short taxi ride."

"Her studio? I wonder if I might meet Takala?"

The woman gave a thin-lipped smile. "I am afraid that Ms Takala is a very private person."

"Okay…" Ella smiled. "But she's still painting, I take it?"

The woman answered elliptically, "The studio is run by her brother Sanu, Ms…?"

"Shaw. Ella Shaw."

"If you wish, Ms Shaw, I will ring Sanu and arrange a viewing? When might be convenient?"

Ella shrugged. "Why… this afternoon?"

"One moment." The woman picked up a phone, dialled and spoke in lowered tones.

Ella strolled back to the paintings, noting the signature in childish capitals: *EMMI*.

Emmi Takala would be in her early fifties now; she wondered how the passing years had treated the artist; whether she would be able to discern, when they finally met, Takala's fey beauty as described by Richie in his journal.

The woman was at her side, proffering a card printed in Finnish. "Sanu will be at the studio all afternoon, and will be pleased to meet you, Ms Shaw. Would you like me to call you a taxi?"

"Please, yes."

She stood before the window as the woman spoke on the phone. It was not yet three o'clock, yet a louring violet twilight had descended over the sea. A raging wind whipped the snow into a dizzying pointillism; the only pedestrian in view was an old man, leaning into the wind. A dark blue police car idled along the harbour front.

A taxi pulled up before the gallery – unfortunately the same freezing Skoda that had brought her here – and Ella thanked the woman and hurried out to the car.

They left the centre of the city and passed through the grey, block-built suburbs, Ella wondering how people were able to endure existence in an environment lacking in the slightest aesthetic appeal. The landscape improved slightly once they were out of the city and into the frozen countryside, following a flat coastline made all the more stark by the occasional bare fir tree.

After twenty minutes the taxi turned off the main road and took a narrow lane along a headland covered in a dense pine forest, and Ella's spirits picked up.

In a clearing overlooking the wintry sea, a large weatherboard house stood beside a long, low building clad in red-painted timber. The house was in darkness, but orange light glowed in the cabin's windows.

The taxi pulled up outside the studio, and the driver told her in broken English that he'd wait and take her back into town. She thanked him and hurried into the cabin, then stopped in her tracks at the sight of a hundred vibrant canvases.

A tall, severely thin old man, leaning heavily on a black cane, turned as she entered. A bleak smile split his face; with his ice blue eyes and rather grim expression, he looked like an elderly general who had fought too often on the losing side.

"Ms Shaw, how pleasant this is," he greeted her in slightly

accented English. "We get too few visitors these days. You are, of course, familiar with Emmi's work?"

"I've admired it from afar for quite some time. Today's the first time I've seen one of your sister's paintings in real life. They're stunning."

"I am delighted you think so, Ms Shaw. Perhaps," he suggested diffidently, "I might take you on a little guided tour. But first would you care for a warming drink. Tea, coffee, or perhaps a little glögg? It's a Finnish spiced wine."

"That's kind of you. I'll try the glögg."

He moved to a side room, and returned with two big mugs of a thick, brown mulled wine. "To be sipped delicately. It will warm your soul on this winter's day."

She sipped; it burned, but with a spicy finish like the best single malt.

They proceeded, their pace dictated by Sanu Takala's limp, clockwise around the studio, taking in the artwork in chronological order.

Sanu talked Ella through the various stages of his sister's artistic life, from the early abstracts of her twenties, to the mature, more representational landscapes of her thirties and forties.

"Her finest period, in my opinion, was in Crete. She was there for more than twenty years, and it was the happiest time of her life. Her paintings, I think, reflect this. Observe the colours, the vitality. I come in here on the coldest days, Ms Shaw," he laughed, "and warm my hands before these canvases!"

"I can well believe it."

"My sister is well respected in Finland, but little known outside our country. She is a special person, Ms Shaw; all who have known her say so. Her friends bewail her lack of fame, but it is a measure of the person she is that fame matters not at all to Emmi."

Ella stopped before a large canvas and stared. The painting showed a tumbledown farmhouse in an olive grove, with the figure of a man in the mid-distance, leaning against a tree.

She stepped forward, peering at the figure, then smiled to herself and backed away to get another view.

There could be no doubting her eyes, or mistaking the figure in the painting: it was Ed Richie.

"You like this one, perhaps?" Sanu asked.

"It's... yes. It's marvellous," she said then hesitantly, "How much...?"

"To you, two hundred euros," he said.

"Then I'd very much like to buy it," Ella said.

"I will have it delivered to the gallery in town," Sanu said, "and perhaps you could return there to arrange payment and collection?"

She regarded the painting, and the tall, sun-tanned man it depicted.

They moved on around the gallery.

"I read," she said, "that your sister returned to Finland a few years ago."

"That is correct. Emmi married a fine man in 2009," Sanu said. "He, like her, was an artist, a sculptor from Norway. They had many happy years together, until four years ago when Bjorn died in a swimming accident. His ashes are scattered on the coast where Emmi lived and worked. She tried to go on, to remain there, but perhaps you can appreciate... Crete held too many memories, happy as well as painful, and so she came home."

"I wonder..." she began. "I wonder if it might be possible to meet your sister?"

That thin, bleak smile again. "Just last year, Ms Shaw, Emmi left Finland again."

Ella looked up at the old man; his bright blue eyes were far away.

"She returned to Crete?"

"No," he said, "she went to England."

"England?" She smiled to herself at the irony of the situation. "To work?" she asked.

"To meet someone," Sanu said, and Ella's heart commenced a thudding that sounded loud in her ears.

"You see," he continued, "before her marriage she met someone, an Englishman."

Ella found her voice. "Do you know his name?"

"Emmi said that he was called Edward, and that he was a writer. I think they were lovers, many years ago, and then last year I think he contacted her. At any rate, she received a letter from England, and she told me that she must go to England to meet him."

"Last year?" she said.

"Last year, in July."

Ella felt dizzy. She sipped her drink, feigning interest in the paintings as her thoughts raced.

Could Sanu have got it wrong? Or could this Edward, a writer who had loved Emmi long ago, be another, different Englishman...? What were the chances of that?

But how *could* it be the same Edward? Five years ago, a small, cold voice said in her head, Ed Richie disappeared.

"Do you know if they met?" she asked.

"I presume so," he said, "though Emmi keeps her thoughts, and her emotions, very much to herself. I received one email from England last year, six months ago. She said she was well, but little else, and she did not mention the Englishman."

"Do you happen to have her current address in England?" she asked, her mouth dry. "I'd like to look her up, when I return."

"Unfortunately Emmi left no address," he said. He hesitated, then said, "Late last year, in December, I received a card. I will show it to you."

He reached into an inside pocket of his blazer and withdrew a postcard showing a snow covered scene of the Yorkshire Dales. On the back was a message written in Finnish.

He read, "To my dearest brother, Sanu, with love. Goodbye... Emmi."

He returned the card to his pocket, his gaze distant.

"Goodbye...?" Ella said.

"And I have not," Sanu said, "heard from her since."

From Ed Richie's journal, 2nd January, 2019

JUST HEARD ABOUT the air crash on the radio. One of those shocking moments I'll recall for a long, long time. I'm assuming it's an assassination – the media in the US are already suggesting that the President's plane was brought down over Kentucky by a bomb in the hold. I can't say I'm that surprised – I recall talking with Diggers in the Bull a year or two back, wondering how long it'd be before the establishment had a stomach-full of the buffoon and decided to get rid of him. Already, not surprisingly, some sources close to the President are blaming it on 'terrorist operatives...' What is significant is that none – *not one* – of the President's aides or advisers was on board the flight with him.

From Ed Richie's journal, 29th November, 2022

I CAN'T WIN. A couple of years ago, T. J. Laisterdyke, reviewing *Distant Relations* in the *TLS*, accused me of writing of a future 'peopled only by a privileged, Western elite...' little understanding that that was the whole point of the satire. And then this week the ignorant little shit, reviewing *A Question of Identity* in the same journal, wrote: 'In his portrayal of Indian life in the 2030s, Richie is guilty of a gross act of cultural appropriation...' I despair!

In the Bull last night, Diggers told me the cowardly bastards at the Beeb might be pulling the plug on *The State We're In...*

CHAPTER NINE

June, 2002

FOR THE SECOND successive time, Richie woke to darkness.

He lay still and considered the events on Crete, and what Emmi Takala had told him. At least, he thought, he wasn't going mad. He was part of some incredible scientific experiment... or that was what Emmi had told him. Perhaps there was a chance that he might meet her again; she had been sent to 'intercept' him, after all, and if it had happened once, then why not again?

Then he saw the flaw in his reasoning. If the phenomenon *was* of his own devising, then of course he might have invented *everything*, the events in Crete and Emmi's explanation included.

So he might still be in the grip of some extraordinary madness...

He lay in the darkness and gradually made out the shape of a window to his left. He was no longer in his Yorkshire barn conversion: there was no window at the foot of the bed. If not Yorkshire, then where? He had lived in London for twenty years from 1982. Judging by the position of the window, and the early traffic noise, he guessed he was now in the capital. He turned his head; he was in a double bed, but by himself.

He reached out to the bedside table, found a lamp, and located the switch on the flex. He turned on the light and looked around the vaguely familiar room. His memory of it did not match the reality; he had thought the walls a bland magnolia, when in fact they were pale green. The Klimt facing the bed he could have sworn had hung on the landing.

He was in the tiny Notting Hill terraced house he'd rented for six months in 2002. He'd lived with Laura Stephenson, a set designer with the BBC and a very strange woman – not that Richie had realised this, at first. For the last month of their fraught relationship, Laura had insisted on sleeping alone on a fold-out bed in his study.

He realised, as he lay in bed, that he felt physically well. His body was not plagued by the joint pains that would begin a decade later, in his early fifties. Nor did he have a hangover; he had drunk relatively little while living in London. Only later, after his move to Yorkshire, had he hit the bottle, when increased prosperity and dissatisfaction with his writing had proved a dangerous combination.

He swung himself out of bed and stared down at his naked body. His belly was flat and his legs bulged with well-defined muscles. He'd still played squash once a week in 2002, and the occasional game of five-a-side football. He stared at his hands. They were younger, the hands of a man of forty-two, not the arthritic, wrinkled hands of a fifty-six-year-old.

His clothes were folded neatly over a chair: faded blue jeans and a colourful shirt he would never have worn in his fifties. He dressed, pushing from his mind the question of how long he might have in this time before he was dragged away again. But it was impossible; he could no more *not* think about what was happening to him than he could cease breathing. He felt like getting drunk.

He looked across the room and caught sight of himself in the mirror. The image gave him pause. He was a stranger. Had he really looked so young and slim? His dark hair was trimmed short and he was clean-shaven. He was flat-bellied and well-muscled around the chest and upper arms. Christ, he'd really let himself go over the years.

He picked up a book from the bedside table: a social history of the 1950s. It was the summer of 2002: he'd been doing background reading for a radio play set in 1955.

Laura would be sleeping in his study, their relationship having floundered on her paranoia. She'd eventually leave him in July, and he'd remain here another week and then, with the lease expiring, rent a cheaper bedsit in Southwark until his move to Yorkshire in December.

He looked at the bedside clock. It was 7.55.

He left the bedroom, moved along the landing and paused outside the second bedroom, which he used as a study. He listened, but could hear nothing from within the room. If it were a weekday, Laura would have left for work already: he hoped so, as he really had no desire to meet her again.

He moved downstairs and along the hallway. The newspaper had been delivered. He picked up the *Guardian* and read the date.

It was Saturday the 15th of June. Laura would walk out a day before her birthday, in early July. It being a Saturday, she would be upstairs.

He took the paper to the kitchen and made himself coffee and toast, moving around the room like a stranger; almost fifteen years had intervened to erase from his memory such minutiae as where things were kept. He was surprised by how much he had forgotten about the small, day to day details of everyday life.

He sat at the table and ate Marmite on toast, the newspaper forgotten before him.

The small kitchen brought back memories of his time with Laura, and especially their last few weeks. She had become, over the six months they had lived together, increasingly suspicious and jealous. She had a fatally insecure personality and saw his every friendship with another woman as a potential love affair; every few days, during their last couple of months, her questions about casual acquaintances would escalate into full-blown shouting matches, with Laura accusing him of infidelity and he questioning her sanity.

The unfamiliar ringtone of a mobile sounded, and it was a few seconds before he realised that the opening bars of Beethoven's Fifth was his own phone. He traced the sound to the lounge and found the device, a ludicrously chunky specimen, on the coffee table.

He slumped on the sofa and took the call.

"Ed," Digby said. "Just ringing to wish you good luck."

"Good luck?"

"You know," his friend said, "that arbitrary state that fate sees fit to bestow on individuals from time to time: the antonym of misfortune."

"Right, but..."

"Christ, did you hit the sauce last night?"

Richie clutched at a possible get-out. "Just a bit."

"Where did you go?"

He floundered for a second. "Oh, just around the corner..."

"Thought you hated the Grapes?"

"You know, any port in a storm."

"Laura been playing up again?"

"Tell me about it."

"Anyway, good luck with Morrison this afternoon. I think your outline will bowl him over."

Awareness crashed over him. Max Morrison was the American director who'd shown interest in a film synopsis, provisionally entitled *VR*, which Richie had pitched to his production company a year earlier. The director was in London this weekend and wanted to see Richie. Even now, so many subjective years down the line, he felt bitter about his treatment at the hands of the director.

"We'll see," Richie said.

"What time are you seeing him?"

"Ah... Good question. I'll check my diary."

"Ed, you're sounding a bit out of it. Don't go into the meeting hungover, okay? Morrison's a shark; he'll have you for breakfast. Take a couple of paracetamol and have a cold shower, hm?"

"Well... I don't know about the cold shower bit."

"Oh – before I go, what are you doing tonight?"

"Nothing planned."

"How about coming over to ours for dinner? We're having a few people around. I have a little announcement to make. Oh, and don't bring Lulu."

Richie blinked. "Lulu?"

Digby sighed. "You really are on another planet today, Ed. I was quoting the song, you know: '*You can bring Pearl, she's a darned nice girl, but don't bring Lulu…*'? I mean, don't bring Laura. Recall the last time she was here? I thought she was going to throw our best china at you."

"No Laura," Richie said. "See you tonight."

He killed the call and stared at the phone.

All in all, he recalled now, the 15th of June 2002 had been a shit of a day. He'd met Max Morrison at an expensive bistro in Chelsea and the big-shot director-producer had proceeded to humiliate him and shred his outline, calling for farcical changes that Richie, desperate for a movie break, had abjectly agreed to make.

Then he had gone to Digby and Caroline's dinner party and his friend had announced that, on the back of landing a lucrative contract to write for Yorkshire TV, he and Caroline had found a place up north and were moving in the autumn. Richie had congratulated his friend on his luck, but had been aggrieved that Digby would be living so far away. They met up a couple of times a week in London, and the idea of not seeing Diggers for their regular sessions was unthinkable.

Little did he know, at the time, that a few months down the line a good word from Digby would land Richie a regular writing job with Yorkshire TV and he'd move to the converted barn later that year.

He'd be able to enjoy the dinner party tonight, this time, and his congratulations would not be hedged with resentment.

He returned to the kitchen, finished his coffee and toast, then considered the imminent meeting with Morrison.

He had only a vague recollection of the film synopsis he'd slaved over on and off for months. He would have to locate the file on his PC and get himself up to speed on the 'latest' version: he must have emailed at least a dozen different outlines to LA over that summer, each one re-jigged and altered at Morrison's overbearing insistence.

The problem was that his PC was in his study, and Laura was famously vitriolic about having her sleep-ins disturbed.

He looked at his watch. It was almost nine. Surely she wouldn't mind if he crept in and quickly turned on his computer? But knowing Laura, that would be enough to set her off.

He was about to make himself a second cup of coffee when a sudden recollection hit him. On the morning of his meeting with the American director, Laura had confronted him with the photograph of Annabelle...

He heard Laura's footsteps on the stairs. The door opened and she walked past him and into the sitting room without a word of greeting. The sight of her, for the first time in nearly fifteen subjective years, was a shock. She was hunched over in a chunky pink dressing gown that emphasised her anorexic slightness, and her thin, pinched face was studiedly turned away from him.

"Make me a coffee, would you?" she called from the sitting room.

He made the coffee on auto-pilot.

The criterion of beauty, he knew from experience, was very subjective. Had anyone asked Richie, years later, if he'd thought Laura Stephenson beautiful, he would have answered with a reserved affirmative, adding the rider that her beauty was of a peculiar variety. He recalled a line from Mervyn Peake's *Gormenghast*, describing Fuchsia Groan as ugly, but that a small twist would make her suddenly beautiful. Now, seeing Laura again after many years, he realised that her face merely required that small twist...

"Toast?" he called.

"You know I don't have breakfast."

Had known, he thought. And forgotten. Come to that, he'd also forgotten how she liked her coffee.

He took a gamble, added a splash of milk, and carried it through to the sitting room.

She was curled on the sofa, her feet drawn up under her small bottom, and was staring with determination into the far corner of the room.

He passed her the mug and moved to his armchair, knowing that she had the photograph in the pocket of her dressing gown and knowing, too, what he was about to endure.

She looked up from her coffee and stared at him. Her thin face was lopsided, the long lips skewed; her left eye was larger than the right. He wanted to reach out, re-arrange those features, and make her beautiful. If only it could be that easy.

"What the hell is this?"

Hell, the coffee... "I'm sorry?"

She held out the mug. "The coffee. It's white. You know I take it black."

He sketched a smile. "Sorry. I forgot."

"Forgot? Christ, how long have you known me?"

That was a good question. He'd forgotten that, too.

She said, "Does *she* take it white?"

This wasn't quite how it had happened before – he'd not got the coffee wrong – but it would lead to the same result.

"I'm sorry?"

She stared at him and said, very deliberately, "Does the woman you're seeing take her coffee white?"

He sighed. "I'm not seeing anyone."

"You lying little..."

"Laura –"

"Don't you dare say my name in that forbearing, patronising tone, you bastard!"

"This is ridiculous."

He should get up and walk out. He almost did so, but stopped himself. If he enraged her, then who knew what she'd do with the photograph? He wanted it back, wanted to see the woman it depicted again, after so long... If he sat tight, weathered her tirade, then he knew she'd throw it at him and storm back upstairs to the study, wailing her pain.

She dug into the pocket of her dressing gown and pulled it out. "Who's this?" She waved the photograph at him.

He took a breath. "I've no idea. I'm too far away."

She surged to her feet and stood over him. "Who the fuck is it, Ed? I found it in your wallet. I needed a fiver to go see Christina yesterday..." She held out the picture of the slim, smiling girl.

He reached out to take it, but she snatched the photo away.

She paced up and down before him, hunched in her dressing gown, barefoot, the photo clutched in her thin fingers. He watched her, willing her not to rip the picture into two, as she had on the first occasion.

"It's the bitch you met at that launch party, isn't it?"

"Launch party?" Then he remembered. His script-writer friend Alan's first novel had launched a few weeks ago, and there'd been a party in Piccadilly. Richie had gone along, and taken Laura, and during the course of the evening he'd got into conversation with a woman he'd known years ago when he'd worked at Waterstone's. They'd chatted for fifteen minutes, catching up on their respective lives, and Richie had made the mistake of allowing Laura to see that he was enjoying the woman's company.

"And a few days later... you didn't come back till late –"

"I told you, I had a session with Digby."

"And on Friday? You were out all day when you'd told me you'd be working here..."

He floundered under her gaze. He had no idea what he'd done on that far-away Friday, and in Laura's eyes his silence condemned him.

"Jesus!" She stood over him, her face twisted and ugly. "Jesus Christ, Ed! You bastard! You're seeing her, aren't you? You're fucking the little bitch!"

"Of course not! Don't be ridiculous... The woman I met at the launch, she worked with me years ago. We were catching up." He pointed at the photo still clutched in Laura's fist. "And that isn't even her."

"Then who the hell is it?"

He sighed. He recalled, dimly, that years ago he hadn't even bothered to explain who it was. This argument was the culmination of a dozen such confrontations with Laura, and he'd not been in the mood to placate her.

"It's a girl I knew, a long time ago."

"You liar! It looks like the Waterstone's bitch."

"It doesn't look anything like her. The woman at the party was much older than this. And if you look at the photo closely, you'll see the girl's wearing flared denims and a cheesecloth blouse, hardly the height of fashion these days."

Laura gave the photo a cursory glance. For a second she looked convinced, then her expression turned to suspicion, quickly followed by rage. "Christ! That 'sixties party you were invited to the other week... You said you we're going out for a pint with Digby instead – but you went to the party and took this bitch, didn't you!"

Richie made the mistake of laughing.

She screamed at him. "You bastard, Ed. You're fucking her!"

She looked at the photo, then compressed her lips and with quick deliberation tore the picture in half and threw it at him.

He caught one piece and retrieved the other from the carpet. As she watched, he pieced the picture together. By good fortune she had not ripped the photograph cleanly in half, so that the image of the slim smiling girl in the flares and blouse was still intact.

Laura stood in the centre of the room, breathing hard, her face red with rage.

Looking up from the photograph to Laura, Richie said quietly, "She was called Annabelle. I knew her *twenty years ago*. I was in love with her, very much in love. She was nineteen, just a kid. We lived together for a few months. She was the first woman I really, truly loved."

Laura asked quietly, "And... what happened?"

Taking a breath, Richie told her all about Annabelle and her death.

He slipped the two pieces of photograph into the back pocket of his jeans and stood up.

Years ago he'd not bothered to explain who Annabelle was, when Laura had ripped the photo in two. He'd let her race upstairs in tears and could not be bothered to follow her and explain.

Now she stood before him, her head hanging as she quietly sobbed.

He hesitated, then reached out and took her into his arms, kissed her forehead and held her for a long time.

"I'm sorry, Ed."

"It doesn't matter."

"I hate myself."

"Don't," he murmured.

"I'm stupid and ugly."

"You're far from stupid, Laura, and I think you're lovely."

She hiccuped on a sob. "No, I'm ugly. Every... every morning I look in the mirror, and do you know what I see?"

"Laura, please..."

"I... I see an ugly cow with a lopsided face, lips too big, nose bent..."

He pulled away, stroked her face, and kissed her forehead, her nose, her lips. "Laura, please don't..."

She sobbed and almost collapsed in his arms. He held her as she wept. "Love you..." he said.

"No you don't," she sniffed.

"That's for me to know, and to say."

She looked up, wiped her eyes with the back of her hand, and shook her head. "I don't know what you see in me. What do I give you? I'm stupid, ugly, and neurotic... I don't deserve you, Ed."

He shook her gently. "Now you're just being silly. You shouldn't think like that. Christ, a million women would give their right arms to have what you've got: a great job, great friends, someone who loves you..."

In a tiny voice: "You're just saying that."

Over her shoulder, he looked at his watch. He still had a couple of hours before he was due to meet Morrison.

He took Laura under the chin and lifted her face, then kissed her and slipped the dressing gown from her shoulders. She stood before him, tiny and white and vulnerable, unable to meet his gaze.

He carried her upstairs, then laid her gently on the bed, undressed and made love to her. At one point, at one treacherous point, he closed his eyes and imagined that it was Emmi he was making love to, then her image vanished as Laura cried out beneath him and bit his shoulder as she came.

She dozed beside him, curled into a foetal ball, and Richie found his jeans on the floor and slipped the ripped photograph from the back pocket. He stared at Annabelle's smiling face, a knot of pain in his stomach.

A month after the original version of this encounter, Laura had left him, and that very same day Richie had lost his wallet to a pickpocket on the underground. The wallet had contained three credit cards and thirty pounds in notes, but most importantly of all, Annabelle's photograph. It had been the only one of her he possessed, and he'd been inconsolable at the loss.

He stared at the sleeping woman beside him, and wondered what would happen to his relationship with Laura when he was whisked off back through time to some unknown rendezvous with his younger self. Would he wake in a day or so with any recollection of what had happened this morning? Or would the time current-him spent here be a blank? Would the Richie of tomorrow or whenever be able to understand Laura, her weakness and vulnerability and the reasons for them, and bring himself to feel compassion for her?

No, he realised. Of course not...

Gripped by a sudden welling of sadness, he rolled quietly from the bed, dressed and moved to his study. He accessed his old, huge PC and found the *VR* file. For the next half hour he read through half a dozen outlines of the synopsis, then a dozen emails he'd sent the director, bringing himself up to speed on the situation.

He closed down the machine and returned to the bedroom.

Laura was stirring. He sat on the bed beside her and stroked her face.

"Got to nip off to meet that bloody Morrison," he told her.

She smiled up at him. "I hope it goes well, Ed."

He kissed her forehead, hesitated, then said, "Look, Digby and Caroline are having a little do at their place tonight. You're invited."

She widened her eyes at him. "I thought Digby didn't like me."

"Silly. Where on earth did you get that idea? Of course he likes you."

She gripped his hand. "Thanks Ed, but I can't. Hanna's having her hen night, and I'm going to that, remember?"

He didn't remember. "Of course."

"But you have a nice time, Ed, okay? And thank Digby for me."

He kissed her again, said, "See you later," and slipped from the bedroom.

He took the tube from Notting Hill Gate to Fulham Broadway. The carriage was hot and crammed with passengers, mainly foreign tourists. It had been almost fifteen subjective years since he'd lived in London. He'd become so accustomed to life in rural Yorkshire, where every time he ventured from the house he saw a familiar, friendly face, that the mass of strangers now made him feel isolated.

It hardly helped that he was, in real terms, a man from another age. Without being able to define the differences, he was aware of the changes in fashion – and there was a certain optimism in the air that, thinking back, he thought he understood. The country was well into its fifth year under New Labour, with the recession yet to happen; did that account for the smiling faces, or was he putting a gloss on the situation, here in June 2002, biased by and based on his own politics?

One thing that he'd forgotten, until seeing a headline in a newspaper, was that just last year Al-Qaeda terrorists had flown two airliners into the twin towers of the World Trade Centre, and President Bush was waging his War on Terror, that glib, empty sound-bite.

He marvelled, as the train rattled along, that he alone on the planet was aware of what was to come, the US-led invasion of Iraq and the terrible repercussions to world peace it would engender.

He fell to speculating what he might be able to do to prevent the futile invasion – but realised that despite the foreknowledge he was powerless. Who would believe him? His warnings that Saddam's weapons of mass destruction were nothing more than US lies, that the invasion would lead to catastrophic destabilisation in Iraq and neighbouring countries, would be derided as the nay-sayings of a lunatic. He might very well be able to change the small-scale events of his own existence and those of people close to him, but on the world stage he was impotent.

It occurred to him, as he alighted at Fulham Broadway and walked back towards Chelsea High Street, that he should suggest to Max Morrison that his outline feature the US-led invasion of a Middle Eastern country, and the future political consequences; they could always be included as a kind of alternate history in the virtual reality sections of the film. He dismissed the idea: the little research he recalled doing into Max Morrison and his politics had suggested that the director was a staunch Republican.

This recollection brought back memories of the meeting with the director, and the man's arrogance and bravado. He'd browbeaten Richie into writing a first draft of the screenplay for a paltry two thousand dollars, having first changed the original scenario – which Richie had sweated over for months – out of all recognition.

In the event this meeting, and all the draft outlines and the hundreds of emails, would come to nothing: Richie would hack out a first draft of the screenplay and a couple of years down the line be reluctantly paid the agreed-upon two grand. But Morrison would shelve the project – probably writing it off as a tax loss – to concentrate on clearing his name in a sex-scandal that would blow up in 2005. He'd fail, be sentenced to fifteen years, and die in jail of a massive coronary a few years later.

The knowledge gave Richie, as he entered the wine bar where he was to meet the director, a pleasing frisson of schadenfreude.

A gargantuan bear of a man, over six-and-a-half feet tall and as broad as a padded quarterback, rose to greet him with a patently insincere grin, hollering, "And here he is in real life, and looking nothing like his picture, eh, EmmaLou? Shit, man, come here!"

He enveloped Richie in a suffocating hug. The American wore a vast pair of brown corduroy trousers held up by bright red braces that described great arcs over his huge stomach, made even bigger by a loud Hawaiian shirt.

He stood back and introduced the girl next to him. "Ed, meet EmmaLou. EmmaLou, Ed. Em's my P.A. and goddamned life support system. Hell, I can't even move without Em's say so, isn't that right, girl?"

EmmaLou showed her teeth in the fixed rictus of a bored air-hostess.

Richie recalled the girl from their original meeting: a small, perfectly-proportioned platinum blonde of the kind that might have been ten-a-penny in Hollywood but who, even in London, turned heads with her tanned, cosmetically-enhanced perfection. She had sat in silence through their meeting, moving only to make notes in a spiral-bound jotter and to grin her agreement with the director. Her robotic subservience had not struck Richie as odd at the time, but now he understood: she hated the man. Three years down the line EmmaLou would accuse Max Morrison of multiple counts of rape, starting when she had been just twelve years old.

"That photo did you no credit," Morrison boomed. "No credit at all. Thought I'd be meeting with some weaselly banker, but just look at you. A lean, mean, writing machine, eh, Ed? Loved your latest draft."

They ordered drinks – Morrison insisting on a bottle of champagne – and then lunch: the Americans had steak, while Richie ordered salmon salad.

As they ate, Morrison regaled Richie with a list of his latest hit films, citing what they'd cost to make and their box-office takings. The man was a crass egomaniac, probably borderline Asperger's, with no sense of humility and zero interest in the views and opinions of anyone but himself.

From time to time Richie glanced at EmmaLou, to gauge her reaction and perhaps exchange a conspiratorially raised eyebrow. But the P.A. attended to her meal without the slightest glance his way.

"Now, *VR*." Morrison tapped the print-out before him: the latest version of Richie's synopsis. "Love the title, by the way. Snappy, punchy, no bullshitting. Your latest draft cuts the shit, so well done you. Loved the action sequences, and the motivation behind OmniGen's cover-up. Nicely handled, Ed."

"Delighted you liked it."

"But... Listen, bud, recent events..."

Inwardly, Richie smiled. He knew what was coming, and thought back to the shock his younger, naive self had experienced when Morrison had said, "Recent events have made the terrorists-as-heroes aspect of the film a little..." – the director grimaced and made a see-saw of his right hand – "a little dubious, get me?"

The younger Richie had just stared, open-mouthed, unable to find a suitable response. Now he sat back casually and said, "So what do you suggest, Max?"

"Thought you'd see it my way, bud. What I suggest is this little tweak. The terrorists are now the bad guys, huh? And the heroine – what's she called, Terri? This Terri kid isn't their leader, but she's employed by the government to root out the bad guys in VR and kick their goddamned butts."

Richie recalled his drop-jawed response to the director's sweeping change. Like a fool, he'd nodded and gone along with them: "O... kay. I get where you're coming from."

Now he held the American's gaze and said, "So just who are these terrorists?"

Morrison spread his hands in an expansive gesture. "Hey, let's cash in on public sentiment, huh? Who'll be paying to see this film? I'll tell you, the good guys across the USA and Europe... And what does the paying public want to see? They want to see the bad guys getting fucked over, Ed. So we make the VR terrorists towel-heads, huh?"

"Let's get this straight," Richie said, "the terrorists, who in all the previous drafts have been the good guys, fighting the vested interests of OmniGen to bring VR to the people, are now Arab terrorists."

"That's what I'm getting at, Ed."

"And the motivation of the terrorists in this version?"

Morrison planted his meaty hands on the table and leaned forward. He looked like a genie, just emerged from the lamp, about to grant the first of three wishes. "They want to bring good old OmniGen, who in this version are an arm of the US government, to its knees."

"And Terri, the lead, who is no longer a terrorist, because the terrorists are Arabs..."

"In this version, Ed, Terri works for the government..."

"To wipe out the terrorists?" Richie said.

"You got it in one, Ed," the director said, "only I want to scrap this Terri character. In the redraft she'll be a *he* – and" – he pointed at Ed – "and I've got none other than Chuck Norris lined up for the part."

Richie smiled. He nodded and kept on smiling, draped an arm over the back of his chair and took a long drink of champagne. He glanced at EmmaLou; she was watching him with a slit-eyed, wincing expression that said, *Oh, please agree with the motherfucker, for your own sake...*

In their original meeting, Richie, like the crawling, greedy coward he had been, had nodded and said, "I think it can be done. Yes, I don't see why not..."

Now he stared at the director and said, "So let's get this straight. The good guys are now the bad guys, OmniGen are now the good guys, and Terri the feisty twenty-year-old kick-ass hacker is now... Chuck Norris?"

The American grinned. "You got it!"

EmmaLou closed her eyes.

Richie maintained his genteel English smile – no need to let the side down with a show of emotion, old boy – reached across the table and picked up the annotated version of his email.

Then, holding the document up over the table, he tore it into two, then four, then eight, and dropped the resulting confetti onto Morrison's plate. "I think your ideas stink, Max. And as we say over here, I suggest you shove your notes, and all the shit they contain, back up your big fat arse."

EmmaLou stood suddenly and, holding a hand to her mouth as if about to vomit, ran towards the toilet.

Richie rose from the table, leaned forward, and said to the dumbfounded director, "And I suggest that, in future, you think twice about fucking twelve-year-olds..."

Morrison, on the verge of apoplexy, or maybe even a coronary, for once in his life found himself speechless. Richie turned on his heel and sauntered from the wine-bar, almost punching the air in triumph as he did so.

IT WAS THREE o'clock and he had a few hours to kill until dinner at Digby's that evening. He took the tube into central London, then to Islington, where Digby and Caroline lived, bought a copy of the *Guardian* and found a quiet pub in a side-street. He settled down in the corner with a pint of Fullers and a packet of dry-roasted peanuts, set the paper on the table before him and stared into space.

In a day or so he would be taken from this time, whisked back to who knew when, and compelled to play out whatever set-piece lay in wait for him... To what end? Why the hell was this happening to him? Had Emmi been a figment of his imagination, along with her talk of scientists, or had there been something in her claim of being sent to intercept him?

He drank his beer, turned to the sports pages and read a report about Yorkshire's victory over Lancashire at Headingley.

His attention wandered. He thought again of Emmi. If she had been more than a figment of an hallucination, and if what she had told him was true, then what was to stop her locating him again?

He wondered if he should attempt to look for her; but how to go about that? Where might he find her, and how, in such limited time available to him? It was an impossible task – even if she *were* real.

He bought a second pint and recalled the man he'd been at the age of forty-two. He had lived in a constant state of apprehension and worry about where the next commission might come from: hence his capitulation to the megalomaniacal Morrison. He was hacking out journalism and fillers for magazines and newspapers, and selling the occasional radio play to the BBC, and while it satisfied the creative urge within him, he craved the next step up: the financial security of regular TV work. He had assumed, at the time, that besides the money, writing for television would prove as creatively rewarding as his radio work. He wished he could have communicated with his younger self and disabused him of the notion: told himself that with money came compromise, and the death of ambition.

He wondered what he might do if, miraculously, he found himself stabilised in this time. For one thing, he could avoid all the dead ends, the synopses and outlines submitted in hope, but which would never come to anything – and devote himself to the projects he knew would succeed. He could curb the TV work, continued writing radio plays and, to flex his creative muscles and ambition, tried his hand at stage plays.

For the next couple of hours and another two pints, he daydreamed the afternoon away.

Towards six he left the pub and tipsily made his way through the expensive, tree-lined streets of Islington, remembering to call in at an Oddbins to pick up a couple of bottles.

He was about to meet the younger version of his best friend, and he experienced a strange, apprehensive curiosity as he climbed the steps to the navy blue, gloss-painted front door and banged the lion's-head knocker three times.

Digby, at this time, was picking up regular TV work with the

Beeb, and several of his one-off plays had received good notices in the press. He would continue with what he called his 'serious work,' but this evening would announce his move north to work on a drama for Yorkshire Television. It would be the start, Richie knew with the advantage of retrospect, of his friend's gradual descent into TV hackdom and eventual dissatisfaction.

The door opened and a tall, blonde, very attractive woman smiled at him. "Edward, lovely to see you." She kissed his cheeks before Richie, a little shell-shocked, realised that this was Caroline, in her mid-thirties now and almost unrecognisable from the woman in her forties he'd last seen a couple of subjective days ago: she'd dyed her hair blonde and wore it long.

"And how was your meeting with the big-shot?" she asked over her shoulder as she led him through the plushly-carpeted hallway, up a flight of stairs, to a lounge dotted with expensive, tasteful, bespoke furniture. "You must tell us all about it over dinner."

A dozen guests occupied the room, drinking wine and chatting in small groups; Richie knew most of them, aspiring screen-writers, one or two already established names, a mid-list novelist and his sculptor wife, and a scattering of TV people: your average Saturday night bourgeois, quasi-intellectual Islington soiree. Talk would be of the arts, the deplorable political situation in the Middle East thanks to US foreign policy, and what everyone was working on. Name dropping would be *de rigueur* and later in the evening the inevitable argument would break out between those who saw television as the opiate of the masses and those who considered it a valid art-form, citing the works of Mercer, Potter and McGovern *et al*.

Richie looked around for Digby, but recalling his passion for cooking, guessed he was in the kitchen preparing his *pièce de résistance*. He found himself chatting to Chubby Passmore, a successful writer of sitcoms, and his partner Helen.

Across the room he noticed, with a mental jolt, a tall, elegantly slim woman with long blonde hair; she wore a black velvet dress and pearls. She was a softly-spoken New Englander, he remembered, called Elizabeth Teller, and he had met her here tonight for the first time... They would talk for a long time, bound by an ineluctable mutual attraction, and would exchange numbers at the end of the evening. In a month, when Laura left him, he would contact Elizabeth Teller and begin an enjoyable, low-key affair until he followed Digby north to Yorkshire.

Now she caught his eye and smiled, and Richie looked away.

Digby emerged from the kitchen, looking faintly ridiculous in a food-stained apron and huge oven gloves. "Ed!" he called. "Do you mind if I borrow him, Chubby? Ed, come and talk to me while I toil in the bowels of hell."

Smiling, he excused himself and followed Digby into the kitchen.

"And ditch that bloody stuff Caroline foisted on you and help yourself to a real drink."

Digby turned to the cooker and lifted a casserole dish onto a work-surface, and Richie opened a bottle of Sam Smith's bitter, leaned against the wall and watched his friend.

This Digby Lincoln was even leaner than he would be in 2008. He had an almost full head of hair and moved around the kitchen with alacrity as he seasoned the dish and added a splash of wine.

"So, how'd it go with old Morrison?"

Richie remembered reporting, the first time he had this conversation, that the director had asked for certain changes, and he'd agreed to them.

Now he said, anticipating Digby's reaction, "Morrison demanded some ridiculous changes to the outline, so I told him to go fuck himself and shove the synopsis where the sun doesn't shine."

Digby turned and looked at him. "And what did you *really* say?"

Richie smiled. "I kid ye not. I told the overbearing bastard where to get off."

"What?" Digby looked shocked.

"Diggers, the man was a cunt. And a nasty fascist cunt, to boot. He wanted changes that would have made the script pro-American propaganda."

Digby sighed and leaned back against the work-surface. "Ed, Ed... have you ever heard of the word 'compromise'?"

Richie restrained himself from telling his friend that the word would almost ruin Digby in years to come. "There's compromise, and there's compromise. On this, I wasn't willing to compromise."

Digby winced. "Please tell me that you said it civilly, so that you can contact Morrison, tell him you've had second thoughts, and agree to his suggestions, hm?"

Richie shook his head. "'Fraid not, Diggers. There's no going back. I really told him to shove the synopsis up his fat arse."

"God preserve me. Look, Ed... This was a foot in the door. So what if he wanted to fuck about with your outline? You should have bitten the bullet, gone along with it, and taken the filthy lucre and everything that followed. Christ, Ed, you needn't have signed the thing with your own name. It was an opening" – Digby pointed at him – "and an opening you need, let me tell you."

Richie shrugged casually, tipped the beer, then said, "I couldn't, Digby. And I'm glad I didn't. Things'll pan out."

Caroline swept into the kitchen. "Edward, go and mingle while I help Raymond Blanc in here. Tell people dinner will be ready in fifteen."

Digby said, "Ed told the American director to go fuck himself, Caroline."

Caroline smiled at Richie. "Good for you, Edward. Now shoo, shoo... Out of here!"

"No, but you don't understand, Caroline..." Richie heard Digby say as he left the kitchen. "Ed needs the damned work, and the kudos."

Dinner was a pleasant affair, helped by the fact that Richie was more than a little inebriated. He sat between Chubby Passmore and Elizabeth Teller, and across from Digby, who was beaming to himself and obviously biding his time to break the news about his job offer and imminent relocation.

At one point Richie regaled the guests with an account of his meeting

with Max Morrison, overplaying the director's obnoxiousness –
though not by much – and describing his expression when Richie
suggested he bugger himself with a furled copy of the synopsis.

"And another thing," he said, wagging a finger round the table,
"I'd avoid any dealings with the man in future, if I were you. A little
dicky-bird told me that Morrison will soon be in big trouble."

Helen said, "Juicy. Do tell."

"That young P.A. of his, EmmaLou… He's shafting her."

Chubby chuckled. "And this is a crime, Ed? I should think that
in LA it's obligatory to have carnal knowledge of one's personal
assistant. The crime would be if one didn't!"

"Except in this case," Richie said, "he started fucking her when
she was twelve."

From the flurry of comments that greeted this revelation, Richie
assumed he'd earned his dinner. He raised his glass. "So, a toast to
Max Morrison, the nasty fascist shit."

Glasses were raised amid much laughter and talk turned to other
things.

Later, over coffee, Digby tapped an empty wine glass with a
tea spoon and called out. "Silence, silence, ladies and gentlemen,
please!"

Drunk, he beamed around the company like a flushed Mr
Pickwick.

"I have a little announcement to make, one and all." He reached
out, gripped Caroline's hand, and went on, "An announcement,
both joyous and at the same time a little sad. For, after all, do not
all changes in one's life, one's circumstances, engender contrary
feelings…?"

"Get on with it!" Chubby called out.

"So to cut to the chase, to cut a long story short and to impart
the glad, if bittersweet tidings, without further ado… my good lady
Caroline and I are moving, lock, stock and barrel, to Yorkshire."

"Good God," Chubby Passmore expostulated, "why the bloody
hell are you doing that?"

"Yorkshire?" someone said. "Where exactly *is* Yorkshire?"

"Just this side of Siberia, so I'm told."

"Isn't it famous for something, so I've heard?"

"Puddings," the novelist said, "and prejudice."

Digby silenced the comments and said, "Yorkshire Television, in their infinite wisdom, have commissioned me to head a team writing a big-budget soap, and to be honest it was too good an offer to refuse. We've found a farm to convert on the moors, and we're moving in a couple of months. Not," he hurried to reassure his friends, "that we're turning our backs completely on old London. You'll be delighted to hear that we're keeping on our little Chelsea pad."

Richie raised his glass in congratulation and watched his friend accept the plaudits.

Later in the evening, Elizabeth Teller cornered Richie and applauded him on his treatment of Max Morrison. "The fellow really needed to be taken down a peg or two," she said in her warm, modulated New England drawl.

They chatted, but Richie's heart was never in the conversation; his thoughts drifted, and he recalled the first time he made love to Elizabeth, how she demanded he undress her and do things to her which, given her ladylike demeanour and elegant manners, rather shocked him.

He smiled absently, and nodded in the right places, and soon found himself in drunken conversation with someone else.

Then he was standing outside the front door in the early hours, swaying a little as he took his leave of Digby Lincoln.

"I really think, Diggers old man, that you should... should think twice about the Yorkshire thing. Don't go."

Digby patted his shoulder. "I'll be down every couple of weeks, Ed. Don't worry. We'll have our regular sessions... only less regular."

"No... I mean." He swayed, focusing on his friend. "I mean, you won't be happy up there, Diggers. You'll regret it. Fifteen years down the line, you'll tell me... you'll say, Ed, I should never have left London. That's what you'll tell me. I remember."

Digby guffawed and hugged Richie. "Tell you what, Ed, I'll put in a good word for you with the producer, get you on the team, eh? That'd be something!"

Richie stared at his friend, then said, "I don't know when I'll see you again, but you're a good friend, Diggers..."

And he went reeling off down the street, followed by Digby's laughter.

He took a taxi back to Notting Hill. He was surprised to find that Laura had arrived back before him, and that she was curled up asleep in his bed.

He undressed quietly, careful not to wake her, and slid in beside her. He pulled her naked body towards him and murmured, "Loves..." before falling asleep.

He awoke to go to the loo at seven o'clock that morning, surprised that he'd managed to get through the night without earlier visits. His older body would have required at least four trips, after the volume of alcohol he'd consumed.

He was making his way back to bed, and anticipating making love to Laura later that morning, when he felt an oddly familiar pain in his head. He leaned against the wall, moaning, "Christ, no..."

Then the white light hit him and he slumped to the floor, unconscious.

An email from Roger Hartnell, commissioning Editor, Vector Press,
2nd February, 2018

DEAR ED,

I've read *Interesting Times*... and what can I say? I love it. It has everything: depth, a great storyline, fantastic characters, and as a parable for our times it's way ahead of anything else out there. It'll go down a storm – but of course the *Daily Mail* will hate it.

I ran it past marketing and acquisition on Thursday, and they gave me the go ahead. That's the good news. The not-so-good news... I can offer you an advance of five grand. I know, I know! It's peanuts. But it is a first novel, after all, and your name isn't really known outside TV circles.

As for rewrites – the odd line here and there, the occasional cut, but nothing major at all. If only all the mss I deal with were this clean.

Now, I suggest you get yourself an agent. I know you had someone for your TV work, before you sacked her, but I'd advise you get someone for the novel, and all the others you're going to write for us.

And how about dinner when you're next down?

Very best,
Roger.

Email from Ed Richie to Digby Lincoln, 2nd February, 2018

DIGGERS, JUST HAD word from Hartnell at Vector, the new imprint you put me onto: as you forecast, they're taking *Times*... What I never suspected was the paltry advance: five grand – that's a third of the brass I got for the last TV script, which took me about three days to write!

I know I shouldn't complain. You always said there's no money in writing novels.

Thing is, having had the Beeb turn down my last few outlines, I really need the novel to sell.

A pint or two tonight in celebration?

From the Guardian first novel round-up, December 2018

INTERESTING TIMES, BY TV and radio script-writer Ed Richie, is an accomplished and readable first novel. What is notable in this seven hundred-plus page dystopia is that Richie eschews the dialogue-driven format, which one might expect from a script-writer, and uses an expository narrative harking back a century or more. This imbues the story of a failing TV writer battling the censors and the powers-that-be in a near-future totalitarian Britain with a learned gravitas. Richie's profound satire is a timely reminder of the fragile freedoms we all take for granted. Recommended.

CHAPTER TEN

January, 2030

ELLA MOVED THROUGH passport control, her progress delayed by having to follow the non-English resident stream, and made her way to the baggage carousel. Snow had fallen in England during the two days she'd been away, and flying over Norfolk Ella had stared down on a landscape that lay lifeless and inert under the white-out, blinding in the bright winter sunlight.

The baggage from the Helsinki flight was slow in arriving, so she took the opportunity to slip to the loo. Easing her way through the press of passengers, she glimpsed a familiar face: a thin, dark-haired man in his mid-forties. Sitting in the cubicle, she wondered where she'd seen him before – and then she had it. He'd been on the train from Manchester three days ago, glowering at her when she offered the little girl her Queers Against the Front leaflet.

A coincidence? But what were the chances of his being on the same train, and the same flight from Finland? Was she being followed – or was she being paranoid?

She took her time in the toilet, and then hung back when she returned to the baggage retrieval area. She scanned the crowd for the man – he'd been wearing a navy blue suit and a grey overcoat – but it appeared that he'd claimed his baggage and departed. She spotted her case trundling along the rubber flanges and managed to grab it before it disappeared back through the hatch.

She was taking a slideway to the rail station, keeping an eye out for the well-dressed man as she did so, when her wrist-com chimed.

Kit smiled up from the tiny screen. "How was the flight, El?"

"Bumpy. Don't tell me, still nothing on Ralph Dennison, right?" They had spoken last night, Ella reporting her findings in Finland, while Kit admitted that she'd hit a brick wall concerning the scientist.

Kit's complicit smile told Ella that she was wrong. "This morning I spoke to Charles Sloane – he was doing his PhD at the same time as Dennison, then worked with him at Omega-Tec Research in Oxford. He lost contact with Dennison years ago, but when I explained that a colleague of mine was interested in doing a piece about the scientist, he agreed to meet you."

"That's excellent."

"He's an emeritus professor at Balliol, and suggested you ring him to arrange afternoon tea. He's free this afternoon or all tomorrow."

"That sounds civilised. I'll do that."

Kit gave her Sloane's number, then said, "Any idea when you'll be back?"

"I'll probably stay down here for a couple of days, then go back to London after Oxford and try to track down a few more of Richie's ex-lovers."

"Ah, the harem…"

"Don't say it in that tone."

Kit smiled. "I think, reading that journal of his, you're falling under his spell."

"No, but I'm certainly coming to understand what kind of person he was."

"A self-centred serial philanderer redeemed only by his right-on political stance?"

"You can read the journal when I get back," Ella said, "and make up your own mind. Anyway, how are things at your end?"

"I'm working hard for SFM and contacted Canongate about the possibility of their publishing my diary of the last five years. I'm meeting a senior editor tomorrow."

"That's great. Good luck."

"Oh, and Aimee's met someone. Or I suspect she has. She's being very secretive and stays out long after her shift at the café is through."

"I'm sorry," Ella said. "Are you okay?"

"I'm as tough as old boots, El."

They chatted for another minute, then Ella cut the connection.

She took the underground to Paddington, then checked the times of the trains to Oxford: there was one every hour, and the next departed in forty minutes. She found a café and ordered a coffee and a salad sandwich. It was one o'clock, and she hadn't eaten since breakfast at six that morning, crispbread, rubber cheese and pickled gherkins. She selected a booth at the back of the café so that she could see everyone who entered; there was no sign of the thin man in the navy blue suit.

She got through to Charles Sloane, gave her name and mentioned Kit's call that morning.

"I'd be delighted," he said in cultured tones. "Tea at my college, that's Balliol. Say three this afternoon? Excellent. I very much enjoyed your book on Corbyn, by the way. I look forward to meeting you, Ms Shaw."

Ella thanked him, cut the connection and finished her lunch.

She pulled Ed Richie's journal from her case and for the next twenty minutes scoured the later entries for mentions of Emmi Takala.

24th August, 2016: *Anna bought me that bloody landscape I half-admired in York last week. She insists I hang it in the lounge, replacing Emmi's canvas. The two are incomparable. So this morning before I put it away under the stairs, I sat and admired it for a while, wondering if I made a mistake all those years ago. How different would my life have been, had I gone*

*back to Crete and Emmi? Would I have found some measure
of happiness, or fulfilment?*

Tuesday! A session with Diggers tonight.

Ella smiled to herself and closed the journal.

The mention of Digby Lincoln reminded her that she'd intended to
call him as soon as she arrived in England.

She raised her wrist-com and spoke his name.

The dial tone sounded, followed by a cautious, "Hello?"

Her screen remained blank; evidently Digby had an ancient phone.

"Digby, Ella Shaw here."

"Ella, lovely to hear from you. How was London, and the delightful
Sam?"

"Sam was as delightful as ever, and working hard. She sends you
her best wishes." She hesitated. "I was wondering if I might quiz you
about something?"

"Fire away."

"It's about Emmi Takala, the Finnish artist Ed met in Crete in
2008."

"Ah, the ethereal Emmi," Digby said. "Ed was quite smitten. I
could never understand why he didn't follow it up. When I tried to
probe, he always changed the subject. Anyway, how can I help?"

"I've just returned from Finland, where I met her brother." She
paused, knowing that she was about to drop a bombshell, then went
on, "He says that Emmi went to England last year – to meet Ed."

Digby interrupted. "Did you say 'meet' Ed?"

"That's right. He thinks that Emmi had a letter from him, and then
she told her brother she was going to England to meet 'Edward'..."

"Could it have been another Edward?" Digby asked.

"That's what I wondered, but her brother said that they'd met on
Crete years ago and that this Edward was a writer."

"Bloody hell!" Digby laughed. "But..."

"I know, if she *did* receive a letter from Edward, a year ago, then
he's still – well, *was*, a year ago – alive."

"Bloody hell!" Digby said again. "But this is fantastic. I'm... He can't be mistaken, or lying, can he?"

"Mistaken? Well, it would be a massive coincidence, wouldn't it? And I saw no reason why he might have lied to me."

"I... I'm sorry... I'm filling up. This is remarkable... The thing is, Ella, if Ed is still alive... then why hasn't he contacted me? And where is he? And why the hell did he vanish?"

"And why, out of the blue, did he write to Emmi Takala?"

The silence stretched, and Ella said, "Digby? You still there?"

"I'm sorry. It's just... I'm quite overcome. This is the most remarkable news. Thank you. The last few years, what with Ed's disappearance, and then Caroline... It hasn't been the best of times, Ella. This... well, this is a light in the darkness."

Ella smiled. "I thought I'd better keep you up to date. Look, I must dash. I'm catching a train to Oxford in five minutes. I'll keep you posted."

"Bless you, Ella. Goodbye."

She gathered her bags, left the café and made her way to the Oxford platform.

The journey took thirty minutes longer than the scheduled hour due to maintenance work outside Reading. She filled the time by listening to one of Ed Richie's radio plays she'd downloaded from the BBC archive. *The Wall* was first broadcast in the summer of 2017, a scathing satire and the last play Richie would sell to the BBC. She wondered if there might be a connection.

When the play finished, she opened his journal and scanned the entries for November and December 2016, and discovered an entry about the play.

13th November, 2016: *Had a long conversation with Shaw at the Beeb this morning, and I mooted the idea of a radio play about Trump. A satire – what else? He said it sounded just the thing he was looking for. Bravo for Shaw! I was expecting the thumbs down.*

The Wall *was inspired by Andrei Platonov's very strange*

novel The Foundation Pit, *set in post-revolution Russia, about a group of labourers digging a vast hole in the countryside, the foundations of a great house for the workers.* The Wall *will be set in a notional future fascist state in which all artists are ordered to abandon their work and build a wall to 'protect' their country. The bricks of the wall will be hollow and, when the artists have been worked to exhaustion, they are summarily shot and placed in these brick coffins... It sounds crude in synopsis, but the play itself will be allusive and subtle, I hope. We'll see.*

Thirteen years later, Ella thought that *The Wall* was still as fresh and affecting as when it was first broadcast. Bravo for Richie!

The train pulled into Oxford station and she took a taxi to Balliol.

CHARLES SLOANE MET Ella at the porter's lodge and escorted her along oak-panelled corridors to his set, two small rooms overlooking the snow-covered quadrangle. The Professor was a tall, cadaverous man in his seventies, with a hesitant manner at once querulous and endearing. He praised Ella's book on Corbyn once again, following up with a few comments about recent British politics. She gained the reassuring impression that they were on the same side.

His sitting-room was full of dark oak furniture, old standard lamps, and much chintz. There was no evidence of a computer, or even a television or softscreen. Ella gazed through the mullioned windows at the changeless scene of the quadrangle: she might have been transported back a few centuries.

"I took the liberty of ordering tea and scones. They'll be here presently. I thought that, a little later, we might take sherry in the Senior Common Room. I have so few guests these days that I rather make an occasion of it when the rare beast turns up."

Ella murmured that that sounded pleasant, and asked the Professor if he still taught.

"No longer, alas, though I supervise the occasional PhD student."

A tap at the door signalled the arrival of afternoon tea. Sloane took control of the trolley and wheeled it in. He poured the tea and offered Ella a buttered scone.

Ella asked him about his college days.

"I was at Cambridge," he said as he settled himself into an armchair. "And then I 'joined the other side' for my PhD here. I wanted to study under Robertson, a great man. When I gained my doctorate, I joined Omega-Tec, just down the road, and spent ten years there before being wooed back into the arms of academe. That was over thirty-five years ago, and for my long service I was allowed to stay on here way past retirement. You know, college life rather spoils one; I'm not at all sure I could survive out there in the real world."

Ella smiled. "I understand you were friends with Ralph Dennison."

The Professor juggled a crumbling scone. "Of course, that's what you came here to discuss! Do you know, I'd quite forgotten that little point, and extemporised by boring you with my *curriculum vitae*. Forgive me. But yes, Ralph and I were great friends. He was brilliant, quite brilliant, while I was never in his league, which I suppose is why I found myself back here, teaching."

"And you knew the writer Edward Richie?"

"Not well, but we got along well enough, I suppose. Ralph, however, was a great chum of his."

"And when Ralph moved to Oxford...?"

Sloane smiled. "I followed him. As I said, I wanted to study under Robertson. Oh, they were heady times, Ms Shaw. We were at the cutting edge of our field, doing some really ground-breaking research, and we'd discuss our work long into the night, and often till dawn. I got to know Ralph even better during that time; I had him to myself, so to speak."

Ella sipped her tea. "What was he like?"

The professor sat back in his chair and held his teacup before his chest, his gaze distant.

"He was intense, phenomenally intelligent, a little distant emotionally, perhaps. Our own relationship was firmly grounded in the intellect, of course. That said, I..." He stopped, gazing at her. "Well, speaking as people who understand each other, Ms Shaw, I will admit that I was a little in love with dear old Ralph."

She smiled. "And Ralph?"

"Was oblivious. And anyway he was hetero – not that he was in the least successful in that department until much later."

"What was the subject of your doctorates, Professor?"

"I was working on cosmological inconsistency, Ralph on exotic matter in the vicinity of black holes..."

"And after gaining your doctorates, you and Ralph joined Omega-Tec?"

"That is correct. Again, I rather think I rode in on Ralph's coat-tails. Ralph bloomed like a tropical plant introduced to sunlight and, to continue the horticultural metaphor, I rather wilted under the intense heat."

"What was the nature of your work at Omega-Tec?"

Winking at her, he tapped the side of his nose. "All rather hush-hush, Ms Shaw. We had to sign the Official Secrets Act, for Omega-Tec was backed by the government." He shook his head. "But as there's been so much water under the bridge since then, I'll tell you that we were doing research into faster-than-light travel – not the mechanics, the hardware and all that, but the theory."

"That's... fascinating."

He smiled. "You're too polite, Ms Shaw. I won't bore you with the details. But it was all rather heady stuff at the time."

"And did it lead anywhere? Are we any nearer being able to send ships to the stars?"

The Professor gazed out at the quadrangle. Snow had started to fall again, sifting from a pewter sky. He withdrew his gaze and smiled at her. "Oh, it was all very theoretical, my dear, and to be honest I don't mind admitting that I was rather out of my depth, though Ralph was in his element."

She sipped her tea, realising that he hadn't actually answered her question. "And he worked with Omega-Tec for fifteen years, I understand?"

"That's right," the professor said. "We saw each other quite often during that time, kept each other abreast of what we were doing – not that I was setting the world alight. Towards the end, the last couple of years, we saw each other less and less – Ralph's work load, you see, was colossal."

"And he left Omega-Tec around 2000?"

"Around then, yes."

"Do you know the circumstances...?"

"Again, this is between you, me and the gate-post, my dear. If you do use what I say, it must be unattributed, do you understand?"

"Perfectly."

"One evening Ralph came here in a bit of a flap. He said his research had gone as far as it could, that he felt inhibited by certain restrictions imposed at Omega-Tec, and that anyway he'd had a better offer."

Ella lowered her cup. "From another country?" she ventured.

"That's what I assumed, at first, but I was wrong. Ralph had been approached by a private individual – a billionaire, no less – and offered what every research scientist in the world would have given both arms and legs for: his very own research facility, a team of hand-picked scientists, and unlimited funding. *Unlimited.* Ralph was beside himself."

"And he accepted the offer."

"Like a shot. Wouldn't you?"

She considered the question. "I suppose it would depend on who would be making the offer. I'd refuse point blank if it were the Americans, the Russians, or the Chinese... Or the English, for that matter." She leaned forward. "Who was behind the offer, Professor?"

He smiled. "That was my first question, too. And one that had vexed Ralph for a time. Suffice it to say that he was satisfied that the billionaire in question was independent, and not allied to any foreign government or political regime. So he left Omega-Tec and disappeared. I saw him once in the next ten years, and he wouldn't be drawn as to the nature of his work."

"And then, in 2010, he really did disappear?"

"According to newspaper reports, yes. He had a flat in London, which he used from time to time, and there was a news item about his not having been seen for a year or more. A question was asked in the House about the whereabouts of 'one of our leading scientists,' and answers were there none. Of course, the gutter press came out with the usual claptrap, that he'd gone over to the other side, to China or Russia, or that he'd been kidnapped and forced to divulge his secrets."

"Were either credible?"

"Ralph would never have worked for the Chinese, the Russians, *or* the Americans. He was an honourable person. And anyway, he had everything he could have dreamed of with the philanthropist billionaire."

"But the kidnapping hypothesis?"

"I can't see it, myself. But I have a theory, my dear."

Ella leaned forward. "Go on."

"I think that his independent research hit gold, that they came across something so extraordinary that it initiated a new stage of enquiry, something that had to be kept so secret that it would be dangerous if it ever became public knowledge. I think the billionaire had everyone involved in the project 'disappear,' assume new identities, and continue their research in total and absolute hermetic secrecy."

"And would you venture a guess as to the nature of this... breakthrough?"

The Professor laughed. "I wouldn't be so foolish," he said, "though..."

"Yes?"

"If you promise not to divulge your source, I would be able to tell you the name of the billionaire behind the project."

Ella was a little girl again, being promised the best Christmas present ever, and she felt like saying, "Yes, please."

"And do I have that undertaking?" the professor asked.

"Of course."

"Very well," he said, "his name is Duncan Mackendrick, and he has his headquarters in your neck of the woods, Ms Shaw: Edinburgh. I am given to understand that he has his base of operations at a certain Hailes Castle. And now," he went on, "I do think a drop of sherry is in order. Should we repair to the SCR?"

She followed the Professor from his set to the Senior Common Room, considering the irony of chasing halfway across Europe and back only to find that the person who could perhaps shed most light on the whereabouts of Ralph Dennison, and perhaps Ed Richie, lived in the same city as herself. She entered the SCR behind the Professor and stopped in her tracks.

He smiled at her. "Yes, it is rather beautiful, is it not?"

She approached the painting that hung above the blazing fire; she took in the vibrant Greek landscape, the gorgeous sunset and the sparks of silver pigment glinting in the rocky headland, and finally the childish signature: *EMMI.*

Professor Sloane was at her elbow. "A gift from an anonymous benefactor, just last year," he explained. "The odd thing is that while Ralph was with Omega-Tec, he often donated artworks to the college." He gestured at the painting. "Wherever he is now, Ms Shaw, I rather think he would approve, don't you?"

She nodded. "Yes, I'm sure he would," she said.

From Ed Richie's journal, 3rd March, 2023

I WAS IN Waterstone's in Leeds the other day when I saw Jeremy Corbyn's biography – a great brick of a book. And what a surprise when I picked it up and saw who'd written it: Ella Shaw. Surely it couldn't be Annabelle's sister, the same Ella Shaw who, as a twelve-year-old, had visited Annabelle and spoke hardly a word to me? But when I turned to the back-flap I saw her photo… Forty years might have passed, but I saw the girl she had been in the determined face of the ageing woman. I bought the book and I'm a hundred pages into it: authoritative, insightful, and extremely readable – the kind of literary biography that isn't often published these days.

From Ed Richie's journal, 1st January, 2025

WILL THERE EVER be peace in our time, or is it a precondition of our being human that we'll forever be at war? It's late, and I'm pissed… Just got back from the party at Diggers'. Breaking news while we were revelling… Neo-Nazi terrorists in Warsaw have slaughtered two hundred hostages – men, women and children – at a shopping centre in the city. No sooner have the religious fascists of Daesh been routed, than Nazi thugs raise their ugly heads. I despair. I need a drink… Maybe this is a suitable subject for the next novel?

CHAPTER ELEVEN

May, 1995

WHEN RICHIE CAME to his senses, he was sitting in an armchair before a cluttered desk and a primitive Amstrad computer, green text glowing on a black screen. He leaned forward, staring at the words, the screen seeming to pulse with unhealthy light. He read a few lines and realised that this was one of his early, unsuccessful radio plays – and the Amstrad the old machine he'd had for years and could never afford to replace.

A trickle of smoke over his right hand caught his eye, and he was amazed to see a cigarette smouldering between his fingers. He swore, leaned forward and buckled the cigarette in an ashtray already half full of tab ends. He'd forgotten that briefly in the mid-'nineties he'd taken up smoking.

He peered at the top right corner of the computer screen, checking for the date. But of course the Amstrad had no such niceties. This was a write-to-disc only contraption, a step up from an electric typewriter. He recalled that he'd had the machine for almost ten years, unable to afford anything more advanced, and had grown fond of the thing.

He took in the unmade double bed, the wonky IKEA wardrobe, and the bookshelf stuffed with dog-eared paperbacks, reference books and dictionaries. He hardly recognised the place; his memory of the room, of this period, was more than twenty years old, and imperfect. He'd completely forgotten that he'd ever had a Greenpeace poster of the *Rainbow Warrior* above the bricked-up fireplace, and he had no memory of the plastic globe on the mantel-shelf – maybe a joke birthday present from an old girlfriend? The notion struck a vague chord, but he was unable to bring either the occasion or the woman to mind.

So this was the room in the Brixton terraced house he'd rented between '94 and '98. He recalled he'd shared the place with two junior doctors, though due to the erratic pattern of their shifts he'd hardly seen them. It was a period of his life he had no desire to dwell upon, never mind relive, having spent much of the time in a futile fog of self-pity. He'd worked part-time at the local Waterstones, seen a few women he hardly recalled, and the radio plays he'd sent off to Bush House had been returned, without comment, with depressing regularity.

He looked around the room for some indication of the date. He wasn't wearing a watch – he'd disdained such personal ornamentation in the 'nineties, he recalled – and he couldn't find a discarded newspaper: he'd lived a frugal life, without the luxury of daily papers. He moved to the window and stared out; it was evidently spring or summer, as bright sunlight bathed the row of cars parked in the narrow street. He moved to the wardrobe and stared at his reflection in the mirror.

He was in his mid-thirties, his hair longer than it would be at forty-two. He had a beer belly and looked unfit – it was still a few years until he took up jogging, resumed five-a-side football, and started eating healthily.

He was wearing frayed, faded jeans and a dark green Fruit of the Loom T-shirt. He wondered who he was seeing now. He'd dated a succession of women while living in Brixton, with long abstinences in between affairs while he concentrated on his writing.

He pulled out the desk drawer and found a cheque book. He looked at the last stub, and found that he'd written a cheque for ten pounds on the 20th of April, 1995. But how long ago might that have been?

A wallet sat beside the Amstrad, containing two credit cards and twenty pounds in ten and five pound notes, and...

With shaking fingers he pulled out the photograph of Annabelle, not yet ripped in two by the jealous Laura. He stared at the fey girl-child, then raised the photo to his lips and kissed it.

He sat down and stared at the computer screen. If the house suffered a power cut while he was out, then he would lose everything he'd written to disc that day. He reached out for the mouse and saw that there wasn't one. His hand hung in the air, bereft. How the hell was he to go about saving his work on the disc and closing the contraption down?

He read a few lines of the text glowing on the screen, then scrolled to the start of the play and began reading. From time to time he paused to alter a line, cut unnecessary dialogue or insert better, pithier phrases. The play was not without merit – in fact, it showed distinct promise – but it was terribly overwritten. It was one of the many efforts he'd finished but filed away without sending off to be summarily rejected.

Perhaps, when he was shunted away from this body and this time, he'd bequeath himself a rewritten play that was saleable... thus changing history.

He tapped away for the next hour, rewrote the ending to his satisfaction, then played around with the keyboard until he worked out how to save the file. He recalled how paranoid he'd been about losing work back in the 'nineties – and rightly so, on a device so primitive – but for the life of him couldn't recall how to copy the disc or back it up.

He left his room and tapped down the narrow, uncarpeted staircase to the equally bare hallway. A jacket he recognised hung alongside half a dozen others on a wall-rack opposite the door to the living room. He was shrugging on the frayed corduroy jacket when the door opened and a vaguely familiar face looked out at him: male, Asian, mid-twenties... But what was his *name?*

Then he had it, as if from nowhere: Az.

"Oh, Eddie... I was just about to see if you were in. That was Tash on the phone, wondering where the B.H. you were."

"Tash?"

"Tash," Az said. "Get a grip. Tash, your boss. You were due to start at one."

"Bloody hell. Lost all track..." Richie temporised. "I was busy... Look." He stopped, knowing how daft he'd sound – but ploughed on anyway, "What's the date?"

"The 19th."

Az made to close the door, but Richie said, "Of?"

The young man gave him an odd look. "May."

"And it's '95, right?"

"Riiight..." Az leaned against the door-frame and stared at him. "Look, if I were you, Eddie, I'd go to fewer of those parties. They're no good for your head."

"Yeah, you're right. Look, one more question. Who am I seeing at the moment?"

Az gave a crooked smile. "I think you *should* be seeing one of my tutors in the psychology department, Eddie. But as for women..." He shook his head. "Pass. I think you're between them at the moment, but don't quote me on that." He made to close the door.

"Thanks, Az. See you around."

The door re-opened a fraction and the young man peered out. "I'm Isfan, Eddie. Az moved out a month ago. Seriously, are you okay?"

"I'm fine," Richie said, colouring as he hurried from the house.

He turned right along the street and headed towards the main road. He was late for his afternoon and evening shift at Waterstones, but he was damned if he was going to turn up. He'd buy a paper, find a pub, and try his best to recall the minutiae of day-to-day life back in May 1995.

He bought a *Guardian* at the corner off-licence and entered the smoke-filled bar of the White Horse. That was another thing he'd forgotten about 1995: the smoking ban had yet to be imposed, and the non-smoking British public was still endangering its collective health with passive inhalation. As he ordered a pint of Fuller's and glanced around the crowded room, he noted another difference. There were perhaps thirty drinkers here, mainly men, and not one of them was in heads-down communion with his mobile phone.

Richie found a table by the window and enjoyed a long mouthful of beer. He read his way through the *Guardian*, finding it an odd experience. He recalled some news stories from the time, while others were as lost as the small events of his everyday life. He read a lengthy report on the Russian paramilitary troops' massacre of civilians in Chechnya, and another of the car bomb in Oklahoma City, USA, which had claimed more than one hundred and sixty victims.

He wondered what Digby would have made of the news; over the years, he'd spent many a happy hour in the pub, dissecting the news with his best friend.

He was thinking that he should get in touch with Digby when it hit him.

In 1987, Digby had completed a long science fiction novel he'd been working on for three years. *A Trove of Stars* was, Digby claimed, ground-breaking hard SF in that it combined cutting-edge, up-to-the-minute cosmological speculation with penetrating character insight. *A Trove of Stars*, he predicted, would take the world by storm.

He'd handed the hefty manuscript to Richie one evening in the Malt Shovel in Islington, full of hope, and over the course of the next week Richie had read it and made copious notes.

The following Tuesday night he'd presented the ms to Digby, along with his critique.

They had long been in the habit of commenting on each other's work. Their respective strengths had complemented each other's weaknesses: Digby excelled at characterisation, and Richie was a dab hand at turning a tight plot.

One thing they had agreed on, however, was total and brutal honesty: what benefit was faint praise when what a piece needed for improvement was constructive, no-holds-barred criticism?

That night in the Malt Shovel, Richie had told his friend that *A Trove of Stars* was a mess, a flabby, overwritten monster with leaden pacing and tedious *longueurs* where the author took needless time out to tell the reader about the characters' states of mind.

Digby had read Richie's notes with an increasingly stony expression; at one point Richie thought he'd even seen tears in his friend's eyes. Richie had expected a certain amount of objection from Digby, the odd argument about aspects of his criticism, but not blanket denial.

When Digby finished reading the notes, he looked up at Richie and said, "I don't agree."

Richie nodded, sipping his pint. "About?"

"All of it."

"All of it?" Richie tested a smile on his friend, to see how he might react. Digby remained stony-faced.

"You don't understand," Digby said. "What I'm trying to do here is bring the concerns of the modern psychological novel to the hidebound format of hard SF."

Richie had restrained himself from accusing his friend of talking pretentious bollocks. He tried to formulate a diplomatic response. "Well... I think that's partly the problem, Digby. You see, in my opinion, while there's lots to admire in the novel – the ideas are first rate, and the line-by-line writing is good – in places the characterisation is weak."

"Weak?" Digby sounded incredulous. "Where, for instance?"

"Okay... How about here, the twenty-page passage from page two hundred? You have Ellory meeting Varda on the shuttle, and when they return to Mars they begin an affair."

"So what's wrong with that?"

"Well... Ellory is two-timing his girlfriend, Lani, but you fail to show what he feels about this. He'd feel some guilt, remorse – but you don't even go into why he felt he needed the affair."

"I do." Digby leafed through the manuscript. "Here. The passage about how Lani had treated him on their last landfall."

Richie tried not to smile. "But it comes over as shallow, Digby. It's schoolboy reasoning. And until now, you've built up Ellory as a seemingly complex, caring individual. But that passage shows him as a shallow, self-centred fool. It's inconsistent writing –"

Digby had surprised him by saying, "But… but it's based on how I felt when I met Elspeth…"

Uneasy, Richie had gone to the bar for another round, and when he'd returned to the table, Digby had vanished.

He'd phoned Diggers the following day, expecting to find his friend hungover and conciliatory, but Digby had slammed the phone down on him.

Hurt, Richie had left it a week, then phoned again. Digby hung up at the sound of his voice. The following week he wrote to Digby and apologised for his harsh assessment of the novel. *I know what it's like to have something I believe in trashed in that way. God knows, it's happened to me… On this occasion, perhaps I was wrong. Can I read it again, try to understand a little more what you were intending?*

His concession had elicited no response, and he'd gone round to Digby's grubby Finchley flat. He'd wanted to say he was sorry, that he was wrong – and that it was stupid to let ten years of friendship end like this.

But Digby had slammed the door in his face – and when, a week later, Richie tried again, he was told by one of Digby's erstwhile flatmates that his friend had moved out without leaving a forwarding address.

Over the course of the next few months, Richie had dropped into the pubs they'd frequented together in the hope of bumping into Digby, but it appeared that he'd moved away from the North London area, or that he was scrupulous in avoiding their old haunts.

Richie had thrown himself into his own writing over the next few years, lost himself in doomed relationships, and continually regretted what he saw as his friend's unconscionable desertion.

The hiatus would come to a welcome end next year, May 1996, when Richie would bump into Digby Lincoln in Piccadilly Waterstones. He'd spot the smartly-dressed Digby, in beige chinos and a suede jacket, staring at the ranked titles in the sci-fi and fantasy section – perhaps pondering, Richie thought, what might have been.

His first urge had been to greet Digby like the long-lost friend he was – his second, to be more circumspect, fearing another rejection. Timidly, he had advanced to Digby's side and said, "Diggers…?"

Digby had started, then stared at Richie, his eyes narrowing with some indecipherable emotion. Then he'd returned his gaze to the glossy covers.

Just when Richie could stand the silence no more, and was about to turn and walk away, Digby said, almost inaudibly, "I'm sorry."

"No," Richie found himself saying, relieved. "I am. I was wrong. I… I shouldn't have been so…"

Digby interrupted. "You were right, Ed. Every word of it. I was an arrogant, pretentious bastard. Your criticism was right, especially about…" He shrugged. "And the longer it went on, not seeing you… the harder it was to get back in touch and apologise. Christ, Ed…"

"How about a pint?"

Digby smiled. "How about several?"

Now, drinking his pint in the White Horse, Richie recalled the feeling of swelling relief, the sensation of walking on air, as he left Waterstones with his old friend and wandered along the road to the St James Tavern.

Over what turned out to be an all-day session at the St James and several other watering holes, they caught up with what they'd each been doing over the past eight years. Diggers announced that last year he'd married a wonderful woman called Caroline, an administrator for the NHS based at St Bartholomew's, and he worked as a freelance technical writer, doing okay financially but feeling far from fulfilled creatively.

Richie told his friend that he'd muddled along from one dead-end job to the next to subsidise his writing, and had sold a few minor radio plays to the BBC but was still waiting for the big break.

After that they'd seen each other every week, sometimes twice a week, for sessions in central London. A few months later, Richie started selling radio plays to a producer at Bush House on a regular basis, and he'd put Digby in touch with the woman. Within a year they were both selling radio scripts to the BBC, and had got back into the habit of vetting and criticising each other's work. If anything, the hiatus had cemented their friendship: they'd been inseparable ever since.

Digby's reaction that night at the Malt Shovel had puzzled Richie on and off over the years, but in his relief that their friendship was back on an even keel, he'd pushed his concerns to the back of his mind.

Now, finishing his first pint and ordering a second, it came to Richie that he'd been a blind, ignorant fool. Why hadn't he seen Digby's rage for what it had been – not indignation at criticism of his novel, but reaction to Richie's criticism of Digby himself?

Back in '86, Digby had been seeing a trainee lawyer, Elspeth, and as far as Richie could see was serious about her. Then, at a New Year's Eve party in Hackney, Richie had introduced Digby to a woman called Hester – who Richie had met casually for drinks once or twice – and had been amazed when Digby had announced, a few days later, that he was seeing Hester.

"So you've kicked Elspeth into touch?"

Digby had looked uncomfortable. "Not yet…"

And for the next few months he'd proceeded to string both women along.

And that evening in the Malt Shovel he'd reacted badly to Richie's assessment of his central character, Ellory, as shallow.

He took a mouthful of bitter and shook his head.

What a fool I was, he reflected; what a blind, ignorant fool…

* * *

HE LOOKED UP as a group of half a dozen youngsters – at least, that was how he thought of them – entered the pub, laughing and joking. They congregated at the bar and ordered drinks. Some of the faces were familiar, others not so. A couple wore the black shirts of Waterstones staff, out for a lunchtime session, and the company's black and white plastic badges on lanyards around their necks. He recognised the others as regulars at the pub.

They saw him, fetched their drinks from the bar, and muscled in around the table – four young men and two girls in their late teens. He'd forgotten the names of most of them, though they'd been workmates and drinking companions in this very pub after work.

"You're in the shit with Tash." This was Jill, and Richie recalled that for some reason she had disliked him intensely.

A plump girl with bright red dyed hair touched his arm. "What the fuck, Ed? You were due in at one. Tash went ballistic. She had to cover for you." Her name-tag identified her as Debs.

Jill said, "You could've phoned in, you know?"

"Well, I forgot."

"What happened?" Debs asked.

Richie looked up from the newspaper. "I was ill."

"Not too ill to drink, though?" Jill said.

He hoisted his pint. "Hair of the dog."

"She'll have your balls," Jill said, "the next time you're in."

"She's welcome to them," Richie murmured, and turned his attention to the paper.

He wished they'd go away and leave him to his beer, but it appeared that they were entrenched for a session. When he came to the end of his pint, he picked up the empty along with his paper and moved to the bar. He found a high stool at the far end, bought a third bitter, and sat drinking with his back to the Waterstones crowd. Let them think him a miserable bastard...

He'd have a couple more pints here, then go for an Indian at a place he recalled around the corner, then he'd pop into a few of the pubs along the high street and get well leathered, return to his room and sleep through the night and hopefully through much of the following day. By then, he suspected, he'd be pitched back again to... when? He was thirty-five now and it was 1995. So would his next port of call be at some point in the 'eighties, in his twenties? Jesus, he had that to look forward to... working in various dead-end jobs while living in filthy bedsits around north London.

Debs appeared smiling at his side and touched his arm. "Ed... you okay? It's just... you don't seem yourself."

He smiled at her, and he vaguely recalled that they'd been friends, though never more than that.

"I'm fine, Debs. Really, just tired and hungover."

She hesitated, her bottom lip trapped between her teeth. "Ed, you doing anything later?"

He smiled at her again. How to put her off without being offensive? "To be honest, Debs, I plan to get royally shit-faced and then descend into oblivion."

"Oh." She pushed her face into a drink and looked away.

He returned to his paper, hoping she'd leave him.

"Hey," she said a minute later, "guess who I bumped into last week?" She held up her left hand, as if this should have told him something. He stared at the bandage around her wrist and shook his head.

"So I was in A&E after slicing myself – accidentally, of course – and I saw your ex there. Helen."

"Helen..."

"She fixed me up, asked how you were." Debs laughed. "Same as ever, I said, getting pissed and writing."

"Helen." He felt dizzy, then sick. He stared at the girl. "When did you say this was?"

"Last week. I–"

"Last week, and it's the 19th today?"

"Yes. So...?"

"Oh, Christ."

"Ed?" She stared at him, wide-eyed.

"Oh, Christ..."

He slipped from the stool, knowing that he was about to vomit, and rushed towards the toilets.

He made it just in time, ejecting five pints of foul-smelling gruel into a hand-basin, then moving to the next and splashing his face with refreshing cold water. He braced his arms against the basin and stared at the unfamiliar reflection of the young man he'd been.

Helen Atkins...

He'd met Helen in a Camden nightclub in late '94, and it had been the start of a torrid on-off-on affair that had lasted almost five months. Its beginnings had been inauspicious and unlikely, in that he loathed nightclubs – only going this time because he was drunk and the Waterstones crowd had dragged him along – and the short, stocky girl who insisted on dancing with him till throwing-out time had not been his type at all. Helen was his height and broad, with a round face, an English rose complexion and a devastating smile. She was from Bolton and worked in accident and emergency at St Thomas's, had a Northerner's down-to-earth stoicism and a nurse's industrial sense of humour. ("I only picked you up, Ed, 'cos I was gagging for a good shag." "And *was* it good?" "So-so.")

They'd shared a disdain of pretension, a love of Ealing comedies, and little else other than a magnetic physical compatibility that had made sex an uncomplicated, uninhibited joy.

She'd left him about half a dozen times in those five months, saying that she wanted someone who would commit to her: he'd refused to move in with her, he said, because he feared that the routine of domesticity might sap his will to write. She'd finally left him after objecting to something he'd written about her in a radio play. He'd called her politically naive, "The kind of institutionalised Labour voter who in the 'thirties would have voted for Mosley had he promised more meat in the pies." She had thrown the typescript at him and yelled that she never wanted to see him again. And she hadn't.

A month later Tash had called him into her tiny office at

Waterstones one Monday morning, sat him down, and said she had some terrible news. A folded copy of *The Sun* was on her desk, with a headline about the passenger plane that had crashed in the Swiss Alps.

Tash had indicated the paper and said, "Ed... That girl you were seeing... we met at a party... Helen Atkins –"

"What about her?"

"The air crash in Switzerland, Ed... I'm so sorry, but Helen was aboard."

Saturday the 20th of May...

He pushed himself away from the mirror, hauled open the toilet door and reeled through the pub. Despite having unloaded all the alcohol he'd downed that day, he still felt maddeningly drunk. He was aware of the surprised attention of Debs and the rest of the Waterstones' crowd as he staggered through the packed bar and out into the street.

He stopped dead, swaying in the hot sunlight, disoriented.

Where had Helen lived – where *did* she live?

He saw a double-decker bus stop-starting down the busy road, with the number 59 and its destination above the cab: Southwark, a couple of miles up the road...

He ran along the street, easily outpacing the bus, and arrived at a stop. Panting, he waited with a dozen others until the bus eased to a stop with a hiss of compressed air brakes and the door concertinaed open.

He bought a ticket to Southwark High Street and slumped into a seat as the bus lunged into motion.

He recalled the sense of cryogenic numbness that had gripped him when Tash passed him the paper. On an inside page he'd stared at a list of some of the known victims. *Helen Atkins, 25, a nurse from Southwark.* He'd hardly heard Tash tell him to go home, take a couple of days off... He'd gone to the pub instead and proceeded to drink himself into a grief-filled, tearful stupor.

If they had still been seeing each other, then Helen wouldn't have gone on the cheap package holiday to Rhodes; he'd detested flying, had done so only once before. They would have taken a holiday somewhere in Britain instead...

He'd attended her funeral, deadening his grief with the anaesthetic of booze, and had gripped her mother's hand and mumbled words of futile consolation to the inconsolable woman, who had so disconcertingly resembled her daughter.

Now it was Friday, May the 19th, and Helen had not yet taken the ill-fated flight to Rhodes.

The bus seemed to take an age to travel the two miles to Southwark High Street. It was Friday afternoon and the traffic was heavy. The heat was intense, making the journey even more unbearable. It didn't help that he'd thoughtlessly taken a seat at the rear of the bus, near the furnace heat of the engine. He got up and made his way to the door as the bus turned into the High Street and stopped. Then he was off and running... He slowed; there was no need to hurry, he told himself; he had a day before the flight.

But it had been many years since he'd last been to Southwark, to the cramped terraced house Helen shared with three other nurses. He had a dim memory of the street's appearance, identical to a dozen others in the area. Kennedy Street, he recalled... He stopped an old woman and shouted, "Kennedy Street?"

She backed off, staring at his vomit-flecked jacket, and pointed vaguely. "Third on your right, luv."

Richie ran on, panting and feeling a sensation little short of elation as he turned the corner into Kennedy Street and slowed to a fast stride, counting off the houses as he passed.

Number forty-four was identical to all the others, with an overgrown privet hedge, a painted gate, and lace curtains at the front window. Richie pushed through the gate and hammered on the front door.

He knocked again, cursing at the delay. He recalled there was usually someone at home, as the four nurses rarely worked the same shifts.

The door swung open and a young black woman, familiar but whose name he couldn't recall, stared at him. "Oh... Ed. This is a surprise."

"Is Helen in?"

"Ah... no. No, not at the moment."

"It's important. I need to see her. It's urgent. Do you know when she'll be back?"

The young woman considered, biting her lip. "Her shift finished at three, so she should be back by four."

He felt his wrist. Damn it, he wasn't wearing a watch.

She smiled. "It's twenty to four."

"Could I possibly – ?" He gestured past her, into the hallway.

"Ed, I'm not sure that she –"

"Please... It's important. Life or death, and I'm not exaggerating."

She relented, and Richie felt like kissing her. She stepped back and ushered him inside.

"I'll make you a cuppa, Ed. Black, isn't it?"

He sat down at the scrubbed kitchen table and stared around the small room. The blue and white hooped teapot was achingly familiar, as was the dusty cuckoo clock on the wall. How many times had he sat here, drinking tea and chatting to the other nurses while waiting for Helen to get ready upstairs?

She passed him a mug and he clutched it. "You're a star."

"Look," the woman said, moving to the door and turning, "Don't tell Helen I let you in, okay? Just say you found the door open. I've got to go."

"Is she...?"

"You hurt her, Ed," she said, and hurried out.

He stared at the black-and-white chequered linoleum, anticipating Helen's return and wondering what to tell her. His memory of her was twenty-one subjective years old, and gone was the affection he must have felt for her back then; all he recalled was that she was a good person, who had deserved better than him, and better than the end that awaited her.

He finished the tea. It was almost ten to four. The time dragged. His heartbeat was louder than the ticking of the cuckoo clock. He stood up, paced the small kitchen, then on impulse hurried along the hall, turned and climbed the stairs.

Helen's room was through the first door on the right. He stood on the threshold, staring at the double bed where he'd made love to her countless times, recalling the hammering on the walls, the cries of good-natured complaint from the other women.

A big navy blue suitcase stood at the foot of the bed, open but not yet packed. He wondered where she kept her passport; as a last resort, he could always steal it.

He heard the front door open. His heart skipped. He stepped back onto the landing and eased the bedroom door shut. He faced the stairs, expecting to confront her, but footsteps sounded along the hall as she made her way to the kitchen.

Dry of throat and with mounting apprehension, he made his way quietly down the stairs and approached the kitchen.

Helen stood with her back to him at the sink, filling the kettle.

She was still in her white uniform, and the silly origami hat that perched on her bountiful blonde curls. She had a thick waist and broad bottom and Richie wanted nothing more than to advance into the room and take her in his arms.

She turned, alerted by something, and stared at him in shock.

Her mouth opened. Her face wasn't as pretty as he recalled. She looked like a startled Cabbage Patch doll. "Ed."

He lifted a hand. "I'm sorry. I just need to warn you…"

"Ed, what the hell? How did you get in here?"

"The door was open."

She placed the kettle on the draining board. "What do you want, then?" That Lancastrian intonation, the broad vowels.

"I know this'll sound crazy…"

"I said I didn't want to see you again."

"This isn't about us."

"I'd had enough, I needed to get away."

"This is important."

"You can't just barge back into my life like this."

He held up both hands, as if to silence her; they were talking at cross purposes.

"Okay." He took a breath. "Helen, please listen to me. You're going on holiday tomorrow."

Her eyes narrowed. "And you're not coming with me, if that's your game."

He said, "Don't go."

"What?" She sounded incredulous.

He found himself blurting, "The plane crashes. You'll be killed, along with the other two hundred passengers."

"Ed… this is sick! What the fuck…?"

"Please, I'm begging you, Helen, don't take that flight. It crashes. I know."

She leaned back against the sink and crossed her arms under her large breasts. "Ed, I know you're afraid of flying, but this is insane…"

He felt like weeping. "This is nothing to do with me, for chrissake! Please, please listen to me. There's something wrong with the plane. A technical failure… I can't remember. But it crashes. Ploughs into a mountainside in the Swiss Alps. Everyone on board is killed… *will be* killed. Please, Helen, just say you won't go…" A thought occurred to him. "Listen… how much did the flight cost, the holiday?"

She shook her head, mystified. "*What?*"

"I'll pay for it. Everything. I'll give you the money to cover the cost – but just promise me you won't go. Please, Helen."

She pulled a strange face, torn by pity and exasperation. "Ed, you've flipped. You're mad. You aren't making sense. No," she said, shaking her head as if something had just occurred to her, "this is some game, isn't it? A sick joke to pay me back. You shit, you bloody little shit! How dare you!"

"No, please, Helen!"

"Get out of my way."

She pushed past him and stormed down the corridor. He thought she was heading for the front door, but he didn't hear it open. He leaned against the wall, resting his forehead against the embossed wallpaper. He felt a nebulous anger, directed at no one in particular, and at the same time a terrible sense of impotence.

He moved into the hall. She was in the front room, speaking on the phone.

He heard the receiver rattle in its cradle and pushed open the door.

Helen sat on the edge of the sofa, legs pressed together, hands clasped on her lap. She averted her face from him. The phone sat on the cushion beside her.

"Helen..."

She looked up at him, tears pooled in her eyes. "What are you trying to do to me, Ed?"

He murmured, "Save you."

"You just can't walk in and say these things." She stared at him. "What made you think...?"

"The plane crashes."

She shook her head, then said, more to herself, "How the hell can you know that?"

He wished, now, that he'd said there'd been a bomb threat made to the airline.

"Helen, why would I lie about this? I want to save you."

She stared at the carpet. "Get out," she said quietly.

"Helen... You mean a lot to me."

She looked up at him. "Mean a lot?" She sounded incredulous. "Then why the hell did you write all those awful things about me? Calling me an ignoramus, a fascist!"

"Helen, that wasn't about you. It... it was an extrapolation."

"Extrapolation my fat arse! I read those other pieces, the plays you wouldn't let me read. What did you call me, a 'fat northern bint obsessed with sex and shopping'...?"

"That was a character, speaking lines."

"But you wrote them, Ed. And they were based on me!"

246

"But they weren't meant to be vindictive."

"No? But this is, isn't it? You didn't like it when I walked out, so this is how you're getting me back."

"Helen…" he pleaded.

"Ed, the police are coming. If I were you, I'd just fuck off before they get here."

"Okay, I'm going. But please, Helen, for chrissake don't get on that plane."

"Fuck off! Just you *get out and fuck off!*" She surged to her feet, her face made ugly with rage and tears.

He backed from the room, turned and hurried from the house.

He found himself retracing his way back to the high street. He ran for a bus going in the direction of Brixton and jumped aboard, slumped into a seat at the front and wondered what the hell to do next.

In the morning he'd return to Southwark, plead with her again and if she still refused to see sense, take her passport…

But what if he was shunted back in time before tomorrow?

No, he had to do something now…

A bomb threat… If he contacted the airline and claimed there was a bomb aboard the flight… He could always exhort the airline to check the plane for a technical failure, but they'd be more likely to take notice of a bomb threat.

It occurred to him, as the bus carried him into Brixton, that he didn't know the plane's flight number, nor even the airline, just that it was heading for Rhodes tomorrow morning.

That was okay, when he arrived home he'd Google…

He closed his eyes. Except this was 1995, and the internet was hardly up and running, and all he had back at his room was a shitty little Amstrad…

So he'd find a travel agent in Brixton and ask them for the details of the flight.

He jumped off the bus in the high street and hurried along, searching desperately for a travel agency. Newsagents, bookies and greengrocers... and then, ahead, a Thomas Cook sign. He pushed through the door.

The woman at the counter smiled at him. She took in his dishevelled, sweat-soaked state, the reek of beer and vomit, and managed to maintain a professionally neutral expression. "How can I help you, sir?"

"I'd like details of a flight leaving tomorrow for Rhodes."

"And would you like to book a seat, sir?"

"No, I'd just like the details, please."

"One moment."

She consulted the monitor and tapped a few keys. "There is only one flight leaving tomorrow, sir, from Gatwick, at seven-thirty."

"And the airline?"

She peered at the screen. "That would be with EuroFly, and there are seats still available, if..."

"No, I just want the details. You don't happen to have the flight number and EuroFly's telephone number?"

"I can obtain them for you, if you'll just bear with me."

He slumped in the seat and closed his eyes. He felt suddenly hungry, and in need of a drink. After he'd made the call, he promised himself, he would buy something from Marks & Spencer's, along with some decent beer, retreat to his room, gorge himself and wait until he was snatched away from this time.

"Here we are, sir," the woman said, passing Richie the flight number and the airline's telephone number on a slip of paper. "Is there anything else I can help you with?"

"No, that's great. Thanks."

He left the travel agency and hurried along the street until he found a phone box.

He fumbled with a handful of coins, then found that he had to read the instructions as he'd forgotten how to use these damned antiquated things. Lift the receiver, insert the coins, dial the number...

He was sweating and his mouth was dry.

He dialled the number and closed his eyes as the dial tone rang out.

"You're through to EuroFly. How can I help you?"

Richie swallowed. How did you go about informing an airline that one of their planes would be carrying a bomb?

"I'd like to speak to someone in charge, please."

"Can I ask the nature of your call, sir?"

He took a breath. "I want to report a bomb threat."

A silence greeted his words. Then, "Would you please repeat that, sir?"

"Okay..." He repeated his words and waited.

There was a click on the line, and then a cool male voice spoke, "Good afternoon, sir –"

Richie interrupted. "There will be a bomb on one of your planes, flight number EF-43576, from Gatwick bound for Rhodes."

"Very well, sir," the voice was calm, professional, "and do you have the emergency code?"

Richie blinked. "Emergency code?"

This was 1995, he reminded himself; was the IRA still bombing mainland Britain?

"Very well, no code... Okay," the operative said. "Can I ask who is calling, sir?"

"That doesn't matter. But I advise you to cancel the flight to Rhodes."

"Sir, I wonder if I can establish..."

"Listen! Just fucking listen to me... There'll be a bomb on the plane to Rhodes tomorrow, and if you don't cancel the flight, over two hundred people will die. Have you got that?"

"I hear you, sir –"

"Good."

He slammed down the receiver.

Sweating, and feeling ridiculously conspicuous closeted in the kiosk, Richie shouldered open the door and stumbled out.

He leaned against the phone box and took deep breaths, calming himself. Would they ground the plane, he wondered, just because of a bomb threat? Perhaps, if he were still around in the morning, he should apprehend Helen before she left for Gatwick?

Recalling his promise to himself, he entered Marks and Spencer's, loaded up with food and beer, then returned to his room.

He ate slivers of smoked salmon and Mediterranean salad, washed down with three bottles of real ale, then stretched out on the bed and looked around the room. At the age of thirty-five, he told himself, this was what his life had amounted to. A shabby room in a run-down Brixton terrace, a few dog-eared possessions, perhaps two hundred pounds in the bank, two or three inconsequential radio plays accepted and three dozen rejected...

He contrasted this with what he would have, years down the line. A big barn conversion in a pleasant North Yorkshire village, paid for lock, stock and barrel, a nice car and thousands in the bank. As well as more than a hundred TV credits to his name. But, he asked himself as he stared at the ceiling, was I happy?

Was I ever happy?

How could he be, with a string of failed relationships behind him and the attendant weight of regret?

He pulled the photograph of Annabelle from his wallet and stared at it, reliving his too-short time with the first real love of his life, reliving that fateful morning.

He suddenly needed to talk to someone who would understand.

He sat up and looked around for his mobile phone, then remembered two pertinent details: he didn't have a mobile, and even if he had, he wouldn't have been able to contact Digby now because they were not on speaking terms. Richie didn't even know where his old friend was living these days.

There was no one he'd more like to talk to now than old Diggers.

He heard the doorbell ring and ignored it. It sounded again, and this time someone answered the summons. He heard a hushed conversation down in the hall, and then footsteps on the stairs.

Someone tapped on the bedroom door.

Two bulky men crowded the narrow landing, a young uniformed constable and a mean-looking bulldog of a brute in plain clothes.

The latter said, "Edward James Richie?"

"That's right."

"We've received complaints from a Helen Atkins... and something about a bomb threat. Would you happen to know anything about this, sir?"

Richie leaned against the door, his heart thudding.

He took a breath. "Flight number EF-43576, from Gatwick bound for Rhodes," he said. "If you don't do something about it, then it'll go down over Switzerland with the loss of everyone aboard."

"And how do you know this, sir?" Bulldog asked. "We understand that you contacted EuroFly and mentioned a bomb to a representative of the airline..."

"That was to get their attention, *your* attention, so job done." He smiled from Bulldog to the uniformed copper. "There's no bomb, but a technical failure will bring down the plane, with exactly the same result."

"Right, we're taking you in for questioning."

Bulldog gripped his upper arm and led him forcefully from the house and into a waiting, unmarked car.

He was driven at speed through the streets of Brixton and over the river. The car slowed in the congested traffic as it approached central London. Richie closed his eyes and leaned back.

The sunlight switched off suddenly and he opened his eyes to find they were motoring down a ramp into an underground car-park. He was manhandled from the car and across an expanse of oil-stained concrete to a lift where two uniformed officers were waiting. He ascended in the lift and was escorted through a maze of green-painted corridors to a tiny cell.

He was left there and the door locked behind him.

The cell was four metres long and two across, with a narrow bunk to the right with a thin foam mattress and a single rough blanket. The obligatory stainless steel bucket stood in one corner.

Richie sat on the bed and waited.

Half an hour later the door was unlocked and Bulldog appeared. He was back-lit by a naked bulb in the corridor, and Richie was unable to make out his features, just the bulging shape of his shoulders and neckless head.

"Up," Bulldog said. "This way."

He was led from the cell and along the corridor to an interrogation room consisting of a desk and three chairs. Bulldog motioned him to the single chair on the far side of the desk, and a second plain-clothes man entered the cell. If Bulldog conformed to the stereotypical image of an overweight, middle-aged career copper, the newcomer looked more like a corporate banker, with a sharp navy blue suit, patent leather shoes and collar-length golden hair. Richie guessed he was in his mid-thirties, and high up in the echelons of London policing, to judge from the way Bulldog deferred to him as they entered the room, nodding obsequiously and pulling out the second chair for him.

Banker leaned back and fixed Richie with a pair of ice blue eyes, his expression emotionless.

Bulldog gave his own name and that of the younger man, but Richie continued to think of them as the two Bs: Bulldog and Banker.

Bulldog referred to his note-book and said, "At approximately four o'clock this afternoon you entered the premises of forty-four Kennedy Road and there informed one Helen Rose Atkins that the plane she was due to take tomorrow at seven-thirty, flight EF-43576 from Gatwick, would crash over Switzerland due to a... 'technical failure.' You then made your way to Brixton High Street where you phoned EuroFly and informed an official there that there would be a bomb aboard the said flight. And yet you later told me that..." He glanced at his notes. "'There's no bomb, but a technical failure will bring down the plane, with exactly the same result.' Now, Mr Richie, just what the hell are you playing at?"

Richie clasped his hands on the table-top and looked from Banker to Bulldog. "I know for a fact that the plane will crash, as the result of a technical failure."

"Then why did you claim to the EuroFly official that there would be a bomb aboard the flight?"

"It seemed the best way to me to alert them to the technical failure – to get their attention. They can't let the plane take off. I... A friend of mine, Helen Atkins, she dies... *will* die, along with everyone else on board if the flight goes ahead."

Without altering his laid-back posture, Banker said, "'Dies'?"

"*Will* die," he corrected himself.

"A 'technical' failure, Mr Richie?"

"Some kind of mechanical fault," he said, "which will result in the plane losing height over Switzerland and crashing into a mountainside."

He had no idea why the plane had crashed, and hoped his explanation sounded nebulous enough to prompt the engineers to conduct a thorough mechanical inspection.

He wished, now, that all those years ago he'd read the report about the crash so that he'd be able to report its exact cause to Bulldog and Banker. But what, he wondered, if the crash was caused by pilot error?

"'Some kind of mechanical fault'?" Banker repeated, his tone dripping with sarcasm. "But you are unable to say precisely what *kind* of fault?"

"I just know that if the flight takes off, over two hundred people will die." He hesitated, then said, "Or it might even be down to pilot error..."

"Pilot error?" Bulldog echoed.

"But *how* do you know?" Banker asked.

"Do you promise me that you'll ensure the plane is thoroughly examined?"

Banker said, "It goes without saying that engineers will instigate safety checks, Mr Richie."

"And the pilots forewarned?"

Banker sighed. "How did you obtain your information, Mr Richie?"

He looked from Banker to Bulldog. He shook his head. "You wouldn't believe me if I told you," he said. "I know what will happen; I've told you, and now the onus is on you to ensure that the flight never leaves the ground. Or you'll have the lives of over two hundred people on your conscience."

Very deliberately, Bulldog leaned forward and said, "No, Mr Richie, you're the one who'll have their blood on your hands. And their deaths on your conscience. How do you expect us to believe a word you say if you refuse to divulge how you came by the information?"

"I *don't* expect your categorical belief; I'd be a fool to hope for that, wouldn't I? What I expect from you is a reasonable degree of doubt, sufficient for you to have the plane thoroughly inspected."

The two Bs exchanged a frustrated glance.

"Be reasonable, man," Bulldog snapped. "Tell us how you know!"

"As I said, you wouldn't believe me. And to be honest, I don't *need* to tell you."

Banker signalled to Bulldog, an almost imperceptible nod, and the two men rose without a further word and left the room.

A pair of uniformed constables led him back to the cell.

He sat on the bed and waited.

A sergeant brought him a tray of food: a mug of tea, a white bread cheese sandwich, and an iced bun; the latter such an incongruously dainty offering that Richie couldn't help smiling. He asked the sergeant the time, learning that it was much later than he'd assumed: almost eleven o'clock. Little wonder he felt so tired.

He drank the tea, ate the sandwich and the iced bun.

He wondered if he'd spooked Helen sufficiently for her to have second thoughts about taking the flight, but doubted it. Her salvation lay in the competence of the engineers, now. Or in the diligence of the forewarned pilots.

A while later the single, low wattage bulb in his cell was switched off; faint light slanted in through the grille in the door.

Richie lay on the bunk and, within minutes, was asleep.

He woke once to use the bucket in the corner, then went straight back to sleep.

When he awoke, disoriented, it came to him that he'd time-jumped again. Then he recalled his arrest and recognised the stark cell. The light came on, and in due course the sergeant brought him breakfast. A bacon sandwich and a mug of tea. No iced bun, this time.

He ate hungrily and drank the tea.

He'd forgotten to ask the time, and he cursed himself. The flight was due to take off at seven-thirty... Had the authorities heeded his warning and cancelled the flight? But if it had taken off, then how long before it would be over the Swiss Alps? An hour, two?

He took to pacing the cell, three strides one way, three back.

Had Helen left for the airport? Had the flight been cancelled? Was Helen dead, or alive? In his mind, she existed in an indeterminate state. Schrödinger's Helen, he thought, and laughed bitterly.

An hour later he was escorted from his cell to the interrogation room.

He was made to wait a long time, panicky with the need to know what had become of flight EF-43576, before Banker and a second, dark-haired plain-clothes man – no Bulldog, this time – entered the cell and sat down across the table from him.

Their expressions were eerily identical: set, frozen, and inimical.

"Mr Richie," Banker said, "thirty minutes ago, flight EF-43576 from Gatwick was reported missing over Swiss airspace, and just ten minutes ago we received confirmation that the aeroplane had pitched into a mountainside in the Alps."

Richie swallowed, unable to ask about Helen.

The dark-haired detective said, "How did you know, Mr Richie?"

Richie swallowed a sob and whispered, "Helen? Was Helen aboard the flight?"

The two men exchanged a glance, and then Banker said, "I'm sorry, Mr Richie."

He surged to his feet. "For chrissake!" he cried. "I *told* you! I warned you. I told you to make the airline check..."

"We relayed the information," the new man said, "and the engineers went over the plane with a fine-tooth comb. The flight crew and pilots were informed, and the engineers found nothing untoward. The plane was passed as airworthy."

Richie subsided back into the chair. "I *told* you," he said, all rage spent now. "I told you…"

Banker leaned forward. "How did you know, Mr Richie?"

He looked from one man to the other. "Go to hell," he said.

He was escorted back to his cell and locked in.

She was dead; fun-loving, filthily-humorous Helen Atkins, despite all his warnings…

He hung his head and wept.

A minute later, and without warning, he felt a pain in his head and was assailed by a familiar white light.

Extract from the review, by R.L. Davis in the TLS, *of* End Days *by Ed Richie, May, 2025*

...E<small>ND</small> D<small>AYS</small>, R<small>ICHIE</small>'S eighth novel, is a work of a writer at the height of his powers. Through the sympathetic characterisation of Sebastian Jones, a good man facing impossible choices in a near-future fascist state, Richie portrays the slow erosion of not only civil liberties, but simple human values of decency and goodness. It's a brilliant conceit – if not wholly original – to portray the moral and ethical decline of a nation through a cast of desperate characters. It is perhaps not surprising that the good man, Sebastian, is brought to his knees, by the end of this harrowing but gripping novel. *End Days* is Richie's latest, and best, work of fiction.

CHAPTER TWELVE

January, 2030

ELLA TOOK THE train from Oxford to Birmingham and changed for Edinburgh.

She was sure, as she boarded the second train, that she caught a glimpse of the thin man in the navy blue suit step aboard another carriage further along the platform. She found her seat and kept an eye on the far door, but the man didn't enter the carriage. She convinced herself that she was being unnecessarily jumpy.

She settled down for the long journey home as the train pulled from the station and rattled through the irredeemably grim industrial Midlands; even the snow here was old and grey, a shade lighter than the sky, adding another layer of misery to the depressing landscape. They passed through a wasteland of derelict factories and empty warehouses, overgrown railway junctions and moribund industrial estates – what had once been the beating heart of industrial England killed by the ongoing recession.

Grim-faced armed police patrolled the carriages, their presence subduing even further the already oppressive atmosphere. Ella read more of Ed Richie's journal and then, as the train was pulling into

Leeds station, got through to Douglas and asked if he could use the influence of ScotFreeMedia to get her an interview with the business tycoon Duncan Mackendrick.

Her editor peered up from her metacarpal screen. "Thought you were working on your book about this Richie chappie?"

"I am, and there might be a link to Mackendrick – but don't mention that to him, Douglas. Just say SFM would like to run a light lifestyle piece, okay?"

"I'll do my best, Ella. When are you coming back to work?"

"Not yet. You gave me a month, remember?"

Douglas grunted and cut the connection.

The train left Leeds and took the east coast line, the grim slurry giving way to an unspoilt rural landscape where the snow, freshly fallen, dazzled in the winter sunlight.

She looked ahead to her interview with the businessman – if Douglas managed to swing it – and wondered at the best way to broach the subject of Ralph Dennison and Ed Richie. Around 2000 Dennison had been lured from Omega-Tec by Mackendrick, and a few years later had vanished completely; in 2025 Ed Richie had likewise disappeared shortly after a series of meetings with his old student friend. There had to be a connection.

As to where the Emmi Takala painting hanging at Balliol fitted into the puzzle... At the moment, that was an enigma beyond her understanding.

The train stopped at the border crossing a few miles north of Berwick-upon-Tweed. The armed English police alighted and gathered on the platform, vaping while they awaited the next train south. Scottish customs officials made their way through the carriages, checking ID and welcoming travellers to the Independent Republic of Scotland. Ella was coming home.

KIT WAS IN the kitchen, cooking at the stove, when Ella entered and dropped her bags. "That smells good," she said.

"Chilli," Kit said. "Aimee just called to say she wouldn't be back until midnight, although her shift ends at eight. You hungry?"

"Famished. And I'd love a glass of wine. You?"

"Silly question." Kit returned to the bubbling pot.

Ella poured two large glasses of Chardonnay. "I'm sorry about Aimee, Kit."

"Don't be. I'm not, on reflection. It couldn't last. The age difference, for one thing, and we're very different people." She turned, leaned against the stove, and smiled across at Ella. "It was a relationship founded on pity on my part, and desperate need on hers, so how *could* that have lasted? It's a miracle we got through a year."

"You two still friends?"

Kit frowned. "I don't know. Aimee's all guilty silences, but she doesn't have the guts, or the experience, to tell me it's over. I think I'll have a quiet word with her, tell her I understand, and that it's time for both of us to move on."

Ella stared into her wine, ill at ease.

Kit served up the chilli and they ate to the accompaniment of Arvo Part's third symphony; her favourite, Ella recalled. She asked Kit how she was getting on as a paid employee of ScotFreeMedia, and the older woman laughed and said she was still adjusting to the liberty of not being censored.

"And the damned thing is, El, I'm catching myself self-censoring, which I did all the time back in the US. I've got to stop and remind myself, on almost every page, 'No, it's okay – I can say that.' And it's nice to be able to walk down the street, hand in hand with your lover... Well," she went on, "it *was*."

Ella changed the subject and told Kit about her trip to England and Finland, filling in the details she'd omitted during their earlier conversations.

"So what we have here," Kit said, pouring more wine, "is *three* disappearances. Ed Richie, Ralph Dennison, and Emmi Takala. And you think that what links them is your Scottish tycoon, Mackendrick?"

Ella pulled a face. "I'm not sure. Maybe. I might be wrong, but it's a strange coincidence that Dennison vanished after being wooed by Mackendrick, Richie met his old friend Dennison just before he too disappeared, and then last year Emmi Takala came to England to meet Ed Richie, according to her brother, and hasn't been seen since. And then her painting turns up at Balliol."

"And what did you say Dennison was researching at Omega-Tec?"

"According to Professor Sloane, the theory behind faster-than-light travel."

Kit laughed. "Well, there you are. Mackendrick has built a starship to take all his rich friends to another pristine world while global warming fries planet Earth. Quiz Mackendrick about that when you interview him, hm?"

"And get thrown out on my ear, sure."

Kit picked up the bottle of Chardonnay and shook it. "Empty. Hell, that didn't last long."

Ella opened another and they moved through to the lounge, where Kit had lit the wood stove and dimmed the lighting.

They sat on the sofa, facing each other..

They chatted for an hour, making headway into the second bottle while Kit outlined a couple of political pieces she'd written for SFM. She was quietly insightful, delineating what she saw as problems of European policy and suggesting her own solutions. Europe was facing a critical dilemma, she said: Brussels was treading a diplomatic middle-way between the US and China, acting as peacemaker between the two super-powers while attempting to finance its military response to an increasingly belligerent Russia. Kit suggested a stronger alliance with China, which would stymie Russian aggression and leave the US out in the cold.

Later, the conversation having moved on to mutual friends from way back, Kit smiled and said, "You know what? This reminds me of old times. You and me, a bottle of wine, good conversation."

"I've missed that," Ella said.

Kit regarded her. "What, the wine, the conversation, or you and me?"

Ella stared across at her old lover, seeing in Kit's homely face the faded beauty of the woman she had been. She said, deliberately, "The conversation."

Kit nodded, as if acknowledging that that was the answer she had expected. "Ella, has there been anyone you were serious about since we...?"

Ella shook her head, not at all liking the direction the conversation was taking. "I've been too busy..."

"What clichéd rubbish!" Kit laughed. "Listen to yourself. 'Too busy'? No one's too busy to find someone who means something to them."

Ella sipped her wine; she was drunk, but she needed to get even drunker. "And you think I deliberately...?"

Kit was staring at her. At last she said, "El, can I ask you a question? Do *you* understand why you left me back then?"

Ella found herself colouring. "I..."

"You never said," Kit said. "I mean, you never really told me the real reason. Just some bullshit about needing space."

Ella shrugged, uncomfortable.

"You know what I think, El?" Kit murmured.

Mute, Ella shook her head, dreading her friend's words.

"I think it had to do with losing Annabelle, all those years ago."

She didn't look up. "That's rubbish! How on earth could that – ?"

"When your sister was killed that day... her death killed something in you, too, El. You loved her; your loss affected your ability to give yourself. You know, the years we spent together... the years I showed you my love... I never felt that it was reciprocated. Can you begin to understand how that felt for me? Loving someone, but not having that love, that affection, returned?"

Ella shook her head. "That's too... too simplistic a rationalisation." She almost said too 'American' a rationalisation.

Kit shook her head. "Or perhaps..." she went on, "it's all to do with guilt. You have survivor's guilt, and it inhibits you, stifles your response to emotion. You can bring yourself to love anyone because you're aware, on some level, that your sister was denied it."

Ella looked up, anger flaring. "What's this all about, Kit? Why are you – ?"

Kit sipped her wine, then said, "Because I'd like us to start over, El. Pick up where we left off. I still feel so much love for you, you know? I think we can give each other so much."

She stopped talking and surprised Ella by standing up suddenly. For a terrible second she thought that Kit was about to step forward and kiss her, but to her relief she moved to the window and stared out.

A minute elapsed, and Ella found it impossible to break the silence.

"I'm turning in," Kit said at last. "I want you to think about what I've said, okay? We'll talk later."

Ella nodded fractionally, and looked away as Kit left the lounge.

She sat in the warmth for a long time, watching the snow fall outside, and finished the bottle of wine. She considered Kit's words.

Her wrist-com chimed: it was a text from Douglas, informing her that Duncan Mackendrick had agreed to see her for one hour at eleven tomorrow morning at his country residence, Hailes Castle, in East Lothian.

Still thinking about what Kit had said, Ella acknowledged the text and went to bed.

Extract of an email from Digby Lincoln to Ed Richie, 19th December, 2022

GREAT MEAL LAST night – we ought to get into Leeds more often.

Well, what I was fearing has come to pass, Ed. The pusillanimous BBC has called it a day with *The State We're In*. I had an email this morning – they couldn't even extend the courtesy of a phone call! That mealy-mouthed turd William Burton claims falling viewing figures… What I detest about the bastard, Ed, is that he can't even be honest. We all know that ministers in the alliance have been putting pressure on him and the board.

What now? I despair.

Reply from Ed Richie:

THE FUCKER! I'M coming over with a bottle of Glenfiddich.

CHAPTER THIRTEEN

December, 1988

"Don't try to move, mate."

He groaned and attempted to lift his head from the cold, hard ground. His skull throbbed as if someone had hit it with an axe. He was freezing and the pain in his head was agonising, and if that were not bad enough he had a debilitating hangover. He lay on his stomach, his cheek resting against an icy cobble. Wincing at the pain, he squinted along a narrow mews with posh houses on either side.

An ugly goblin squatted beside him, his face a gargoyle mask with missing teeth and sunken cheeks. He gripped a can of Tennant's extra strong lager in one hand and a smouldering roll-up in the other.

"Don't move, mate. There's an ambulance on the way."

Overwhelmed, he murmured, "Thank you."

"Good job I came along, mate, or you'd've froze to death. Reckon someone done you over. I saw you lying there and hammered on a door. Rich bastards wouldn't answer. Then a posh bint sticks her head out and asks what all the din was about. Practically had to beg her to ring an ambulance. Cunt!"

"Thank you."

"You'll be right, mate. Get you to hospital and checked over. You'll be fit and well in no time."

He managed to move his right arm and lodge it beneath his face, like a pillow.

"Remember what happened?" the goblin asked.

He thought about that. "No. Nothing."

"Out for a drink last night, eh? On your way home and some bastard jumped you, that's what it looks like to me, mate."

Last night? He tried to think back, work out where he'd been, what he'd been doing, but his mind was a complete blank. He had flashes, visions that came at him like images from a nightmare: a big house on the edge of moorland, a sun-lit island, a small house on a typical London street... none of them the stuff of nightmares in themselves, but nevertheless imbued with a terrible sense of foreboding.

"Good news is the bleeding's stopped. Reckon you were knocked out. Don't think your skull's fractured, not that I'm a doctor." The goblin thought this funny and chuckled to himself, then took a long swig of beer.

"Where am I?"

"Just off Fulham Broadway, mate."

"London..."

"'Course, London. Where'd you think you were?"

He tried to smile. "Really no idea."

"Here, you know who you are, mate?"

He thought about it, long and hard. Who was he? A name came to him. Ed... Edward? That seemed somehow appropriate. He wondered if he should be more concerned about his inability to recall anything about his past... but it seemed oddly irrelevant. He had the strange feeling that he was all right now, that he had somehow escaped from a nightmare that had been haunting him. But when he tried to probe the feeling, tried to work out exactly why this should be so, his mind slipped and slithered around a nebulous intuition that refused to coalesce into anything definite.

"Edward," he said.

"And I'm Migger."

Migger? What an odd name. Perhaps his ugly saviour *was* a goblin, after all?

"And here's the bloody ambulance at long last. Hey!" Migger yelled, standing up and waving. "Down here!"

The vehicle backed down the mews and stopped. The first paramedic in lemon-yellow fluorescent jacket examined his head, murmuring reassurances, while the second questioned Migger.

"Nasty gash. Concussion," the first paramedic reported to his partner. Then, "What's your name, son?"

"Edward."

"Edward. Got a second name, Edward?"

He said, "Can't think."

"Do you know if you're on any kind of medication, Edward?"

He tried to laugh. He had no idea. "I don't know."

"Okay, we'll take you in, get that head sorted out. Your memory will return in time. You'll be fine."

He heard a crackle as the second paramedic spoke into a cell-radio on his lapel.

He was eased onto a stretcher and lifted into the back of the ambulance, Migger in solicitous attendance, clutching his Tennant's.

"Thank you, Migger," Edward called out.

"Watch how you go, mate."

Then the doors were slammed shut and the ambulance drove off.

The medic unbuttoned Richie's jacket and shirt, and applied a monitor to his chest. He closed his eyes and heard a constant bleeping above the thrumming of the ambulance's tyres on the road. He felt a prick in the back of his hand, and soon the pain in his head abated; he seemed to be floating, in the grip of a wonderful lassitude.

The next thing he knew, with a dreamlike transition, he was being wheeled down a hospital corridor, watching the fluorescent strip-lighting strobe overhead. Then he was in a small room, sitting up, while a nurse did something to his head. He knew she was applying stitches to the wound, but the sensation wasn't at all as if needles were piercing his scalp: it was dull, and oddly reassuring.

"There, that's you patched up and as good as new."

He was back on a trolley, then, with something thick and padded beneath his head. At one point a medic shone a bright light into his eyes, left and right – and he experienced that odd, nightmarish intimation again, associating bright white light with something to be feared. Then the sensation was over and the young woman doctor was saying, "And I'm told you can't recall much at all, Edward?"

"No... Very little."

"Very well. Now, I'm going to ask you a few questions, and we'll see how we get on, hm?"

"Okay."

The doctor was slim and blonde and beautiful.

"How old are you, Edward?"

He shook his head. "Sorry..." He stared down at his hands; he was young – in his twenties? But why, then, did he have the odd feeling that he was much older than this?

"Do you know your address?"

"No, sorry."

"Are you from London?"

"Ah..." He thought not, though he had half an idea that he lived in the capital now.

"Very well..." She wrote something on a clipboard. "Now, can you recall if you have family, friends who might recognise you?"

"Family?" He thought hard. How did he know that his parents were dead, without being able to visualise anything about them? And friends? He saw a big, round-faced young man with a neat drooping moustache... His face was familiar, reassuring, but for the life of him Edward could not summon a name.

"One moment," the young woman said. She moved off; Edward saw her in murmured consultation with a grey-haired doctor, who glanced his way from time to time and nodded.

The woman doctor returned. "Very well, Edward. You're suffering from what I fully expect to be temporary amnesia. You've had a nasty blow to the head, but there should be no lasting ill-effects, so don't worry yourself on that score. Now, what we have to do is keep you under observation for a while. There isn't a bed free for the moment, unfortunately, so we'll have you on a comfortable trolley in the corridor for a short while. Do you understand, Edward?"

He nodded, then thanked her.

He lay back on the trolley and was wheeled into a quiet corridor and left. Someone asked him if he would like a cup of tea, and he said that he'd love one. A nurse took his pulse and looked into his eyes, then an auxiliary appeared with the promised cup of tea and assisted him into a sitting position so that he could drink it.

The tea was sweet and milky, and he thought vaguely that this was not how he liked it.

He wondered if he should be worried that the attack on him had left him with next to no memory – had, in effect, temporarily robbed him of his identity. The odd thing was that he felt no real concern. He wondered if this were a consequence of his head injury. At any rate, the lovely doctor had said that his amnesia would be only temporary. Not to worry.

But the niggling sense of unease that assailed him in waves from time to time whenever he tried to concentrate on his past – what did that mean?

Something moved him to slip a hand into the left pocket of his jeans... but his wallet was gone. He felt a surge of panic which, he was aware, had nothing to do with his money and credit cards. They could be replaced, after all.

He leaned to his left, eased a hand into his back pocket, guided as if by instinct, and surprised himself by finding something there: a bus-pass holder carrying the photograph of a slim, elfin girl. She appeared to be in her late teens or early twenties, with high cheekbones and a pointed chin. She was smiling out of the picture, directly at him, and his heart surged.

But who was she? Try as he might, he could not supply a name, nor any associated memories.

He returned the photograph to his back pocket, oddly comforted.

He was transferred from the trolley to a bed in a four-berth ward, and a curtain was pulled around the bed for privacy. At some point he must have undressed, or been undressed by a nurse, as he was wearing a ridiculous hospital gown now. Every twenty minutes a nurse came and checked his pulse, looked into his eyes, and asked him the same set of questions, to which he gave the same answers. He slept.

He dreamed. He was on an island, swimming in a lagoon with an impossibly pretty blonde woman… and then he was in a bar, drinking with the moustached young man he partially recognised… Then he was no longer in the bar, but talking to the slight, fair girl in the photograph.

He woke up suddenly.

Annabelle…

Was that her name? For some reason he was sure that it was, but he knew nothing about her, who she might be, or his relationship with her. He recalled the fading, elusive images of his dream, and felt that odd shiver of unease again.

Later, the attractive doctor returned.

"And how are we getting along, Edward?"

"Feeling a little better, thank you."

"And that memory of yours?"

He pulled a face.

"Again, I'm going to ask you a few questions, to see how you respond."

She went through the same questions: his name, his age, where he lived, if he recalled family and friends. Then she asked, "And do you know the date, Edward?"

Something moved him to say, "May…? May, 1995?"

She quirked her lips in a smile. "Not quite, Edward. We're getting a little ahead of ourselves, aren't we? It's December, 1988."

"1988?" Why did that seem wrong?

E. M. BROWN

"And do you know the name of the Prime Minister?"

"Ah…" He racked his brains. "Major? John Major?"

The doctor frowned. "Well," she murmured to herself, "that might be a *slight* improvement. No, Edward, it's Margaret Thatcher."

He repeated the name, aware that it had negative connotations, but was unable to define them.

"Very well, Edward, what we're going to do, seeing that you're coming along reasonably well, is allow you to get dressed and sit in the day room. We might have to transfer you to another hospital, but first: how about something to eat?"

He dressed and was assisted by an auxiliary to an open-plan area lit by shafts of wintry sunlight. He was alone here, and the auxiliary returned with a tray of food: he ate hungrily, lasagne followed by sponge pudding and custard, and more milky tea.

His head no longer throbbed and his hangover had worn off; he felt much better, if a little abstracted from the reality going on around him.

He withdrew the photograph from his pocket again and stared at it.

The sight of the girl, Annabelle, produced an ache in his heart, a sadness he could not source. He thought of the moustached young man, and knew – without quite knowing why – that the oddly familiar stranger might be able to help him.

He stood up and walked to the window. He felt well, and the last thing he wanted was to be transferred to another hospital. He was seized by the conviction that if he were to be allowed to walk the streets of London, the things he would see, buildings and landmarks, would somehow provide associations, somehow jog his memory.

He moved to the door of the day room and looked up and down the corridor. When there was no one around, other than a shuffling fellow patient, he walked casually along the corridor, came to a double door and pulled it open. As he stepped out into a wider corridor and followed an exit sign, he felt both a quick stab of guilt at absconding, and a sense of relief.

He came to the exit and left the hospital. The sun was still shining, but with little warmth; he buttoned his jacket and turned up the collar. He came to a busy main road and saw a sign for Trafalgar Square. He turned left and headed down Charing Cross Road.

He wondered if he should be more frightened, cut adrift in the capital without an idea as to his identity, other than the name 'Edward,' a set of vague, uneasy memories, and a photograph. The odd thing was that he felt liberated, free of fear: he tried to analyse why, and had the strange notion that he'd escaped something dreadful.

He was penniless in London, without a home to call his own or much of an idea who he was, and yet he felt curiously light-hearted, almost relieved.

He caught a fleeting glimpse of his ghostly reflection in a shop-window, and stopped to stare at himself. The face of a stranger stared back at him: young, lean, and handsome, with shoulder length dark hair and a five o'clock shadow like emery paper. The bandage around his head made him look like an Apache brave. He moved on, meaning to find a window where he could get a better look at himself, but found himself staring instead at a display in the window of a bookshop.

A pile of hardback books, as thick as bricks, formed a ziggurat, but it was the paperbacks piled at either side of it that caught his attention. The large format paperbacks were entitled *A Trove of Stars*, by Digby Lincoln. A sleek starship graced the cover, flying by what looked like an exploding planet.

Digby Lincoln...

On auto-pilot, he pushed into the warmth of the bookshop and moved towards the display. He picked up the thick, eight hundred page hardback and stared at the author photograph on the back of the book.

The photograph matched his memory of the Italianate, moustached young man. Digby Lincoln was his friend, his best friend, and his girlfriend was... He could visualise the elegant, sophisticated young woman, but could not recall her name.

Above Lincoln's name on the front cover a banner declared Lincoln a *New York Times Best-Selling Author*, and the blurb on the back announced that *A Trove of Stars* had been optioned by a major Hollywood production company. He flipped through the vast tome and was brought up short by the dedication. *To Ed Richie, the best of friends, whose harsh words made it work.*

Ed Richie. He was Ed Richie...

Something stirred in his sluggish memory. Why did the dedication sit so awkwardly with his elusive recollection of reading the book? He recalled commenting on the first draft of the novel, as if it were years ago, and felt uneasy at something. Digby Lincoln's reaction to his criticism?

His memories were maddeningly intangible. He replaced the book on the pile and knew that he had to find Digby, question him, and perhaps come to some understanding of who he was.

But where did Digby live? He racked his memory but came up with nothing.

He picked up the hardback; the publisher was Gollancz, and its offices were just around the corner in St. Martin's Lane.

He left the bookshop, stepped out into the freezing December street busy with tourists and Christmas shoppers. He asked a newspaper vendor for directions to St. Martin's Lane, then made his way back along Charing Cross Road, turned right and hurried along an alleyway. It was odd: he had no idea where he might live in London, or where Digby Lincoln lived, but he made his way around central London as if by instinct.

He came to the imposing glass-fronted tower block across the road from The Ivy restaurant and pushed through the swing doors.

A uniformed attendant behind a desk did a double-take at the sight of his bandaged head, and asked, "Can I help you?"

He found himself saying, "I have an appointment with my editor at Gollancz."

The attendant pushed a thick ledger across the counter. "Just sign your name, and put the time there."

He did so, thanked the man, and crossed to a silver-fronted elevator. A silver sign beside the lift said that the offices of Gollancz were on the third floor. He stepped into the lift and rose, rehearsing what he would say to the receptionist.

The lift bobbed to a halt and the door slid open to reveal a foyer with a potted fern and, opposite, a glass-plated door. Beyond, he made out a reception area, a high counter, and shelves of new books.

A young woman like a fashion model sat behind the counter; she gave him a dazzling smile as he approached.

He found himself stammering. "This is rather unusual... I suspect you won't give out the addresses of your authors, but I'm a good friend of Digby Lincoln. The thing is..." He smiled ruefully and touched the bandage, "I was mugged yesterday and... Well, I can't recall a thing... Could you possibly contact Mr Lincoln, explain that Edward Richie would like to see him, and ask if he could possibly come here?"

Throughout his explanation the woman had tried to maintain a neutral expression; by the end of it she was frowning. "Would you mind if I spoke with a colleague briefly, Mr Richie?" She pointed across the foyer. "Please take a seat."

He sat in a comfortable padded chair while the woman slipped from her high stool and pushed through a swing door to an open-plan office.

She returned with a tall, stooped, grey-haired man in his fifties who regarded Richie over a pair of half-moon glasses as if he were a vagrant. "Mr Richie, I understand?"

Richie stood and held out a hand. Reluctantly, the man took it.

He found himself repeating himself, gabbling that he was a good friend of the author Digby Lincoln and needed to see him. "Look," he said in desperation at the man's dubious expression, snatching a copy of *A Trove of Stars* from a nearby shelf and opening it at the dedication page. "Digby dedicated the book to me. Ed Richie. If you could just ring him and say I need to see him..."

The man looked from the dedication to Richie's bandaged head.

"Do you have any proof of identity, by any chance?"

"Look, I was mugged, robbed. My wallet was taken, and... to tell the truth I don't know where the hell I live. I need to talk to a friend. Please, if you could call Digby..."

"I'll see what can be done," the man said, and turning to the woman murmured, "Leave this with me, Amy."

The man returned to the office and Richie resumed his seat. He caught the young woman's glance and smiled, but she looked away quickly.

He was still clutching the copy of *A Trove of Stars*. He opened it and began reading.

The starship Prometheus *was still twenty-five thousand light years from the galactic core when xeno-biologist Lani Choudry made the discovery...*

He looked up as the swing-door opened and the tall man spoke quietly to Amy. To Richie he said, "We have Mr Lincoln on the phone, if you'd care to..." He indicated the receiver Amy was holding out to him.

Richie set the book aside and took the phone, smiling his thanks and relief.

"Digby...?"

"Ed? What the hell – ?"

"Digby, am I glad to hear your voice! Look, I need to see you –"

"Charles said something about you being mugged?"

"Knocked unconscious and robbed. That's not the worst of it. Seems as if..." Strangely, he was on the verge of tears. "Digby, my memory's gone. Can't even recall where the hell I live..."

"Right, I'm on my way. Sit tight and don't move. I'll be there in... say, thirty minutes. Is Charles still there?"

"Yes. Thank you!" Richie almost sobbed. He passed the phone to the tall man. "Digby would like a word."

He returned to the padded chair and sat down.

Charles spoke with Digby in lowered tones, then nodded to Richie and pushed through the swing door. This time, when Richie caught

Amy's glance, she smiled and said, "Mr Richie, would you care for a tea or coffee?"

"I'd love a coffee, thanks."

Digby would rescue him, fill him in. He had a vague notion that he, like Digby, was a writer, but certainly not a sci-fi writer as he'd never cared for the stuff. Digby would put him right. Presumably, in time, his memory would return.

Amy returned with a cup of coffee. Richie held it in both hands, warming himself and sipping: it was excellent. He smiled at the woman.

She said, "Digby's mentioned you, Mr Richie. He said you read the first draft of *Trove*. Weren't you at the launch last year?"

He smiled and indicated the bandage. "I might have been. So... Digby's a *New York Times* Best-Seller...?"

"He's big, Mr Richie. One of our biggest sellers in all genres."

"Good old Diggers. He's always wanted to write a sci-fi blockbuster, combining hard science with great characterisation." The words came, backed by knowledge, but from where?

"He's a fine writer, Mr Richie. I mean, I don't like SF, but I can read Digby's books." The phone rang and Amy said, "You're through to Gollancz. How might I help?"

Richie sat back and closed his eyes. The headache had ceased; all he felt now was a dull ache that seemed to permeate his entire body, and an all-encompassing tiredness. What he needed was a hot bath and a long, uninterrupted sleep.

He had a sudden flash vision: a view through a window – a study window, he somehow knew: sheep in a sloping field, a distant copse. And he knew, somehow, that he was no longer in his twenties. He was approaching sixty...

"No!" He sat up quickly, opening his eyes.

Amy looked at him, fixed a smile in place, and turned to her monitor.

The doors to his left swung open and Digby Lincoln stood there, staring at him. He wore an immaculate blue suit, a white silk shirt and red tie.

"Christ, Ed! What the hell...?" His friend winced at the sight of the bandage, sat beside Richie and gripped his arm.

Richie found himself holding Digby's hand and squeezing. "Great to see you. I... You don't know how..."

"You should be in hospital –"

"I was."

"This amnesia? What did they say?"

Richie tried to think back. "I... I'm not sure. I gave them the slip. I... I hope you don't mind me getting in touch like this? I needed to see a friendly face. I don't even know where the hell I live."

"Christ, Ed... You mean, you discharged yourself?"

"Not even that. Just walked out. I had to get away."

"Right. I know someone. I must have told you about Mick. He's a doctor, our neighbour. Anyway, I'll give him a call and have him give you a once over. You're coming back to my place."

"I don't want to impose..."

"For chrissake, Ed, don't be so bloody daft. Look, a taxi's waiting."

Digby crossed to Amy, spoke a few words, then took Richie's arm and assisted him into the lift.

"What the hell happened?" Digby asked as they descended. "You said you were mugged?"

"Apparently. Woke up this morning in a mews off Fulham Broadway. A homeless guy found me and raised the alarm. An ambulance took me to Charing Cross hospital."

"You've no memory of being attacked?"

"Nothing."

"Bloody hell, it was sub-zero last night. You could have frozen to death."

Richie laughed. "I was a bit cold when I came to my senses."

"And this amnesia... You said you don't know where you live? But you know *who* you are, of course?"

"Not at first. I mean, I knew I was called Edward... then I left the hospital. I saw your books in a shop and something clicked. I knew you were a friend."

"Thank Christ for that. You might've been wandering around all bloody day."

Digby escorted him from the lift, across the foyer, and out to the waiting taxi.

He collapsed into the back seat and they were whisked away through the streets of London.

"Just got back from a meeting, which is why I'm dressed like this." Digby indicated the suit. "Can't wait to change into jeans and a T-shirt. I called Pam, and she's bringing in a Thai, your favourite."

"Pam?"

"You know, Pamela?"

Richie shook his head. "I'm sorry."

"'Posh, pulchritudinous Pam, all pashmina and pearls,' you call her."

"I do?"

Digby smiled uneasily. "Don't worry, it'll come back to you."

He stared out at the passing traffic. "Caroline..." he murmured.

"What?"

Richie shook his head. "Strange... I could have sworn you were with Caroline. I... I can see her, but... No, it's gone."

He saw a tall blonde woman, smiling at him, but the image was as fleeting and elusive as something glimpsed in a dream.

Digby smiled again. "Don't know a Caroline, Ed. You sure she wasn't one of your many conquests?"

He turned to his friend. "Do you know if... I mean, am I seeing anyone at the moment?"

"You mean you can't recall Jemima?"

Richie shook his head. "No. Nothing."

"Perhaps that's just as well. It ended a month ago and you took it badly, hit the bottle. Right, here we are, home." He leaned forward and said to the driver, "Anywhere around here."

He paid the driver and helped Richie up the steps of a big townhouse on the corner of a tree-lined square. Try as he might, Richie remembered nothing of the house from the outside. And, on entering the lounge and sitting on a vast floral sofa, he recalled nothing of the interior, either.

"I'll fix us a couple of coffees and ring Mick," Digby said, and slipped from the room.

Richie stared at his hands resting on his lap, and turned them over to examine his palms. They were the hands of a stranger, and yet he must have seen them millions of times in the past... They should be familiar: why did he recognise areas of London, and know his way around, when his own body was unfamiliar to him?

He looked around the room. The painting above the mantelpiece was familiar, a rural French scene, which he recalled Digby buying on holiday. He recognised the statuette of a leaping hare, and the Hockney prints – and not just as cultural icons: he remembered seeing them before, on many a late-night session with Diggers. But surely not here, in this palace?

Digby returned with two mugs of coffee. He'd changed into faded jeans and a Levi's T-shirt; he looked slim, and no longer carried a beer belly.

No longer...? Now where the hell had that come from?

"Mick says he'll be around inside the hour," Digby said, passing Richie a coffee and sitting at the end of the sofa. "How are you feeling?"

Richie touched his head. "Fine. Well, there's no pain. A little tired."

"And... your memory? What can you recall?"

"Not a lot."

"Short-term, and long-term?" Digby asked. "I mean, can you recall coming here last week, the party for Pam's thirtieth?"

He shook his head. "Nothing. Not a thing." He sipped his coffee.

"Okay... what about your play?"

"My play?"

"You do know you're a writer?"

Richie nodded. "I... dimly, yes. But as to what I wrote..."

"Radio plays, Ed. Your second was broadcast a fortnight ago

on the Friday afternoon slot. Decent reviews. You don't recall coming round here last week, waving the letter from the production company who wanted to talk to you about your adapting it for TV?"

Richie smiled. "No, nothing."

"Bloody hell, Ed. Okay... you recall uni? Meeting me, the sessions in the Mitre, the parties in that grotty little house I rented off Mill Road?"

"The place with the patch of mould on the sitting room ceiling, like a map of Africa?"

"That's the place! So your long-term memories still function..."

"I remember the Mitre – and the first time I met you, wasn't it at a rehearsal for the Footlights? I froze like a dummy and you breezed through it like a natural."

Digby smiled. "And what I liked about you, Ed, was that you didn't bear a grudge in the pub afterwards. And it wasn't long afterwards that we discovered we both liked... Well, you tell me."

Richie pointed at him. "Plays, specifically for radio and TV. We both loved David Mercer's work. It's strange, the more I speak about it, Digby, the more I remember – the more things come back. But as to what happened a few days ago..."

"You went to a party at Camilla's last night – or you said you were going."

"Camilla?"

"That blonde with the studio flat in Chelsea you're nuts about – the blonde, not the flat."

"Means nothing to me."

He drank his coffee and considered the visions, the dream-like glimpses of Digby and himself as older men, and images of a foreign land he had never visited.

The doorbell chimed, distracting him.

"That'll be Mick."

Digby returned to the sitting room with a small, plump man in his late twenties, whom he introduced as Mick Canning. Dr Canning's casual dress – paint-stained jeans and a Hawkwind T-shirt – clashed oddly with his pristine black bag.

"So…" Mick said, sitting beside Richie on the sofa and peering into his eyes, "Digby says you were mugged, taken to hospital, from where you absconded. And your memory's shot, right?"

"Pretty much," Richie said.

"Long-term's okay," Digby put in, "but his short-term memory is kaput."

Canning opened his bag, pulled out an ophthalmoscope, and shone a bright light into Richie's eyes. "Do you have any idea when you were assaulted, approximately?"

"Not really. Late last night, early this morning, perhaps. I might have been to a party in Chelsea. I came to my senses somewhere in Fulham."

"Any double vision?"

"No."

"Vomiting?"

"No."

"No other episodes of unconsciousness since?"

Richie shook his head. "No."

"And did they x-ray you at – ?"

Richie shook his head. "No."

"So you have long-term recall, but no short-term, right? How far back can you go? How about last year? Christmas, say?"

Richie concentrated. "No, nothing."

"What's the last thing you remember?"

Richie thought back; it was like being asked to do an almost impossible physical exercise. He came upon a memory, and mentally winced… No, he didn't want to concentrate on that, still less talk about it.

"Memories of uni, with Digby, the pubs we went to…" He shook his head. "The odd thing is that ever since waking, I've had… I don't know what to call them. Visions. Almost like… images from a dream. Only…"

He looked from Canning to Digby.

"Go on," Canning said.

The more he thought about the visions, the clearer they became. "It's as if I have memories of being older... in my fifties. I'm... I'm living in Yorkshire, on the moors, and Digby's not far away... and we're both writing for TV. And then..." He shook his head. "And then it's as if I've flipped back in time, to my forties, on holiday on a Greek Island, and I met someone, a woman..." He gasped at how real the images became as he concentrated, and how they came with attendant emotions, a melancholy at the TV hack he would become, the love he felt for the blonde woman...

Canning heard him out, nodding. "The brain is a very strange organ, Ed. It's the part of the body we know the least about. You've had a hell of a blow on the head, and quite naturally it's affected you. You're suffering hypnagogic hallucinations – seeing images, feelings things, that haven't happened even though they seem real to you. I wouldn't worry about it; the mind does odd things to you when you're asleep, after all. Think of all the surreal dreams you have. This is something along those lines, though brought about by trauma." He replaced the ophthalmoscope in his bag and snapped it shut. "Right, what you need to do is rest. No alcohol. If you vomit or feel like vomiting, call 999. Have a restful night and – this is an order – first thing in the morning get yourself along to CC and explain the situation to someone there. There'll be formalities to go through, they might even prescribe medication, and they'll certainly make a follow-up appointment."

"I'll drive you there myself," Digby said.

"I've no doubt that, given time, your memories will return, Ed. Just take it easy." Canning rose and shook Richie's hand. "And do get yourself back to the hospital, okay?"

"I'll do that."

Digby saw his friend from the room.

"It's strange..." Richie said when Digby returned.

"What is?"

Richie shook his head, as if marvelling. "My 'memories' of the future, of my older self... they seem more real than my actual memories of university. I was *there, living as an older person, and* I have real nostalgia, real regret..."

"You heard what Mick said, the brain is a strange organ. What you mentioned reminds me, in a different way, of those people who claim to have regressed to previous lives and retain crystal-clear memories, recalling sights and sounds and smells... And yet it's all a product of the imagination." He tapped his head. "All happening up here."

"It's reassuring," Richie said, "but disconcerting at the same time."

"As Mick said, the 'memories' will fade and your short-term ones will return. It's all a question of time."

"I have one particular 'memory,' Digby. But it's of a past that never happened." He concentrated, and little by little it came back to him. "You showed me a draft of *A Trove*, and when I criticised it..." He shook his head. "You couldn't take it, Digby. You told me to get out, that you never wanted to see me again."

"I did? What a shallow, egotistical fool that Digby Lincoln must have been!"

"And yet..."

Digby smiled. "Ed, the fact is that, without your comments – which I admit were hard to take at the time – without your comments, *A Trove of Stars* might never have been published. It's an indication of a writer's maturity, Ed, when he can take criticism and use it." He smiled. "Now, I could murder a beer, and normally I'd feel guilty about drinking when you can't. Another coffee?"

A little later Pam arrived with the take-away, and Richie had the odd experience of spending the next couple of hours – over food and then coffee – in the company of someone who, he'd been told, he'd met many times before, but of whom he had not the faintest recollection. It must have been odd for Pam, too, being treated as a stranger by someone she knew well, but she put on a good show of accepting his reserve.

It was odd to watch Digby and Pam together, effectively, from Richie's point of view, for the first time: he was surprised at the pair, at how Pam's extrovert character contrasted with his friend's introversion; she was bubbly and loquacious, while Digby was much quieter, more self-contained. Opposites attract, he thought.

Pam took herself off the bed at eleven, and Digby fetched more beer from the kitchen.

"Now, Ed, I'm going to ask you what you thought of Pam, and see if it's the same as what you told me originally, when you met her back in spring."

Richie winced. "Was I uncomplimentary?"

"Not exactly," Digby temporised. "Go on, then."

"Well, she's nice. Obviously very bright, and talented."

"I sense a *but* coming."

"Not a *but* at all. That said... she's not the type of woman you usually go for. You usually like less... demonstrative types. And tall women."

"You see... your memory is coming back."

Richie frowned. "The odd thing is... I have nothing at all to back this up with. I can't recall a single one of these tall, quiet women. Except..."

"Yes?"

"No, it's nothing."

"You mentioned someone called Caroline."

Richie sat in silence and stared across the room to the painting above the hearth. He said, "The odd thing is that this Caroline seems more real to me than any of the others. And she's no more than a product of my imagination."

They talked of other things for a time, and on Richie's prompting Digby outlined the plot of his next novel; usually he was loath to discuss his work... another detail that Richie remembered.

Towards midnight, when Richie thought that his friend was about to suggest they turn in, he said, "There's a cut-off, Digby. I've just realised it. Earlier, when Mick asked about the long-term memories...

The last thing I recall wasn't university."

Digby looked at him. "What was it?"

Richie slipped a hand into his back pocket and pulled out the plastic bus-pass holder containing the photograph.

He stared at it until he felt tears stinging his eyes, then passed the photo to Digby.

His friend took it in his thick, clumsy fingers and stared down at her smiling face in silence.

"Annabelle..." Digby said.

Richie said, "I recall everything about that last day, Digby. Everything. Every last detail. What I said to her, and how she responded. It's as if it happened yesterday. And I can feel the guilt."

"Ed... Ed, for chrissake. We've been over this time and time again."

"Have we?"

"Believe me, we have. And it wasn't your fault."

"But it *was* my fault, and I know it. And nothing I can do can make up for it." He took the picture from Digby and slipped it back into his pocket. He wished he could return the memories just as easily to wherever they came from.

"Strange, isn't it, Digby, that I recall nothing else from around that time, but that very last day is branded on my memory."

"Perhaps it's not so very strange at all, Ed..." Digby said.

They talked late into the night, discussing Annabelle's death, and Digby resorted to the platitudes he must have used again and again in the past, no doubt to little effect; and they made not the slightest difference this time, either.

Richie went to bed at one and slept well, waking only once at dawn to use the toilet, then sleeping again until bright winter sunlight woke him at nine o'clock. He rolled out of bed and dressed, and a phrase came suddenly into his head. *The first day of the rest of your life...*

He was looking forward to going back to the hospital, perhaps receiving medication. He wanted his memories back, which in turn would return his *life* to him.

He smelled coffee and bacon, and realised he was very hungry.

He made his way to the bathroom, then halted... He felt suddenly unwell, and it came to him that he had to alert Digby: he had to get to hospital, and immediately.

He felt a strange pain in his head, then staggered as a white light hit him full in the face.

From the Daily Mirror, *22nd July, 2030*

Whatever Happened to Ed Richie?

IN JULY 2025, best-selling novelist Ed Richie vanished without a trace from his luxury Yorkshire barn conversion in the village of Harrowby Bridge. Police were mystified at the time, and are no closer to solving his disappearance five years later. Detective Inspector Ralph Graham, from Leeds CID, who led the investigation at the time, said recently, "Sadly, we've had no further leads on the whereabouts of Mr Richie."

Speculation is rife as to the writer's fate. A doyen of the Left, he was reviled by the Right for his outspoken criticism of the Tory party and the rise of the UK Front, and some have speculated that Mr Richie might have been the victim of far-right thugs...

CHAPTER FOURTEEN

January 2030

Ella woke early the following morning and left the house before Kit or Aimee were up and about. She breakfasted on coffee and a granola bar at a café in Waverley station, and took the ten o'clock train out to Haddington on the new line. Last night she'd spent an hour Googling the man she was about to meet.

Duncan Mackendrick had made his millions in the information technology boom of the late 'nineties, selling a controlling share in his cyberware company to the Chinese in 2008. He was accused of selling out at the time, and pilloried as a traitor by the British press. Since then, however, he'd used his millions to start a dozen new companies and fund as many lines of scientific research, all the while pouring funds into the Scottish National Party. Now, with the SNP governing the country, he acted as their official scientific advisor and kept his fingers in a dozen high-tech pies. In his mid-sixties, online photographs showed him to be a stout, grey-haired man with the weather-beaten face of a Highland farmer – an image he was fond of playing up to, as his ancestors had been crofters on the Isle of Lewis.

The train drew into Haddington station, just to the south of the county town, and Ella took a taxi out to Hailes Castle. She wondered what her imminent interview might yield. The businessman would deny all involvement with the disappearance of Ralph Dennison and the whereabouts of Ed Richie, of course; but Ella liked to think she could tell when someone was lying or concealing the truth.

The taxi passed through a security check at the gate, rolled up the long gravelled driveway, and deposited her before the great oak door of the refurbished fourteenth-century castle. Through small windows in the rebuilt east and west wings, she could see open-plan offices and people working at softscreens or standing in consultation before wallscreens. As well as being Mackendrick's country residence, the castle was the hub of his business empire.

The thick timber door swung open before she was halfway up the steps and a bearded young man in a T-shirt bearing a mathematical equation waved her in. "Ella Shaw? You're a bit early, but Mac'll see you. I'll show you up."

That was something else she'd read in his online profile: Mackendrick didn't stand on ceremony. He ran his business on democratic lines, liked to be known as 'Mac,' and had a healthy disregard for punctuality.

He led her up a timber staircase, and at the top hammered on a door, opened it without awaiting a reply, and ushered her inside. He closed the door behind Ella without announcing her arrival. She found herself in a large room with windows on three sides, giving magnificent views of the surrounding snow-covered countryside.

She didn't see Duncan Mackendrick until he extricated himself from the depths of an ancient settee, dabbing his mouth with a napkin.

"Caught me indulging in my daily ritual – tea and tattie scones at ten-thirty." He spoke in a soft Highland burr, as welcoming as his smile. He shook her hand. "Now, we could stay in here and chew the fat over tea, or how about a turn about the garden? It's such a lovely morning with the sun shining and frost on the ground, why not take advantage of it, hey?"

When she smiled her assent, he led her not to the door but to a lift in the corner of the room. He grabbed a threadbare overcoat from the back of a chair, along with a stout walking stick, and limped into the lift. They descended, and the lift door opened onto a gravelled path at the rear of the tower. Mackendrick pointed his stick at a flight of steps that led down into a vast sunken garden.

They walked across the lawn, leaving dark footprints in the frosted grass.

"Douglas said you wanted a lifestyle piece," the businessman said. "Five hundred words of cliché on how the reclusive, self-made billionaire bachelor spends his days in the lap of luxury, hey?"

"Well..."

"It's been done before a hundred times, with varying levels of vitriol depending on the political bias of whichever paper or newsfeed the reporter is employed by. What I don't understand is why ScotFreeMedia sends Ella Shaw to do the dirty work. Come to that, I don't understand why Duncan wants a lifestyle piece on me. He knows me personally and could write the rubbish himself. Down here."

She followed him down another shallow flight of steps to a flag-stoned area surrounding a circular pond, its surface sealed with a sheet of fractured ice. They walked around the pond, Ella matching her pace to Mackendrick's limp.

He glanced at her, sideways. "So, Ms Shaw, what kind of piece *do* you intend to write?"

"You're notoriously reticent when it comes to speaking publicly about the various scientific projects you fund."

"And rightly so. These things are often top secret. Don't want our rivals to get their dirty mitts on our hard-won knowledge, do we?" He stopped and stared at her. "So that's why you're here? You really want to know about the research?"

"Not all of it. Just certain aspects."

Mackendrick led her away from the pond and down a long, paved walkway between frosted lawns.

"'Certain aspects,'" he said, almost to himself. "Now, I wonder what you mean by that?"

She took a breath, aware that she was taking a risk. "Okay... I'd like to know a little about the research done by the scientist Ralph Dennison, and what bearing it has on the disappearance of the novelist Ed Richie."

She watched him closely as she spoke, but his expression didn't flicker in the slightest.

"And what makes you think I have anything to do with these people, Ms Shaw?"

"I have it from a reliable source that you hired the services of Dennison way back in 2000. He has links with Ed Richie, and met the novelist a number of times just prior to Richie's disappearance five years ago."

"Who told you this?"

"I can't reveal my sources," she said.

Mackendrick seemed unperturbed. He pursed his lips, staring across at the distant hills. "What do you know of Dennison's work?"

She blinked, surprised. She had expected a blanket denial from the businessman, followed by a swift dismissal.

"I understand that his work for Omega-Tec, back in the 'nineties, involved the theory behind faster than light travel."

He smiled at her. "That's highly classified information, Ms Shaw. I think that perhaps only twenty people in England and Scotland, and the rest of the world, know that."

"So..." she ventured, "you're funding work in this area?"

He refrained from replying as they walked on. At last he said, surprising her, "You're a Scottish national, aren't you?"

"That's right."

"Came up here in 2020, naturalised a couple of years later. I like what I've read of yours."

Ella wondered where this might be leading.

He turned to her. "Who do you think our enemies are, Ms Shaw?"

The question wrong-footed her. "Why... principally the US and Russia."

He nodded. "And when you say the US, you also mean their lapdogs, the UK Front. The difficulty of having the enemy on your doorstep, so to speak, is that infiltration is very difficult to prevent, or detect. We've shared such a common culture for so long that chameleons find it easy to adapt." He smiled at her, then laughed. "Forgive the metaphors, Ms Shaw. What I mean to say is that I have to be very, very careful."

He swivelled and gestured back at the castle with his stick. "The chill's getting to my bones. Time I was getting back inside. It's been pleasant chatting with you, Ms Shaw."

And that's it, she thought; a polite brush off, rendering her trip out here futile. Mackendrick certainly had *something* to do with the disappearances of Dennison and Richie, but why admit as much to her?

Instead of returning to the tower, Mackendrick walked her around the castle to the gravelled drive.

He turned the lapel of his tweed coat and spoke into a tiny microphone, "Greg, would you be so good as to drive Ms Shaw back to the station? Oh, and if you could give her one of my cards."

They waited before the steps, Ella wondering where she might go next in her investigation. Back to tracking down and questioning Richie's lovers?

Mackendrick said, "Give me two days, Ms Shaw, so that my people can do the requisite background checks."

She peered at him. "And then?"

"And then I might be willing, once I am assured that I can trust you, to tell you a little more about certain aspects of the research I fund."

"And about the disappearances of Richie and Dennison?"

He ignored her. "Ah, here he is..."

The bearded young man emerged from the castle and hurried down the steps. He passed Ella a silver metal rectangle, embossed with Duncan Mackendrick's name and contact details.

"Use this number to give me a call in two days," Mackendrick said. "Have a pleasant journey back to Edinburgh."

They shook hands, when all Ella wanted to do was hug the businessman.

Greg led her across to a small electric runabout, and as they rolled down the drive he said, nodding to the card in her hand, "You're privileged. Mac doesn't give out many of those."

She nodded. "I think we got on very well."

"Mac's astute. He makes snap judgements about people. If he likes you, you're in."

As they turned along the old B-road towards Haddington, Ella stared at the steel card in her hand, then slipped it into the inner pocket of her parka. She was excited, but cautioned herself about getting too carried away; the businessman might tell her something about his research, eventually, but whether that might lead her to discovering what had happened to Ed Richie was another thing entirely.

"Hello," Greg said. "Looks as if there's been an accident."

Ella looked up. A car was slewed across the road before them, its driver staggering from the vehicle with a hand pressed to his bloodied head. She had no idea what struck her as odd about the scene – only later did she realise that there was no other vehicle in sight, and that the injured driver was vaguely familiar.

Greg braked and reached for the door.

Ella said, "Wait..."

"What?" He opened the door. "He's injured –"

Greg jumped out and ran towards the car.

Only when he reached the driver, and knelt over him, did Ella recall where she'd seen the middle-aged man before: on the train, and at the airport terminal.

But by then it was too late. The man lifted a hand and sprayed something into Greg's face. The young man fell as if pole-axed.

At the same time, someone hauled open Ella's door. She turned, crying out, and a balaclavaed figure raised a canister and sprayed her in the face with something foul-smelling and acidic. She felt dizzy, then sick. Hands grabbed her, pulled her from the car and carried her along the road: she guessed there was more than one person. She heard a door open, and was lifted into a confined space that stank of oil and petrol. Someone forced a hood over her head and pulled a cord tight around her neck. She heard an engine start up, the floor vibrating under her cheek.

Someone bound her arms and legs as she lay on her left side. She was in the back of a van of some kind, aware only of the sound of its engine and the strange sensation of passing in and out of consciousness.

At one point she came to her senses as the vehicle passed over what might have been a speed bump. She had no idea how long she'd been in the van, and no way of telling. She wanted to struggle, but the drug made her sluggish. Even rational thought, as she tried to work out why she was being kidnapped, was too much of an effort.

Later she heard traffic noises, and the vehicle stopped and started, and she guessed they were driving through a city: Edinburgh. The engine stopped and the van came to a standstill. Ella tensed herself for whatever might happen next.

The doors opened and she felt hands on her upper arms, hauling her out. She was placed on her feet and someone untied the ropes around her ankles. Then two people gripped her arms and dragged her, staggering, away from the van. The only indication of her environment was the texture of the ground underfoot: from the cold, gritty concrete of what might have been a garage, to the creak and give of old floorboards. She heard a door open and was assisted through it and made to sit on what felt like a dining chair. Someone secured her arms and legs to the chair with parcel tape. Footsteps retreated and a door closed.

She sensed that there were people still in the room, watching her. She felt terribly vulnerable.

For the first time since her abduction, she found her voice, "What do you want?"

She heard whispered voices, away to her right, and then someone was unfastening her wrist-com and going through the pockets of her parka and jeans.

"What the hell do you want from me!" she cried.

She heard footsteps, a door open and close, and then silence.

The only sound, as she sat bound hand and foot to the chair, the hood over her head, was the pounding of her heartbeat. The air was cold; she was aware of the faint scent of machine oil. Was she in a garage?

She struggled to free her hands and feet from the tape, but they were tied tight and there was no way she might free herself.

She felt a spasm of panic when she realised she wouldn't even be missed until she failed to return home that evening.

She heard the door open.

Footsteps approached: more than one person. She heard a chair being placed before her, positioned exactly, and then another. Two people, then. This was the interrogation.

A man's voice, with an English accent, "Now, Ms Shaw, in your own words, tell me about your meeting this morning with Duncan Mackendrick."

"Take the hood off and I'll talk."

"As if we'd be so foolish. You'll tell us what we want to know, Ms Shaw, if it takes all day... or all week."

"Like hell."

"Why did you see Mackendrick?"

She hesitated. "An interview."

"About what?"

"A short lifestyle piece. A filler for SFM."

The man laughed, cynically. "As if the esteemed journalist Ella Shaw would do lifestyle fillers for SFM."

"Needs must."

"Don't give me that, Ms Shaw."

She heard whispering, as the man consulted with whoever accompanied him.

He said, "A week ago you interviewed the television writer Digby Lincoln, and then the actress Samantha Charlesworth. The following day you flew to Finland and spoke with the brother of the artist, Emmi Takala. On returning to England, you interviewed Charles Sloane at his college in Oxford."

"What about it?" she asked, trying to keep the tremor from her voice.

"Why, Ms Shaw? Why your interest in these people?"

Inside the hood, she licked her lips. "I'm writing a book, the biography of the novelist Ed Richie. I'm interviewing the people who knew him: his friends, acquaintances, lovers."

"I wasn't aware," the man drawled, "that Ed Richie had any connection at all with Duncan Mackendrick."

Ella thought fast. "That wasn't anything to do with the book. As I said, it was a filler for SFM."

"You're a far from convincing liar, Ms Shaw."

The man and his accomplice conferred again, and this time Ella heard the second person's voice. The tone was low, and with a terrible shock of recognition Ella realised that she had heard the voice before: a woman's voice, American.

She must not, she knew, give any indication that she was aware of the identity of the woman. If she did, then she might never get away from here.

The man said, "What do you know about the work conducted by the scientist Ralph Dennison, Ms Shaw?"

She was about to deny any knowledge of the scientist's work when she heard a cry from outside the room. The door burst open and someone yelled, "Move it!"

A window to her right shattered. Something hit the floor and skittered across the bare floorboards.

The man hissed, "Christ..." and she heard chairs falling as the pair jumped to their feet. "How the – ?"

The man grabbed her arm and attempted to drag her from the room. He stopped, then cut the tape binding her legs. Ella stood, twisting to free herself from his grip. She felt the woman's hands clutching her shoulders, grunting viciously as she steered Ella towards the door.

Crying out, Ella swung her arms, still attached to the chair, and more by good luck than judgement hit the man. She heard his grunt as he staggered across the room. She swung again, freeing herself from the woman's clutches. She stumbled against the wall and slid to the floor, the chair dragging painfully on her wrist. She managed to pull her hands free from the twisted tape; she was reaching to remove the hood when she heard a second window smash. Something bounced across the floorboards and came to rest very close to her.

Then she was deafened by an explosion, the shockwave knocking her sideways. She lay very still, stunned.

She heard the hissing of something like escaping gas, and above it the sound of the woman, sobbing.

Then an acrid stench hit her and she passed out.

SHE WOKE TO find herself in a wonderfully warm bed.

She felt as if she were floating, and wondered whether this was the effect of the mattress or of the gas still in her system. She struggled upright and looked about her. She was in a Nordic timber-clad room, with a big picture window at the far end overlooking a scene of snow-capped mountains and a lake. She wondered where she might be – Scandinavia, the Scottish Highlands? Next to the bed was a chair with her clothes folded and piled on it; and on top of her parka was Duncan Mackendrick's silver card.

She lifted her right hand. Her wrist-com was missing.

She tried to sit up further, and swing herself out of bed, but was overcome with dizziness and passed out.

She was not alone in the room when she came to her senses again.

A small blonde nurse stood at the foot of her bed, reading from a softscreen. She smiled when she saw that her patient was awake.

Ella struggled into a sitting position, and the nurse hurried to bank her pillows.

"Where am I?"

"You're fine," the woman said. "You're safe now."

"But where...?" she began. "Who...?"

She felt drowsy, closed her eyes and slept.

When she next came awake, a familiar figure in Harris tweeds was seated beside the bed.

Mackendrick took her hand briefly, squeezing her fingers. "Good to have you back in the land of the living, Ms Shaw."

"Where am I?"

"I am afraid your whereabouts, for reasons of security, must remain a secret."

"My wrist-com...?"

"Again, for security, Ms Shaw, it must remain in our safe-keeping."

She closed her eyes, framing her next question. She still felt drugged, drowsy. "Who...?"

"Who snatched you? The Americans, of course. With the help of the English."

The Americans... She recalled the voice she'd heard while being held captive, and felt sick.

"Aimee Carter," she said.

Mackendrick looked surprised.

Ella explained. "While I was being held, I heard them talk. I recognised her voice."

Mackendrick said, "The woman using the name Aimee Carter was an employee of the US government, initially tasked with keeping tabs on your friend, Kit Marquez. When you told Kit Marquez about Ed Richie and Ralph Dennison, quite naturally Marquez had no reason to suspect Carter. She must have mentioned your enquiries to Carter, who relayed them to her handlers. The Americans are very interested in Dennison's whereabouts."

She thought of Kit, and Aimee's betrayal. "Have you informed Kit about – ?"

"Carter was arrested yesterday," Mackendrick said.

"But how long have I – ?"

"You've been unconscious for almost twenty-four hours." He pointed across to his card on top of her piled clothes. "And it was only thanks to the card that we were able to trace you."

"The card?"

"A surveillance device. When the police informed us that Greg had been found unconscious by the side of the road and that you had been abducted, we instituted a search for you. We were able to track the card, and I had a team effect your release."

She tried to sit up. "Greg...? How is he?"

Mackendrick nodded. "He's fine, Ella."

She collapsed back against the pillows. "The card..." She smiled. "That was devious of you."

"We needed to listen in on what you might have said to Douglas, and anyone else, when you returned to Edinburgh. While you've been unconscious, we've been able to delve pretty comprehensively into your past."

"And?"

Mackendrick smiled. "And I'm pleased to say that my initial judgement has been proven correct. So..."

"Yes?" she said, her voice catching.

"So I can tell you what happened to Edward Richie," he said. "I'll leave you to get dressed now, Ella, and then I'll take you down to the lab."

He moved from the room.

I can tell you what happened to Edward Richie...

Ella climbed from the bed and dressed quickly.

From the Breitbart News *online, 17th October, 2028*

Gone and Forgotten...

REMEMBER FAT-CAT HACK Ed Richie, caviar-commie beloved of the liberal chattering classes for his overblown, overlong novels satirising all things good and patriotic? No, you probably don't. He might have been a best-seller back in the day, but few read his tub-thumping agit-prop in these enlightened times.

Well, Richie did a bunk in summer 2025, vanishing from his North Yorkshire pad, never to be seen again. Some say he saw the writing on the wall, the fall of his beloved Labour party and the rise of the Right – so he did a runner with all his ill-gotten gains.

And get this. Our Asian reporter has credible info that Richie, 70, has been seen living it up in Phuket, Thailand, indulging his passion for prostitutes and... wait for it... lady-boys.

In fact, check out the photos, right, of handsome fat-cat Richie as he was in 2005, and what he looks like now, bloated on the good life and weighing in at three hundred pounds...

CHAPTER FIFTEEN

June, 1983

WHEN RICHIE CAME to his senses he was lying in a comfortable bed. He knew from the position of the pale grey rectangle of the window to his right that he was no longer in Digby's Islington house.

He had all his memories intact. He recalled himself at fifty-six, a journeyman TV writer with a house on the Yorkshire moors; he recalled sessions with Digby at the Black Bull, and his last row with Anna Greaves, where all this had started...

He recalled finding himself shunted back in time a year, and his fear that he was going mad; and then the second time-jump back to 2013. He remembered the holiday in Crete, and how he had manipulated events so that he'd met Emmi Takala earlier than he had on the first occasion; he recalled their love-making in the lagoon, and later in bed at her farmhouse... She had stunned him by saying that he was part of some experiment, as she was herself. But had that been his own imagination, playing tricks?

He recalled 2002, and Laura and the party at Diggers' Islington pad. He remembered awaking in 1995, attempting to save the life of Helen Atkins, and failing... and then waking from concussion in a Chelsea mews, in an altered time-line where Digby Lincoln had taken his criticism of *A Trove of Stars* on board and become a successful science fiction writer.

But the question he asked himself, again and again, was: was any of this *real?* Was he actually being shunted back in time to inhabit his own body at various ages, or was it all the delusion of a comatose mind?

He lay very still and tried to discern exactly where he might be; the room was indistinct in the pre-dawn darkness. He made out the window, and the table before it. Next to the bed was a small cabinet, with a thick book beside a digital clock. The clock read 6:20, and gave the date: 20/06/83.

He lay paralysed, sweating, grappling with his thoughts.

He was in the tiny three-room apartment in Hackney he'd shared with Annabelle from July 1981, after they'd graduated from university, until June 1983.

The happiest time of his life, until the morning of the 20th of June. *This* morning...

He felt sick at the realisation of where he was, *when* he was... He could not bring himself to turn his head and stare at the young woman sleeping beside him in the darkness.

Annabelle? Could it be? Was she really there, beside him, alive again?

Was it truly the 20th of June, or was his mind playing one last, sadistic trick on him, as punishment?

Very carefully he sat up, found his clothes on a chair beside the bed and dressed, still unable to turn and look at the sleeping woman... But he could hear her shallow breathing on this miraculous summer's morning.

Still not turning to look at the bed, he moved to the door, hesitated, then looked back.

The sight of her slim form, naked in the pale dawn light, with the sheets twisted around her lower legs, made him gasp. A part of him wanted to rush forward, take her in his arms, and verify what his eyes were telling him. Another part of him, stupefied by the consequences of finding himself here, could not bring himself to shatter what might be no more than a cruel illusion.

For more than thirty years he had lived with the knowledge that Annabelle Shaw was dead; he had relived this morning, and his part in it, countless times; he had lived for years with the knowledge that the woman he had loved no longer existed, was no longer part of a reality that for him had become a punishment.

As the light strengthened, he saw her sleeping face on the pillow, her lips slightly parted; her small breasts rising and falling as she breathed.

He moved into the small living room, closing the door quietly behind him and drawing the curtains to admit the early sunlight. The sight of the room brought memories flooding back: there was the ancient sofa where they'd made love a hundred times; there the rickety table where he'd pounded out his early, immature plays, believing they were excellent. There, in the opposite corner, stood Annabelle's desk, where she worked sometimes in the evening, writing reports and exhibition notes for the Kensington gallery where she worked.

He collapsed on to the sofa and raised his right hand; it was shaking uncontrollably.

He had met Annabelle Shaw during his final year at Cambridge – and wondered why he'd not noticed her sooner. She was tiny, bird-boned, quiet and terribly shy, and she glowed with a singular, radiant beauty. His first sight of her had stunned him, brought him to a halt in the café across from King's College. She'd been bending over her book, a coffee at her elbow, and Richie had stared at her until someone tapped him on the shoulder and told him to get a move on. Too shy to speak to her, he'd bought a sandwich and hurried back to his room, but had been unable to concentrate on his essay.

For the next week he could think of nothing else but the need to talk to the young woman; he bored his friends with paeans to her beauty, until one of them had said, "For Christ's sake, Ed. Look, I know a friend of hers. I'll put in a good word, say you'd like to meet for a drink."

They had met at a pub called the Pickerel across the street from Magdalen College, and he'd responded to her shyness by being uncharacteristically talkative; she later said that that was what she initially liked about him was his ability to expound interestingly on any subject, and his insightful questions about her and her Classics degree. At the end of the evening he'd known, with a certainty he'd never experienced with anyone else, that he was in love with Annabelle Shaw.

They'd met for a drink again a few days later, and then a few days after that for an Italian on Hills Road. Annabelle, like him, was in her final year at Cambridge, and hoped to get a job in London on graduating. She possessed a strange, soothing calm, a warm sense of humour, and an intelligence that often left him in awe: she brought a singular perspective to every conversation, and made him see the world anew. A month after their first date, they made slow, hesitant love in her room in a house overlooking the Cam, and for the next few months after that they were inseparable. When they graduated, she with a first, Richie scraping a 2:1, they rented the flat in Hackney, and Annabelle started work for the gallery while Richie tried to sell radio plays to the BBC. Despite his lack of success – he'd found part-time work in a local bookshop to tide him over – it had been the happiest nine months of his life.

He found a tissue in his jeans pocket and dried his cheeks. The shaking had stopped, giving way to a profound calm. The sunlight strengthened, promising a warm day, and picked out the details of the small room: the threadbare carpet, the faded Rothko poster, the ancient two-bar electric fire... But none of these things had mattered in the slightest: neither he nor Annabelle had been materialistic; for nine months they'd had each other, and that had been enough.

He made himself look across the room at Annabelle's desk. In the top right-hand drawer was the manuscript of his latest play, which he'd given her for evaluation yesterday afternoon. For the rest of the day – a Sunday – and into the evening, she'd curled on the sofa and read the manuscript, making occasional notes in her tiny, impeccably neat handwriting. Richie, too nervous to settle at anything, had busied himself around the place, doing the weekly washing and cleaning the bathroom, from time to time looking in on her to see if she seemed to be enjoying the play. It was, in his opinion, the finest thing he'd ever written, a ninety-minute three-hander about a doomed love affair set in post-war Germany – a subject and a place, he realised in retrospect, about which he knew nothing. He had high hopes for the play, and planned to adapt it for the stage... At dinner that evening Annabelle had told him that she was halfway through the piece, and would not be drawn to tell him her thoughts; at bedtime, having finished the play, she had been reflective, telling him that she needed to think about it. He remembered his confidence that Annabelle would confirm his certainty that the play was little short of brilliant.

He moved across to the desk, opened the drawer, and took out the play-script.

He sat on the rickety dining chair before the desk and leafed through the script, tears streaming down his cheeks.

He read her tiny printed comments: *This doesn't work... Too trite... Motivation? This scene is way too long – see my notes on page 30... Would someone like James really say this?* On and on, page after page, a litany of criticism that was insightful, constructive, and brilliant.

Not that the young insecure Ed Richie had thought this at the time.

He closed the script and replaced it in the drawer.

He looked at the clock on the mantelpiece. It was seven-thirty: Annabelle would be getting up for work very soon. His heart crashed at the thought, and he worked to prepare himself.

He moved back to the bedroom and stood in the doorway, staring at the naked woman on the bed.

She stirred, turning onto her back. His stomach felt as if he had been gutted by a very sharp knife. He would have to work to appear normal, when she awoke; he could not show his wonder, his joy, at her existence.

She opened her eyes, reached out her right hand to the empty area of bed, and then saw him by the door and smiled. Oh, her smile... Had he forgotten its effect, the tilt of her lips, the off-centre twist? He swallowed.

"Oh," she said, "there you are."

He made himself say, "Couldn't sleep. Got up and read. Breakfast?"

"That'll be lovely. I'll just get a quick shower."

"Toast and scrambled egg?"

She beamed at him, swung out of bed and danced, tiny and naked, to the bathroom. "You're a sweet."

You're a sweet...

He was weeping again as he moved to the kitchen and prepared coffee, eggs and toast.

He was going through the motions, doing exactly what he'd done this morning, all those years ago...

In fifteen minutes she would emerge from the bedroom, stunning in a red summer dress and white cashmere cardigan, and over breakfast he would brace himself and ask her for her verdict.

But this time, he told himself, it would be different.

Very different.

As he stirred the eggs, he thought back thirty-four years, reviewed his memories of that time long ago, and relived what had happened...

IN HIS NERVOUSNESS to hear what Annabelle had thought of his play, the Richie of old had burned the first lot of bread. He'd toasted another two slices, perfectly this time, and she'd hurried into the kitchen, stood on tiptoe, and kissed the back of his neck.

He had served her a plate of scrambled egg on toast and sat down at the small Formica-topped table. She took a mouthful, smiled at him, and said something about a meeting she had this morning. Evidently she had no intention of mentioning the play.

He forced himself to eat, and then said, "So... the play. What do you think?"

She nodded, smiled again – a fleeting quirk of her lips – and frowned down at the process of cutting her toast. "Well..."

He said, "You think it still needs a bit of work?"

"Do you?" she asked.

"Maybe here and there, a little tweaking, maybe a scene or two that could be tightened." He cleared his throat. "But I want your opinion."

She sighed and said, "Ed, I don't think it's the best thing you've done."

He recalled feeling genuinely shocked. "You don't?"

"Not by a long way."

Defensively, he snapped, "Then what do you think *is* the best thing I've written?"

"That fifteen-minute play you did a couple of months ago for the BBC competition."

He stared at her, amazed. "That? But that was trite, a light piece of entertainment."

"But it worked, Ed, its characters worked –"

"And you think this doesn't work, you don't think the characters – ?"

"I honestly think it needs work."

Stunned, reddening, he said, "How much?"

"A lot."

"You're joking, aren't you?"

"Ed, you asked for my opinion, and I'm giving it."

"So..." He was aware that his voice was shaking. "Why do you think it doesn't work?"

"I think two of the main characters need rethinking. James's motivation, especially in the second act, doesn't ring true. I don't think he'd react as he does – I can see why he *needs* to, from a narrative point of view, but as it stands it comes over as authorial convenience. I think if you foreshadow his reaction to Gemma's rejection of him by rewriting a few of his earlier scenes –"

He interrupted bluntly. "I think he works. His reaction is a sign of his insecurity."

Annabelle bit her lip, nodding. "Okay. But Ed, we're given no indication of his insecurity in previous scenes, and I think you need to be more subtle in your depiction of him. It…" She hesitated, not meeting his eyes. "It's his reaction to Gemma, Ed, his inability to see her as a person, to empathise with her, that –"

"I'll think about it," he said. "So who else, in your opinion, doesn't work?" It was almost a sneer.

"As it stands, Gemma's a cypher. She doesn't have life, depth. It's a particularly male view of a woman, how she reacts. I don't for a minute believe she'd fall for someone as unfeeling as James."

"But she is shallow, that's why she *seems* not to have depth."

"Ed, her shallowness comes over as… how to put this… not as authorial intention, but as authorial lack, a lack of…"

"Go on. Say it."

She stared at him. "Ed, you asked for my opinion. I want to see this play succeed. I want you to sell it. Nothing would make me happier."

He drew a breath, shaking with barely suppressed rage. "Okay, I can fix the characterisation. That's no problem. I was going to look at it, anyway. But what about the plot?"

She stared at her plate. "Ed, if you're going to take that tone, I'd rather not read your plays."

"What tone? Do you think I should sit here, mute, while you tear apart something I've sweated blood over the past six months?"

"I'm not tearing it apart. I'm trying to offer constructive criticism. Look, perhaps it'd be better if you read my notes. I've annotated the script, and gone into more detail on separate sheets." She pointed through the kitchen door to her desk. "Maybe read them while I'm at work, okay, when you can take your time and think about what I've said?"

ocococrrr r I okk

"I can think about what you're saying now. Why don't you think the plot works?"

She held her head very still, her knife poised in her elegant hand just above the plate. Her jaw clicked to one side as she contemplated what to say next. "The first act drags, it lacks dramatic tension. The second act is a little better, but needs cutting, and the third act..."

"Do you know what I think?"

She hung her head, sighed, and then looked up. "No, Ed," she said wearily, "what do you think?"

"I think you're jealous."

"What?" She looked astounded.

"You're jealous. You wish you could write like me, but you can't. This is payback for my criticism of that short story you wrote earlier this year."

She was shaking her head. "*What?*"

"You know you can't write, and you hate me for pointing that out, so this is how you show it."

Tears filled her eyes, and to his eternal shame the sight of them had pleased him. "But... but I agreed with you, Ed! I agreed with you, for God's sake! I knew my story was terrible. I said so, remember? I said I'd stick to art reviews..."

"But you didn't mean that, did you? You resented me for undermining you. You just *said* that!"

She opened her mouth, speechless. Then the tears fell, rolling down her cheeks, unchecked, as she stared at him.

She whispered, "I can't take any more of this. I'm going."

He glanced at his watch. "You'll be early," he sneered. "Doesn't that ponce of a boss of yours open the doors at nine?"

"So I'll sit in the car for twenty minutes."

"Do that."

She placed her knife and fork down, very gently, on either side of the plate. "I'll see you tonight."

"If I'm still around," he said.

She appeared to be considering her reply, but perhaps knew, in her wisdom, not to provoke him when he was in such a mood. She just nodded and hurried from the room. He heard her in the hall, getting her bag ready and selecting a jacket. Then he heard the front door open and close and, a minute later, the sound of her MG starting up and moving off down the street.

He moved into the sitting room and kicked the sofa. "Fuck!"

He paced the small room, enraged. He channelled his anger at Annabelle, calling her a jealous, callous, selfish bitch.

He moved to her desk and pulled out the play-script, flung himself onto the sofa and read her notes. "Wrong!" he said. "Wrong! *Wrong!* She doesn't get it!"

Christ... didn't she realise that he'd worked *months* on the fucking play, going through a dozen drafts, ditching scene after scene in an effort to get it right? And then she comes along, gives it a cursory read through, and makes these superficial criticisms...

His analyses of her criticism led him, over the next hour, to question what he saw in her; he'd thought he'd loved her, but how could he feel anything for someone who didn't understand him and his work? The sex was still great, but Christ, he could get that anywhere.

He was still fuming when the doorbell rang. He ignored it. The fuckers could piss off.

The bell chimed again, and again, and when it was obvious that the bastards wouldn't go away, he charged to the door and hauled it open.

Two uniformed police officers, a man and a woman, stood on the doorstep. He sighed. "Wrong house," he said. "If it's about the drugs, you want next door." He was already closing the door.

"Mr Edward Richie?"

That stopped him. "Yes?"

"Can I confirm that Annabelle Jane Shaw is domiciled here?" the woman asked.

"That's right."

She spoke again, but Richie didn't take in the words; the WPC, accustomed to repeating herself to shocked citizens, said, "I'm very sorry, Mr Richie, but Annabelle Shaw was fatally injured in a road traffic accident at approximately eight-forty this morning."

Richie stared at the police woman. "What?"

Fatally injured... He heard the words, but they made no sense.

The man said, "Annabelle Shaw died instantly when her car was involved in an accident with an articulated vehicle on Victoria Park Road at eight-forty."

Richie said her name, and then, "Dead?"

"I'm sorry, Mr Richie."

"No!" It was a cry of disbelief.

He turned and staggered into the house. He recalled very little of the next few minutes, but he attacked his desk in the sitting room, dragging it over and kicking it to pieces, and when the copper came in after him, repeating his name and making soothing gestures.... Then he recalled being spoken to by a couple of oddly powerful paramedics who called him Edward, over and over, and sedated him with an injection. He recalled shouting Annabelle's name as he was stretchered out to the waiting ambulance, and then nothing more until he awoke in a hospital bed hours later.

He slipped in and out of consciousness, and once, on waking, was aware of a small, shrunken couple seated beside his bed in silence.

He recognised them, through the numbness of his grief, as Annabelle's parents.

He reached out mutely and gripped their hands.

All he recalled of their visit was something Mrs Shaw had murmured to him, "Annabelle loved you, Edward. You made her very happy. Thank you."

He was assessed, kept in overnight, then given the name and number of a counsellor and discharged. Digby Lincoln and his current girlfriend were waiting for him at the Hackney house, and took him home. He lodged with them for the next two weeks, gave notice to the landlord of the Hackney place, then found a bedsit in Maida Vale, around the corner from where Digby lived.

Six months later, in a Chelsea wine bar he'd taken to frequenting, Richie approached and started chatting to a small, blonde Australian, the first in a succession of doomed liaisons with women who resembled Annabelle Shaw.

Now, more than thirty subjective years since Annabelle's death – still an hour away – he relived that fateful morning and cursed himself for the shallow, selfish, egotistical fool he had been.

And now Annabelle, stunning in a red summer dress, came into the kitchen as he stood at the cooker, raised herself on tiptoes and kissed the back of his neck.

HE DID NOT burn the toast, this time.

He turned and watched Annabelle as she seated herself at the table. It was all he could do to stop himself from pulling her to her feet and holding her tight.

Christ, he thought; what a fool I'd been back then: so caught up in my own concerns that I'd been blind to Annabelle. He recalled what she'd said about the play, *"It's his reaction to Gemma, Ed, his inability to see her as a person, to empathise with her…"*

Only now, years later, did he see the truth of her words; only now did he acknowledge that she had been criticising the man that Ed Richie had been.

He served her a plate of scrambled egg on toast and sat down. She took a mouthful, smiled at him, and said something about a meeting she had at work this morning.

Her soft voice brought back a slew of memories.

He reached across the table, touched her cheek with the back of his hand, and murmured, "I love you, Annabelle."

She smiled, perhaps a little uneasily. "Love you too, Ed," she said in a small voice, her eyes downcast.

"And before you say another word," he said, "I know you're dreading telling me how poor the play is."

Her eyes widened, her expression turning to surprise and relief.

"It's not that poor, Ed."

"Yes, it is. I thought long and hard about it during the night. James's characterisation is terrible. He's superficial and self-obsessed, unable to understand or care about anyone but himself. And Gemma wouldn't fall for someone so egotistical."

She stared at him, then murmured, "Those things can be fixed, Ed."

"And it needs cutting. The first act drags, and the third lacks dramatic tension."

She tipped her head, a smile playing on her lips. "You've read my notes."

"Just a peek. And you're right. It needs a lot of work. But I can do it, and I will. Thanks to you, it'll be a much better play."

She shook her head, as if in wonder. "Ed... This isn't like you. You can't take criticism."

He recalled something Digby had said... or would say, years later, when he himself had had time to look back and reflect: That an indication of the maturity of a writer was his ability to accept criticism.

"I got up early this morning, Annabelle. I couldn't sleep. For a long time I just stood in the doorway, watching you as you slept. And I realised something." He took her hand. "I realised how much you mean to me."

She said, very softly, "Thank you."

They talked about the play for a while, and Richie told her how he hoped to rewrite it, and make James a more sympathetic character. Their conversation brought back memories of their time together, when he'd told her all about his ideas for plays, his hopes and dreams.

At eight-fifteen, she looked up at the clock and pulled a face. "Gosh. Look at the time. I must fly!"

"No!" He reached across the table and grabbed her hand, almost in panic. "No. I'll drive you this morning."

"But..."

"I need to go into town. It's on my way. And later... I'll pick you up and we'll go for a meal, okay? Just the two of us, in celebration."

"Celebration?" She laughed.

"I want to thank you for all your work on the play. You don't know how much it means to me."

Moved almost to tears, she took his hand and kissed his knuckles.

He drove her into the West End, avoiding Victoria Park Road, even though it was well before eight-forty when he made the detour. She chatted about the meetings she had arranged this morning, and a forthcoming exhibition, and Richie lost himself in the sound of her voice.

He dropped her outside the gallery and watched her cross the pavement and turn at the door, smiling at him and waving. He drove on into central London, exulting. Tonight he would pick her up and take her to a restaurant of her choice, and then they would return to the house and make love with the bedroom window open and the lace curtains blowing in the summer breeze.

He spent the day in London, like a tourist in this strange, earlier age... He bought a paper and found a quiet pub, had lunch and a pint and read all about a world he recalled but dimly. He found, as he read, that he was hardly taking in the news reports; the events would not touch him, anyway. He was a traveller, passing through. He had done his duty to Annabelle, and saved her life. Tomorrow, or whenever, he would be whisked away to another time, and then another... until, what?

He hardly cared. He wondered if this was what this had been about: saving Annabelle. In that he had succeeded, and his fate hardly mattered now, even to himself.

Or was he fooling himself? Was this no more than an hallucination, brought about by his terrible guilt, and was his saving of Annabelle his subconscious mind's way of assuaging that guilt?

No, he told himself. This was all too real to be the product of his guilt-stricken conscience. He really *was* here, in 1983, and he really had saved Annabelle's life.

He wondered how their relationship might continue when he was taken from this time. He would soon relinquish this body to the immature, egotistical Ed Richie, leaving Annabelle with the inferior version of himself. He regretted that – she deserved better – but consoled himself with the fact that she was alive now, with all her future before her. She could always leave him, he thought, and find someone who might truly appreciate her...

That evening he took her to a Cypriot restaurant in Greek Street, and they ate moussaka and drank retsina. She told him all about her day, the meetings and her plans for the exhibition, and Richie listened in wonder, drunk on the simple fact of the woman before him.

They took a taxi home, a little tipsy, and in the bedroom with the window open and the warm breeze lapping at the curtains, he undressed her slowly and he made love to her as if for the very last time.

From Ed Richie's journal, 3rd May, 2023

I'VE BEEN THINKING about Annabelle a lot of late: it goes in cycles, like pain, or like grief... Sometimes it seems bearable, while at others the very thought of her pitches me into the blackest despair.

CHAPTER SIXTEEN

January, 2030

ELLA STOOD BESIDE Mackendrick as they descended in the lift.

The door slid open and he led her down a short, carpeted corridor to a polished timber door. He entered a code into the security lock, then eased the door open and waved her through.

The lab was a long, white-tiled room illuminated by fluorescent strips. At the far end of the chamber stood two cylindrical tanks, each as long as a family car.

At their entry, a tall man turned from a computer screen on a desk to their right.

"Allow me to introduce Ralph Dennison," Mackendrick said, "Ralph, this is Ella Shaw."

The scientist reached out a hand and took hers in a firm grip. He was thin, in his seventies, with a benign expression and snow-white hair. His thin lips curved into what might have been an ironic smile.

Ella said, "It's good to meet you... at last."

His smile intensified. "I've heard so much about you," he said, "these past few days. Welcome to my lab."

She looked around the chamber, her gaze fixing on the cyclinders; they appeared to be filled with swirling grey gas.

I can tell you what happened to Edward Richie...

Mackendrick said, "The march of science is not so much a steady advance, Ms Shaw, as a staggering dance. We take two steps forward, and then several back, and often several to the side. How many discoveries have been made by scientists looking for something entirely different from what they eventually happened upon?"

She looked from Mackendrick to Dennison. "And you're telling me that this was the case here?" She stared across the lab at the smoky cylinders, suddenly aware of the chill in the air.

"I lured Ralph from Omega-Tec, thirty years ago, with promises of his own lab, the best technicians, and unlimited funds. The irony is that all his work, all his research, might have come to nothing – or who knows, might have alighted on a different discovery entirely – had it not been for a chance meeting with other research scientists in my employ."

Ella looked at Dennison. "You were researching faster than light travel?"

"The *theory* of FTL travel," Dennison replied. "Tachyon vectors, and the activity of sub-atomic particles, and dark matter..."

"And at an informal get-together in this very establishment," Mackendrick went on, "Ralph fell into conversation with Obi Ozaki and Gina Ventura."

"Whose specialisms were...?" she asked.

"Ozaki specialised in neurone-mapping," Mackendrick said, "that is, creating means by which the content of the human brain could be downloaded into mimetic gelware."

"And Ventura?"

"She is a specialist in quantum string theory, the study of what may lie beneath the sub-atomic reality of our universe."

Ella smiled. "Heady stuff."

"I recall the very instant," Ralph Dennison said, "after we'd been chatting for an hour, when something clicked. It occurred to Gina and Oz almost at the same instant: that there was a link between our theories, that I might apply my research into the behaviour of tachyon vectors to Gina's theory of the nature of 'reality,' and to Oz's work on mind-body duality and the possibility of downloading the human consciousness." His thin lips described a beautiful smile. "Ms Shaw, that moment was indescribable, perhaps the most intellectually thrilling moment of my life. What followed, as we put our theories to the test, was even more amazing."

"Which is no exaggeration," Mackendrick put in, "considering what Ralph, Gina and Oz accomplished."

Ella swallowed, bracing herself. "Which was?"

Smiling, Dennison glanced at Mackendrick, who gestured towards the far cylinders. "This way, please."

Feeling a little dizzy, Ella accompanied the men across the tiled floor towards the cylinders.

"To explain," Mackendrick said as they walked, "I shall have to resort to metaphor. Now, think of the universe, of reality, as made up of countless tiny grains, like sand – with every grain connected to every other grain by invisible matter, so what you have is a vast – so far as we can tell, *limitless* – interconnected nexus of pulsating matter. This matter exists even below the sub-atomic level, below even the 'strings' that we thought underlay the universe. This matter – we call it Dennison-Ventura-Ozaki space – is the medium through which reality flows... and also through which flows the passage of time."

She stared at him. "Time?"

They came to the cylinders and stood between them; the temperature in the chamber seemed to drop even further as they did so. Ella peered into the cylinder on her right, but made out only a depthless, swirling grey medium. At the end of each cylinder, until now concealed, was a seated technician monitoring softscreens and touchpads, intent on their tasks and oblivious of Ella and the men.

Dennison said, "Working with Oz, we effectively developed a means of unshackling the mind from its temporal prison."

"Meaning?"

"Meaning, Ms Shaw, that we developed a form of time-travel."

Ella looked from Dennison to Mackendrick, who was smiling at her reaction. She felt a little dizzy, and leaned against the stainless steel plinth on which the nearest cylinder rested.

She repeated, "Time-travel?"

Mackendrick spoke to one of the technicians, who nodded and ran a hand across a touchpad. The smoky haze in the cylinder before Ella swirled, and through the wisps she made out the prostrate form of a naked man. He appeared to be suspended in the cylinder, his shaven head trailing a mass of leads and wires. His long, drawn face was serene. Even without his characteristic shoulder-length hair, Ella recognised the old man as Ed Richie.

She felt dizzy again. She raised a hand towards the tank. "What...?"

"You see before you the man you have been seeking," Mackendrick said. "Ed Richie is travelling in time."

She shook his head. "But... but he's still *there*..."

Mackendrick went on, "Recall the metaphor: the universe, made up of countless interconnected grains – the very substance of space and time. Just as we in our corporeal forms travel one way through time, Ralph and his colleagues realised that it would be possible to send the mind of a subject in the reverse direction. But it was Oz and Gina who developed the means of downloading human consciousness into Dennison-Ventura-Ozaki space and shunting it back through time."

She shook her head. "I'm sorry...?"

Dennison said, "Stated simply, we made a copy of Edward Richie's consciousness and sent it back through the reality nexus to... *augment* the consciousness of his earlier self."

"Augment?"

"We theorised long and hard about what happened to the 'original' mind of the person whose mind was supplanted by that of the subject," Dennison said. "Were we, in effect, committing some kind of... of murder... in doing what we were doing? However, we discovered that the mind of the host, if you like, is subsumed into the consciousness of the subject. The subject's memories are overlaid on the host's, augmenting the mind, for want of a better word."

Ella stared at the scientist. She was struggling. "You've sent him back…?"

Mackendrick said, "The idea was to send him to a certain point in the early 'eighties, and stabilise him there. However, we suffered a certain dysfunction in the transference mechanism – a glitch that we have since rectified. The dysfunction resulted in Richie's consciousness being shunted arbitrarily back through time, so that he inhabited 'himself' at various random periods over the course of the past thirty odd years, beginning in 2017. In the January of that year he suffered a comatose episode and was hospitalised – this was his 'arrival,' if you like, in his 'past' self."

She struggled to get her head around what Mackendrick was telling her. "So he found himself in his old body…?"

"For periods lasting a day or a little longer, before being shunted back to another equally arbitrary time. From the year 2017 he was shunted to 2016, and then to 2013, then 2008, 2002, 1995, 1988, and finally 1983."

"It must have been terrifying," she said.

"All the more so, Ms Shaw, as Richie had no idea what was happening to him."

She stared at Mackendrick. "How can you be certain of that?"

"Because we were able to visually monitor, routing through the temporal nexus, what Richie was seeing, and view his reality on our screens, though we were unable to establish an aural link. In 2016 Richie met with his friend Digby Lincoln and explained what was happening to him, and we were able to analyse Lincoln's responses – through the agency of a lip-reader – and have our fears confirmed: Ed Richie didn't know what was happening to him. Although he'd entered into the project in full knowledge of what he was undergoing, in the process of transference he lost all memory of his life from 2017 onwards. Oz worked out that it was the same dysfunction in the transference system that had affected the memory of Richie's 'copy.'"

She struggled to take this in. "Okay... I see. But... but why Ed Richie? I mean, he seems a strange subject to select as the first..." She gestured to the body in the tank.

Dennison said, "He wasn't the first, Ms Shaw. Six other men and women went before him, beginning in 2015. The first three – they were all volunteers, by the way, who knew the risks – died in the process of the shunt. Our fourth subject was successfully shunted to 'inhabit' himself at the age of thirty, in 1980, but in the process all temporal telemetry was lost, so we had no means of monitoring his progress. Our fifth subject was successful, and this time the telemetry lasted for a week before the connection was lost. We were dealing with situations entirely new to us, and the complexity of the theory and the reality of what we were doing was staggeringly difficult to comprehend.

"We transferred our fifth subject over a decade ago, and then waited another five years – working to refine the system and iron out the glitches, before looking for someone who would consent to be our sixth subject." Mackendrick gestured to his colleague. "Ralph had known Ed personally, and suggested him as a possible subject. He made overtures, assessing Richie's suitability. When Ralph made the proposal, and Richie agreed, we arranged his disappearance in 2025. Richie wanted to contact his old friend, Digby Lincoln, to explain the situation, but of course we could not allow it. Richie understood, and consented, though not without a certain regret – the lure of being sent back to inhabit his younger self was too great."

"When we became aware that Ed Richie had suffered memory loss through the transfer," Dennison said, "and had no notion of why he was undergoing the phenomenon, we attempted to rectify it. We feared that Richie might suffer an irreparable mental breakdown – madness – as a result of what was happening to him.

We tried everything within our temporal-technological means to do so, without success. There was only one thing we could do: send another subject back to inform him of what was happening. Last year, having perfected the transference technique, we approached the seventh subject."

Ella nodded, suddenly understanding. "Emmi Takala."

"It was Ed Richie himself who suggested her as a possible candidate as a future subject," Mackendrick said. "They'd had an affair, many years earlier, and I think Ed Richie saw it as a way of giving something to the woman, the gift of renewed life... As it happened, four years ago she lost her husband. It was Ralph's idea that I approach her to purchase one of her paintings – which I later donated to Ralph's old college – and apprise her of the situation regarding Ed Richie." He murmured to the technician working at the second cylinder, and the mist cleared to reveal the floating form of a pale, slight woman in her fifties, her head a Medusa-mass of leads.

"She agreed to the process, and we transferred her to the time of her liaison with Richie in 2008, to tell him about the project and his part in it."

"And?" she asked. "It was successful?"

Mackendrick shook his head. "Before Takala could tell him, he was shunted back from 2008 to 2002."

"And you couldn't send Takala back to the same time?"

"We looked into it," Dennison said, "but, you see, we had set the limit of Takala's transference to 2008 – expressly to prevent the possibility that she would suffer the same arbitrary dysfunction as Richie."

She stared at the floating, prostrate bodies in the tank. "And now? They're still alive? Why don't you decant them, allow them to continue...?"

Mackendrick interrupted. "They are, technically, brain-dead. The reason we keep them tanked is that they are acting as, for want of a better word, transponders for the temporal signals coming up-line;

without them we would have no visual link to what is happening to Richie and Takala."

She looked from the naked, emaciated forms to the scientist, and formulated her next question. "And… and the reason you're doing this; is it merely to push back the boundaries of scientific understanding, or" – she looked from Dennison to Mackendrick – "or there's another reason, right? You" – her thoughts swirled at the possibilities. – "you want to change the past? Perhaps, by altering events back then, to change the present?"

"Why are we doing this?" Dennison asked. "Well… one answer is that we did it because we *could* do it. Another, because we wished to test a theory, or a number of theories. What would happen when we sent a subject back to the past? Would their actions cause changes in the present? So the answer to your question is, we sent a subject back in time simply to find out what might happen."

"And," she said, "did you find out?"

"Indeed we did," Dennison said. "What we discovered proved a theory that I and one of my colleagues had formulated. We found that reality consists of a limitless number of parallel timelines, and that when we sent a subject back, we then had no control over the timeline they were entering. The realities that Ed Richie found himself in often differed, to varying degrees, from the timeline he recalled. We also discovered that by sending back a subject to a certain point in time, we created an entirely new timeline in the reality of the universe; a branching in history, if you like. A subject going back to a certain time doesn't change *this* timeline, the here and now, as that would be an impossibility, a paradox – but it does create *another* future, elsewhere."

She shook her head. "I can't begin to comprehend…"

"By sending Ed Richie back," Mackendrick said, "we hoped to prove Dennison's theory; we hoped that Richie might effect a change in his own, personal timeline… and so prevent something from happening, something which had had terrible repercussions for one certain individual, and for the person he became."

Ella swallowed.

Mackendrick went on, "Why do you think he agreed to take part in the project? He was a highly successful novelist, rich and feted, with an enviable lifestyle and many friends. Of course he would have his life to live again, and find himself inhabiting a new, younger, fitter version of himself" – he smiled – "but there was something more, something even more important, that lured him into the past. We hoped he would be able to change an event that happened when he was twenty-three... Of course, there was always the possibility that in *this* time-line, Annabelle did not die that morning, but we could not take the risk of returning him to after the time of the accident."

Ella leaned back against the cylinder, tears streaming down her cheeks.

"Annabelle...?" she said.

"Despite the temporal dysfunctions that had shunted Richie randomly through his past, he did indeed arrive at the date we'd pre-programmed as his destination: the 20th of June, 1983. The morning your sister died, in our timeline, in a car accident on Victoria Park Road. Richie blamed himself for her death – they had an argument that morning, and she set off for work earlier than she normally would have done. Annabelle was killed, and Richie had to live with the guilt for the rest of his life."

"But did he manage to...?" Ella gestured towards the tank, aware that her hand was trembling.

"Richie came to consciousness that morning in 1983, and prevented the argument, and in so doing brought about a timeline in which your sister survived."

He nodded to the technician at the foot of Ed Richie's tank, and the woman ran her hand across a touchpad. Mackendrick took Ella's elbow and assisted her towards the array of screens; the technician vacated her seat and Ella slumped into it.

"Watch," Mackendrick said, indicating the big softscreen at the end of the tank.

The screen was black, but shot through with lines of interference;

then a hazy image appeared, its colours muted to shades of pastel. The interior of a restaurant, dim and candle-lit.

"This is a recording we made of the evening of June the 20th, 1983, in Ed Richie's new timeline – hours after, in our own timeline, your sister died."

Ella leaned forwards, her tears flowing freely now, as the image of the restaurant as seen through Ed Richie's eyes swung and he looked across the table.

Ella gasped.

On the screen, Annabelle laughed at something Ed Richie had said to her. Her sister was twenty-three, and elfin-beautiful, her eyes glowing in the candlelight. The girl reached out and took Ed's hand across the table, and her lips moved as she silently spoke.

Ella wept as she recalled that day, all those years ago. She had been twelve, living in Peckham with her mother and father. She'd felt sick that morning and her mother had allowed her a day off school, and just after eleven o'clock a police car had drawn up outside the terraced house. A constable came to the door and spoke to Ella's mother, and as she came down the stairs from her room, Ella had seen her mother collapse against the door frame, caught by the constable, and heard her anguished cry. She recalled little of the hours that followed, other than being hit by the stunning realisation that she would never again see her sister.

And now here was Annabelle, on the night of that same day, enjoying a meal with Ed Richie – who, Ella thought, would be rejoicing in the salvation of the woman he loved... and no doubt wondering at the miracle that had brought it about.

Mackendrick murmured something to the technician, who reached past Ella and tapped the touchpad. The image on the screen went blank, flickered, then was replaced by another scene.

Ed Richie was sitting on the side of a bed, staring at the sleeping Annabelle. Ella could only imagine what must be going through his mind.

Mackendrick said, "This is a little later that evening."

Richie's gaze lingered on the sleeping form of Ella's sister, her chest rising and falling, her long blonde hair fanned out across the pillow. As Ella watched, Richie reached out and stroked the sleeping woman's cheek.

Ella looked up at Mackendrick, wiped her eyes and said, "Why...? Why have you shown me this?"

He smiled. "Can't you guess? We would like Ed Richie to know the truth behind that 'miracle'; we failed once, when we sent Emmi Takala, but we have honed the system since then, and we know where we went wrong. We would not make the same mistake again."

"Again?" she echoed.

"With our increased understanding of the phenomenon, we can send you back to Ed's timeline, so that you can tell him all about the experiment here in 2030, and reassure him that he is now stabilised in his own time."

Ella stared at the screen as Richie turned and watched her sleeping sister.

"Send me back...?"

To live her life over again, to avoid the mistakes of her youth, to navigate the uncertainties of growing up, with the knowledge of the adult who had already done the growing...

"But Kit...?" She had left Kit once before, all those years ago, and still felt guilty at doing so; could she desert her all over again, just when Kit hoped that there might be a possibility of their getting back together?

She stared at the screen and the young woman on the bed.

To see her sister once again, to hold her in her arms and tell her that she loved her...

She felt Mackendrick's hand rest briefly on her shoulder. "We will leave you for a while, so that you can come to a decision."

She watched the two men walk away between the tanks, and returned her gaze to the woman on the bed.

She could return to inhabit her younger self, she thought, and work for a better future in a new timeline...

She smiled. But what had changed, she asked herself? Wasn't that, after all, what her life had always been about? To do one's best to make your world, this world, a better place?

On the screen, Annabelle rolled over to face Ed Richie, and smiled.

She looked up and watched Mackendrick and Dennison in conversation across the chamber.

"I don't know," she murmured to herself. "I just don't know…"

From Ed Richie's journal, 20th June, 2023

I RECALL READING somewhere – I can't remember where; it might have been in a novel – that grief is like a physical wound. It heals, in time, but always there is scar tissue.

   The 'scar tissue' of grief is psychological trauma, which manifests itself in all manner of devious ways when you least expect it. For years after the accident, I'd see small, blonde women and convince myself that they were Annabelle. Even now, more than forty years later, the sight of someone resembling Annabelle brings me up short and fills me with a bitter, corrosive guilt.

CHAPTER SEVENTEEN

June, 1983

THREE DAYS AFTER arriving in this time, three days after saving Annabelle's life, Richie awoke early and lay rigid in bed. He thought, for a terrible few seconds, that he'd jumped back in time yet again: the sunlight slanting in through the gap in the curtains made the room appear somehow unfamiliar. Then he saw the alarm clock on the bedside table, and the novel he was reading, and he calmed himself. He reached out, touched Annabelle's warm, reassuring body, then slipped out of bed and dressed quietly. He moved to the sitting room and sat at his desk in the corner.

He pulled a book from the shelf beside the desk, the collected works of Oscar Wilde, opened it at the bookmark and for perhaps the hundredth time read the astounding quote.

Was it too much to hope, he wondered, after three days, that he would remain here for good? Or, as he feared, would his stay of execution come to an end and he'd be whisked off to inhabit the body of a younger version of himself? He lived in fear of being taken from the bliss that his life had become.

But even more painful than that was the thought that Annabelle would be left with the person he had been.

The day after saving Annabelle's life, he had awoken on what he presumed would be his last day here, and then again yesterday, and again this morning... thinking always that *this* day would surely be his last.

On the second day he'd been leafing through the collected Wilde, and happened to read a line in *An Ideal Husband* that brought him up short, stunned.

Even you are not rich enough, Sir Robert, to buy back your past. No man is.

He'd hardly dared hope, since then, that perhaps he was that unlikely man...

Now he set aside the Wilde, opened his notebook, picked up his pen and began writing.

A little later he became aware of Annabelle, leaning in the doorway. "Ed," she said sleepily, "what are you doing?"

He looked up and smiled at her. Limned in the doorway by the sunlight, she was an angelic vision, and he swore to himself that, no matter how long he might have in this time, he would show Annabelle Shaw his love and live every day as if it were his last.

"I'm writing a story," he said, "about a man who buys back his past with the hard-won currency of experience."

Annabelle crossed the room and stood beside him, then caressed his shoulder and kissed the top of his head.

"Love you, Ed," she murmured.

She returned to the bedroom, and later Richie finished writing and joined her.

From Ed Richie's journal, 10th May, 2024

JUST BACK FROM a late session with Diggers at the Bull. Really shouldn't be drinking that much at my age.

I'm sitting at my desk. It's almost two, and the house is very quiet. Ella Shaw's *Corbyn: A Life*, is open on the desk where I left it before I set off to the pub. The sight of it, Ella's picture on the back-flap... it brings back memories of Annabelle.

I really ought to contact Ella Shaw, tell her how much I'm enjoying the book, and perhaps talk to her about Annabelle. I need to talk to someone about her, someone who knew her...

CHAPTER EIGHTEEN

July, 1988

ELLA AWOKE IN the body of her eighteen year-old self.

Born again...

She lay very still, as if too frightened to move, as sunlight streamed in through the bedroom window. Her last thought was of being inserted into the Dennison-Ventura-Ozaki chamber, the freezing touch of the gas as it enveloped her body, the telemetry leads being attached to her shaved skull. She recalled experiencing a moment of supreme terror at the thought of what could go wrong. There was always the chance that she might not survive the shunt, that this would be her very last thought.

Mackendrick had elected to shunt Ella into Richie's new timeline in 1988, when she was eighteen. She had finished school with three A levels and was about to start a course in journalism at the London School of Economics in autumn. At eighteen she was on the cusp of adulthood, coming to terms with her sexuality: it would be a good place to 'start.'

She was startled by a call from downstairs. "Are you ever going to get up, Ella?"

Her mother's voice made her throat tighten with emotion. No amount of mental preparation, back in 2030, had readied her for the fact that she would meet again her mother who, in 2010, had died... *would die*... of a cerebral haemorrhage at the age of seventy.

"Did you hear me?"

"Coming!" Ella called.

She dried her eyes on the cuff of her pyjamas, then looked at her hands and laughed: they seemed ludicrously young. She sat up and swung herself from the bed, staring across the room at her reflection in the wardrobe mirror.

So young, so fair and slight and... *unfinished*. That was the word that came to her. She appeared, sitting on the edge of the bed, to be physically innocent of the traumas that life would heap on her in the years to come: no lines on her face, no stoop, no habitually downturned mouth: all the signs of age that had greeted her when looking in the mirror at the age of sixty.

She had never recalled being so impossibly pretty – she had always downplayed her looks, eschewing make-up and wearing dowdy clothes, and ignoring the attention of the boys in the sixth form who asked her out. It had only come to her, very gradually in her sixteenth year, why she felt nothing for boys. That slow learning experience, that coming to terms with what she was, and having to face the consequences of her mother and father finding out, was something that, now, she had no need to fear. She had lived through it once, traumatically, and now with the wisdom of years would know how to negotiate the emotional pitfalls that had made her life, back then, so fraught.

She found her clothes on a footstool beside the bed and dressed: old jeans and a grey sweatshirt.

Taking a deep breath, preparing herself, she left the bedroom and made her way down the narrow stairs.

Even this short descent, on garishly patterned carpet, past dowdy old-gold wallpaper from the nineteen-fifties, past the dusty cuckoo clock in the hallway and the wooden globe on the telephone table, brought back a slew of long-forgotten memories.

And now to face her mother in the kitchen: her mother, whom she hadn't seen for more than twenty subjective years.

She was standing at the sink with her back to the door, washing dishes. Ella collapsed onto a dining chair.

"Make yourself some tea and toast. I'm not doing it for you. I don't know what time you call this. You know what your dad said? Up at eight all summer, and you work on your studies. Prepare yourself for a working life, girl."

Listening to her mother's litany now, Ella wanted to weep. As a young girl she was frustrated by the admonitions, but now they came to her ears like poetry.

When her mother turned, leaning back against the sink and drying her hands, Ella just stared.

Her hair was not as grey as Ella remembered, and her face was without the lines of grief that had etched themselves since the death of her eldest daughter. In this timeline, Ella told herself, her parents had been spared that tragedy.

Her mother was small, slim, in her late forties now, with a head of blonde curls and a thin, not unattractive face.

And it was like staring into a mirror and seeing her future self. The resemblance was unnerving: the thin, pretty face, the small nose and wide lips.

"I don't know what you're staring at, Miss. Didn't you hear me? There's the bread, and you know where the kettle is." She finished drying her hands and hung up the towel. "I'm popping round the corner for a coffee with Doreen and Pat."

Ella could only nod.

"Pop out to the Co-Op, Ella. Get some milk and eggs, would you?"

"Of course."

"That's a miracle. No protests?"

Ella smiled.

Her mother busied herself round the kitchen, putting things away, and then hurried into the hall. She came back holding her overcoat, a thick brown thing that looked at least fifty years old. "Your dad's back early today, so tea's at five. I won't be long."

Her father...

Ella took a breath and said, "I might... I might go and see Annabelle and Ed later."

Her mother gave her an odd look. "You know Ed will be writing all day? He won't want to be bothered. And Annabelle won't be back till after six."

"Oh, I forgot," she said.

Her mother gave her a concerned look. "Ella, are you feeling well? You're acting odd."

"I'm fine. Honest. A bit tired."

Her mother laughed and shook her head. "I don't know..." she said. "Well, drop the latch when you go out, and don't forget to take the spare key."

Her mother pulled on her coat and hurried from the room. The front door slammed.

She sat very still in the sudden silence.

Mention of her father brought back another rush of memories. Her father had always been a remote, emotionally reserved figure. He'd worked as a clerk for the local council, earned enough to keep a roof over the family's head and put food on the table, and probably considered that the extent of his familial duties. Ella could not recall his once avowing love for her or her sister, and he was not the kind of man to hug or kiss his daughters. Ella's relationship with him during her later teens had been fraught with mutual misunderstanding. In just ten years from now he would die from lung cancer at the age of fifty-nine, the result of a twenty-a-day cigarette habit from an early age.

She would work to make her relationship with him easier from now on: it certainly couldn't be any worse.

Also, she told herself, she would attempt to stop him smoking.

She started, then, as she realised that her promise to Mackendrick and Dennison had slipped her mind. She moved into the hallway and stood before the mirror. She mouthed *Thank you*, then remembered the pre-arranged signal to assure the observers in the future that all was well. She held up her right hand, three fingers spread, then one by one folded her fingers until only her fist remained. I'm well, I have my memories...

She leaned towards her reflection, as if this would make it easier for Mackendrick and the others to read her lips, and said slowly, *Thank you so much.*

She didn't feel like anything to eat. She'd grab something later.

She'd need money for the bus... but where had she kept her savings?

She ran up the stairs, marvelling at her renewed athleticism, and crossed her bedroom to the fat yellow pig sitting on her bookshelf. She raided its belly for a few pound coins and some small change, grabbed her anorak from the hall, then stopped suddenly.

She sat on the settle beside the telephone table and leafed through her mother's address book until she came to Annabelle's entry.

There was the address, written out neatly in her mother's tiny hand-writing.

Annabelle and Edward: 22 Marlborough Street, Camberwell.

She found her father's dog-eared A–Z of London, located Marlborough Street, and plotted her route. She tucked the booklet into her pocket, remembered to take the spare key, and slammed the front door behind her.

It's July 1988, she reminded herself as she almost skipped along the pavement to the bus stop. The ogre is still in Downing Street, but will soon be deposed by her own party: the invasion of Iraq is yet to come, along with all that that would bring. Donald Trump was not yet President of the USA; and the rise of the far-right in the UK, the appalling civil war in Nigeria and much else... All those horrors lay in store. Or perhaps not.

She took the bus to Camberwell and sat on the top deck, right at the front, and watched the passing world.

She wondered if, in this timeline, she would meet her first love, Terri Rivera-Sanchez, later this year; would she fall hopelessly in love and for three months be blissfully happy, until Terri told her she'd met someone else? Ella had been devastated, almost suicidal; if it did happen this time, she thought, she'd handle it better. She'd understand that it was inevitable and that, despite the superficial physical attraction, they were mentally incompatible: she was only eighteen, for pity's sake!

She thought of Kit Marquez, and wondered what her old lover was doing now: she would be eighteen too, starting student life at Princeton. The world had yet to hear from the feminist firebrand she would become.

And the Kit Marquez Ella had left behind in 2030?

More than anything, Ella had wanted to see Kit one last time, to explain what was happening, and apologise. But that was impossible, of course: Mackendrick had made that plain. No one could be informed of what was happening there, deep beneath the Cairngorms.

In Kit's future, Ella Shaw would suddenly disappear, mysteriously, without a trace... She eased her conscience with the knowledge that Kit was strong: she would survive.

But that had hardly made her leaving any easier.

The bus stopped at Camberwell High Street, and Ella jumped off at the next stop, hurried along the street and turned the corner into Marlborough Street. She stopped outside number 22 and stared at the navy blue front door.

At some point in the very near future, tonight or tomorrow, she would meet Annabelle.

The thought constricted her throat, tightened her chest.

Her dead sister, dead for almost fifty subjective years.

Annabelle, back from the dead, now twenty-eight...

But, first, she had something important to tell Ed Richie.

She hurried up the front path, lifted the knocker and pounded three times. So what if she interrupted Ed's writing? She thought he'd understand.

No one answered. She knocked again, harder this time.

She saw the outline of a figure through the pebbled glass, and the door opened.

She took a breath. Ed Richie... the man she had pursued, in the future, until she had found him here, in the past...

He was slim and dark, with a piratical five o'clock shadow and dark eyes – and he was intimidatingly tall as he smiled down at her.

"Oh, Ella..." He raised a finger to his lips. "Annabelle's in bed. She was sick in the night. Come in. Coffee?"

Ella swayed. "Annabelle's at home?" she said stupidly.

"Too ill to go to work, but she'll be fine. Must've been something she ate. Come on, don't stand out there all day."

In a daze she followed him along the hall, past a small, book-crammed study, to the long kitchen at the back of the house.

Ed fixed coffee in a percolator at the cooker and Ella sat at the scrubbed kitchen table.

"I'm not interrupting...?"

"No, not at all. I was just rewriting something, but it's not urgent."

She stared at Ed Richie, this man who had found himself pitched back in time, inhabiting ever-younger versions of himself. He must have thought, at one point, that he was losing his sanity. And now here he was, living in a new timeline in 1988 with the woman he loved, a twenty-eight-year-old man with the memories of someone almost sixty.

He exuded a strange sense of calm, as he moved around the kitchen, a wise bearing altogether at odds with his youth. The only other person she had met who had possessed this ineffable *centredness* had been a Zen master. In her youth, Ed Richie had overawed her with his intelligence and intensity; and now she felt herself in awe of everything this man had experienced.

She looked across the room at the Welsh dresser, and what she saw there made her catch her breath. She stood, crossed to the dresser as if in a trance, and picked up the framed photograph.

Annabelle and Ed, embracing. Annabelle staring out of the picture, laughing, ecstatically happy – looking a little older than when Ella had last seen her. She backed to the table, still clutching the photograph, and sat down heavily.

Ed turned from the cooker and stared at her. "Ella? What...?"

She looked up through her tears and appealed to him. "I want to see her, Ed."

He looked bemused. "Of course. But..."

She shook her head, laughed through her tears. "Oh, Christ, Ed, I'm sorry. I'm so bloody happy!"

He smiled uncertainly, as if she had gone mad.

She said, "Ed, sit down."

He nodded, poured two cups of coffee, and carried them to the table. He sat down before her. "Ella?"

She reached out, her tears still flowing, and clutched his hand.

"Oh, you poor, poor man... What you must have gone through."

He was suddenly very still. He turned his head slightly sideways, staring at her askance. "What do you mean?"

She cuffed her tears, sniffed, and smiled at him. She nodded, took a breath, and said, "I know what happened to you, Ed. I know everything. More even than you know. And I've come to explain..."

His eyes widened. "Ella...?" he said again, an appeal in his voice.

"You see, like Emmi Takala in Crete in 2008, I've been sent back to tell you what happened."

He opened his mouth to speak, but no words came. He slipped further down in his chair, staring at her, and then found his voice, "For so long, Ella, I thought I was going mad. I... I'm not, am I?"

"No, you're not." Ella reached out and took his hand, and began, "In July 2025, Ed, you disappear..."

"EVERY DAY," RICHIE said a little later as he sat, clutching her hand, "every day I've wondered if it might be the last. I've learned to live from day to day... to live every day as if it *would* be my very last."

She said, "You're safe, Ed. You're safe in this time. Nothing, and no one, can take that away from you."

He sat very still, staring down at their linked hands.

"I've lived in great fear," he murmured, "and, at the same time, in great joy." He looked up and smiled. "Come on," he said, "I'll take you to Annabelle."

He led her from the kitchen and up the narrow staircase, then paused outside a bedroom door and gestured. "I'll just see if she's awake."

He opened the door and slipped inside, and Ella felt her throat constrict.

She took a step forward, pushed the door open with her fingertips, and stared across the bedroom.

In the half-light she saw the figure in the bed, and watched Ed kneel and take Annabelle's hand, and kiss her fingers.

She thought she had never seen anything so beautiful in her life, and when Ed looked up and nodded, and Annabelle lifted her head from the pillow, smiled and said, "El, what a lovely surprise. Come here..." Ella stepped into the room, crossed to the bed, and took Annabelle in her arms.

EPILOGUE

From Ed Richie's Journal, 24th August, 1988

I'M TAKING ANNABELLE and Ella to the Clarke Award ceremony this evening. Diggers' *A Trove…* is nominated, and I think the novel might receive the first of many accolades. We're meeting Diggers and Caroline for a Chinese afterwards, and intuition tells me that my friend just might be announcing his engagement.

I bought Annabelle a new dress yesterday, especially for the occasion, a short, jet black, off-the-shoulder affair, and she looks stunning in it.

Oh, and the latest in Ella's complicated love life… Following her mysterious trip to the States last week, she announced on Monday that she has a new lover: a young woman called Kit Marquez.

She told me, yesterday, that she'd known Kit in her previous life.

E. M. BROWN

E. M. Brown has previously published bestselling novels under the name Eric Brown. An award-winning name in science fiction for over thirty years, in that time he has won the BSFA award twice for his short fiction, while his novel *Helix* was a bestseller, and *Helix Wars* was short-listed for the Philip K. Dick award. He's divided his SF output between action-adventure novels including *Helix*, the *Bengal Station* trilogy and *Binary System*, and more character-based work such as *The Kings of Eternity*, *Starship Seasons* and *The Serene Invasion*. *Buying Time*, under the name E. M. Brown, falls into the latter category and explores the life and times of Ed Richie, reluctant time-traveller...

FIND US ONLINE!

www.rebellionpublishing.com

/rebellionpub   /rebellionpublishing   /rebellionpub

SIGN UP TO OUR NEWSLETTER!

rebellionpublishing.com/sign-up

YOUR REVIEWS MATTER!

Enjoy this book? Got something to say?

Leave a review on Amazon, GoodReads or with your
favourite bookseller and let the world know!

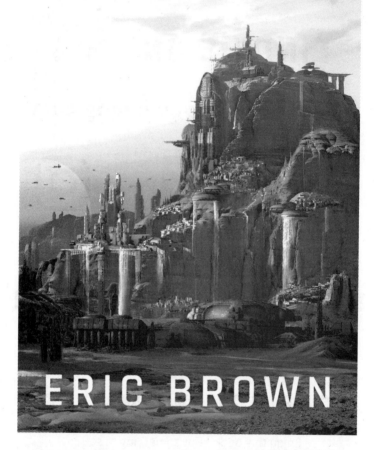

BINARY/SYSTEM

ERIC BROWN

On what should have been a routine mission to the star system of 61 Cygni A, Delia Kemp finds herself shunted thousands of light years into uncharted space. The only survivor of a catastrophic starship blow-out, Delia manages to land her life-raft on the inhospitable, ice-bound world of Valinda, and is captured by a race of hostile aliens, the Skelt. What follows is a break-neck adventure as Delia escapes, fleeing through a phantasmagorical landscape.

As the long winter comes to an end and the short, blistering summer approaches, the Skelt will stop at nothing to obtain Delia's technical knowledge – but what Delia wants is impossible: to leave Valinda and return to Earth.

 WWW.SOLARISBOOKS.COM

Follow us on Twitter! www.twitter.com/solarisbooks

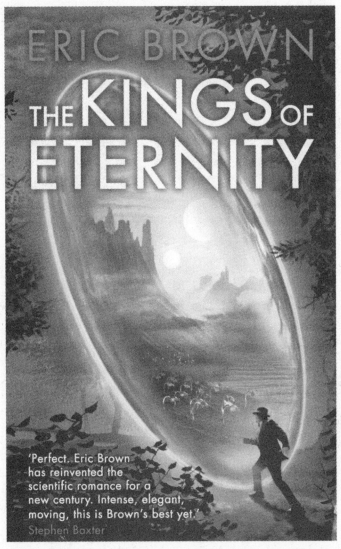

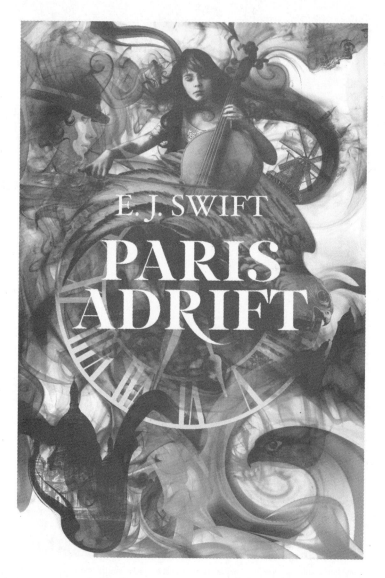

There's a strange woman called The Chronometrist who will not leave her alone. Garbled warnings from bizarre creatures keep her up at night. And there's a time portal in the keg room of the bar where she works.

Soon, Hallie is tumbling through the turbulent past and future Paris, making friends, changing the world — and falling in love.

But with every trip, Hallie loses a little of herself, and every infinitesimal change she makes ripples through time, until the future she's trying to save suddenly looks nothing like what she hoped for...